Vampire Whore II:
Blood & Lust

Also by Adenike

Vampire Whore

I Love Him, He Loves Me Not

Tales of Intrigue

Birthright

Adenike

Presents…

Vampire Whore II: Blood & Lust

Literati Media Group

ISBN 978-0-9895223-4-2

Printed in the United States of America

*All characters, events, most establishments, and organizations mentioned in this book are complete works of fiction. Any similarities to any person, either living or deceased, are both coincidental and unintentional.

Cover Art Provided by:
Adenike

Content Edited by:
Literati Media Group
LiteratiMediaGroup@gmail.com

Media Content Provided by:
Literati Media Group
LiteratiMediaGroup@gmail.com

Dedicated to
What it could have been… (But God!)

A Quick Note from the Author…

The moral of the tale you are about to read is that your past should not define you. Your journey, with all its twists and turns, has shaped you into the resilient, powerful woman you are today, but it does not define you. Embrace your past experiences, triumphs, and challenges and use them as a stepping stone towards greatness.

I use vampires as a metaphor for human emotions and the experiences that come with them. My main character is a young woman vampire who has been emotionally abandoned and emotionally wounded. Women vampires in literature have long been portrayed as complex, intriguing characters with a dual nature— both seductive and deadly. Much like these mythical creatures, women who have experienced past trauma often exhibit a similar duality in their personalities and behaviors.

As you delve into this story, remember that your past, though it may have been filled with pain, trauma, and struggles, has also been a catalyst for your revival. It has made you stronger, wiser, and more compassionate. Use your past as a source of empowerment, not a burden that holds you back. Your journey is a testament to the transformative power of embracing your past.

Accept your unique story, share it with pride, and inspire others to do the same. Your voice matters, your experiences matter, and your presence in this world is invaluable. Let go of guilt, shame, and regret, and step into the bright future that awaits you.

You are a queen, a warrior, and a beacon of hope for those who come after you. Own your story, learn from your journey, and know you are worthy of all the love, success, and happiness the world offers.

The story of the **Vampire Whore** *is the celebration of the dual nature of women as a reminder of the beauty and complexity that lies within every woman, no matter her past experiences. Embody your inner vampire— aggressive, fearless, and fiercely resilient— and know that you are capable of rising above your past traumas to shine brightly in and after the darkness.*

But remember... the importance of the journey is to heal. Do that, above all things.

Vampire Whore II: Blood & Lust

I

The Night Kilion Died...

"Let me love you tonight," Mahlon whispered in the pretty girl's ear with the long and slender legs. His deep, thick voice poured effortlessly into the ear closest to his soft, naturally puckered lips. The timbre in his velvety baritone resonated through her like the low hum of a strummed cello reverberating in a chamber hall. His alluring request made her eyes flutter while he continued playing with the soft wet pussy of another woman sitting on the other side of him in the darkened booth. He was sandwiched between two beauties.

The gorgeously tanned woman he currently had his fingers in was a young, sultry blonde who'd been flirting with him from the bar. Earlier in the evening, they locked eyes and made an instant connection when she spotted him gyrating unapologetically with a petite, big booty hottie that had approached him on the dancefloor. The air throbbed with energy while the techno-infused beat pumped from the ten-foot-tall speakers pulsated through their bodies, but he left her there when the blonde from the bar beckoned him to her.

The woman with the long, slender legs was the friend of the pretty blonde who was currently getting exquisitely finger fucked. Her closed eyes, which were rolled under their lids, told the tale of the man with the wide solid fingers between her vaginal lips, was experienced in satisfying a woman's desires.

When Mahlon had asked the woman with the slender legs, "Let me love you tonight," he knew she'd say yes without hesitation. Initially, he caught her looking shyly at him and her friend, fooling around in the dark booth behind the dance floor. He could tell by the way the woman crossed her toned legs she wanted to play, too, but wasn't bold enough to ask. So, like a gentleman, he took the initiative and requested her presence, saving her from missing out on the fun. He liked making it easy for women to get what they wanted, and all he had to do was make the first move, which is what a woman looking for a story to tell wanted anyway— a sexy, mysterious gentleman to ravish them without feeling remorse.

Mahlon pulled away from the slender-legged woman with longing in his eyes once he whispered his want, turning his attention to the pretty blonde who now quivered and moaned a bit louder as she edged towards her climax. The girl with the slender legs bit her lip with curiosity as she watched her friend magnificently cum from his assertive but gentle touch.

"Yes…" was all she could say when he removed his hand from between her friend's legs and allowed his sticky but slippery fingertips to outline the slender-legged woman's bottom lip. Without any further hesitation, he then slipped a cum-glazed finger between her craving and slightly parted mouth. Her tongue flickered on his fingertips, demonstrating the level of pleasure he could derive from her mouth. At that moment, he knew she was experienced in fellatio. Sucking a man to climax was not new to her.

Mahlon pulled his now wet finger out of her mouth and hungrily inserted his tongue directly, jutting it in and out, and slipped and slid around hers. He felt her lean in for more foreplay. He accommodated her nonverbal request by gripping her hair and tilting her head backward, exposing her beautiful, elongated neck. A mischievous glint of desire danced in his eyes as his thoughts ran wild with sexual possibilities. "My dear, I must have you." His nefarious chuckle as he spoke his intent hinted towards the dangerous liaisons the slender-legged girl triggered.

Mahlon scooped her up, causing the pretty blonde to topple to the floor in a drunken and unconscious sexual afterglow. The slender-legged woman blushed that the strength of his arms could cradle her seemingly weightless frame.

She looked at her passed-out friend, overjoyed she too would experience that type of orgasm. "You're next." He smiled devilishly at his second course. The blonde he'd fingered and left in the dark booth was no more than a mere appetizer for his hormones to awaken, but nothing he would insert his penis in. The blonde had looked delicious when he spotted her earlier that night. However, after engaging her with flirtatious musing and then getting her drunk, the alcohol fumes emitting from her pores were a mixture of rancid blood and decomposition, exposing her as a drug user and on the verge of death from habitual abuse. *Looks can be oh-so deceiving...* He thought to himself as they touched each other inappropriately when cuddled in the booth.

Mahlon despised dying blood. The taste and feel of it swirling around his mouth lacked the girth, consistency, and warmth of a healthy human's intoxicating blend. Sure, in desperate times, it could be a meal, but why settle for subpar libations when top-shelf offerings were all around? But for all the sexual tension he and the blond had built up, he couldn't leave her without a tale of ecstasy to remember him by. He felt obliged to satisfy her— not just wanting desires but also for his arousal. He found that foreplay excited him more than it excited his prey, and he was going to use the energy he expelled on the pretty blonde to appreciate and enjoy the healthy mortality of the next beautiful one.

The color of his emerald green eyes flashed in the dimly lit nightclub as he turned away from the booth he'd occupied with the two women. As he began his walk toward the private rooms available to high rollers like himself, the bulky patron who'd roughly passed by forcibly nudged his shoulder. The patron then stopped in his tracks and slowly turned when he heard Mahlon say, "It would be a guy like you who has no respect for the precious cargo I carry."

"What you say to me?"

Mahlon smugly walked over to the brute, exposing the angelic face of the beautiful woman.

"Jack!" The woman jumped out of Mahlon's arms, surprised to see the man standing before them.

"What are you doing with my woman?!" The brute named Jack asked as he poked Mahlon in the chest.

Mahlon looked at the woman, slightly confused, but then quickly understood the moment. He gave them both half of a smirk and a chuckle. "Look…" Mahlon raised his hands as if innocent of the presumable charges against him. "She just wanted me to fuck her. I'm sure she was going to get right back. Isn't that right, sweetness? Just wanted a little thrill?" Mahlon turned his head towards the woman with the beautiful legs whose once tanned complexion was now strawberry toned from embarrassment. Mortified, she quickly changed allegiance and stood by her brutish Jack, grabbing his hand and stumbling over her excuse.

"Babe… I was— I was drunk… and I— I thought it was you… I mean sort of… ev— everyone looks alike in a dark club…"

"Yeah, sure they do." Mahlon's response to the blonde's defense was filled with condescending laughter. This wasn't his first time being confronted by a beautiful woman's mate. He never could understand why society felt the need to be monogamists all the time since being polyamorous caused less turmoil.

Jack stepped in front of his girlfriend to confront Mahlon in a thin attempt to defend her honor. "You calling my girl a liar?"

"Of course not… no woman ever lies about what they truly want…" Mahlon glanced over Jack's shoulder, catching the woman's eye contact. He gave her a knowing wink and a smile before continuing his conversation with her boyfriend.

"No hard feelings, my good man! Let's toast your pretty young thing we've both had the privilege to touch… you more than me, shall we say!" While Mahlon belted out another laugh and reached for a glass of wine floating by on one of the hostess girl's gold trays, unexpectantly, he heard a sickening crack as Jack's hairy knuckles delivered a blinding blow to his jaw, which rattled his teeth and left it slightly off center.

Mahlon stumbled to the floor and then touched his bruise delicately so as not to make it hurt more than it did. Fortunately, the pain was slight. Had he been mortal, the hit may have possibly produced swelling or even a missing tooth, but being immortal afforded him immunity to common pains. A trickle of his thick black blood dripped from the edge of his mouth even though the punch felt more like a slight. He wiped the blood trail away before getting back up, his smile catching Jack off guard since he thought he knocked him out with just the one blow. "So, we're doing this now, knowing your girl's a hoe." Mahlon stated rhetorically.

"What'd you say, bro?!" And before Mahlon could respond, Jack lunged at him, tackling Mahlon at the waist, forcing them both to the ground in a chaotic ball of rage. Loud shrills and screams of women standing close by could be heard throughout the posh nightclub. The DJ mistook the screams and movement of the fight and changed the music from techno to hip-hop, which fueled the partygoers, breathing more life into the brawl taking place in the back of the club.

Not soon after the fight between Mahlon and Jack started, smaller fights from other club patrons began to spring up around them, causing more confusion, which then bred more fights. With the bustle all around him, Mahlon managed to leap from the floor and onto Jack, ripping his shirt open. Revealing Jack's bare chest, Mahlon saw an opportunity he couldn't refuse. "You've ruined my dinner. I guess it's no fine dining for me tonight!"

Mahlon's eyes flashed amber in color as his desire for hot, warm, thick blood would now be fulfilled by Jack instead of the pretty hoe with the long legs. His incisors grew long and thin as they protracted downwards. Mahlon dove back into the fight, ready for his drink, knowing the tussle between him and his assailant was merely a charade to cover his real intention.

Mortals were never a match fist-to-fist for Mahlon; however, he enjoyed the adrenaline rush of hand-to-hand combat. Engaging in a good street fight was his favorite sport. One punch to Jack's gut had him bellowed over in pain. Mahlon lunged and pinned Jack to the floor and nuzzled up to his throat. He then took his bite. His razor-sharp canines easily pierced Jack's thick, muscled neck. He suckled forcefully, drawing a red stream into his open mouth while the massive chaotic brawl loomed around him, allowing no one to question or care about Mahlon and Jack's entanglement.

"Alright, you two break it up!" Mahlon's teeth were forcibly yanked from Jack's neck as the burly bouncer pulled the two to their feet. The heavyset security guard, whose thick muscular arms were squeezed into a standard black t-shirt that looked linty under the club's black lights, turned Mahlon around to get a good look at him. His face then turned to a scowl with remembrance. "Didn't I put you out last week and the week before that?" The bouncer pushed and shoved Mahlon and Jack through the crowd, headed towards the back alley door.

"Has it really only been these three times? I'm sure I can count at least two other times this month when you've grabbed me by the collar, ripping a Keith Walker original that I had to fly to him to get fitted for. Mind you, I still need to send you the bill for that."

"Yeah, yeah." The bouncer opened the back door and shoved the two out. The slam from it echoed, and the sound from it bounced off the wet cobblestone streets and the neighboring buildings. Jack stumbled over to the club's back door and banged on it mercilessly.

"Let me back in! My girl's in there! She needs me! Let me back in!" He pounded a few more times before realizing his attempt to reenter the club was futile.

"It's no use, my guy. We blew it. We're out of the club and in the streets." Mahlon threw his hands up in a what-can-you-do kind of way as he looked around his surroundings, momentarily reflecting on the night's transgressions. "You wanna go grab a beer or something? We can meet up with your trashy girlfriend later and have a threesome. Let's at least end the night as friends, right?"

"Are you high, drunk, or both?" Jack looked at Mahlon, agitated and stupefied. "Why would I grab a drink with you? You macked on my girl and got me kicked out of the club. I paid $150.00 on this outfit you ruined, and my girl's in there drunk and probably scared."

"Not scared, dude. She's a hoe. Actually, she's probably in the corner fucking a dude who paid more money on his outfit than yours, so let's go have a drink. We can call her from there and tell her to bring the fella she's probably sucked off, and we can run a train on her. My condo's not too far from here." Mahlon motioned for Jack to tag along as he began to walk out of the alley.

"Dude! Stop ragging on my girl! She's not a hoe!" Jack attempted to tackle Mahlon with all his might, but with the lack of blood from the unbeknownst vicious bite he received in the commotion, his attempt was a mere lean-in. Instead of landing a punch, his face planted on Mahlon's torso. And before Jack could raise his fist in a feeble attempt to fight, he was pinned to the cold, wet wall in the alley. Feeling merciless, Mahlon stared at him with a hint of cruelty in his eyes.

"I tried to be nice about it and make the last moments of your life enjoyable— grab a beer, have a few laughs, and then run a train

on your hoe for fucks sake, but nope. You want to be combative."
Mahlon flashed a devilish smile, exposing his terrifying fangs under
the unknown dim light source in the alley, forcing Jack's eyes to
widen and him to squirm, trying to free himself from Mahlon's firm
grip.

"Dude… what the fuck's wrong with your teeth?" Jack said
in a shaking voice.

Mahlon let his tongue slowly lap his mouth and teeth before
smiling once again. "Why, nothing's wrong with them. They are
perfectly designed to rip through flesh… human flesh when it's time
for me to feed. And Jack, you're on the menu…"

"Awww, man! Not me, man! What are you?! You some kind
of freak?! Some kind of monster! What are you!" Jack began to
whimper and struggle. His body moved wildly under the strength of
Mahlon's one arm that held him to the wall. Mahlon watched him
with delight, knowing the adrenaline and agility would warm Jack's
blood, making it more enjoyable once he began his dining experience.

"No need to worry about what I am, Jack." Mahlon ripped
the rest of Jack's tattered shirt away from his body, baring his
smooth, hairless, sweaty flesh. Mahlon's hunger grew at the
anticipation of tearing through Jack's well-toned abs and
unblemished skin. "Be more concerned about how much this is going
to hurt." Usually, Mahlon wouldn't kill his prey. The art of the bite
kept his victim alive and him satisfied, but Jack's infractions and the
alcohol he'd consumed during the night fueled him with power and
destruction, making him a very sloppy drunk.

No longer able to resist his carnal instinct, Mahlon drove his
teeth into the side of Jack's neck and directly into his jugular. The
surge of blood flowed swiftly into his mouth, sifting through his teeth
and down his throat. The first gulp of Jack's healthy secretions felt
glorious; satiety had set in, and Mahlon knew from that moment on
he could enjoy the different metallic flavors and the aroma Jack's
blood offered. Jack's dying screams became white noise for Mahlon,

equivalent to the melody one would hear mindlessly while grocery shopping or riding an elevator. The soothing tone of Jack's fear only made his experience with his victim even more exquisite.

Unfortunately, Mahlon's moment of delight was short-lived. Moments like these always were. Jack's screams, which were once robust, were now a faint whisper, and as Jack's blood became chunky and sludgy, the taste changed, quickly ending the meal Mahlon so much enjoyed. He glanced at Jack's glazed-over eyes of death and then, for good measure, checked his dinner's wrist for a pulse. *Can't have you coming back as a zombie vamp, can I?* Mahlon felt the faint heartbeat slow to a stop. He loosened his teeth of the clamp-like hold on Jack's neck and let his victim's body fall limp to the ground.

"You were delicious, Jack. You didn't disappoint. I'd say I'd see you around, but... well... I can't see that happening with you being dead and all." Mahlon reached down and brought Jack up to his feet— like a puppeteer manipulating his marionettes. "It was a pleasure to have devoured you." Mahlon then gathered Jack's head between the crevice of his elbow, and with his free hand, he twisted Jack's head violently to one side, severing his brain's connection to his spine. Mahlon chuckled as he turned and walked away, only to be startled by the frightened pair of eyes peeking from behind the dumpster.

"Who's that in the shadows over there? Come here. Come see me." Mahlon demanded.

The eyes became startled and then fully hid behind the dumpster. "Now, don't be shy. I can't say I don't bite, but maybe I won't bite you. Take a chance on an old dead soul and show yourself."

Mahlon casually walked over to the dumpster. The click of his heels echoed as they connected with the pavement. The bags behind the dumpster rattled slightly as the person who belonged to the frightened pair of eyes scampered to find a better hiding spot. Mahlon's pace came to a halt, and he stood in front of the ramshackle garbage. He folded his arms playfully and said, "Show yourself, or I'm going to get you out."

The bags didn't move right away, but they soon began to tumble from each other, falling towards Mahlon's leather loafers. Finally, a young boy emerged from the pile— grungy skin, tousled hair, and tattered clothes. He knew straightaway that the boy's home was where he found him. Mahlon motioned with his finger for him to come closer. However, he could tell by the boy's scared expression that Mahlon must have looked horrific. He'd never wiped Jack's blood from his face and hands.

"Never mind what you see." Mahlon waved his hand as if shooing a fly that obscured his view. "Don't look at me closely. Come to me and see me for what I am." Mahlon smiled meekly, and his eyes sparkled as the boy began to relax while gazing into Mahlon's now dark black eyes, which also had a tint of shimmer. Staring into them was like looking into space, watching the stars dance and twinkle. Driven by a sense of wonder of who or what stood before him, the young boy began to walk slowly towards the mysterious man… no longer scared but with a look of captivation and intrigue. The boy's obedience made Mahlon smile humbly. He held out his hand, and the boy placed his hand in it.

"Thank you, my child. Thank you for seeing my true self." A trickle of a blood tear slid from Mahlon's eye, humbled by the child's innocence. Not always the menacing predator of lore vampires are constantly portrayed as, he pulled the boy closer to him and embraced the malnourished little one, holding him in the folds of his arms. The moment felt pure for Mahlon assured his humanity was still intact after such a horrific act with Jack. He released the young man from the clasp of his cold, hard body and looked over him fondly.

"My dear boy. This is no longer your life." Mahlon pulled out his small notepad, scribbled a message, and handed it to the young one.

"Take this note to the shop on 15th and Main. Hand it only to Arthur." The boy took the note, slipped it into his pocket, and then continued to stare into Mahlon's hypnotic gaze. "Now, once you give this note to Arthur, you won't remember me or what you've seen here because none of this is real. You will do what Arthur says because Arthur is a good man, and you will grow up to be a fine gentleman. Once you have finished your schooling, you will come to work for me, Mahlon Jamison. All will be explained then." The boy nodded his head slowly while absorbing his directive. "Now, run along and start your new life." Never turning his head to look back or question Mahlon's instructions, the boy walked hastily out of the dark, wet alley and made a left once he made it to the street. Right behind the boy, Mahlon headed the other way towards his car to turn in for the night.

"Good night, Jack! Thanks for an exciting time! Your hoe would have been better, though!'

II

"Alexa… power up the Lambo." Mahlon heard the pleasant notification ding from his phone while walking to his car. *"Your Lamborghini Veneno is now on,"* Alexa responded. The lights on his car flickered as the Italian Stallion readied its charge, and the driver's side door slowly began to open. The speed racer engine revved in anticipation of pulling from the sidewalk's curb. Mahlon hopped in while the door descended and locked.

The pleasant ding of an Alexa notification came through the car's speakers, which was one he would surely dread. Mahlon rolled his eyes in annoyance, irritated by what he knew was coming. *"Your alcohol level is above the baseline standard for non-inebriated motorists. Please exit the driver's seat. Do you have a designated driver, or would you like if I called you an Uber?"*

"Fuck off with the drunk talk Alexa! I just live up the street!" His court-ordered breathalyzer powered by Alexa didn't require him to breathe into a tube. It was sophisticated and sensitive enough to analyze vapors coming from pores. The technology was still in beta mode and limited to high society's repeat offenders, and he had enough money to pay for the Alexa parole app to keep him out of jail for recklessness.

"Driving is prohibited. Please remove yourself from the driver's seat. Would you like an Uber?"

"No, you stupid bitch, I'm not getting out of the car! These are my best loafers! I can't walk in these!" Mahlon hit the steering wheel repeatedly with his hand, unable to contain his annoyance with this type of supervision.

"Car deactivated." Alexa powered down the car, and the interior went dark. Frustrated, Mahlon got out of the Lamborghini and hit the button on his key fob to shut and lock the door. Surveying the area, which was vacant of partygoers or neighborhood dwellers, he spotted a lone man walking down the sidewalk and rummaging through his jean's pants pockets. From the breast pocket on his black seal-skinned blazer, Mahlon pulled out his nickel-brushed silver flask and took a few swigs of the aged cognac it held. He put the flask back into his jacket pocket and crossed the street to walk beside the man.

"Hey, my guy. You headed home?"

More focused on pulling out his keys, Mahlon had startled the man as he wasn't paying attention.

"Um, yeah. Geesh… you scared me for a sec." The man jiggled his keys and hit his car's key fob, making the lights blink on his Mercedes coupe.

"Nice ride, dude. Let me drive it home, and you can take a taxi or something to yours."

"What? No way, man. I don't even know you." The man walked over to his car with Mahlon not too far behind.

"C'mon. Alexa won't let me drive mine because she said I'm too drunk. I'd catch an Uber, but I don't like some stranger just driving me around like I'm lost and helpless." They had both arrived at the guy's car. He'd opened the door, but Mahlon leaned on it to shut it and casually plead his case. "Let me drive your car home, and

I'll have someone from my team return it to you tomorrow with a full tank."

"Are you crazy or something? I said no." The guy had now locked gazes with Mahlon's dark black pupils. His vision blurred, and his muscles relaxed, making him feel as if he was floating, and the world around him disappeared, only leaving Mahlon's voice as his god. Mahlon knew then that the driver had surrendered his will. He leaned in, grabbed the man's arm, and let go of it to see it drop loosely by his side and his mouth slightly agape.

"You can just hand over the keys and catch an Uber, like I said, and all will be better tomorrow. I'll return your car with a full tank of gas, and you won't even remember me or this moment." Mahlon smiled as he spoke the trance, and the guy nodded and handed over the keys. He nudged the guy away from the car, opened the Mercedes door, and hopped in.

III

Mahlon pulled away from the curb and immediately stepped on the gas. The speed of the car's take-off and the engine's rumble excited him as he enjoyed the smoothness of the ride. As he drove, he signaled to make a right and head to his condo, but the car felt so freeing, and he didn't want the ride to end as soon as it started. Instead, he made a left to take the car on a joyride down the coastline. Mahlon hit the console button to retract the coupe's roof and transform it into a convertible. He pulled his flask out of his pocket once more and took another swig of his drink. The alcohol was warm in his chest, which contrasted with the breeze on his face.

Pressing on the accelerator, he sped along the winding, hilly road out of town. The car raced towards the dark shoreline. As he sped along, he admired the stars twinkling like tiny dancers on dark water. The sky shimmered a deep midnight black under the night's cloak. Mahlon breathed in deeply to enjoy the smell of the sea air. He closed his eyes and imagined himself soaring in the heavens as fast as the Mercedes sped down the road. The smoothness of the ride gave him a sense of freedom that he enjoyed after devouring a meal. Human blood rushing through his veins provided a vigor that vampiric blood never could.

In the moments after feasting is when he felt most alive. He was most human with live blood coursing through him. He could taste food better, having sex felt more intense, and his real feelings about love and hate were at their peak. Real blood made him human, such a contrast from lurking in the darkness and shadows. So different than infinite power and an everlasting life.

The blare of a horn startled Mahlon from his daydream of flying. He swerved just in time to miss the oncoming car. The blare echoed as the car whizzed by, barely crashing into him. Mahlon chuckled to himself at the mishap. He pulled out his flask once again, pouring the last of its contents into his mouth. *Liquor, one more thing that tastes so good after I've eaten.*

Mahlon threw the empty flask out the back and pressed his foot harder on the accelerator. He turned the music up, allowing the upbeat tempo of the rhythmic melody to set the pace. Mahlon sang along to Jay-Z's classic, "Money Ain't A Thang" as the odometer reached 100mph. The night felt good to him. Life felt good. He veered smoothly into the opposite lane to pass by the slow-moving truck in front of him. He then swerved back into his lane when a car rounded the corner, and they were face to face on a course to collide. An angry horn blasted from the car's driver, scolding him for his carelessness. Mahlon laughed at how cautious humans could be. Then, he sped up to glide down the hill, which felt like a rollercoaster.

"What a thrill!" He shouted at the top of his lungs. He took his hands off the wheel and lifted them above his head. His arms stretched high to the sky as the Mercedes descended its slope. The car's speed began to escalate. His fingers felt the air whip between them; Mahlon closed his eyes to feel the rush. *Life… I can feel it…* The blare of another horn as the car it belonged to sped by brought him absolute joy, but unexpectantly, an overwhelming sadness came over his soul. A sadness that made him collapse into the driver's seat and grip his heart like it was falling out of his chest. Grief had suddenly set in, and the zeal for life slowly drained from his head and out of his feet. His shoulders slumped in hopelessness, and his dark red tears began to stream down his face. He'd made it down the hill and finally grabbed the wheel, wondering what could have caused the despair he now felt. *Maybe it was a bad batch of blood? Jack smelled clean, and he looked pretty healthy. His blood could not have been tainted where I couldn't detect it. What the hell is wrong with me?*

A rising warmth began to surge within Mahlon, and he grabbed his chest, surmising the heat originated around the placement of his heart. Without warning, his arm burst into flames, painfully searing his skin. Startled, Mahlon tried frantically to use his other hand to pat the flame out as he saw his skin redden and blister from the growing heat. The Mercedes picked up speed as it rounded a curve at 120mph, flipped over, and smashed into a tree. Mahlon was immediately ejected from the car as he began to combust into a horrific agony of flames. He landed in the nearby ditch, and the unscrupulous flares continued. The fire he was now overcome by ignited every nerve in his body with unwavering torment. Every second of the scolding heat felt like he'd been burning in the pit of hell for eternity. Even with his body engulfed in flames, it still quickly tried to heal itself with its regenerative abilities. Still, the fire consumed Mahlon faster than the body could repair itself. He let out a loud scream in pain as he rolled on the ground to smother the blaze.

"KILION!!" Mahlon hadn't uttered his name in so long that the word sounded foreign. His brother's name resonated in his head, and he realized the fire was because of his brother. "KILION!!!" He said once more. It was all he could say as the pain took all of his other thoughts. All he could think of was his brother, and he realized this was the end of both of them. Whatever his brother felt, Mahlon also felt. They weren't twins as humans, but they were born from the same monstrous blood that created them in death. The fire overwhelming him was not something he could stop. Whatever Kilion had done was also the demise of him.

"Brother... You didn't need to allow this! You could have prevented our death!" Mahlon lay helpless in the ditch as the flames continued to scorch his skin and bones. Finally, the fire ended. His burnt flesh blistered and pussed, oozed, and then melted off his bones, leaving him as a burnt caucus with a good suit. The acrid smell of his burning flesh filled the night air, mingling with the metallic tang of his powerful and ancient blood. He lifted his arm to see the damage, surprised the flames did not kill him. He looked at his hand. Smooth dark brown skin was now replaced with charred decaying blackness.

"I'm not dead." As he rolled over on his stomach to stand, the feeling of the raw and tender seared flesh from the burns gave him the certainty that he'd made it through the fire. "I'm not dead." His full lips had melted off his face from the heat of the fire, making his words muffled. "I'm not dead." He looked down at his feet. The impact with the tree had flung his shoes off. Painfully searching near the wreck, he spotted his loafers. Despite the damage, they were still wearable, and he slid them onto his peeling bare feet. Mahlon wrenched in discomfort as they were tender and blistered. He walked over to the car to see the damage, which couldn't be seen from the road. It was still too dark, and the ravine he'd gone in was deep enough that he may not have been found any time soon. Unbeknownst to him during his time behind the wheel, The road he'd taken had veered away from the shoreline and was deep in the hills. Mahlon looked at the tree he hit and saw the point of impact.

Mahlon sat down beside the car. The sadness he'd felt was no longer part of him, but he could undoubtedly feel the loss of his brother, Kilion. His long-lost brother. The one he hadn't seen in at least six centuries. They were close before they'd been bitten. Living together. Marrying sisters. And even after the bite unalived them, their bond grew closer. They promised they would be there for each other, but after thousands of years together, they grew tired of each other's company. Kilion craved love and stability, and Mahlon wanted to live in the now. Their bond may not have been physical anymore, but they were emotionally tied. They could still feel each other no matter where in the world the other was, and that bond was all that was needed to ensure the other was still around.

Mahlon continued to sit as he thought the moment through. He was still alive, but his brother, for as much as he knew, was gone. He'd seen other vampires spontaneously combust, and that combustion usually meant eternal death.

He, on the other hand, was still alive. His brother, dead. "Why am I still here?" He lifted his hand and looked at it once again. The skin that was once charred and black had begun to rejuvenate itself. The new skin was dark and smooth, like it had never been burnt. He was pleased to see the new skin but knew he'd have to find a place to heal completely. The darkness of the night helped, but he'd need to bury himself to recharge.

He looked over his shoulder, peering at the sky to see dawn approaching the horizon. He didn't have too much time before the sun would be up. He surely would die in the sun, and even though he'd escaped death once in a night, he wasn't going to take any chances with a new day. He walked away from the mangled Mercedes and further down the ravine, where he found the beginnings of a hollowed-out burrow. Using his healed fingertips, he dug the burrow out just enough to curl into it and cover himself with dirt. *I must find out what happened to my brother before my death catches up with me.*

Chapter 1
Back on The Block...

The heels of Minah's Louboutin stiletto platform pumps clicked the bumpy cobblestone as she traipsed the sidewalk. The darkness of the night contrasting the dim light of the streetlights highlighted her slim physique while passing under them. Her curves were accentuated more by her knee-length fuchsia bodycon dress. Her diamond-encrusted clutch was held by her manicured hands, and the full set of French-tip gel nails was swung by her side as it pinched the half-smoked blunt between her other. Her natural wavy hair extensions, which were pressed long and straight down the middle of her back for the night's escapades, swayed in the opposite motion as her hips. The energy of her vibe set the tone for the type of trouble she wanted to get into.

"I see you, baby girl." The man hung out the window like a happy dog on a joy ride when he saw Minah walking his way. He blew the horn at her. She glanced his way but didn't respond. She and him both knew the code— you see me, I see you. No other cordials needed to be expressed. The man made an illegal U-turn in the middle of 24th Street and Bells Road, where the shipping containers are held once they make it off the port of Richmond. The man parked his car at the corner and got out. He locked his doors, checked his surroundings, and then scurried to catch up with her before she disappeared around the corner.

He sent out a cat-calling whistle when she turned her head to look his way. She then flashed a smile with her juicy, shimmering lips and winked with her left eye, her lashes batting slowly, almost covering her "come hither" stare. He picked up his pace, rounding the corner mere seconds after she did.

"Yeah, I seen you, baby girl. Looking all fine and what-not." He pulled her hand towards him, slowing her in her tracks. "I heard 'bout you. Yeah, my pat'na told me he fucked with you a month ago. He said you the baddest one down here, so I had to come see for myself."

"You said your friend told you about me?" Minah smiled coyly. "Your friend shouldn't be running his mouth about his lady." She let a giggle escape her lips and pulled her hand from his.

"He got a big mouth, but I'm not gonna tell anyone about you. I promise." He stepped closer to her and pulled her in, closing the space between them. He allowed his hand to roam down the side of her thigh and then back up so he could cup her round and firm backside. "Umph. That apple nice, but I want to know about that peach you got in the front."

She stared him in his eyes and slowly licked her lips before she responded. "You can. It'll cost, though."

"It's Friday, I got a pocket full of cash, and my bitch ain't home. I'm ready to play with you, baby girl. How much it cost for me to lick it and stick the head in?"

"Five hunnid." Minah put her hand on his dick and began to stroke it above his jeans softly.

"Damn, baby girl! That's a lot of money for some run-through pussy. How you gonna play me?"

Minah dropped her hand and her smile before she pulled away from him. Irritated, she folded her arms across her chest. "Look. Don't talk shit about my pussy. You either eating it or fucking it but you not gonna run your mouth about what I do with it. It's mine, and if I choose to charge YOU five to put that tiny ass dick in my good shit, then you gonna pay me what I say. Now it's five hunnid like I said, or you can get the fuck out my face."

"Easy, baby girl! Sweet thang with a pretty mouth like yours got some fire to it! You nasty inside and out. I like that in a bitch." He laughed at how feisty she turned out to be. He dug into his pocket, pulled out five one-hundred-dollar bills, and handed them to her. Minah put them in her clutch and placed it next to the garbage can close to where they were.

"You just gonna leave your money lying right there? Where your daddy at so he can hold it for you?"

"Ain't no daddies 'round here. But keep talking, and I'm sure Big Mama will pop up and cut your tongue out for slowing up this transaction. Now, pull your pants down so I can suck that lil' dick you hiding."

"Man, you feisty!" He laughed once more before dropping his jeans. His dick sprung to attention once his boxers were down his legs and crumpled on top of his denims. Minah stepped towards him and squatted to where her face was centered with his johnson. She grabbed it as if it were a mic and slowly wrapped her fingers around it. She looked up at him before saying, "This the best and last head you 'bout to ever have."

"You right about that. wifey don't do this shit. That's why I'm here." He laughed again before closing his eyes and anticipating her lips brushing against the tip.

Before Minah could perform, the shadows behind him shifted. Heels clicking from behind startled him out of his moment. While kneeling, Minah glanced up and then retreated with a timid step. The man looked behind him to see the most stunning woman standing in tall, liquid leather lace-up thigh boots, a black floor-length hooded cape, a white, three-inch wide diamond necklace, and nothing else. The entire mound of her breast and her shaven crotch were exposed by how the cape draped her tightly framed body. She dropped the hood from her head, exposing her wild, long, curly hair. Her eyes slanted upwards and were accentuated by her feathered lashes. Her pupils were dark pools of sensuality. She licked her lips with desire to see him so eager. The man smiled and turned to face her, forgetting Minah, who had scurried to the back corner of the alley.

"My, my my…. You fine as hell. You came to watch, or can I play with you, too?" The man turned to look for the pretty young one who was about to perform. "Hey, baby girl… Where'd you go? Looks like one of your friends just showed up. That's why you charge so much? You gotta split the bill with her?" Minah didn't answer. The man shrugged his shoulders and turned back to the mysterious woman. He greedily rubbed his hands together.

"Two-for-one or just the one of y'all. I. Don't. Give. A. Fuck. Y'all both fine. But you… You different. Something ain't right about the way you staring at me, but I fucking love that shit." Bianca walked closer to him and wrapped her fingers with her pointed black lacquer fingernails around his neck, squeezing it just enough to feel the buoyancy of his meaty neck. She then peered down at his aroused and swollen dick. Pre-cum dripped from its tip like a leaky faucet. The drool of lust for it formulated in the corners of her parted lips. She fell to her knees and grabbed his phallic with only her mouth and then swiftly slurped him into the back of her waiting throat, making the tip of him touch her tonsils.

The first stroke of her tongue wrapping around his pole sent quakes through his thighs. Her mouth slid slowly back to the tip before she sucked him back in suddenly. His knees buckled, and his eyes rolled back.

"Oh my god… girl! Who is you!" He whimpered out of pure bliss and allowed himself to give in to feelings he'd never experienced during sex. He looked down at her to see his juices slipping and dripping from her mouth. He began to shake in horror when he noticed the creamy red stream falling from him and her mouth. He tried to push her off his dick but failed. "What type of hold do you have on me?! Stop! I— I've had enough! Let go!"

Her teeth dug in further as the blood rushed into her mouth. She squeezed his balls with her fingertips to help pump the blood in faster.

"Let go of me, bitch!" He beat his fist on the back of the mysterious woman; however, his poundings became weak and undisruptive. "Baby girl! Come get your girl! I know you see her over here fucking my shit up! Help me! Don't let me go out like this!"

"I can't help you." Minah said as she meekly crawled from the corner. "No one is going to help you. You should have never come down here." Minah stood up and leaned on the wall beside her. She relit the blunt she'd thrown beside her and began to smoke as she tried not to watch her bait die in agony.

The man's head began to swirl as he lost consciousness. He fell to his knees and slumped to the side, no longer able to hold himself up. Bianca lifted her free hand and grabbed him by the neck, clenching tight enough that her nails broke his skin. His blood oozed between her fingernails. She undid her grip on his dick and pounced on his neck. Mangling it with her teeth, tearing through flesh and bone while sucking the blood from his main vein. The last of his plea to live and be set free gurgled softly in his throat. Still conscious and eyes wide awake. Bianca stood up and spit his grisly flesh from her teeth and onto his face, covering his opened mouth.

Chapter 2

"Did you call the boys to come get them already?" Bianca approached Minah, stepping her slender stiletto heel into the man's eyeball. The squish of the impact splattered on the stem of her shoe and stuck to it while she continued to walk. She forcefully grabbed Minah closer and wiped her bloody hands across Minah's cheeks and lips. She then grabbed her small melon-sized breasts and fondled them aggressively, cleaning the rest of her hands in the process.

"Yeah." Minah said uncomfortably, trying not to look at the mangled men or Bianca. "They haven't hit me back yet." She took one step from Bianca, not wanting to inhale the smell of death and bloody carcass that came from the mess around her mouth.

"You told the fellas I was hungry tonight because it's a bunch of dead niggas in the corner."

The stench of guilt and remorse for assisting in their patron's demise swirled with Bianca's four-course meal, making her nauseated. But Bianca pulled her closer and gripped her face, forcing Minah to look into her eyes so she could answer.

"Not tonight, Bianca. I ain't got it in me to hook up with you." Minah winced when Bianca squeezed her nipple for denying her advances.

"Change your mind." Bianca smiled menacingly. She squeezed Minah's nipple harder and then turned it ever so slightly. "Change your mind and give me a kiss. You know I like fucking after I've eaten."

A solemn tear rolled down Minah's face as she held back on voicing her pain and humiliation. She opened her mouth to resist Bianca's advances, but she saw where Bianca had bitten her own tongue, and her dark, thick blood sat atop like a little pill waiting to be swallowed. Bianca's blood still appealed to her. She was, in fact, an addict to it. She licked her lips as she gazed at her desire. Bianca's mouth turned into another smile, and she slithered her tongue out for Minah to lick.

Minah took the bait. She shoved her tongue into Bianca's mouth, lapping the droplet of blood from its place, and began kissing her forcefully. Bianca allowed Minah to chomp down on her plump bottom lip to taste more of the delectable nectar. Bianca's thick, sweet serum ignited a desire in her she thought was extinguished when she saw her kill another victim. Still, that was forgotten when Bianca's powerful blood seeped into her tastebuds. Nothing mattered after that first taste. She felt her nipples tighten and her clit swell with every swallow of the nutrient. The constant itch under her skin, reminding her that her body craved the blood, began to subside once the serum flowed swifter down her throat.

Minah pulled back from Bianca and looked at her mistress with desire. Her vision was keen from the clarity the blood gave it. Its powers were limited in her body, but it did enhance her sensual desires as well as heighten her senses to give a full erotic experience. "I'm ready to play my lady." Minah lay on the ground on her stomach and arched her back. Her petite bottom now tooted in the air. She wound her hips, mesmerizing Bianca at the site.

She lowered herself to Minah's derriere and placed a hand on each of her winding hips, halting their movement. She slowly bent closer and breathed in. "You smell fresh." Bianca stuck her tongue out and slid it between and down Minah's butt crack. The moisture from the hidden crevice was infused with body salt and the Dior Poison perfume Minah had sprayed earlier. Bianca's hands shifted position, allowing her fingers to open Minah's backside as if peeling an orange to reveal Minah's tight hole. Bianca drew some saliva from the back of her throat and spat it out on Minah's sphincter, making her clench.

"Nah-ah." Bianca shook her head at how Minah's body's responded and then playfully tapped Minah on her bottom. She smiled slyly. Bianca was oh so horny for her petite minion. "Keep that hole relaxed for me, or it's going to hurt when I open you up." While still gaping Minah's cheeks, she stuck out her pointer finger and licked it. She then used her fingernail to slice a thin 'X' across Minah's anus and pulled Minah's cheeks further apart. Minah winced slightly as she felt the ripping sensation coming from her backside. "Shhh… Minah… This will only hurt for a minute." Bianca leaned in further. The saliva still dripping off Minah's ass hole. She stuck her tongue in the orifice, loosening Minah just enough to let her know the experience wasn't going to be as bad as she thought. "Good girl, my little slut." Bianca said as she began to let her tongue tickle Minah's insides.

Minah arched her back even further as the sensational experience overwhelmed her sense of pleasure. Bianca reached around and used her fingertips to stroke Minah's clit, instantly making Minah groan in delight, and her sex juice began to stream down her leg. Suddenly, she felt a prick where Bianca had opened her hole. Bianca wrapped her lips where the blood from her teeth punctured and began sucking the blood from her wound while massaging Minah's pink sphincter.

"Bianca..." Minah whispered as she concentrated on being pleasured.

Bianca then let her fingertips slide from Minah's clit and into her waiting slit and began thrusting two of her appendages in and out of her.

"Oh my god..." Minah said in a deep guttural moan as she sexually exploded over Bianca's hand and overflowed into the space on the ground where she was posed doggy style.

Once Minah came to Bianca's satisfaction, she stood from behind her and finally wiped her mouth. "Good girl, my pet." She said to Minah as she stroked her minion's head.

"Bravo!" Lance clapped his hands enthusiastically as Bianca walked away from Minah. "Man, every time y'all hook up, it's a show!" Marco, Polo, Rell, and Phaizo, who were part of Lance's crew, began to clap and laugh along with him. Brothers Marco and Polo slapped hands in agreement that the sexcapade was, in fact, enjoyable. Rell grabbed Minah's clothes and bashfully handed them to her. She snatched them from his hands and began to put them on. Bianca smiled coyly and curtsied at her applause. Blood-smeared handprints could be seen all over her body. Phaizo handed the cape she was draped in previously back to her and stepped away cautiously, uncertain if she was hungry for a second helping.

"Thanks, fellas. I'm not here for your amusement, but I'm glad you found some pleasure in mine." She strolled past them on her way out of the alley and snapped her fingers to call them back to her attention. "Lance, walk with me. The rest of you freaks, get to cleaning. There are three bodies in there tonight. Pile 'em at the end of the block so they can go out with the trash tomorrow." Lance picked up his pace to match Bianca's stride. The other four guys got to work clearing the bodies Bianca had fed on from the night's engagement. Minah finished dressing and caught up with Bianca and Lance but walked behind them, not wanting to be too involved in the conversation. Sex with Bianca had always been humiliating, but them watching her being taken advantage of was just demoralizing.

"Catch me up on tonight's business." Bianca pulled a cigarette from her cape's pocket along with a lighter. She put the cigarette to her lips, and Lance took the lighter from her hand and lit the cigarette for her. She'd grown accustomed to having a pull from one after her night outs. Since cancer was no longer a factor and she couldn't get addicted to them, the after-dinner cigarette had become her ritual and a habit she'd picked up from Lucy, her long-dead mentor and nemesis. She took a long inhale of the Virginia Slim and then exhaled the smoke into his face. Lance coughed and then waved the vapors away.

"We did good tonight, Boss. The crew managed the dope boys, and they made a couple of stacks. The twins will drop that money off later at your place. Rell and Phaizo already got the cash from Roxanne and the girls. Phaizo said the money sack was a little light. Rox told him clientele been scarce. The girls are hearing rumors on The Block that word about you being a monster roaming around getting out, so people starting to be scared to come round here. Plus, with all these demos and renovations going on around here, it's not too many places the girls can take their dates."

"Little bitches." Bianca scoffed at the idea that men were actually fearful of coming to get pussy. "Minah. Meet up with Roxanne and let her know she and the girls need to come up with something to get the clientele back, or they gonna start losing one girl a night to me."

Minah nodded and then lowered her head, keeping her eyes on the ground as she continued to walk behind them.

"What else is going on out here? Any word about Richmond's Finest?"

"Nah. They don't come down here no more. They still complaining about the bodies you keep leaving on the curb though. They say we need a better way of disposing them."

"Tell 'em shut the fuck up and figure it out themselves. Ain't nobody gonna tell me how to run my shit." Bianca laughed at the police's audacity. "Hell… they should be paying me for getting these degenerates off the streets." Bianca passed a woman on the sidewalk as she made her way back to her place.

The woman looked down at the ground before her, not wanting to gawk at the tall, scandalous beauty wearing only latex boots and hardly anything else. However, Bianca was enraptured by the woman's scent of stale cigarettes, dark liquor, and Chantilly perfume, which reminded her of a past she'd long forgotten. However, the blowing horn of the green sedan pulled her out of her trance. She looked over to see Marco, Phaizo, Rell, and Polo signaling for Lance to join them.

Lance lifted his brow inquisitively at Bianca, ignoring her curvaceous but tight and toned body. Her nakedness never aroused him. He'd grown accustomed to her walking freely without clothes inside and outside of the penthouse that any appeal it would have had was lost on him. He wanted to keep his relationship purely professional, and desiring the boss made him feel weak. "We done here? The fellas and I are headed downtown for a bite to eat and then a house party."

Bianca waved him away, and he quickly made his way to the open car door to jump in. She turned back towards them and said, "And don't blow your motherfucking horn at me no damn more! Do that shit again, and it's your ass!"

"Sorry, B!" They burst into laughter and sped off. She liked them. They were like her brothers in a weird way, but they lacked discipline. However, she needed them to manage the affairs of The Block. She'd learned she had no desire to do it like Daddy did, but The Block needed a leader, and that spot was hers. The crew kept things moving so she could indulge in what she wanted most, and that was blood and sex.

"Hello, Bianca." She turned towards the woman who'd just passed her on the street with the reminiscent smell. When the woman said 'hello,' it hit her why her scent brought back the memories of her old home. Her eyes widened in shock and then dimmed coolly when she recognized who it was. Minah looked at the woman as well and then at Bianca in wonderment.

"What you doing here?" She looked the woman up and down, determining by her worn outfit, run-over shoes, and the old-school wrap hairstyle with the curled-under ends she finally hit bottom. Unconsciously, she closed the opening of her cape and walked closer to her. Minah followed behind.

"You look good." Vivian raised her hand and touched a loc of Bianca's coils. Irritated by her fake sensibility, Bianca smacked Vivian's hand away. Vivian frowned, figuring by her nurturing gesture Bianca wouldn't be receptive to any more affection she tried to show. "I've missed you, daughter."

"Daughter…" Minah whispered in shock. Bianca gave Minah a quick look, reminding her to keep her comments to herself. Minah lowered her eyes and stepped back behind Bianca as the two women continued to talk.

"Yeah, well, I wasn't expecting you to find me."

"I figured. You left so fast… I didn't know you were really gone for like a week."

Bianca rolled her eyes. "Don't give me that shit. You ain't look for me. We both know you didn't give two cracks of an egg 'bout where I was and what I was up to. Something or somebody else sent you to find me."

Vivian shook her head in denial. "No. Nothing like that. Ain't nobody send me and I don't know that much about you. I mean… there's a rumor about you I've heard, and I was able to put two-and-two together, and that's how I found you, but before that, I didn't know a thing."

"Well, now that you've found me and you know I'm here, you can go on back home. I'm good without you." Bianca turned to walk away, but before she could, Vivian pulled her arm just enough to stop Bianca and pull her back.

"Don't be like that to me. I came all this way to see you, and I just want to talk. I want to see how you doing and maybe apologize and make things right between us. Yeah, I was a bad mama. I screwed up big time with you. Come on home, and I promise ain't nothing coming between us again. Not nothing. Not even a man."

Bianca stared at her mother long and hard as she mulled over Vivian's words. *No man... Derrick must have really died.* She smiled slightly at that revelation but shook her head 'no'.

"Nah. I ain't leaving here. This is my home now." Bianca stretched her hands in opposite directions to signify her domain. "I run all this, and I ain't got to run scared from nobody here. I'm good. Now go on back home. You've made your peace. I'm good." Bianca picked up her pace as she headed back towards the Hoe-tel.

Vivian followed behind, not ready to give up on being with her. "But what if I stay here with you? What if I come live with you? Truthfully, I don't have a place at home anymore. I lost it in foreclosure. Can I come stay with you 'til I get back on my feet? I can find a job and get a little apartment around here, and we can see each other and work on our relationship?"

Bianca halted once more and turned back to Vivian. She scoffed at the thought of them making nice and being friends. "I don't know about that... you coming to live with me over here."

Vivian could see she was losing her. She nervously looked around and spotted a corner diner with the light on. "Let me treat you to a slice of pie and coffee; we can talk more. As you can see, I'm here by myself. Ain't no Derrick no more. Plus, I can tell you how I found you— and about that rumor I heard."

Bianca thought about it for a moment and nodded her head in agreement. "Alright, buy me some pie."

Chapter 3

The bell above the diner's door chimed as they walked in together. The regulars checkered the restaurant and stared with confusion and a hint of fear when Bianca passed the threshold. She paused, surveyed the room, and then led the way to the booth, hugging against the wide-paned window facing the main street of her territory. Minah hopped into the booth, choosing the space at the door and beside the window. Bianca sat beside her and begrudgingly gestured for Vivian to sit down in the booth across from them.

The waitress on duty hesitated but finally chose to make her way over to take their order. She kept her head low as she stood there. It was peculiar for the waitress to see what they knew as the Devil Bitch at the diner, and she feared Bianca's every move. "What y'all gonna have?" She said as she tried to steady her pencil against the order pad.

"Just some water for me." Minah replied.

"I'll have a coffee— black. And she'll have the pie." Vivian said as she nodded towards Bianca. Bianca half-smiled at her mother and waved the waitress away, who immediately scampered back to the kitchen to fill the order.

Vivian took a deep breath and exhaled as she looked around the diner, noticing that the eyes of its patrons darted their way or just plain out stared. The click of the jukebox turning on could be heard, allowing everyone to revert to their plates in front of them. Vivian returned her attention to the table, where she met Bianca's cold glare.

"Why? Why are you here now? I left that trash dump you called home years ago. You didn't find me then, and just like that," Bianca snapped her fingers. Her threatening, long, daggered glossed nails clicked when her fingertips connected. "you're here wanting to fix things between us."

"It wasn't just like that, B. I struggled with the decision to look for you." Vivian fidgeted as she struggled to find the right things to say to a daughter she was never close to. "I admit it. I wasn't the best mom. Hell... drinking and drugging didn't make it better either."

"You're right about that." Bianca waved the waitress over, who'd been standing nearby with their order for several minutes. She hurriedly placed their orders in front of them and quickly disappeared into the kitchen only to peek out the door to watch them for any signs of discontent.

Vivian huffed out her frustration for stumbling over her thoughts and how she should begin the conversation. "Look now, this ain't easy for me. I ain't see the wrong in my actions back then. I mean... I was working two jobs, trying to raise you, and trying to keep a cheating, low-down, trifling man."

"You ain't lied about that cheating man part." Bianca stabbed her fork into her pie, bringing a piece to her mouth and chomping down on it. She chewed it slowly as she reminisced about that last night she was home with him. His attempt to rape her was foiled by her quick thinking. She hated him for what he'd done, but she hated her mom for leaving her to fend him off. She blinked slowly, and as her eyes closed in those quick seconds, she saw the room filled with his blood and him lying on the floor. Dead? She didn't know for sure. She just knew it gave her the opportunity to leave him and her mom in her past and start over.

"Derrick wasn't my best decision by far. Luckily for the both of us, he's gone."

"Gone-gone?" Bianca stopped chewing and swallowed her pie hard. It was odd to her that she still felt nervous about taking his life when she's so comfortable doing it on The Block. In some strange way, Derrick was family to her. In that moment of desperation living in that rank home with him, she wanted him dead, but he'd been around her for so long that there was a familiarity that tugged at her heart. She despised him. However, she never wanted his murder on her hands.

Vivian felt Bianca's uneasiness when talking about Derrick. She reached across the table and grabbed Bianca's free hand and stroked it soothingly before she updated her on his condition. "He survived... Barely survived." She patted her hand, then let it go. Bianca sat back in her seat and let out a small sigh of relief.

"Now, don't get me wrong. He deserved that beating you gave him." Vivian chuckled, remembering seeing him sitting at the table nursing his wounds and the blood all over the living room. Shocked initially, she assumed he'd murdered Bianca, and she'd put up a fight that she lost. That was the first time she'd ever felt how much she'd actually loved her only child. The instant agony she felt when she thought she lost her without making things right between them rushed through her body and shook her violently.

Then anger set in, and all she wanted to do was end Derrick's life. She grabbed her walking stick that rested behind the door and charged Derrick with it. She violently beat him while he yelped and hobbled around the room to get away from the brutal flogging. Through her uncontrollable tears and jumbled curses spun his way, she heard the words, "She's not dead! She ran away! I didn't hurt her!"

She collapsed on the floor after actually hearing him beg her to stop and realizing Bianca was gone without a trace.

"Nah, he didn't die that night. After I realized you fucked him up, I started to see him different. I thought his ass killed you. He tried to spin it like you just went crazy on his trifling ass, but his story didn't add up. And then his drunk ass slipped up and told Nod en'em that you fucked him up 'cause you ain't give him no pussy but don't mind giving it up to them boys behind the school. When I heard that shit, I felt worse 'cause all those times you told me he was coming on to you, I never listened." Vivian shook her head in shame before she continued. "Had I heard what you was trying to tell me, you would not had never left, and we could have kicked his ass together."

Vivian tilted her head back and laughed at the thought of them both beating up on Derrick. But Bianca didn't laugh. Unfortunately, Vivian's realization came too late for her. Her mother's love was too late. She'd been transformed and was more powerful than before she left that shit-hole town, and nothing from the past affected her any longer.

Vivian brought her head back from her laugh and was opposite her stone-faced daughter. She shifted her eyes, coughed out the last of her laugh, and fiddled with her coffee mug in shame of the horrible past her daughter endured. She then suddenly lit up at the thought of Derrick's actual demise and wanted to share, hoping if Bianca heard it, she'd lighten up.

"But he did die." She nodded in satisfaction and waited for Bianca's response, but her expression didn't change. Nonetheless, Vivian continued. "After a few months of healing, he returned to work, and on his first day back, he showed up drunk and fell off a scaffolding lift." Vivian slapped her thigh and let out another laugh. "Girl, I'm so glad that nigga died!" She laughed harder. "Bad thing about it is, he ain't have insurance. They tried to stick me with the bill, but I let the county burn him up and forget he ever existed." Tears of joy slid from the crevices of her squinted eyes while continuing to be amused by his fate. She wiped the tears away with the back of her hand once the memory passed.

Bianca watched Vivian enjoy her own story, and it hit her; she'd never seen her mother this happy. In all her life, she'd only seen her mother sad and bitter. There were never any hugs, never a 'I love you,' or moments where they enjoyed each other. This was the first time she'd ever seen her mother laugh out loud as if there were no worries in the world. Bianca's face softened as she continued to watch her, and then the thought of stumpy old Derrick screaming as he fell to his death put a smile on her face as well. What made her laugh out loud was thinking of him splattered and plastered on the dusty concrete like a cartoon character. Bianca barreled over in amusement, joining her mother in a celebratory joy of Derrick's death.

Minah watched the two of them share the moment and became jealous. She sucked her teeth, folded her arms, and looked out the window. She never had a chance to be light-hearted with Bianca for as long as she'd been with her. Bianca always kept her on pins and needles or bled out so she couldn't do anything but rest and rejuvenate— for Bianca's pleasure. Her life with Bianca was miserable, but she needed her for the blood, and Bianca seemed to need her because she always kept her close... almost like a favorite toy. She was loyal to her owner, and even though Bianca treated her badly, they belonged to each other. Vivian coming into the picture could mess it all up. Minah grabbed the pie plate and began to eat the rest of the pastry she knew Bianca was not going to finish. Irritated by them still laughing at Derrick's mishap, Minah decided she'd interject and change the subject, hoping Bianca would remember why she despised her mother.

"So, if you couldn't figure out where she was, how you find her?" Bianca shot Minah a cold look, which made Minah lower her eyes and sink into the booth, trying to disappear. Minah's comment made Bianca remember her repressed resentment. She wasn't there to make nice with Vivian. Derrick's death was not something to bond over. It wasn't going to make up for years of neglect and rejection. Bianca folded her arms and tilted her head in discontent.

"Yeah, how you find me. I ain't leave no note or nothing. In fact, I made sure I covered my tracks."

"You did. And at first, I wasn't looking for you. I didn't know how to hire no detective or nothing. And for a little while, I just prayed you'd come back, but then you never did so; I just tried to not think about you. And like I said, Derrick died, and ain't have no insurance policy. I needed his paycheck to get by. My job ain't pay me enough to keep the house, so I sold everything and lived in my car for a bit and just drove around from city to city, surviving. Finally, I ran into a friend from Richmond, and she let me come chill with her. I been in Richmond, on the Northside off Brookland Park, near the Chicken Box for some months." Bianca's stare grew harder at the thought that her mother had been living so close to her without her knowledge.

"And, ain't nothing you said told me how you found me."

"Right… so my homegirl… she works at some fancy club named Mama Jo's. You came in there some time ago. She remembered your face from a picture I showed her when I told her you'd run off. She couldn't get to you, though. She said you were with some guy named Daddy and he won't no good."

"Yeah, he dead too. That muthafucka had it coming."

"Well, she told me he died, and then she didn't see you no more and didn't know how to get in contact with you. But then…" Vivian shifted in her seat uncomfortably as she continued her story. "But then she said, dead bodies were showing up over here, which wasn't too big of a deal because this side of town is like Murderville. But she said the bodies had bite marks on them, and they won't dying of bullet wounds or anything else." Bianca smiled at her known malevolence.

"And then she said there was some rumors about you taking Daddy's place and running The Block. But you also a… monster. Like you have some type of devil in you and that everyone over here saw you rip your friend up in the middle of the street. I asked her to bring me here because I didn't believe it, but she wouldn't, so I went to the police station and asked did they have information on you and they told me the same thing. They said to stay away from here because you are not what I think you are. But I had to see for myself. So, I came down here to see for myself. And tonight… I saw it. I saw you— the new you."

"And what do you think?" Bianca said.

Vivian's smile spread across her face while looking Bianca up and down. "Baby, you are glorious." She said proudly. "I saw you for what you have become. A beautiful bitch who don't take no shit from none of these half-assed niggas looking to use you up." Bianca smiled slyly at the description. "You the baddest bitch on this side of town and probably walking this earth. My baby girl a queen on these streets and these niggas and raggedy bitches bow down to my baby." Vivian tipped her head in honor of her daughter's authority and then raised it to meet Bianca eye-to-eye. "All hail the queen." She said in a low, sultry way, dripped in satisfaction.

Bianca acknowledged her mother's honor and bowed back. "Yes, all hail… me. 'Cause I run this shit."

Vivian reached over the table once more and stroked her cheek lovingly. "My baby…" she said the words softly as the glimmer of her tears began to flood her eyes. Bianca leaned into the stroke as if this moment was what she'd longed for. She briefly closed her eyes and exhaled in a show of relief for all the years she was hated and berated. Minah watched as the scene unfolded between the mother and daughter and rolled her eyes out of Bianca's eyeshot.

Vivian sat back in her seat and looked Bianca over again with pride before speaking. "Let me come stay with you a while."

Bianca's eyes widened, and her mouth dropped at the request. "Are you serious? You think I'm going to let you come live with me?"

"Why not? I said I was sorry. We can start over, and I promise I won't be in the way."

"Nah." Bianca rapidly shook her head no as she thought of all the things that could go wrong. "I got a lot going on, and I could see you fucking my shit up. Nah. Let's call it even. We good and everything but I'm not trying to have you live with me. It's stuff about me you not ready to learn. I'm not that girl that ran away years ago."

"B, I know you not. I know what you do."

"Nope. It's not about the bodies that they telling you about. It's bigger than that."

"Bianca, trust me when I say I know what you do and I know what you are." Their eyes met. Vivian noted the unusual color of her daughter's clear golden eyes, the claw-like fingernails, and the richness in her brown tone skin. Even her hair was unusually full. Her physique, tight and toned. At a glance, one would admire her beauty, but up close and compared to other females, Bianca's presence teetered on the other-worldly. As her mother, and even after several years of being absent, Vivian could tell the difference in her child was something time did not affect.

"For the first time, I see you. I see everything about you. You not just gorgeous, you a weapon and I want to be a part of what you got going on. I just want to be there when you come home and just be your mama. Be that mama you need right now. I'm sure this lil' girl you got following you around can't replace me… your mama."

"Don't come up in here disrespecting me! You don't know me!" Vivian's words offended Minah. She scooted up close to Bianca and put her hand over Bianca's. "I got what she wants… and that's something you can never ever come between. Minah leaned in and kissed Bianca seductively on the lips. Bianca began to kiss her in return while her hand made its way up Minah's back. She then grabbed her hair, pulling Minah off her.

Minah winced at the pain as Bianca pushed her back close to the window. "Don't ever do that shit again. I'm not yo' bitch."

"Sorry." Minah mumbled while rubbing her head where Bianca had pulled it.

Vivian stifled her smug chuckle before she continued her thought. "So just let me come with you. I'll make that place you stay in a home. I promise I won't get in the way."

Bianca sat quietly for a moment as she thought the proposition over. She never would have believed she and Vivian could be a real mother-daughter duo like she longed for as a child. However, the degradation she endured under her mother's "careful" watch overshadowed the euphoric desire to have her mother with her.

"I don't know about that. You really fucked me up."

"True. But I'm not that person anymore. I've changed so much. Just let me prove it to you."

Bianca looked over at Minah, who sat sulking by the window and then looked around the diner at the customers who tried not to stare at her. *All these people are scared of me. They don't like me. They just scared of me. Mama act like she not, though.* She eyed Vivian, who continued to smile lovingly at her. A look of remorse drove the expressions on her face, and Bianca made a decision.

"Alright, you can come." Vivian's smile lit up, and she clapped her hands with enjoyment. Minah folded her arms in a huff knowing she'd lost the battle to keep Bianca to herself. "But don't get in my way. I ain't got time for you to be all up in my business. Just know that I run this shit, and you just a spectator."

Vivian nodded her head in agreement. "I get it. You the boss. I'm not going to interfere. I just want to be around you. That's all."

Bianca took one more hard look at her mother and then threw her hands up. "Well, it's agreed. Come on. I'll take you with me."

Chapter 4

Minah opened the door to their twenty-second-floor penthouse at River Towers, affectionately known as the "Hoe-tel". When Minah opened its door, Bianca breezed in, handed her the dark cape, and traipsed through the foyer. Her bare, bronzed backside sashayed as she moved towards the kitchen to wipe the dried blood from her body. Vivian stood in the door in awe of the penthouse's lavish décor. The ample open living space was flooded by the night's starlit landscape, shaped by the six-foot-tall windows. Hanging from the ceiling were three chandeliers. One chandelier hung in the middle of the main living space, its individual diamond-cut pieces dangling from its gold hoops refracted the room's light, allowing it to sparkle. The other chandelier was styled in an abstract group of circles and could be seen hanging in the dining space. The last chandelier was a small box shape and hung above her in the space designated for the penthouse's entrance. Vivian peered to her left and saw the gourmet kitchen with its massive twelve-foot white marbled top waterfall island. All of the appliances in the kitchen were black matte to match the dark black slate floor. The fixtures for the sink, the knobs on the eight-burner gas stove, and the handles for the cabinets and refrigerator were a matte gold tone with a contemporary streamlined style. Over to the right and through the living room was a covered balcony held up by a thick, dark black metal railing. The floors throughout the main living space were rustic, brown-colored wood.

From the outside, the River Towers crumbling building did not reveal how well Bianca lived. When Daddy was in charge, the residence was exquisite inside and out. A manicured lawn, a smooth cemented driveway, and an elegant lobby included a doorman and front desk personnel. Over the years, the building became unkempt, and the amenities Daddy prided himself on fell into disrepair. Bianca's mind wasn't clouded by elegance and frills like Daddy was. Her desires lay within the hunt and kill of anyone she deemed inadequate to live. However, she liked a level of glamour Daddy denied her when he tossed her out of her ninth-floor apartment when he had no use for her.

"Well, don't just stand there. Come on in and find somewhere to sit." Minah said as she shut the door when Vivian finally made her way in. She headed to one of the two Chesterfield-styled couches facing each other and sat down, adoringly rubbing its expensive pearl-colored leather.

"I'll be back." Minah said as she headed towards Bianca's bedroom door but turned back around to address Vivian before being out of earshot. "Everything in here is expensive so don't touch nothing and don't break nothing." Vivian smiled over clenched teeth before Minah walked away. As Minah made her way down the hall, she heard the water from the shower coming from Bianca's bathroom. She could also smell the lavender spice oils she used on her skin after bathing the night's blood from her body. Minah entered her room and grabbed Bianca's gold plush bathrobe and pedicure slippers.

Just as she entered the white-on-white marbled bathroom with the gold fixtures that matched the kitchen's, Bianca stepped out of the shower with the steam from the hot water escaping from behind her. Bianca dripped water from head to toe. Her hair was wet, wavy, and long down her back from being saturated by the shower head's waterfall-effect sprout. Her skin was effortlessly moist and glistening. Minah grabbed the towel hanging on the bar beside the shower and slowly dried Bianca. Bianca ran her fingers through her hair to detangle it as Minah made her way up towards Bianca's tresses, her hands paying close attention to the crevice between her bottom and her puss. Minah felt Bianca's knees buckle slightly as she rubbed her soft pubic hair dry.

"Stay right there." Bianca removed her hands from her head and placed them on Minah's, coaxing her to place her lips on the ones between her thighs. Minah dropped the towel and used her two fingers to expose Bianca's tight-feeling bulbous clit.

With Minah's free hand, she reached over to the bathroom sink and picked up Bianca's favorite toy with the bumpy ridges on the lengthened end. She pressed the 'on' button of the toy, and it began to vibrate with a low hum. Minah pinched Bianca's clit and rested the toy slightly at the very tip of her enlarged button. Bianca began to squirm and moan with delight as the vibrator brought her to her quick climax. Minah stuck a finger into Bianca's vagina opening right when Bianca began to explode. Minah made the hole wider by stretching it slightly, allowing Bianca's cum to pour out of her and spill onto the floor.

Bianca's chest heaved as she regained composure. She stared at Minah with satisfaction as she grabbed her towel. "You can clean that up now." She pointed to the wet spot on the floor, and Minah leaned into the cum spot and licked it up, understanding exactly how Bianca wanted it to be done.

Bianca then pulled Minah from the floor and insistently kissed her. Minah tried to pull away, but Bianca held the back of her head and forced her to remain, sucking Minah's bottom lip into her mouth and in between her teeth. With just enough pressure, she forcibly bit down, piercing her skin and drawing Minah's blood down her throat. A tear from the pain rolled down Minah's cheek. Bianca finally let go and pushed Minah to the floor with a smirk on her face. "Next time you get the idea to kiss me like you own me, just remember you belong to me and not the other way around."

Minah wiped her tears and her lip with the back of her hand. "Yes, Miss…" Minah said in a low sorrowful voice. She then grabbed the gold slippers and slid them onto Bianca's feet. She stood and grabbed the robe and held it open for Bianca to put on. Bianca then walked out of the bathroom, and Minah followed, grabbing the heated lavender spice oil posted on the sink. Bianca sat on her round, king-sized bed and allowed her robe to drape off her body as she watched Minah prepare the room by lighting candles and turning on her favorite slow jams playlist. Minah then approached the bed, knelt before Bianca, and placed her toes on Minah's lap. Minah pulled out her pedicure set and began clipping and shaping Bianca's toenails. Once done, she poured the lavender oil into her hands, rubbed them together, and massaged it into her feet. Bianca let out a low moan and relaxed back on the bed as Minah started her nightly rub down.

"So, what you think?"

"Think about what?" Minah poured more oil into her hand and began massaging Bianca's legs.

"About her showing up."

Minah shrugged her shoulders without care. "I mean, if you want her here, I guess it's alright."

"You lying. I saw how you looked at me cross-eyed because I let her come back here." Bianca chuckled a bit, remembering how hard it is for Minah to keep her emotions from her.

"I mean… I was confused as to why you would let her come here. I didn't even know your mother was even alive. You never talk about her."

"Because it's nothing to talk about." Bianca quickly retorted.

Minah slowed her manipulating hands, hesitant to continue the conversation but curious about the things said at the diner. "You seemed relieved to hear about that guy not dying…" Minah said. She then felt Bianca's body tense with her statement.

"Like, aren't you relieved you didn't kill that guy?"

"I couldn't give a fuck about that guy."

Minah picked up the pace of the massage and moved up Bianca's thighs, kneading them deeply to get her to relax again. "Well, it sounds like he deserved what he had coming. Glad she was able to tell you he really is dead and gone. Is that why you feel she needs to stay here? 'Cause now he is not coming between you and hers relationship?" Minah rubbed her stomach with the oil and then began rubbing upwards to her breast. Her areolas were a darker shade than her nipples, sitting erect as she worked the fatty tissue around them. Bianca let out another moan, which sounded more like a cheetah's purr.

Minah massaged her neck and arms, then flipped her over and rubbed her back and then down towards her butt. "How do you feel about her being here? Do you want her watching your every move?"

Bianca turned her head to the side and said, "She's not going to be up in my business. Like she said, she knows what I am, and she probably doesn't want to get on my bad side. We cool, but we not cool like that."

Minah used her fingertips to spread Bianca's bottom cheeks apart, massaged the oil into the groove between her derriere, and then brought the cheeks back together. Then, in one swift motion, she used her knuckles to push the meaty cheeks up in her palm and brought them back down in a slow and steadied motion to knead on the muscles in her backside.

"Well, don't be so sure about that. You know mama's have a way of always being in your business whether you want them there or not. My mama stayed in my business… always meddling and telling me what to do. I got tired of that, so I left. She loved me and everything, but she was just too nosey." Minah shook the thought of her good-hearted mother out of her head. She knew her mom's meddling was just love and attention, and at times, she wished she could go back to her, but that was over three hundred years ago. All of her loved ones were dead and gone. Besides, she could never let her mom see who she'd become. It would break her heart.

"Well, Vivian ain't yo mama. Vivian a whole bitch, and she only cares about herself. I know what she wants. She just wants a few dollars, and once she gets it, she'll keep her mouth shut— probably get bored and leave anyway." Bianca rolled back over once Minah was done and stood up so Minah could help her back into her wrap.

Minah began to tie up Bianca's robe as she continued speaking. "Well, I don't trust her. I can already tell she up to no good, and I don't think she should be here with us. Just give her some money and put her out. It's not like you ain't got it to give." Minah finished fixing Bianca's attire and met her angry glare, realizing then she'd said too much again. "My bad... I didn't mean what I said about your ma—"

Bianca swiftly raised her hand and brought it across Minah's face with tremendous force. Minah hit the floor, and Bianca pounced on her, grabbing her by the head and exposing her neck. Enraged, Bianca's teeth bore down into Minah's neck, forcibly drawing the blood into her mouth. Minah let out a scream as she struggled to free herself, but she quickly became weak and stopped resisting, allowing Bianca to place her into a heroine-like induced trance.

Satisfied, Bianca stood and wiped her mouth, and spit the residue of Minah's blood onto her.

"No one asked you about my mama no-ways." Bianca turned around to head out of her room to see Vivian standing at the door with a crooked smile across her face.

"Don't mind me, baby. Sometimes, 'the help' needs to be put in their place. You want me to fix you something to drink to wash her down with?"

Chapter 5

"…And you better come back with some money tonight!"

Minah shut the door of the penthouse after Bianca's last demands. For days, Minah lay in bed, recouping from the massive drainage she endured the night Vivian arrived. Bianca also wouldn't let her out of her room as punishment for vocalizing her opinion about her mother staying with them. For those days she was in confinement, she could only hear the murmurs of Bianca and Vivian's voices in conversation with each other. Now and again, Minah could catch the faint sound of an unfamiliar light-hearted laugh, which she could only assume came from her mistress. Bursts of happiness that only good memories could bring were more frequent than before her mother arrived, and Minah definitely felt like an outsider because of it. In those lonely days, locked in a dark room with barely any food and only a sparse supply of blood, Minah was hooked again. In those early mornings of captivity, after Bianca came back from hunting, Bianca would hungrily ravish Minah, draining her and then refilling her with only her addicting blood. The continuous cycle only kept Minah dependent on Bianca. In past years, she tried several times to run, but either Bianca, the blood, or her selfish desires called her back. To escape had become a futile attempt no one took seriously. And lately, her half-baked efforts to leave were mocked by Bianca, and the crew would laugh at her when she'd come back more broken than when she left.

"Daddy taught me how to break a bitch well." Bianca had told her in the past. Daddy had been Bianca's pimp, who used not just brutal but psychological tactics to keep Bianca in her place. Minah had never met him, but his heir of tyranny could be felt through Bianca's actions. Had it not been for Kilion saving Bianca from the streets, she wouldn't be who she was. However, Bianca never saw Kilion's "Gift of Forever" as an act of love or kindness. Even though Minah was jealous, he chose to bless Bianca as his successor and not her.

She'd been Kilion's "woman" for several hundred years, allowing him to feed on her when he was hungry and find refuge and shelter within her home when he needed healing. She knew in her heart he saw her potential and the love she had for him, but he overlooked all of that and chose Bianca to carry on his legacy. Minah harbored a hidden resentment towards Bianca for being the chosen one, and her heart shattered when she sensed his death through their own blood connection.

Despite the pain of his blood flowing through Bianca's veins and not hers, she couldn't abandon her mistress, not out of love but because she was loyal to the blood. As much as she felt she loved Kilion, it was he who got her hooked on the lust for it, but he never abused that bond. He allowed her to indulge in his alluring nectar but never permitted the use of it to cross over into addiction. The line between her love for Kilion and her desire for the blood was thin, though. When he left her by dying in the morning sun, she knew she couldn't live without Kilion and the blood. She had to seek Bianca out to at least satisfy her need for the liquid lifeline. Once Bianca knew how addictive the blood could be, she abused it to keep Minah attached to her.

Out in front of River Towers, Minah hopped in an Uber and headed down to her favorite corner across from the diner, where she first encountered Vivian. The Uber parked, and she walked across the street to the diner, where she saw a glimpse of herself in the window's reflection. Her wig was laid flat to her head, and her Twenty-two-inch Malaysian wavy bust-down slinked towards the top of her butt. Her feathered lashes were in place, and the hue of her makeup matched the bubble gum pink skirt and bra outfit with which she adorned her slight frame. Her clear plastic knee-high boots slightly sagged down her legs and the clear plastic style of the boot showed her chipped pink pedicure that she hadn't had time to refresh because Bianca had her locked in the room. Her shoulders slightly slumped as she stared at her reflection, which showed what no one but she could see. She was alone, unloved, and wasting away. *If Kilion had stayed and just loved me…*

Not wanting to think about what could have been any longer, she straightened her shoulders and shook off her woes. Then, she ran her fingers through the synthetic strands of her lace front and went through the diner's door.

"Frank, you got my usual ready?" Minah said to the bartender, who didn't look up from pouring drinks but knew who it was by the time of day and her high sing-song voice.

"Yeah, go on and head to the kitchen's counter. It's sitting over there. Holla at Kiki and let her know you picking up your order."

As she passed him, she tapped the bar twice with an open hand to acknowledge his instructions.

"Hey Kiki! I got my special. I'll be back in the morning for my coffee."

"Alright, then girl. I'll see you in the morning."

Minah grabbed her fruit smoothie soda concoction Frank always made for her. Frank would make it right before she got there, and Kiki kept an eye on it until she picked it up. She then turned around and headed out the way she came.

"Hey girl, I ain't seen you around in a while. Where you been?"

Minah halted in her tracks to see her friend sitting in the booth alone. She smiled brightly at the sight of him. He smiled back, took a fork full of food from his plate, and placed it in his mouth. "Hey, Kingston." She put her drink down and sat across from him. "Yeah. I've been at home. You know how Bianca can be."

Kingston rolled his eyes at the toxic relationship Minah hinted at. "Girl, don't I know. I don't even understand how you put up with her."

"I feel ya, but it ain't all bad. She just a little jealous, that's all."

"I can't tell you what to do, but you can up and leave her if you want."

"Now, Kingston, you know that ain't true. You know how she can get. If I leave, then who going to keep her from fucking with y'all?"

"Humph… you think you protecting us, but girl, you ain't no match for her. She gonna do what she want to do."

Minah took a sip of her drink and thought about his words. "Maybe you right Kingston, but we'll never know 'cause I don't plan on leaving no time soon." She took another sip and stood up to leave. "I got to go. My shift starting in a few, but I'll catch up with you in the morning."

"Alright, girl. I'll see you then."

Minah headed out of the diner and back across the street. The sun was beginning to set, and she wanted to be on her favorite corner to watch the hustle and bustle of the people winding down and heading home. *These are the people I keep safe*, she thought, hoping to convince herself she was a type of hero.

There was a time when Bianca first took over, and no one would be out on the streets when the sun went down. After a while, though, the people who lived on The Block understood they were fair game if Bianca was out hunting. Eventually, Bianca and the people who lived around them came to an unspoken understanding, and soon, the nightlife came somewhat back. However, they knew once the sun went down, Bianca could make her appearance at any moment, and if she was in a mood to exercise her dominance, anyone in eyeshot could be a target. Most people who were left hanging on the streets after the evening set in were the ones who were just visiting. Those were the prey. Minah would watch to see who took the hint and left and those who intentionally lingered.

As the evening began to settle in, Minah watched familiar faces disappear behind closed doors and groups of strangers stagger out of bars to their car. Her eyes followed two girls as they slipped into a nightclub that stayed open until dawn on purpose, but then she instinctively spotted the man who would be her victim for the night.

She locked eyes with him and smiled sweetly. He was across the street, standing with unflinching composure, watching her as she put her finger to her mouth and winked his way. "Come here…" she mouthed at him and used her finger resting on her bottom lip to signal him over. He crossed the street and got close enough to her that she wrapped her arms around his neck. He used her hug to get up close and sniffed her neck with a long, hard whiff. Minah giggled as his beard and mustache tickled her.

"What you want me to do for you tonight, Baby? I got a bag of tricks I want to show you."

"You aren't the one I want." He unwrapped Minah's arms from his neck and pushed her away with slight force.

Upset with his treatment, Minah balled up her face and angrily responded. "Nigga you ain't all that to be brushing me off like I ain't shit. If you want one of these raggedy ass hoes 'cause you can't afford me, just say that!"

Minah tossed her hair off her shoulders and began to walk away, but he grabbed her arm and pulled her back towards him.

"Let go of me, fuck boy!" Minah struggled to get loose, but his grip was very firm.

"How do you know my brother? I can smell him all over you, but you are not who I'm looking for."

"Fuck your brother. I don't know what you are talking about."

"You do know him. His blood is flowing through your body. Now tell me who you belong to because they are the ones who killed my brother Kilion, and they are the ones who will have to pay."

Minah stopped struggling and intently stared him in the face. Through him, she could see her lover's eyes were finally staring back at her. Minah began to anxiously tremble with how much the man resembled her real master, and she burst into tears of remembrance.

"You're a vampire like him? He didn't tell me he had a brother." She said through her tears and whimpers.

"Just tell me where I can find his killer." Mahlon let her go and stepped back to look her over.

"If I take you to her—"

"Her?!" Mahlon said with astonishment that someone as strong as Kilion was taken down by a woman.

"Yes, Bianca. If I take you to her, will you promise me you'll kill her? I can't take it no more."

Mahlon nodded his head in agreement. "I promise to gut that bitch for what she did to my brother."

Chapter 6

Peeking out the elevator doors, Minah quickly looked down the Hoe-tel's empty hall leading towards the penthouse. Nervous, she peeked back at Mahlon, who stoically stood behind her, his smoldering glare covered by his dark shades. "You sure you ready to do this? She's powerful, and I've seen her rip people and younger vampires to shreds."

"Trust me. I'm stronger." Mahlon stepped past Minah and headed down the hallway. She quickened her steps, making it to the entrance before he did. She put her ear to one of the solid wood oak double doors, listening for the crew or Vivian on the other side of it, but was met with silence.

"I think the place is empty. Bianca is in there, though. It's not time for her to wake up." Mahlon nodded his head. He then opened his black leather jacket, exposing the shiny silver blade attached to his pants belt loop.

"Open the door and lead me to her."

Minah put her key into the lock and slowly turned it. She stuck her head into the darkened home, reassuring herself there was no one on the other side to attack her. She stepped into the penthouse and then looked back at Mahlon, who continued to stay ready to confront his nemesis. She waved him in, pointed down the hallway, and whispered, "She's down there… Last door on the left."

Mahlon crouched slightly, then took half a step toward Bianca's layer and hesitated. "Wait…" He took account of the air around him and smelled the ancient blood and the hint of lavender, unlike Minah, who smelled more human when the aroma of the blood radiated from her pours. Mahlon stood upright and listened to the silence, noticing the dark space had been invaded, and they were no longer alone.

With his hand, he moved Minah behind him and then quickly drew his knife from his belt loop and swiped the air in front of him.

"You missed." The soft voice whispered in his ear. Just then, Mahlon felt a foot to his gut and he went flying across the floor. The pictures hanging on the wall fell on top of him.

"Minah, get out of here!" Mahlon yelled as Minah headed for the door.

Bianca switched on the light, exposing him stumbling out of the corner. "Who the fuck are you coming up into my house like you run it."

Angered, Mahlon's voice rumbled deeply, and he positioned himself like a panther poised to pounce. He then lunged at Bianca, both crashing into the glass coffee table. The shards of its remains could be heard crunching underneath their weight. Bianca's brown eyes flashed the color of gold as her cutting teeth extended for her attack. She opened her mouth and took a ferocious bite from Mahlon's neck while he had her pinned.

"Fucking Bitch!" Mahlon tore himself from her mouth. His dark, thick blood ran down his neck and body. Bianca took the time to lick the residue of his blood from her lips and realized how familiar he tasted. The recognizable flavor slowed her fighting response and gave Mahlon enough time to strike again. With his blade in hand, he came down on Bianca, barely missing his target. She rolled away from the assault and was back on her feet. Mahlon dived for Bianca once more but missed again as she stepped out of his way just in time. She then jumped on his back and used her nails to shred his jacket and shirt. Mahlon grabbed her arm and flung her over his head, and she slammed into the wall in front of them. Mahlon removed his tattered shirt and ran over to Bianca with his blade ready to strike.

"Why are you here!" Bianca kicked her foot into Mahlon's chest, sending him flying across the room, crashing into the seventy-inch television mounted on the wall.

"You killed my brother!" Mahlon regrouped and came for Bianca again. He threw a punch that she blocked with one hand, and he used his other hand to grab her tresses and wound her hair around his knuckles, forcing her to the floor. Bianca screamed out in agony as he continued to yank her hair and drag her down the hall into her room.

"You killed my brother, and now his blood runs through you! I will avenge his death by putting an end to your life! You have no rights to what is ours!" Mahlon punched Bianca across her jaw and then threw her on the bed. His chest heaved in anger as he stared at her wounded on the bed, waiting on her next move. However, she remained seated as she rubbed her jaw. Her hair tousled across her face. She slowly turned and looked at him, her eyes wandering slowly as they descended his body. She noticed how he struggled to stifle the anger within his chiseled physique. From his arms to his legs, his muscles bulged and remained tense to react to any move she tried to make. She looked back at his face and finally saw who his brother was. The love of her human life lived within her foe.

"Kilion… Kilion was your brother."

"And you killed him, and now his blood flows unrightfully in you. I will take your life for what you have done to him!" Mahlon began walking to the bed with his blade in hand.

Bianca put her hand up to stop him and stated, "You got it all wrong. I didn't kill him."

Mahlon grabbed her neck and squeezed it tightly, restricting Bianca's breathing. She began to choke, and Mahlon squeezed tighter. His grip making his knuckles pale.

"No…" Bianca struggled to say. "We loved each other. He put himself in the sun." Mahlon squeezed tighter not approving of her response.

"Lies! My brother would have never done that! You killed him!"

"I'm… telling… the truth..." Bianca struggled to say. "He killed himself because he changed me into this…" Her eyes fluttered as she slowly began to fade. "I never… wanted… to be… this…" The color of her eyes paled to grey, and her dark brown skin lost its luster as her life source began to leave.

Mahlon slowly let go of Bianca's neck as he realized her words. Her eyes stopped fluttering, and her body lay still from his crushing grip. *She didn't kill my brother. The reason why I didn't die when he burned himself in the sun is because his blood lives in her. He killed himself for harming her.* Abruptly, Bianca's body tensed, and her eyes widened as she gasped a breath of life. She coughed violently and sat up beside Mahlon. She looked by her bed, grabbed the glass of water on the nightstand, and drank it. She looked over at Mahlon, who was still deep in thought.

"You two look alike. Except he had braids."

Mahlon nodded in agreement. "We look like our father."

"He didn't tell me much about you."

"We lived separate lives. I hadn't seen him in many centuries."

They sat in silence for a few minutes as they gathered their thoughts on the other. "I didn't kill your brother. I loved him, and he was the second person to love me back." Bianca said matter of factly.

Mahlon looked at Bianca and finally saw her beauty. Her hair was the color of the darkest night. Her coils cascaded past her shoulders, covering her like a drape. He stroked the hair away from her face and tilted her head up so their gaze could meet. Her brown eyes were surrounded by long, thick, luscious lashes that batted at him slowly when she blinked. Her full lips were naturally tinted with a slight hint of pink, contributing to her "come hither" allure. A small dimple on her left side accentuated the structure of her high cheeks. Her skin was bark brown, firm, and butter-soft. He imagined being entwined in her form and drowning in her love. "I can see why he chose you." He leaned in to kiss her, and she kissed him back, their lips connecting softly with little pecks. They then embraced. Their caresses began to linger and soon became filled with passion and infinite desire.

She smiled sweetly once they pulled away from each other, both in awe they'd found each other. "My beauty wasn't the only thing he loved. Lay with me, and I can show you better than I can tell you."

Chapter 7

Outside the penthouse doors, Minah sat nervously, waiting for Mahlon or Bianca to come out to be declared triumphantly victorious. The thrashing and banging she'd heard had ceased, and the stillness of the noise around her was deafening. She could only think they killed each other, and then her worst fears would finally be realized— *the blood is gone.*

The elevator bell rang, and the doors glided open. Vivian and the crew stepped out of the elevator and into the hallway. The smiles and laughter from the group starkly contrasted with the worry and woe she felt. Crouched by the penthouse's front door, Minah immediately stood up and rushed over to them in a panic.

"Slow down, girl! What's wrong with you?"

"Phaizo, it's Bianca— she—"

"Boss Lady in trouble?!" Phaizo's eyes widened at Minah's revelation.

The crew pushed by her and opened the front door, and they all entered in silence.

Lance looked around in shock, surveying the damage. "Marco… Polo… fan out."

The twins cocked their guns and began creeping around the main room. "Rell… follow me."

Vivian pulled Lance's elbow before he and Rell could make it down the hall. "Has anyone ever tried to attack her before? Who could have done this?"

"Ain't no one that know us stupid enough to try to kill Bianca. Whoever did this is not from around here." Vivian let go of his elbow, and Lance and Rell continued down the hall. Lance turned back and said, "Phaizo, hold onto Minah. Matter of fact, take them both outside. We gonna need to talk to Minah about what happened here." Phaizo gripped Minah's arm and led her out of the penthouse while Vivian followed.

Both Lance and Rell heard rummaging coming from behind Bianca's closed bedroom door. Lance slowly turned its handle and opened it, exposing the lovemaking taking place. "Boss Lady! Who the fuck in here with you!" Lance and Rell pulled their guns from their belts and held them at the ready as they stormed in on Mahlon, straddling Bianca and both hands clasping her throat. His body clenched with every muscle flexed while thrusting his member into her honey pot. Sweat flew from his brow and from both of their bodies as Mahlon rapidly hunched on his new sex mate. Marco and Polo rushed the hallway, falling in line behind Lance and Rell with their guns locked and loaded.

Without interrupting the moment, Bianca looked over at the crew while being flipped over by Mahlon. Before he could shove her face into the pillow and raise her hips high enough her ass could meet his mast, she yelled at them, "Get out of here! Can't you see I'm getting fucked! And this time, I don't want a gotdamn audience!"

The crew looked at each other, confused, then slowly put away their weapons. "Yo, Boss Lady, who is this cat?" Lance had never seen Bianca "getting fucked". Be it a man or a woman, Bianca was always the one who controlled the moment. Lance's perspective walking in on Bianca having sex contrasted with what Rell saw. What Rell saw was a dom-type being sexed by an Alpha male… somebody he'd always wanted to be for her. Lance looked over at Rell, who eyed the scene hungrily. Lance couldn't help but screw his face up in revulsion at his boss being someone's snack.

"She said get the fuck out of here." Lance pulled himself from his thoughts when Mahlon stopped his stroke to address them. Lance glared at Mahlon with disgust and tilted his jaw upward in a show of acknowledgment but also with disdain. He then tapped Rell on his shoulder and said, "Let's go." Mahlon turned his attention back to Bianca and continued pounding himself into her backside as she moaned in pleasure. Polo shut the door behind them.

"What the fuck was that in there?"

"I don't know, Rell. I ain't never seen that dude— ever." Lance said, slightly baffled.

"Did you get a good look at him though?"

"Yeah Twin, he something like she is. But not like these weak ass ones she be recklessly making. Them bitches don't last, and they look sick as a muthafucka. This nigga strong as hell."

"Yeah… like he gonna be a problem. I'on like dis nigga already."

"Me neither, Polo."

They walked back to the front of the penthouse and surveyed the destroyed room. "Yo twins, holla at dem bitches hanging out front and tell they asses to get up here and clean this shit up. And on your way down there, tell Phaizo to send Minah in here. That bitch know what's going on, and she 'bout to let us in on what's up with that nigga in the bedroom."

"Igotchu, Lance." Marco said in a low growl of a voice. When he opened the entrance door, he spotted Phaizo guarding the women; his 6'6" stature and expansive frame blocked their view as the two women stood behind him while detained in the hallway's corner.

"So, what happened in there?" Phaizo asked but not surprised by much anymore.

"Man…" Polo wiped the woe from his face before he could respond. "Boss Lady got a nigga in there dicking her down. They in her room sex funky. I ain't never seen her getting piped laid… The shits crazy." Polo walked past a now bewildered Phaizo and hit the down button for the elevator to pick him up. "And however that shit started, they done fucked the crib up getting it in."

"Yeah," Marco chimed in. "And the only one that can fill us in on this bullshit is Minah." Marco yanked Minah from behind Phaizo and stared at her with a menacing glare.

"Me?" Minah said sheepishly.

"Yeah, you. Get your ass in there." Marco shoved Minah through the open door. Wanting to hear what Minah knew, Vivian hurried behind her into the penthouse. The bell for the elevator chimed, and Marco headed to it to go down and wrangle up the women who waited out front for last-minute dates and nothing else to do. Phaizo followed, but Marco turned to him and shook his head no.

"Nah, man, stay up here and guard the door. This nigga Bianca in there with might trip out, and they may need you for backup. Just chill out in the hall for a bit and see what Lance 'bout to do."

"A'ight playa. Dap up." Phaizo and Marco did their custom handshake goodbye before Marco caught the elevator down with his brother.

"Go on down the hall to Lance. Boss Lady in her room with some company." Rell shooed Minah in the direction of Bianca's room as she walked slowly, surveying the ramshackle mess in the front room. "Don't look like you shocked! You bought the muthafucka in here! You knew this shit was going to happen."

"But I don't even know wha—" Minah looked bewildered as she tried to explain.

"You bought someone in here to kill my baby?!" Vivian's voice escalated at the thought of losing Bianca. Vivian rushed past Minah and down the hall to Bianca's room. Her eyes widened, and she put her hand over her mouth while she gasped in surprise at what she saw. Minah quickened her step and made it down the hall to see what the others had already witnessed. What she saw made her quickly turn away in anger and disappointment.

"This ain't no got-damn show! Why y'all staring at me like I'm a bitch on TV? Don't y'all got some work y'all need to do tonight?" Bianca spat her words as Rell, Minah, Lance, and Vivian gathered and gawked at her and Mahlon lying peacefully in her bed. Blood from both of them splattered the walls. Hung pictures were either crooked or crashed into the floor. The room was destroyed just like the rest of the house, but Bianca and Mahlon looked peaceful in their chaotically damaged space.

"We don't mean to stare, B. It's just... you know... we ain't see you with no man like this before. Usually... you know... they be dead— or dying." Rell shrugged at his explanation for staring, and Lance shoved him on the shoulder for his imbecilic response. Rell turned toward him in a huff for being disciplined. Lance mouthed to him to "shut up". He did as instructed and then turned back around meekly.

"We sorry for staring, Boss. We are going to get back to work and let you carry on however you want to. You comfy? Y'all need a drink or sum'?" Lance offered.

"Just get out." Bianca rolled her eyes at them as they staggered away from the bedroom's door.

"Baby, if you need anything I—"

"Bye, Ma."

Vivian nodded her head in understanding, and as she turned away, she revealed Minah, who was hiding behind her before she could disappear with the others.

"Nah, bitch. Bring your ass into this room."

Minah knew Bianca was talking to her. She halted, turned around, and headed into the bedroom. Vivian hung outside the door, out of sight, listening to what Bianca had to say.

Minah lowered her eyes as she approached the bed, not wanting to make eye contact with either Mahlon or Bianca. "Yes, Mistress… Would you like me to join?" Minah reached up and pulled down the strap of her shirt, letting it fall off her shoulder, and unbuttoned it.

"Nah, hoe. Keep your damn clothes on."

Never looking up, Minah ceased undressing upon Bianca's orders.

"How the fuck this man know how to find me? How the fuck he get in here so easily? You let this man in here, didn't you?"

"I— I—" Minah began to fidget as she thought of an explanation. Looking at them lying in the bed after having sex was disappointing to see. Minah wanted Bianca dead so that she could be free of the blood, and she felt Mahlon was the only way. But he did not defeat her and was now her lover, which meant she'd lost the woman she adored to a stranger. Her dreams of living a normal life were now deflated. And not only that, but she'd also had to explain to Bianca how she tried to have her killed. A cold sweat moistened her brow as she thought of what to say about the whole plan.

"Hey Baby…" Mahlon sat up and softly kissed Bianca's cheek. "Don't be mad at her." He kissed her softly again, noticing her body responding to his sweetness. "I'm a powerful and persuasive monster. She had no choice but to bring me up here." He kissed her again, and a slight smile slinked across her face. She draped her arm around him and kissed him on his lips. Her tongue darted in and out of his mouth passionately. Minah lifted her head slowly, relieved Mahlon had lied for her. Thankfully, she'd been spared.

Bianca gave Mahlon one last peck before rolling her eyes towards Minah. With a bit of skepticism, she looked her over for a flaw in Mahlon's story but was too distracted by her desire to fuck him some more to care about the matter any longer. "Take yo' ass out my face and get on The Block and make me some money tonight. I'll deal with you later."

Minah silently exhaled, assured tonight was not her night to die before she responded. "Yes, Mistress." Minah bowed her head and hurried towards the door.

"And shut the damn door behind you!" Bianca said before covering her and Mahlon with her satin sheets and them laughing with excitement.

Once Minah closed the door behind her, she turned to walk away and was met by Vivian, whose arms were folded and her face riddled with scorn.

"You thought you was gonna have my baby killed, didn't you."

"Leave me alone. I have to get to work." Minah grumbled as she pushed past Vivian.

Vivian grabbed her shoulder, pulled her back, and pointed her finger at Minah with disdain. "You see what you did? You done bought that man up in here, and now he gonna ruin it for all of us. You think her happiness is our happiness? You think she gonna treat you right because he's around? You think shit changed? I see how you look at my daughter like you can't stand her. It's real obvious you tried to have my baby killed, but all you did was fuck shit up for all of us. I blame you for all of this."

Minah lamented Vivian's accusations with a piercing glare, and her lips curled into a tight, thin line. Vivian then relaxed her stance and smiled with a sinister grin, realizing that what she accused Minah of had half a bit of truth.

"I got work to do." Minah turned around and walked off as Vivian said her last words.

"You about to see a bitch you never wanted to meet. Bianca going to figure out you double-crossed her and then your ass is grass."

Chapter 8

I'm so tired of this shit... Minah wiped the tears from her face as she exited the elevator at the ground level of River Towers. The girls who were headed to the penthouse to help with the cleanup pushed her off their path as they entered the elevator on its way back up. *Don't nobody respect me here. Even these funky-ass hoes think they better than me.* Minah clicked her tongue in annoyance, her eyes rolling in disdain at the girls she'd rather have been than be in the position she was in with Bianca. Out on the sidewalk, she headed east on Creighton, passing the graveyard on her right, and surveyed the tombstones closest to the gate she walked by. *These dead muthafucka's have more freedom than me. Hell... they ain't got that crazy ass vampire sucking off them like some hung-up feedbag. Besides, I'm tripping hard off some blood that don't even taste like Kilion's no more. His made me feel warm, like he was hugging me while I floated on a cloud. Her's taste like it's got a hint of week-old spoiled milk to it.*

The spring breeze had a bit of a chill, so she picked up her pace when she crossed the street, continuing to consider her situation. *Bianca can be such a bitch. She doesn't know how to treat anyone. If*

I left her today, she wouldn't have nobody to pick on... no one to trust. No one to look after her. Does she think those dummies would take care of her? Lance and his stupid goons couldn't find their way out of a wet paper bag.

The buzzing of her phone interrupted her train of thought. She dug in her bag to answer it and looked at the name of the incoming text... *It's Rox. I'll meet up with her in a minute...* As she put her phone back in her purse, she felt herself bump into a solid mass of a person. "Nigga! Watch where the fuck you walking!!" Angrily, Minah looked up at the figure towering over her. She changed her disposition when she realized she slammed into his waist and not into a regular-sized chest of a regular-sized man. Her glare softened as her eye timidly made its way to his shadowed face. She took a step back to view the massive man she'd just berated.

"Excuse me, miss. I would have moved out of your way had I known you hadn't seen me." The shadowed man dressed in all black took off his draping hood and dark sunglasses, which he now clutched in his fist. His long, silky salt and pepper locs were plated loosely to the back. Some of the escaped strands draped his rigid, emotionless expression. The curl of a welcoming smile never crossed his lips, and his dark glare never softened apologetically, making his request for forgiveness feel more obligatory than heartfelt. The solid man stood in front of her, seemingly not wanting to pass. Minah stared at him awkwardly as she waited for his next move or word, but nothing changed between the two.

Minah cleared her throat before hesitantly speaking. "Did you want something? You looking for someone?" She fiddled with the strap of her pocketbook as she waited for his response. However, he continued to stare at her with curiosity. "Well, if you don't want nothing, I gotta go. Got work to do. She did a side-step to get past him, but he stepped in her way.

"Look, guy. I ain't scared of you, but you making me nervous, and my type of nervous will get you cut, so tell me what you want or get the fuck away from me."

"My bad." He spoke the words in a low, deep, hoarse tone with very little expression. "I was just checking out the merchandise." He continued to stare at her blankly as he pulled out a wad of money and tossed it on the ground. Minah looked at the cash, which showcased the hundred-dollar bill on top of a roll.

Minah sucked her teeth at the disrespectful act and folded her arms. "No dice. You not gonna knock me over the head with those gorilla fists once I pick up that money." Minah side-stepped him once again to make her way down the sidewalk. She turned around to see him picking up the currency he'd thrown. "Yeah, you go on and pick that up, trick. I may be a hoe, but I'm a muthafuckin' lady first, and you gonna treat me like one." She blew a kiss his way before turning back around to head for the diner and meet up with Roxanne. He blew a huff of air from his nose at her arrogance and gathered the now wind-strown dollars.

"See, that's why you can't get pussy. You don't throw money at a woman unless you are at the titty bar. This is the streets, Bud. You hand them the dough like you have manners when picking up a pro."

"Money is money, Mahlon. If they are working for it, how they get it doesn't matter."

"To these ladies, it does matter, Sawyer. You gotta be smooth like me... Even if you're paying for it."

Back on his feet, he returned the money to his pocket and began walking with Mahlon at his side. "So, I guess you struck out with Minah."

"Yeah, I'll have to try another way."

Mahlon patted Sawyer on the shoulder with pity. "No need to. I already bagged Bianca." Sawyer paused, looking at Mahlon to see if he was joking. "You already killed her?"

Mahlon doubled over in laughter, knowing Sawyer would not have understood what he meant. "No, you self-inflicted monk! I bagged her!" Mahlon said as he pumped the air in front of him and gyrated. "I fucked her! She gave up the pussy, and I kilt it!" Mahlon laughed harder as Sawyer shook his head in disgust.

"Typical..." Sawyer mumbled. "The mission is to kill her. Not fuck her."

"That's your mission. I do things my way." Mahlon pulled out his blunt and lit it before catching up with Sawyer's pace.

"So, then what's your plan if it's not to get laid."

"Much better than your plan of getting Minah on your side. Well... yeah, that was a good plan." Mahlon tapped Sawyer on the chest in approval. "I mean, I did tell her I was going to kill Bianca if she took me to her— and I had all intentions of doing that on sight— but MAN! She so FINE!! I mean... I started out fighting her. You should have seen us." His pupils began to dilate with the thought of his desire to murder the beast who killed his brother. "Blow-for-blow, she was my equal... squared up like men at war."

He shook his head and chuckled at the fighting match between him and Bianca. "Neither one of us was going to win that fight." He shook his head again in humble defeat at the thought. "We destroyed her place though." He turned his head towards the high rise where Bianca resided and used his thumb to point it out to Sawyer while walking in the opposite direction. "Her girls and her henchmen are upstairs cleaning it now." He took a deep breath as flashes of his encounter with Bianca jumped into his train of thought.

"But during the fight, something sensual happened. Something so cataclysmic neither one of us could stop the impact, so you can't blame me for my actions after all of that!" Mahlon threw his hands up to show his innocence. "I could smell that human blood in her— 'cause you know she'd just eaten, and human blood is just a complete turn-on when you're excited. And then those titties..." Mahlon squeezed the air in front of him as if fondling a voluptuous woman. "The nipples on those beautiful brown titties were hard like small rocks, and don't get me started on those lips!" Mahlon giggled with delight when he began to visualize the moment Bianca subconsciously licked her lips and smirked before she punched him in the jaw, sending him flying into the kitchen cabinets. "Her lips looked so juicy... Man, I just... I just couldn't help but try her before ripping her into pieces." He ran his hands on top of his head in an effort to wipe the memory of his moment with Bianca away from his thoughts. "That was one hell of a meet-cute."

"A what?" Sawyer asked with frustration.

"Oh!" Mahlon laughed. "I forgot you don't partake in the enjoyment of romantic comedies. See, a meet-cute is when the featured couple meets for the first time in a quirky way. See... the term originated in the nineteen-thirties in a movie about—"

"Would you shut up about a meet-cute and get back to business?" Sawyer said, shoving Mahlon in the shoulder out of irritation.

"Well, aren't you testy!" Mahlon said as he recovered from the shove and returned to walking pace with Sawyer. "I was just trying to bring some culture to your boring vampire hunter life.

Ignoring his comment, Sawyer brought the conversation back to its original point. "We agreed that you would help me kill her. The Council has instructed me to neutralize this woman, and you said you would help in exchange for eternal immunity."

"And I plan on helping you. But I do things my way. And I wanted to have some fun first. Don't worry. I'll get her the next time." Sawyer stopped walking once again to stare at Mahlon in disbelief. "Again? You plan on seeing her again?"

"Yeah. How else am I supposed to kill her."

Sawyer shook his head and began walking once more. "The Council requires her head for her reckless destruction of humankind. If she is not unalived, they will have you destroyed." He looked off into the distance as he contemplated the predicament Mahlon had put himself in. "Since it's your brother's blood in her veins, it makes her your kin, which makes her your responsibility."

"Yeah, yeah. I know." Mahlon puffed his blunt and passed it to Sawyer, who pushed it back to Mahlon in refusal. Mahlon shrugged and took a few more puffs before putting it out and putting it back in his pocket for later. "And once we're done with this, we can go back to being enemies; me living my best life and you hunting innocent vampires for your stupid, petty, player-hating employer, The Council."

"No vampire is innocent."

"Personal opinion!" Mahlon said defensively.

"When the job is done, just stay out of my way."

"Gladly. I've gotta go." Mahlon turned back the way he came, leaving Sawyer to watch him depart. "I told Bianca I was hungry and needed to eat so I could come out here and meet you, so that's what I'm about to do… grab a bite to eat." Mahlon chomped his teeth at Sawyer playfully before looking both ways and taking off running at a blurry, eye-defying speed. Sawyer re-covered his head with his draping hoodie and put his shades back on before disappearing into the nearest alley.

Chapter 9

The bell above the diner's door rang as Minah entered. She smiled, and the cook frying food in his stained apron waved at her. As she approached, her smile grew bigger, seeing two of her favorite people sitting there.

"Don't even pretend like you happy to see me. I knew you saw my text, hoe." Roxanne folded her arms in a huff and pretended to pout as Minah sat down in the booth beside her. She gave Roxanne a peck on the cheek, which made Roxanne smile.

"I was busy when you texted. I knew I was going to see you soon. That's why I didn't respond."

"Well, how I'm supposed to know that? You ain't been coming around. Where you even been?"

"Long story. Bianca tripping, and now her mama here—"

"Mama?! That crazy bitch got a mama?!"

"Ssh, Kingston, don't talk like that in here— you don't know who listening— what will get back to her."

Kingston sucked his teeth at being reprimanded for speaking with irreverence. "You know I ain't stressed or pressed about that crazy girl. I knew her before she became that scary-ass vampire. I knew her when she was Kilion's girl. I was the one who showed Kilion where she was beat up and lying in the gutter. She can't put on no airs for me, chile, and that's why I say and does what I want around here." Kingston snapped his neck and rolled his eyes declaratively before he sipped his water.

"Well, say what you want then, but don't say it around me. Y'all relationship different than my relationship with her."

"Aww, don't be salty, Kingston. Yeah, she killed your mentor, and yes, you not living the good life no more because he was your ticket into high society, but at least he's dead and you're not... And she continues to let you live for whatever reason."

"She only lets me live because she knew she was wrong for killing that fine, sexy, chocolate man, Rox!"

"You are probably right about that. 'Cause we damn sure know she will kill you dead if that's what she finna do."

They all laughed in agreement before Minah changed the subject. "So, what are you guys up to tonight? I had to get out of Bianca's place and get some air; plus, she put me on the corner this evening."

"I know she did." Roxanne pulled out her folded piece of paper with a list of names for the night's working schedule. "I got the call from Twin that Lance said that B said to put you on shift." Roxanne browsed her list as she spoke. "Looking at the schedule, you got Bubbles corner to work. Her spot easy though. She out on a special appointment so it was simple to find you a place." Roxanne put a check by Minah's name on the list, folded the paper back up, and returned it to her purse.

"Lawd... Bubbles and those damn appointments." Kingston chuckled at the misadventures Bubbles had with her clientele.

"Yeah, her customers be wanting some weird shit!" Roxanne laughed at the thought. Kingston and Roxanne slapped hands as they laughed in agreement.

Minah watched their energies play off each other, brightening her spirits. "Well, what do her customers want? What… fuck her fat rolls or something?"

"Nah, Chile! That's an old trick!" Roxanne said. "She done found a new way to keep it fresh for them fat girl lovers!" Roxanne was laughing so hard by then she had to wipe the tears from the cracks of her eyes.

"Well, what is she doing!" Minah asked.

"Well, you know the bitch done gained another fifty pounds just so she can do this new move right, so you know Doctor Now would definitely tell her she needs to come to Texas." Kingston leaned over sideways in his chair as he laughed silently until he was able to gasp. He then boisterously laughed at the Doctor Now comment. Roxanne repeatedly slapped his leg playfully, knowing the reference would have him on the floor laughing uncontrollably since it was his favorite show. Minah watched them cutting up and shook her head at their antics.

When Roxanne and Kingston finally regained enough composure, she continued her story. "My bad…" She said as she breathed hard from laughing so much. "I got off track." Her breathing finally slowed down. "Okay… where was I?"

"Girl, you were saying she gained fifty pounds." Minah said while chuckling to catch Roxanne up.

"Oh yeah… and what she does is dust up her pussy and booty crack with confectionary sugar and baby powder, the dude be laying on the bed on his back, and he wait for this bitch to plop down on his face and smother him. And when she sit down, it be a poof of white smoke that come from under all that ass!" Roxanne began to laugh again but tried her best to stifle her giggles until she finished telling the fat-tastic routine. "Then, when this bitch sit on his face he go to town eating and licking, licking and eating!" Not able to hold it any longer, Roxanne, Kingston, and Minah were now doubled over in laughter, envisioning their five hundred-plus pounds, blonde-haired, blue-eyed friend with the porcelain skin performing such a strange act to satisfy a customer's request.

"Stop the madness! It just sound so messy! Why she got to go through all that for a damn dollar!" Kingston said through his laughs.

"We do what we got to do!" Roxanne said as she wiped more happy tears.

"Well, if he like it, I love it!" Minah said while holding her stomach from the laughing pains. "But Seriously..." Minah stated as their laughter began to subside. "I'm really thinking about leaving Bianca. You know... get out of the city and get clean. I'm tired of her. She really ain't feeling me now. Especially if she got me on The Block working."

"Girl, stop playing. You know you ain't going nowhere. You go through this every couple of months, and then she treat you a little nice— buy you a new shoe, take you to a movie, take you dancing, and get you some jewelry, and you back in love." Kingston retorted while rolling his eyes at the notion.

"Now, now Kingston. Give her a chance. She might be serious this time." Roxanne patted Minah's hand and then gave it a squeeze. "I believe you, sweetie, but what makes this time so different? Why are you thinking about running now?"

"Well, for one, it used to be just me and her. And yeah, she was tough back then, but she was still new to being a vampire. She was a little bit sweeter. But then she started hanging with Lance and his crew, and they started gassing her up."

"Umph... That whole crew too fine!" Kingston said as he sipped his drink. "What them twins up to? Especially Marco. Every time I see him, he makes me sweat!"

"Boy, stop calling them twins! They just half-brothers born on the same day and they got the same daddy. You and everybody around here keep calling them twins like y'all okay with that level of triflence!"

"Shut up about my future husband and his brother! They can be twins if they want!"

"Y'all stop bickering about them boys and focus on what Minah got going on." Roxanne said, irritated they always go off topic when it's time to be serious.

"Sorry, Rox." Minah said, returning to her solemnness to plead her case. "So anyway, at first, the crew was just sticking people up for her and managing the drugs 'cause she didn't know that much about how Daddy ran the business, and they did. But now, they like her best friends and shit!" Minah said in a huff. "And they all crack on me and laugh at me because Bianca only fusses at me and uses me when she's hungry."

"It's got to be the pits, honey. Nobody wants to be disrespected, but honestly, you seem to like the abuse. You never really leave. It's like you go away only so she can show you a little bit of attention, and then you go back, and you're happy until you get mad again." Roxanne reminded her.

"I don't like it! I just stay and put up with it because what else am I going to do? I'm so strung out on her and that blood I can't function if I go too long without it." Minah slumped in her chair in defeat.

"It's not your fault, Minah. You know I would never talk ill about Kilion because he was a good guy, but real talk, it's his fault. He should have turned you or killed you a long time ago. All he did was make you a pretty feen because addiction is hard." Kingston nodded his head while agreeing with his truth.

"Maybe. But he treated me nice, so I can't be too mad."

"Well, what about her mom? Mom's not helping?"

"No. She's worse than the dudes. She wants me gone so she can have Bianca to herself. But I doubt it will happen, though."

"Why? You think B not listening to her?"

"Nah. This man came up to me asking where Bianca was 'cause he was going to kill her for killing his brother Kilion."

Both Roxanne and Kingston dropped their jaw.

"Whatchu say? Kilion got a brother?!"

"Nah! Go Back! You said you tried to have Bianca killed?!"

"Ssh! Don't say that shit too loud!" Minah said.

"Girl, spill the tea fo' I knock your head in!" Kingston commanded.

Minah took a big breath in before she began. "Soooo... I found out today Kilion has a brother, and he's mad that he's dead. I was mad at Bianca for all the shit that's going on and what she been putting me through. He just so happened to have approached me thinking I was her because he could smell his brother's blood in me, but I told him it was Bianca he was really looking for, so I took him to her because he promised to kill her. Well, they fought, but then they started fucking, and now I'm out walking the strip."

"What in the entire hell..." Kingston said, bewildered.

"This some crazy shit, Minah."

"I know. I'm scared because Bianca don't know I tried to have her killed by him. He didn't tell her it was me wanting her dead that got him so close to her. Kilion's brother covered for me."

"Well what he look like?"

"I don't know Kingston!" Minah said, irritated.

"Well, introduce me to him."

"No!"

"Yes! I miss Kilion! I miss the parties! I miss those fucking little macaroons they let you eat while you shop at that fancy-ass boutique Kilion used to get his expensive ass socks from in Carytown! Fuck! I miss Carytown!" Kingston said in a whiney voice. "I know his brother money got to be long like his was! If I can get in good with the brother, then maybe he can get me back on top, and I ain't got to run around this dump of a block with my face screwed up no more."

"No, Kingston! I have my own issues to think about!"

"Do it! You ain't gonna leave that girl, and if she wanted you dead, you'd be dead! Do this for me, and if you serious about leaving, I have a number to a good rehab place for you." Kingston let his bottom lip pout out as he put his hands together to beg.

Minah couldn't resist and giggled a bit. "Fine. I'll see what I can do about an intro."

"Just make sure Bianca, The Bitch don't come. I really can't stand her."

"We all know." Minah and Roxanne said in unison and laughed once again at Kingston.

Roxanne checked her watch and tapped Minah playfully on the nose. "Alright, girl. Whether you like it or not, you got work to do. Your shift about to start. And I'm in charge of the girls. If your ass ain't out there working, then it's gonna be my ass that gets handed over." They all left the booth, and Roxanne dropped a twenty-dollar bill on the table to cover the drinks and the tip. They headed out the door and paused to say their goodbyes.

"Keep your head up tonight, Minah. She only got you out here to remind you that you got it good up there." Roxanne tilted her head towards River Towers to reference it. "In a couple of days, I'm sure you and her will be back like that, and things will have calmed down."

"You may be right Rox, but this seem different. I ain't never seen her laid up with no man— or vampire before. She let this man get the best of her, and that shit don't happen— ever. You do remember how they found Lucy, don't you?"

"Don't remind me. Lucy was my friend, and she ripped that girl into so many pieces it was like putting a puzzle together to get her ready for her fune."

"Right, so the most she did to this dude was give him some good head."

"You know a man with some good dick will calm the meanest of bitches..."

"But if he can do that for her, I know things about to change, and I don't know if it's for the best or for the worst."

"Well, don't think about it tonight. Just go on and make that money and see what tomorrow brings."

"You right." Minah shuffled her feet as she thought about the possibilities. She pulled a cigarette out of her pocket, lit it, and walked to her post. "I'll see you guys in the morning. Breakfast on me."

Chapter 10

The morning of the next day began to peer over the city's skyline as Minah hopped out of the passenger's side of her customer's car. Without saying goodbye, she tucked her cash in her bra and watched him drive off. Bubbles regular customers weren't too thrilled with her being a stand-in for their cushiony companion, but as the motto goes in the business, beggars can't be choosers. If anything, she took care of their needs as asked but without the extra fluff. Minah didn't have the same voluptuous frame as Bubbles, and she was also a bare-bones type of service provider. Minah didn't care if the customer didn't enjoy their experience. She was only there as a punishment. She only had to do enough to get paid, and she did only that.

During her appointments, if Bubble's customers complained about her lack of enthusiasm while she was servicing them, Minah would slap them across the face and threaten them with the lie of abuse or, worse, nonpayment. If she reported them, they'd have to answer to Bianca's goons, who were notorious for enjoying their torturing duties. That night, she only had to slap two customers and call the goons on one.

Minah stretched her arms high to the sky as she yawned and began her walk back home. While she had been out all night, she didn't catch a glimpse of Bianca. Usually, they trolled the block looking for victims, but last night, Bianca or her tracks could not be traced.

As she slowly strolled home, she nodded and waved at familiar faces. Faces she hadn't seen in years. Normally, she would be in before the sun came up, attending to Bianca's needs as she prepared her for her day's rest. Walking back to River Towers afforded her friendly smiles from Tony and Tracy, the couple she'd met when she first moved over there and who bought her groceries a few times when she was penniless. Then there was Bible-thumping Juanita. She turned her nose up at Minah as she swept the sidewalk in front of her apartment. Mrs. Juanita never liked Minah and made it known how she was living with "that nasty vampire gal" and those "funky hooligans" that followed her around making trouble. She hated that meddling woman with equal force, but on that morning, she was glad to see she was still around, being judgmental.

As she shook her head at Mrs. Juanita for still being the same, she caught a glimpse of someone staring at her. She did a double take to see the brooding stare of the stranger from the night before. No longer intimidated by his stature, she put her hand on her hip and walked over with all the attitude she could muster. When she was finally as close as she could get, she reached up and slapped him as hard as she could across the face. Her eyes widened with surprise when he didn't flinch in response.

"You know it's rude to stare, and I only slapped you because this is the second time you've been disrespectful!"

"When was the first." He stated.

"When you didn't introduce yourself."

"I'm Sawyer."

Minah gave a hint of a smile while she ran her fingers through her hair. She reached up and affectionately patted his cheek where her hand had landed, pinching it after for good measure.

"Now, the next time we meet, Sawyer… speak. And if you want my good pussy, hand me the money." Minah turned and continued towards home.

As she walked up to its front steps, she saw Kingston leaning on the wall, watching the girls going in and out. Minah could tell he was silently judging the clothing choices of the people who passed by when his mouth twisted and his eyes rolled once the woman with the tangled and matted wig walked by.

"Boy, stop. Ain't nobody here trying to dress to impress but you."

"Girl, I could make a killing getting these hoes together. I swear I could change their lives with one outfit." He pointed to his crisp white sneakers with the red and green stripes. "See these? Gucci." He said before pointing to his dark blue jeans. "You see these? Ksubi." He said without missing a beat. He leaned in close to Minah. "Smell me. It's Burberry". He then pointed to his white cotton collared shirt before turning the collar up and close to his ears. "And this is Versace." He tilted his glasses towards his nose and stared intently at Minah. "And don't trip on my Tom Ford glasses." He slid them back up his nose to cover his eyes from the morning sun after making his point. "And this just my morning fit."

Minah chuckled at his aspiration. "Just 'cause you wear high fashion from the thrift store don't mean you have what it takes."

"Bitch, please ain't nothing thrift about it. Kilion was my masterpiece. When he burst out on these Richmond streets, I had him dripping like a GAWD, and you know thisssssss."

"Anyways…" Minah said to change the subject. "I know you not out here to watch these girls. So, what do you want?"

Kingston dug into his wallet, pulled out a card, and handed it to her.

She looked at it, confused. "What's this for?"

Kingston shrugged his shoulders and looked down at his clear, painted, manicured nails while picking over them. "It's that number I told you I was going to give you if you hooked me up with Kilion's brother. Well, girl… You are my friend, and I want the best for you whether you give me the hook-up or not."

Minah saw the sincerity in his action and hugged him. "Thanks. I promise I'm going to use it."

"Well, I got to go. I promised Roxanne we would go boosting at Macy's down at Short Pump before it get crowded in there."

"Y'all gonna get caught one day." Minah said through her laugh.

"But not today though! The security guard on duty this morning one of Roxy's tricks! See you later!" Kingston waved goodbye as he hopped onto the city bus headed out of the neighborhood.

Minah got on the elevator and got off at the penthouse. She took a deep breath of sadness. She didn't want to go back in there with Bianca and the fellas, but she had nowhere else to go or a desire to be elsewhere. She unlocked the door and was greeted with silence and the shades drawn. She shut the door behind her and began to make her way to Bianca's room to help her prepare for her rest when the light of a lit cigarette caught her eye. She hit the light switch on the wall, revealing Mahlon sitting comfortably on the couch.

"Why are you here? Aren't you supposed to be sleep or something?"

"I should be, but I must unwind from such a busy night." Mahlon smiled in remembrance of their fun night hunting in a county not too far away. "Do you mind if we go to the hall and talk?"

"Can't, I gotta get Bianca prepped for bed."

"No need. I took care of that. She's already resting."

Minah rolled her eyes. "So now you taking my job when you could have just done what I asked."

Surprised at her words, he jumped up and put his finger over her mouth to silence her. "You know, even though she is asleep, she can hear you. Let's step outside and have a conversation." He pulled Minah out the front door and made his way to a secluded corner with her. Once there, he removed his hand from her mouth.

"Now, keep your voice down."

"You should have killed her."

"Plans changed."

Minah folded her arms in a huff and turned to the wall.

"Look... I'm going to make sure you are taken care of. Think of me as your guardian angel."

"I wouldn't need one if you had killed her."

Mahlon turned Minah towards him. "Look. Sorry, I couldn't help, but I have a real shot at changing her for the better— someone we both can deal with. Just be cool and let me handle it."

Minah rolled her eyes. "Whatever, Mahlon." She dug into her pocket, pulled out a piece of paper and pencil, scribbled down a number, and handed it to him.

"What's this?"

"It's info to a guy who used to hang out with your brother. Get up with him. He can connect you with some high rollers, and he'll tell you more about your girl in there."

Mahlon looked at the number approvingly. "Thanks. I'll give him a call for sure."

Chapter 11

Kingston impatiently checked his watch. He'd meticulously planned the night out for him and Mahlon, but with Mahlon now being an hour late, his reservation at Bateau was null and void, and his 10 pm entrance time for Tryst was now in jeopardy. He checked the time on his phone, confirming how tardy Mahlon was, and then sucked his teeth in frustration. Fed up, he dialed Minah's number. The line rang twice before she answered.

"What, Kingston."

"Don't what me, hoe. Where that man at? Didn't you tell him 8 pm at Bateau?"

"Yeah. I told him. It's 10 pm. Kingston, you been waiting around that long?"

"Yessss." Kingston stated with unwavering conviction, ensuring that his response carried the weight of his aggravation. "I've been standing out here waiting for him. We done missed dinner, but I be damned if we miss getting into Tryst. I had to almost sell my soul and suck a lil' dick to get put on the schedule!"

Minah laughed at Kingston's misfortune before responding. "Ain't nobody tell you to suck dick! You did that for you 'cause you nasty!"

Kingston laughed in spite of his annoyance with Mahlon. "Yeah, girl. You know I don't mind drooling and tea bagging, especially if I'm getting a present for my skills." They then both laughed at his comical response.

"Boy, you crazy." Minah continued. "Well, call his trifling ass. He ain't here with me and B, so maybe he still coming and just had to make a stop first. You know these vampires don't give a fuck about time management."

"Kilion did. That's why me and him vibed. He was sweet like that."

"Boy, please. He was trifling, too. There were plenty of times he would be late coming to see me, don't show up at all, or show up unexpected. Vampires are all the same— only caring about their selves."

"I guess you right." Kingston checked his watch again in disappointment as he shuffled his feet, pondering his next move.

"So, what should I do now? Should I go home? Maybe he'll call me later."

"Don't even wait for him. You've waited long enough. Take your ass home, put your bonnet on, drink some wine, and then go to bed."

"I'm more mad about this appointment we about to miss. Tryst so hot, I couldn't believe I was able to get in. Luckily, the owner remembered me from my days in Carytown with Daddy. You know, Tryst offered me a job as club manager? I might take them up on that."

"Yeah, that might be good for you. It might even get you back in that social life you want."

"Probably, but it's not like I really want to work; you know I ain't built for all that." Kingston picked at his nails and thought before he continued his statement. "I guess… for the sake of leaving this dreadful lifestyle, I'll give the manager a call tomorrow then."

"Good for you."

Kingston began walking away from Bateau to catch the bus back home. He was disappointed he wouldn't get his introduction to Mahlon but optimistic about his opportunity at Tryst.

"Now, where do you think you're going? I thought we had plans?"

Startled, Kingston turned around to see the handsome, broad-shouldered man who could only be Mahlon. His low-cut caesar, with the deepest of waves, laid slick to his head. His hazel eyes sparkled as he smiled, a charming, crooked smile that instantly brightened Kingston's mood. "Umm... I'm not the one who's two hours late." Kingston's words purred with a teasing lilt when he spoke.

"Oh, he must have showed up. See. Told you. They move on their own time. I'll call you later." Minah said before ending the call and not waiting for him to say 'goodbye'.

Kingston put his phone back in his pocket, walked over to Mahlon, and stuck his hand out to be greeted. "So, you're the infamous Mahlon?"

Mahlon grabbed Kingston's hand and shook it warmly. He looked Kingston up and down as he pumped his hand 'hello.' He smiled enthusiastically and then took Kingston in for an embrace.

"Ooh! That's third base for me, sweetie!" Kingston giggled as Mahlon let him go.

"Oh, I'm sorry, Kingston. I couldn't help myself. You are a very good-looking guy. He turned Kingston around to get a full view. "I can see why my brother kept you around; style and grace are very becoming on you."

"Why, thank you." Kingston beamed as he watched Mahlon gush over him.

"But your flattery doesn't excuse you missing dinner."

"Ahh…Dinner. An important meal… I guess." Mahlon shrugged. "I personally hate dinner. I prefer dessert." Mahlon said with a mischievous, all-knowing wink and a smile. "So, take me to get something my taste buds would enjoy."

"Well, you could have told me—"

"Kingston, my friend, stop nagging; I'm here; you're here; we want to go do some nasty things, so let's go do them."

Kingston laughed. "Minah was right. Y'all don't care nothing about what us humans got going on." They both laughed at the true statement. Kingston folded his arm around Mahlon's, and they began to walk. "Well, dessert is right up the way. We'll be just in time for our appointment."

"So, I can do what I want in there?"

"Sort of. You must be discreet. I know you want to fuck but the biting part? You'll have to keep that on the low."

"Umm, I can do that."

"Good. So, the rules of the club are simple."

"Rules, rules. I can figure it out once I'm in there."

Kingston paused his pace and tugged Mahlon back one step to catch his attention. "No, Mahlon, there are rules. These are high-end people, and if we play by the rules, I can get invited back and make new friends and get out of this hell-hole life I've been forced to live since Kilion was murdered. So, play by MOST of the rules tonight."

Mahlon put his hands up surrendering to Kingston's request. "Fine. I'll play by the rules."

"Good. Now, the rules are simple. First rule is you have to fuck. If they don't see you fucking, you are banned right on the spot. Second rule. No kissing in the mouth unless it is the partner you came with. Third rule, you can't only fuck your partner. Fourth rule, protection needs to be worn."

"But I can't catch or give diseases."

"Well, act like you human tonight and wear a condom."

"Fine. Is that all?"

"No means no. That's another rule."

"Nobody will resist me, so I don't have to worry about that."

"Well, if they do, don't get offended and try to mesmerize them with those vampire eyes. Just move on until you get a yes."

"Good, let's go play then." Mahlon and Kingston picked up the pace as they got closer to their destination.

"So, your girl let you out to play?"

"Who?"

"Don't play. I know you and Bianca hooking up."

"Oh, yeah. She's pretty cool, and the sex is intense."

"She know you with me and we out? I don't want her showing up and causing a scene, killing everyone because her man fucking and sucking someone else. You know she a bitch like that."

"She's good on our relationship status. We're not exclusive. I'm sure she's gonna eat Minah's pussy before the night is out, and you don't see me tripping about it."

"Yeah, I guess you right about that."

"So, there's nothing to worry about then."

Mahlon unhooked his arm from Kingston's and led him to the door of Tryst. "So, let's go in. Are you ready?"

Kingston checked his watch, surprised he and Mahlon were right on time for their entrance appointment. He smiled coyly, then placed his hand on Mahlon's affectionately. "Mahlon, it's officially time to play…" Kingston pushed the buzzer on the building, which was vacant of defining marks. Mahlon looked around his surroundings and patiently waited for someone on the other side of the door to respond to the bell ringing.

The area they'd come to wasn't a far walk from the restaurant they met up at, but the atmosphere around Tryst felt quieter since it wasn't on Broad Street like Bateau, one of the busiest main roads in Richmond, but was nestled in the sleepier part of Church Hill. Mahlon looked at the ground and noticed the cobblestone it was paved with. He reminisced on how much he enjoyed the roughness of a horse and carriage over cobblestones in the old country. It reminded him of times riding in England when plagues were rampant and death was everywhere. In those times, he didn't hide in the shadows. He could kill and feed, and no one would know the difference.

The door cracked open, and a pale, thin young man stuck his head out. His trendy tinted circular wire glasses were posed closer to the tip of his nose, exposing his pale blue eyes. He looked Kingston up and down and then at Mahlon, scrutinizing both of them with his glare before he spoke. "What."

Kingston didn't respond right away, thrown off a bit by the young man's greeting. "Yeah, umm... we have an appointment?"

The man looked them over once more and sucked his teeth. He pulled his head back in the door and shut it without another word. Kingston looked back at Mahlon and shrugged his shoulders in bewilderment. Before he could say anything else, the door opened just enough for the thin man to stick his head through. "Your appointment has been canceled. You're late." He stuck his head back through the crack and shut the door. The locks could be heard from the inside, turning to secure the door.

Kingston billowed up in frustration and began banging on the door. "You little scrawny-ass BITCH! Ain't nobody miss their muthafuckin' appointment! Get Rae-Rae out here! Tell Rae-Rae to come to this crusty-ass door!" Kingston continued kicking and banging on the door until he heard the locks turn again. The thin man's face appeared once again.

"Lay off the door." He said with very little emotion.

"Go get Rae-Rae." Kingston commanded.

"Rae-Rae is gone."

"Well, get me someone; I'm not late."

"Um-um... I checked, and you are."

"Nah-ah, Bitch. I'm on time."

"No Bitch, the rules say be here early, like fifteen minutes early, So... you're late."

As the man began to stick his head back in the door, Mahlon glided in front of Kingston and wedged his foot in before it closed. The thin man looked at the foot and then up at Mahlon in disgust. Mahlon smiled slowly as his eyes glistened. The thin man's annoyance with the two began to melt as he stared into Mahlon's eyes, which turned into a spellbinding kaleidoscope of different colors. "Do us a favor and let us in, will you? Rae-Rae set the appointment, and he really wants us to be here. Don't disappoint Rae-Rae and leave us out here."

Entranced, the thin man nodded in agreement and opened the door wider so they could walk past him.

"Now, tomorrow, you're going to work on that attitude of yours... Be nicer to people and not make yourself feel more powerful because you work the door at a hoity-toity whorehouse." The thin man nodded slowly as he continued to stare in a euphoric state. Mahlon smoothed over the man's floppy hair, pushing it out of his face. He then straightened his glasses, pushing them back onto the bridge of his nose. "Just remember, friend. You are the help. You aren't that important." Mahlon continued through the entrance and caught up with Kingston. The thin man shut the door as Mahlon continued down the narrow hall behind Kingston. "Oh!" Mahlon called out to the thin man who stood in front of the door, still in a trance, "Go grab you some more food. Gain twenty pounds. You'll feel better. I've never known anyone nice on an empty stomach." The thin man nodded again in a slow, methodical way before walking to the left of the entrance and into a dimly lit room. Mahlon laughed at his persuasion before turning his attention back to Kingston.

"Why you play so much?" Kingston asked with slight irritation as they made their way into a room where the walls were upholstered, and the light was dark, red, and low. "Why you got to make him gain weight? Why couldn't you just leave it at 'change your stank-ass attitude!?' Why you had to fuck with his weight?"

Mahlon laughed and patted Kingston on the back before answering. "He's unappealing that pale! I like a meal with some meat on their bones. I couldn't sink my teeth into that."

"Did you plan on making a meal of him?"

"Maybe, I mean... I usually like to suck on women, but some men have had the pleasure of enjoying my bite."

"Oh, so anyone can get it." Kingston said slyly.

"Hey, I'm an opportunist. If your delicious blood pheromones are teasingly seeping through your open pores, I will gladly oblige the temptation to bite the hell out of you." By then, Mahlon had cozied up to Kingston's ear. His lips grazed the tip of his lobe as he spoke his utterances in a deep, low tone. Kingston could feel the heat of his breath warming his body, causing his knees to struggle from bending.

"Lawd have mercy…" Kingston whispered as he swallowed his breath while trying to compose himself.

"Don't worry, Kingston. I won't bite— at least not tonight." Mahlon chuckled before licking the dewy sweat that had emerged on Kingston's neck.

Kingston exhaled in relief and then giggled. He then playfully pushed Mahlon away from him. "Boy... you act like you are so irresistible, but I promise you, you not even my type. I like my men a lil' dirty. You too fancy in the pants for me." Kingston allowed his eyes to stroll and then stop his gaze at the noticeable bulge resting humbly in the middle of his dark blue jeans crotch. He licked his lips with slight desire and then brought his gaze back up to meet Mahlon's shimmering eyes. "And you fill those pants oh so well." Kingston puckered his lips and blew Mahlon a kiss. He then turned his focus back to the door in front of them. Kingston breathed out the rest of the air left in his lungs quietly, inhaled hard, and then released the air, relaxing him and recentering his thoughts in preparation for the night's main event.

Unlike the grey steel bolted door that allowed them into the inconspicuous club. The door they faced in the dimly lit room with crushed dark red velvet walls and lighted sconces surrounding them was painted a shimmery dark gold. The door also looked heavy, and a round black iron knocker was in the middle of it. Kingston held the weighted handle in his hand for a moment while he subdued his excitement about finally making it through the most exclusive entrance on the East Coast. The experience had him trembling with excitement.

Mahlon could smell the adrenaline rush through Kingston's body. He gently touched his new friend's shoulder and whispered empathetically, "Calm down. No one likes an Eager Peter. And you won't get your dick sucked if your balls are sweaty."

Kingston swiftly turned his head back at Mahlon, agitated by his jovial comment.

"Why you play so much!" Kingston hissed his angry words and then snatched his face back towards the door. Once again, he took a deep breath and exhaled before letting the knocker thunk against the door. Instantly, he heard the batches of locks on the other side of the door release, and then, finally, the door began to open slowly. As it did, dense white fog came rushing towards them. The cloudy haze was tinted by the red, pink, and blue lights coming from behind the door's opening. The smell of a heavy, incensed fragrance began to fill their nostrils, inviting them to come in and explore. Nervously, Kingston grabbed Mahlon's hand as he took their first steps in. "Don't let go of my grip, Mahlon." Kingston whispered. "I can't see a thing and don't want to get lost just yet."

"Don't you worry." Mahlon squeezed Kingston's hand hard for assurance. "We're in this together. I'll make sure you are comfortable before I find me a playmate."

"Fellas... Welcome." Mahlon and Kingston turned around to watch the door shut, and a curvaceous woman stood before it. Her long rope-like braids cascaded over her shoulder and dangled inches from the floor. Her feet were pedicured but bare. Her toes adorned with rings. Her ankles were wrapped in thin gold anklets. Her toenails were encrusted with jewels and ornate shiny trinkets. Her thick calves supported her thunderous thighs. A tiny gold-sheered angled skirt covered her private area, and a shimmery chain rounded her soft and flat waist. Her breast bulging, her nipples shielded by her gold bra top that tied around her neck and back appeared to want to force their way through the gold lamiae fabric that stifled them. Her honey-colored skin shined and shimmered all over, just as the makeup on her lips, cheeks, and eyes did the same.

"Oh, my Lord... God is a woman..." Mahlon said, awestruck by the temptress' beauty.

She smiled at the compliment and slowly made her way over. "Welcome to my home." the woman said. She held her hand in front of them and opened her closed palm, exposing two black pills.

Mahlon and Kingston looked down at them and then back at the woman.

"Hi. I'm Kingston, and this right here—"

"Ah-ah. No names, gentlemen. You are known and unknown once you make it through the door. I know who you are, and that's all anyone needs to know."

"I definitely like that." A smile crept across Mahlon's face as he listened to the beautiful goddess speak. He looked down at the chalky black pills and then pointed at them. "What are these for?"

The woman smiled slyly as she began to explain. "These pills are a patent blend I created to help you relax and enjoy the night care-free. Take one. I insist." She held her hand up to them a little further, and without hesitation, they both took one, swallowing without water. "Very good. Now follow me." She pushed between the men, and they followed her intently while noticing the rounded but firm jiggle of her derriere.

Mahlon jabbed Kingston with his elbow and pointed to the woman's backside with excitement. "Bruh, I ain't looking at no girl's tail. That ain't my fish."

"But I'm sure you can appreciate it?"

Kingston watched how her booty swayed while they walked down the ornate hallway. "I mean, I'm sure it's nice if that's what you like..."

"And I do like." Mahlon said as he greedily rubbed his hands together.

Finally, they stopped at the entrance of another door, where the woman pulled a badge the size of a credit card from the waistline of her skirt. She swiped the card, and the door slid open with a whoosh. Music bellowed out, and people could be seen walking around with drinks in their hands. Kingston relaxed, happy to see a familiar atmosphere.

"Gentleman, you have made it to Tryst. Please enjoy yourselves. Nothing is off limits, and the drinks are on me. Whatever you desire in a sexual encounter, you will find it here. Don't be shy. The guests are willing participants and eager to give and receive. As mentioned before, you are known and not known all at the same time. The people here have already seen your faces via our vetting process. You have been chosen to be fucked however you like, but please return the hospitality by fucking however they like.

Kingston beamed with excitement as he asked, "All these people in here want to fuck lil' ol' me?!" smiling as he asked.

The woman giggled and then said, "Yes. All of them are ready to pleasure you."

"Thank you, Jesus!" Kingston stated with his head turned high. He let go of Mahlon's hand and headed in. As Mahlon followed behind him, the women stepped in his way. Their eye contact was intense; breathing heavily, their chests rose and fell succinctly.

Without hesitation, Mahlon understood. He allowed his finger to stroke her exposed thigh slowly, adding pressure to his touch and then grabbing the inside where her flesh was most sensitive.

"Is there a problem with me going into the club?" He asked.

"No. There's no problem."

"Is there something I can help you with then?" He asked as he unhanded her soft thigh meat and pulled her close by the waist."

"No, but I can help you."

"And how is that?"

"I choose you... Follow me up to my suite. My friends and I have a private party just for you."

"There are more of you? Do they all look like you?"

"They call me The Ugly One"

"Ummm... Excuse me? Are you coming?" Kingston interrupted.

"I think I'm going to take my chances with her." Mahlon said while never taking his eyes off the seductress.

"Wha— Oh no, you not standing me up again!" Kingston said. The woman grabbed her badge and tapped it on the scanner, shutting Kingston behind them and ending his complaining.

"Let's head up to your place and meet those friends of yours."

"Yes, Let's."

Chapter 12

Kingston buttoned up his black silk dress shirt and then checked the time on his all-black *Verso* Movado watch. *It's 5:00 IN THE MORNING...* surprised but unbothered by the hour of day since he had the time of his life. Kingston looked around the half-empty sex den, focusing in on somewhat familiar faces from the orgy he participated in, in search of Mahlon. He tucked his shirt into his black pleated slacks and slipped on his chunky sole Prada loafers. As he rummaged through the half-naked partygoers sleeping in the last moments of their ecstasy, trying not to step on any of the lying bodies, Kingston softly hissed Mahlon's name in hopes he would answer and wouldn't disturb the guests of the club.

"Mahlon!" He hissed once more in frustration. "Mahlon! Come on and stop playing. It's time to go!" He said as he continued to look around.

"Try the fishbowl." He heard someone say while stepping over them.

"Huh... fishbowl? Mahlon, is that you?" Kingston doubled back to where he first heard the response.

"Try the fishbowl. Tantra probably has him with her and her girls." The lazy-tongued speaker rolled over and pointed to the dark-tinted windows above them on the back wall. "Tantra probably has him up there. I heard some pretty amazing shit happens with her in that fishbowl. She probably changed your friend's life up there."

"Not if he took their lives first." Kingston mumbled before saying, "Thanks," and the partygoer turned back over to cuddle up to a pair of faceless bare breasts.

Tipping past both sleeping and still sexually active club members of Tryst, Kingston made it to the fishbowl's door. He purposefully barely knocked in hopes of not startling Tryst's alluring host, Tantra.

"Come in." Kingston heard the soft, slow voice say. He grabbed the handle and cautiously opened the door, peeping only his head in guardedly.

"My bad Miss Tantra. I'm just looking for my good friend, Mahlon. Someone said he may be in here..." Kingston quickly surveyed the fishbowl, noticing it was a bird's eye view of all the action taking place in the lower den.

Tantra glided over to an empty stool, her naked body exposing the sparkling ornamental nipple piercings resting on the mounds of her breast, and her soft bushel of curly hair tried to hide her pronounced pussy lips. She crossed one leg over the other casually as her relaxed smile began to show. "He'll be down in a minute." She said in a tone Kingston knew only came from a Southerner who experienced good sex.

He glanced at the spiral stairwell in time to see Mahlon sauntering down as he buttoned his shirt.

"My guy Kingston! Is your dick exhausted from all the fucking you did, or are you ready for another round?" Mahlon laughed heartedly while patting Kingston on his back.

"Oh, my dick is satisfied. Little sore though. But it's because I fucked this white nigga so hard I caught a cramp."

"Yeah. We watched you have your way with that guy. I could tell shit got brutal."

As Kingston and Mahlon made their way to the door, Tantra slipped in front of Mahlon and forced a kiss on his plump lips. Mahlon grabbed a handful of her round backside and squeezed it intensely, and then parted the cheeks enough to tickle her tight anus, which made Tantra giggle from the sensation. The act made her release her tongue from his. She stepped back and patted her belly with satisfaction and pride.

"Thank you, my darling, vamp. Soon, you will be the father of the child we have created together."

Kingston's eyes got big as he quickly turned to Mahlon for an explanation. "What in the hell is she talking about, Mahlon?!"

Tantra ignored Kingston's outburst and continued. "And our child will have seven other siblings to grow up with. Because of you, me and my harem of sister-friends have sealed our bond by sharing the same man and conceiving at the same time." Tantra wrapped her arms around Mahlon, and they embraced.

"I know y'all fucking lying! You telling me y'all gonna have some vampire babies running around the city like that's normal and shit? Oh, hell the fuck y'all not!" In shock by the thought, Kingston sucked his teeth and folded his arms together, and began to pout.

Mahlon and Tantra released each other quickly and kissed once more. "I have to go, but call me when the babies are born. Come on, Kingston, let's bid the beautiful Tantra adieu. It's getting to be light outside."

Mahlon grabbed Kingston by the elbow, leading him out of Tantra's layer. Once out of the doors of Tryst, they both got in the Uber they ordered. The two men sat in silence for a moment before Kingston turned to look at Mahlon.

"What the hell was that shit back there?" Kingston asked.

"Tantra and her friends are ovulating and want hybrid vampire babies. They wanted me to impregnate them." Mahlon pulled out his pack of cigarettes and began to smoke one.

"That is the dumbest bullshit I have ever heard! You giving these dumb bitches babies?? What is Bianca going to say?!"

"Chill out, my guy. Bianca's not going to say anything because there's no babies."

"Huh? She just said you are the father to her half-breed."

"Yeah, she thinks a baby is in there."

"Oh, you didn't nut."

"Oh... I nutted. I nutted down their throats and in their asses. On their asses, on their juicy titties, in the small of their backs, and all up in their fat coochies. I nutted so much…"

"You are so gross."

"And their faces," Mahlon said with a blank gaze plastered on his face as he recalled the amazing moment he exploded on each of the erotic beauties. "I nutted on their beautifully divine faces."

Kingston shook his head, knowing at that moment Mahlon had no shame.

"So yeah, I nutted, but that's not why they are not carrying my hybrid spawn. You see, I'm dead." Mahlon said as he put his hand to his chest in a matter-of-fact way.

"Vampires can't create children during sex. My sperm ain't worth nothing."

"Well, why didn't you tell her that? You got that girl thinking she having the next Blade."

"Why would I tell a gorgeous female with seven stunning wives who all want to fuck me 'til my dick fall off that I can't give them some designer babies?"

The Uber driver pulled over at the curb of Jefferson and Mimosa, one of the four entrances to The Block. "A'ight, fellas, this is as far as I go. You'll have to get out and walk from here."

"Sir. Look at me." Mahlon caught the driver's eye through the rear-view mirror. "You will take us to our destination without hesitation. Kingston has on Prada loafers and can't ruin them." The driver nodded his head, pulled off from the curb, and continued down Mimosa to River Towers.

"Mahlon, you just as scandalous as these alive niggas on these streets."

"Yeah, but I can get away with it. I'll go around there for dinner one night and take care of their memory. It'll be like it never happened."

"Oh, that memory eraser thing you do."

"Yeah, that thing. It just helps clean up messy memories."

"And dodge eight baby mama's."

Mahlon laughed and nodded his head in agreement.

Chapter 13

The dawn of the new late spring day seemed to reveal The Block as it indeed was. At night, no one could scrutinize the crumbling and once-thriving businesses that now stood silent. In the morning light, boarded-up storefronts and buildings displayed "For Lease" signs that have long been ignored were mixed between apartment buildings, many of which were built decades ago.

Even the streets were a stark reminder of the neglect by the city's elected officials. Mahlon and Kingston's slow ride to River Towers was filled with jolts and jerks because the roads were a patchwork of potholes and cracked asphalt. Litter and debris lined the filthy gutters, and the sidewalks were uneven and overgrown with dried-out brown and yellow colored weeds. Passing the only playground in the area, Mahlon wondered if the kids in the neighborhood found any joy with the rusted swings, the slides with graffiti painted on them, and the cracked pavement of the basketball courts that have the hoops missing their nets.

The Block's deterioration was lost on its residents, who had gone blind to their surroundings. They lived their lives one day at a time, not realizing they were trapped mentally by the desperation they lived through. Bianca and her crew were in a fight to keep a place that was on the brink of being a lost cause. Mahlon couldn't understand the desire to stay in an area that mimicked the worst of its people. He shook his head at their futility and prepared himself to turn in for the day. Mahlon and Kingston finally pulled up to River Towers. "Thank you, my good man!" Mahlon said to the driver. "Now, once you leave here, go take a self-defense class—"

"Nope! Nah-ah! Don't even try it with him! You ain't God!" Kingston opened the car door and pulled Mahlon out with him. "You can't just go around fucking with people's head 'cause you can! Take yourself on in that building!" Kingston playfully shoved Mahlon towards the Hoe-tel and then turned around to the driver, snapping his fingers to shake him from Mahlon's trance. "Hey!" He clapped his hands quickly and repeatedly, and the driver shook his head and rubbed his eyes as he tried to focus while coming out of his stupor. "Hey! You see me." Kingston said and clapped a few more times.

"Yeah… what happened?" He looked around him and noticed he was on The Block. The one place he never wanted to be. His breathing picked up as he panicked, but Kingston snapped his fingers at him again.

"Hey! Focus. Look at me. Don't pay attention to nothing going on around you. Just focus on me."

The driver nodded, worried that if he didn't, something awful would happen. "I'm listening."

"Good. Now, hold on. I got something for you." Kingston reached into his pocket, pulled out a twenty-dollar bill, and handed it to him. "Here's our money for the ride. Take this and go on head about your business. But don't come back over here thinking you can… 'cause you can't. This was a once-in-a-lifetime thing."

"Sure, sure. I understand." He put his car in drive and headed out of the neighborhood as fast as he could.

Kingston turned to Mahlon, putting his hand on his hip. "It ain't that hard to get people to do what you want them to do. Stop hypnotizing these innocent folks." Kingston walked over to Mahlon, and they continued towards the building.

"Oh Kingston, it is that easy. I can only do that to people who are willing participants. I can't 'romance' a person unless they want it…whether they realize it or not. Just like I can't come into your house unless you invite me."

Kingston thought on that last statement before he responded. "So that parts real? You can't come in my house unless I say so? I thought that was a myth."

"Yeah, no. It's real. And it really fits with a vampire's character. We do have a bit of pride about us. Why be somewhere you're not welcomed?" Mahlon said with a chuckle.

"Well, in that case, I'm never inviting you in. You don't know how to act." They both laughed as they approached Roxanne, Minah, and Danette, who watched them as they exited the Uber.

Danette shifted her body seductively, hoping to catch Mahlon's attention. She leaned over to Roxanne and whispered, "Ummm… is that Bianca's new boo because, girl, I would handle him for real."

Minah overheard Danette when she asked about Mahlon, and she shot back quickly, "There ain't no new 'Boo'. That's just some nigga she fucking. And don't look too hard at him, and don't be asking questions about some nigga you neva going to fuck." Minah spat out angrily at Danette. "I can already tell you plotting, but you plotting on the wrong one. Your ass gonna catch it if you keep on."

"Damn, bitch! You act like YOU fucking him! All I want is for that nigga to do is bite me so I can be the baddest bitch like Bianca." Danette continued to stare at him devilishly as he got closer to them on his way into the building.

"I might fuck him if I want, but don't nobody want that fake ass wannabe Kilion nigga. Fuck him." Minah said with disgust.

"Ladies…" He nodded hello as he walked past. Danette waved flirtatiously and gave a wink. Mahlon did a double take because of the cute greeting from the beautiful coco-brown beauty with almond-shaped eyes, the platinum blonde pixie cut, and a Coke bottle shape to match. She smiled brightly when she knew she had his attention. Captured by her good looks, Mahlon paused his cadence to find his way back to the lovely woman. But without hesitation, Roxanne stepped in between their eye contact, blocking their instant attraction for each other.

"Ah-Ah! Not on my watch! Roxanne locked eyes with Mahlon, which made him stop in his tracks. "You... gon-on-up-there to ya girl. What you not finna do is get my chick tied up in ya bullshit with Bianca. I need Danette staying pretty so she can fuck these niggas and get this money. Bianca would tear her ass up if she EVER thought one of us was messing around with her nigga!" She pointed towards the building's front door, making her demand very clear. Mahlon shrugged his shoulders in surrender, turned, and headed up the stairs into the building.

She then spun around and sternly looked at Danette. Danette shrunk back and covered her mouth as she giggled. "And as for you! You know better! We trying to survive out here for real! Don't get that girl mad at you 'fore you be laid up in a pile of body parts like Lucy was. If you want to stay out here— ALIVE in these streets, you better know she ain't playing with you."

"My bad! It just looks like fun to be a vampire sucking dick and fucking niggas up. Bianca living her best life! I want to be just like her."

"Tha fuck you don't! That bitch cold-blooded. Only thing good about her life is how pretty she is."

"Yeah, if B wanted us to be vampires, she would have made us all vampires by now." Minah said as she reflected on her life as someone who had never been bitten to become as strong as Bianca or Kilion but used as a meal when it was convenient or a last resort. She lowered her head as she slipped into sadness, thinking about how pitiful she must look to all the other girls around her. "Look at me. I ain't never been chosen to be one of them, and they been sucking on me for as long as I can remember. Like three hundred years long." They all became quiet, not knowing how to respond to Minah's situation. Suddenly, she remembered her orders from Bianca and shot into the building after Mahlon and Kingston, who were both standing around waiting in the lobby for the elevator.

"Aye… Kingston, Bianca wants you to come up and see her before she goes to bed."

"Me? What for?" Kingston said in defiance.

She shrugged her shoulders, not knowing the answer to his question. "She said for me to tell you to come up when you and Mahlon get back." She and Kingston hugged their goodbyes before she eyeballed Mahlon with disdain. "Umph… bye, Mahlon." She said before turning on her heels to go back outside to hang out on the steps with Roxanne and some of the other girls still staggering in from a night's work. Mahlon chuckled and shook his head at Minah's dislike for him, knowing his fate and connection with Bianca was much stronger than Minah's with her.

Kingston rolled his eyes at the command but knew he had to oblige. Even though he wasn't under her rule like the others who lived on The Block, he still understood he could only get away with just a little disregard for her power. Had he brushed off her direct orders to come see her in her penthouse, he'd surely pay for his disrespect… and death would not have been an option for atonement. Tight-lipped, he defiantly folded his arms and began rapidly tapping his toes in irritation.

Mahlon saw Kingston's mood change and asked, "Why so mad about going to see her? I know you don't like her, but anything she does or says really bothers you. I'm still getting to know her, but honestly… she isn't that bad. Yeah, she has a horrible temper… much worse than any vampire I've ever engaged, but other than that, she's just a girl with a broken heart. Can't you at least find some sympathy for that?"

In shock at his request, Kingston turned his head swiftly towards Mahlon with an appalled stare. "Are you serious right now? You want me to feel some type of way for that crazy hoe? Have you seen the level of fear and tyranny she oppresses these folks with? A hoe nor a gangster can't even make an honest living around here because she got them walking on eggshells. Hell, a regular guy just looking to get his dick sucked by one of these broads can't enjoy the moment if she chooses to chomp on his ass!" Kingston shook his head in disgust, thinking about how terrible Bianca is to the people on The Block. "It's a damn shame she acts the way she does. And can't nobody and won't nobody stop her. I wish 'fore God, Kilion hadn't chosen her to be his wife. I wish he would have had a bit more discretion with who he fell in love with 'cause he picked the wrong bitch to die for."

The ding of the elevator and the swoosh of air as its doors opened signaled them both to get in and ride it up to the twenty-second floor. Kingston hit the button for their destination and leaned against the elevator wall while pondering his summons.

"Well, tell me, was I a good date or not?" Mahlon said to break the silence.

Glad to be pulled out of his thoughts about his frenemy, Kingston smiled slyly, looking Mahlon up and down. "I mean… after I got over you almost standing me up for the night, I was feeling you." Kingston chuckled, thinking about their meetup and escapades in Tryst. "At least for the little time we were together. Your ass left me, but that's okay. I got to meet so many more interesting and sexy ass people anyway." Kingston allowed the tip of his pinky fingernail to rest on his sharpest tooth in a coy and mischievous way.

"You know we could have fucked last night." Mahlon stated.

"No, we couldn't have." Kingston said just as blunt.

"You're right. You're like a brother to me now."

"Don't try to bench me. I know you still want this." Kingston turned his body's profile towards Mahlon and tooted up his booty while rubbing it seductively.

Mahlon raised an eyebrow to the statement and then shook his head no. "Never ever, bro. You and I…" Mahlon rapidly pointed his finger back and forth between them. "Me and you… never in a million years."

"And why not?!" Kingston pouted and stomped his foot.

"Because of this!" Mahlon said jokingly and motioned his hand up and down towards Kingston. "You are very bratty and way too high maintenance for me." They both laughed at the honest statement.

"Yeah, I guess I'm way too much for you. Besides, you not my type anyway. I like my men secretive and thuggish. You too groomed for my taste." They laughed again as the elevator bell announced they'd arrived on the twenty-second floor.

While walking towards the door, they could see Bianca's crew standing around it. "Oh god…" Kingston muttered under his breath. "These niggas always got something to say when I come up here…" Mahlon looked at Kingston and then at the crew of men standing around. He then felt Kingston's uncomfortableness the closer they got.

"What up, Kingston." Lance nodded at them both as they approached.

"Hey, guys. I'm just here to see B real quick. She said for me to come up when I got back."

"From what… your date with dis nigga?" Phaizo said, using his thumb, nonchalantly pointing at Mahlon.

"Nigga, I ain't know you was gay?" Rell said to Mahlon.

"You gay nigga? How you fucking B, and you like pole?" Marco joined in.

"And you gay for this scrawny ass dude?" Marco said.

Mahlon proudly put his arm over Kingston's shoulder before responding. "What… you want me to be gay for you?" Mahlon removed his arm from Kingston's shoulders and swiftly grabbed Marco by his neck, squeezing it enough to make him gasp for air.

"Yo, man! Let my brother go!" Polo shoved Mahlon's taught extended arm, hoping it would loosen the grip his hand had on Marco's neck, but Mahlon flashed him a menacing glare, signaling Polo and the others to back off— which they did.

Mahlon turned his attention back to Marco's clutched throat. His thumbnail slowly grazed his sweaty skin, opening it just enough to allow a sliver of crimson blood to brighten the slit. Mahlon methodically pulled Marco towards him, stuck his tongue out, and slowly lapped up the blood that began to pool and dribble. "Mmmmm…." He pulled Marco closer. The hardness in his groin butted against Marco's leg, forcing Marco to squirm a little harder to get away. "Nah… you don't want me to be gay for you. You don't seem to handle my flirting too well." Mahlon chuckled and let Marco drop to the floor as he began struggling to catch his breath. Mahlon opened the door to Bianca's home and waved Kingston in. "After you, my friend…" He said with a smile.

Kingston chuckled at the scene and walked in while Mahlon closed the door behind them, leaving the crew as they were helping Marco regain his composure. "Bae-Bae!" Kingston laughed. "Why you had to jack my boo up like that?!"

"After all that you still want that man? I thought I was defending your honor."

"Chile, that shit they talk when they together don't mean nothing. I see him checking me out when he by himself. I may act like I'm scared, but I promise you they not ever gonna lay hands on The Doll." Kingston snapped his fingers twice in declaration and then gave Mahlon a friendly peck on the cheek. "Thanks for having my back, though. Ain't no man ever done that for me before."

"Yeah, well… now that I know you're not really scared of them, it probably won't happen again."

"Whatever." Kingston said as he stuck his tongue out at Mahlon. "Take me back there to go see this wench so I can go on about my day."

"You betta watch your mouth about my girl." Mahlon slightly tagged Kingston in the chest for his insult. "You know her bark and her bite are worse than mine."

When they entered the bedroom, they saw Vivian helping Bianca with getting dressed for her morning sleep. Kingston rolled his eyes once again in irritation before finding a chair to sit in and wait for Bianca to address him. He crossed one leg over the other and began picking at his nails.

"Oh no, my love, don't get dressed. Let's sleep in the bed naked with my dick inside that sultry pussy of yours for the next twelve hours. How does that sound?" Mahlon walked over to the mother-daughter duo, grabbing the silk chiffon robe from Vivian and tossing it across the room. Bianca turned around to him. Her smile brightened as she draped her arms around his neck and kissed him passionately on the lips. Vivian rolled her eyes at the embrace and walked away from the two.

"Did you have a good night at Tryst?" Bianca asked after she'd finished planting kisses all over his face.

"I did. It was a great welcome to this little sleepy city of yours. Who knew there were so many freaks in Richmond?" Mahlon allowed his hand to slide down Bianca's backside until he was able to cuff a handful of her bountiful bottom and use his fingertip to tickle her anus.

"Yeah, Richmond has a lot of freak spots. It would have been nice if you had invited me to come along, but I guess your lil' friend over there has an issue with me."

"Leave him alone. We needed some time to bond, and you needed some rest."

Kingston huffed in annoyance before responding. "Ummm… what did you want? I have something I gotta do soon."

"Don't rush me nigga! You act like you can say shit and it not get back to me, but guess what, it does! Keep my name out your mouth, or I'mma rip that mouth open wide enough for you to eat your damn words!" Bianca said in anger.

Kingston threw up his hands in annoyance before saying, "Fine. Is that all you called me up here for?"

"Yeah. And don't act like you the shit in these streets. I'm the shit in these streets! You ain't above getting fucked up!"

"Aight, B. Whatever. Can I go?"

Bianca waved her hand to dismiss Kingston and went back to tending to Mahlon. She grabbed his hand and led him to the bed. He laid down, and she straddled him eagerly. Vivian cleared her throat to signal she was still in the room.

"Ma… um… you can go. I'm busy."

"I thought you were going to tell me about that job you wanted me to work on?"

"We'll talk about it tomorrow."

Irritated, Vivian left the room, shutting the door behind her. Making her way out of the penthouse, she slammed the door behind her and pushed through the crew, who continued to bicker about their encounter with Mahlon not too long ago.

"Ma, what you all mad for?" Phaizo asked.

"Mahlon has got to go, and we need to be the ones to get him away from her because if we don't, we are going to be the ones she gets rid of.

"Yo, say less. I'm down." Marco said as he rubbed his neck.

Chapter 14

"Minah!" Bianca yelled as she lay in bed after waking from her day's slumber. Sitting up, she stretched, yawned, and yelled again, "Minah!" She got out of bed, groggily walked out of her room, and opened Minah's bedroom door. Not finding her there, she went back to her room and sent her a "Where are you" text. She stared at the phone for a moment, assuming Minah would respond immediately, but she didn't. Bianca dialed her number, and the call went straight to voicemail. She sucked her teeth loudly and tossed the phone to the floor in frustration. The thump of it landing interrupted Mahlon's sleep.

"Dear, could you please keep it down? I don't wake up this early." He turned over and nestled the edge of the blanket under his chin.

"Get up. I want to go out." Bianca lightly nudged Mahlon on the shoulder to wake him.

"No, Darling. It's barely evening. Besides, I'm still tired from last night."

"Yeah, I can see you used all your energy with Kingston. Y'all fucked?"

"Darling?!" Mahlon said with irritation. "Please don't be crass with me. You know he's just a friend. Do I ask you how Minah's pussy taste? No. So don't ask me about my liaisons." Mahlon yawned and turned over.

"Minah's not responding to my calls. I don't know where she is."

"Use your telepathic abilities and call her to you. I'm sure she will answer then." Mahlon mumbled.

Bianca shook her head no. "Nah. I don't like opening my mind to her. I can tell she like to linger trying to read other thoughts. I'on like that." She scrunched up her face at the thought.

"You're so fickle about her, Darling. Either open your mind to her or go walk the streets looking for her. I'm sure she won't be hard to locate." He put the pillow over his head and said, "I'll meet you later this evening, and we'll go hunting together. I promise."

***

Minah heard the ding on her phone and saw there was a text from Bianca. She looked at the message and stared long and hard at it, trying to resist the urge to respond instantly. She knew it would be best to reply to at least say, "I'm out hunting for you" or "On my way back to meet you at the penthouse." But either of those responses would have gotten her into deeper trouble with Bianca. There was no correct answer when it came to her. Minah knew she should have been at Bianca's side when she was ready. Bianca hated having to ask her where she was.

She put the phone back into her pocketbook, no longer scared of the consequences of not texting back. She chose to live in the moment with Sawyer. She rolled over in the bed in their rented hotel room to see him staring at the ceiling in deep thought.

"You okay?" Minah asked. She touched him softly on his bare shoulder. Their bodies naked beneath the covers they lay under.

"Yes… I just… I never thought I would be here… In this place emotionally or physically with anyone."

Minah nodded in agreement. "I understand. I don't even remember being touched so sweetly in the way you have touched me. It's been a long time since I've had sex without fear."

Sawyer slowly sat up in the bed and looked down at Minah. Her delicate frame and petite features made him think of a broken bird who needed nurturing to fly again. He smiled sweetly at her and lightly brushed the back of his hand across her cheek.

"We've definitely bonded. I know it's only been just a few hours before we ended up here." He used his hand to gesture at the room and the bed they both currently occupied. "But even from our first encounter where you educated me on how to talk to you to our moment today, you have been on my mind. So, when I approached you today— not because I wanted your body but because I wanted to know more, I was prepared for anything that could happen next. I've never felt this way about anyone. I live in solitude… because what I do requires never feeling for anyone."

Minah sat up in the bed beside him to listen intently. "Yes, what you do is hard. As long as I've been around them… those vampires, I've never met a vampire hunter. How come I've never met you before now?"

"It's complicated, but understand we knew of you. We keep our distance until it's time to respond. And that's why I have to do what I have to do to Bianca. She is out of control. Because of her, people are spooked by things that go bump in the night."

"I know she is." Minah bowed her head in sorrow. "I'm part of her problem. I'm the one bringing her victims."

"You aren't the problem; you suffer by her hands. My job is to neutralize her, but that would leave you without a way to recover from the havoc she has brought to your life. I can't do that. I can't kill her knowing you will hurt with the loss of her… not after what we've shared today."

Minah blushed as she thought about their morning. After getting Bianca settled in for her rest for the day, she made up her mind to run away from the life. She knew there was a good chance Bianca would have found her, but she was going to be prepared this time for death by her hands. She knew she wasn't going to go back. Sitting at the bus stop waiting for the next one out of the area, Sawyer pulled up and offered her a ride. In his car, it only took the one question, 'Where are you headed?' for her to break down in a bucket of tears, and that's where she poured her heart out to a man she didn't know. He had to pull over just to try and comfort her, and once she calmed down enough, she told him everything.

Her life story spanned hundreds of years, just like his. She spoke of how when she was young, she wanted to be free, but her parents wanted her to stay with them and work the land. They were all enslaved beings, and she could no longer settle with just being a worker. She left her home like many did… in the night to escape to the north, where she found her freedom and Kilion, who wanted to build her up.

Kilion found her story of escaping to freedom intriguing and took her under his wing. He built her up by giving her the means to own a place to live and a skill to make money with, and when she was ready to get her family, she found them all dead. The land they worked when she lived there with her family had been scorched. The people and everyone who lived there were hung. Kilion was all she had. She begged him to take her life. Kill her or make her like him, but he wouldn't. Instead, he kept her as his distant companion, and she agreed to the way he chose for her because she had no one.

Sawyer listened to all of it. He listened through her tears, her pain, and her anger. He never heard anyone's story quite like hers. She was different; she was strong, and she was also vulnerable. She was unseen, just like him. She worked in the background of life, trying to keep order and balance in any way she could. Minah touched a part of his heart he never thought was there. She exposed a vulnerability he didn't know he had, and he felt safe with her even though she was in need of a real hero. She saw it, too. And when she did, she knew he would allow her to protect him. Finally, she was someone else's strength.

She directed him to the hotel they were now in and made love. Real love full of passion and desire. He was careful with her. His large frame bared down on her, but he was cautious not to crush her. He allowed her to be on top and control his movements while he lay underneath her, willing to take orders. He laid her out, spread her legs, and kissed her softly in between her hidden lips. She bent her knees, allowing him to stand strong as she swallowed his manhood in honor. After they both succumbed to their bodies' will to naturally release, they knew their bond was solidified.

Minah's body began to tingle thinking about their lovemaking. Sawyer saw the blush in her face and leaned in to kiss her passionately. "I have to go." Minah said while her lips were pressed to his.

"Why?" Sawyer said as he pulled himself away from her.

"I'm not going to run away. I have to go back. She texted me already. I'm sure she's going to come looking for me."

"Well, if she does, I'll kill her. I must. It's part of The Council's orders."

"But isn't Mahlon handling that? You said Mahlon is trying to change her."

"He is. I'm waiting around for him to let me know."

"Well, once she changes and agrees to peace, we can leave together." She gave him a kiss and put her clothes on. I have to run. Once she goes to sleep tomorrow morning, we can see each other again." She picked up her bag and left the room.

✳✳✳

Dejected, Bianca quickly put on a pair of red leggings, a matching halter, and her red retro Jordan 5's. She pinned her hair in a high bun, grabbed her silver bomber fur, and checked her look in the mirror. "Perfect." Since it was a bit too early to be out in the evening sun but not too early that she would burn to death if she were outside while the sun was setting, she put on enough sunscreen to protect her face and any skin not covered by her attire. She then blew a kiss to herself and grabbed her hoop earrings to put on as she made her way out of her room. "Don't keep me waiting outside for your ass." She paused her exit to hear Mahlon's response, but he only snored heavily. She shook her head in dissatisfaction and left the room, shutting the door behind her.

Heading down the hall, Vivian opened the door to the spare bedroom and headed to the bathroom, but she slowed her walk when she saw Bianca coming her way. Bianca rolled her eyes with disgust, knowing her mother wanted to talk and she was not interested in listening.

"What, Ma."

"Nothing. Just headed to the bathroom. Saw you coming. Hadn't spent any time with you in a couple of days. Seems like Mahlon has been keeping you busy."

"Say what you gotta say, Ma. I don't want to wait around here all day for you to tell me you don't like him."

"Who said I didn't like him? I never said I don't like him. I'm just wondering when are we going to have time to hang?"

"What you not good at is lying. You don't like him."

"Listen, if you like him, I love him… but…"

"But what?"

"You don't see what he's doing?"

"He not doing nothing, Ma"

"Of course he is. He's taking you away from me. Look at us. I just got here, and we haven't had any time together."

"Ma, that has nothing to do with this."

"Doesn't look like that to me. If y'all ain't fucking or biting the shit out of somebody, you go the other way if I even look at you too long." Vivian folded her arms across her chest as she huffed in frustration.

"I haven't spent no time with you because I don't trust your trifling ass yet."

"Bianca!" Vivian threw her hands helplessly in the air as Bianca spoke her truth.

"Don't give me that shit, Ma. When I was a teenager living with you, your ass left me to fend for myself 'cause you were caught up with that short-ass, drunk-ass, bitch-ass, rape-ass nigga, and now you mad 'cause this nigga getting more quality time than you. Don't be thirsty, Ma. When I'm ready to spend some time with your begging, free-loading 'Mother-of-the-Year'-ass, you'll know." Bianca stared coldly as her mother stood in front of her with a shocked and blank face. She sucked her teeth and then gave a half-cocked smile before she began to walk away.

The slick and shady response Bianca gave brought Vivian back into the moment of their contention, and she yanked Bianca's arm, pulling her back into the conversation. "Now, hold on one minute, daughter. I'm still your mother, you little bitch. You think because you the baddest thing walking around here that I won't beat your ass up and down these streets? You think I'm scared of those fucking fangs in your mouth?! Bitch, please. I will knock those ungodly teeth so far down your throat; they'll snag your asshole when you shit them mutha-fuckers out! Don't you EVER think you done got so grown you above me! I'll beat your ass!"

Bianca's eyes flashed with rage as she listened to her mother's tone as it went from meek to threatening. She swiftly grabbed Vivian by the throat and slammed her against the wall behind her. Bianca allowed her nails to sink into her mother's neck slowly, piercing the skin as she deliberately and methodically squeezed her neck. Watching her mother squirm under the crushing pressure she applied to her throat and the way her eyes bulged while struggling to breathe made Bianca's mouth water with delight, her sharp fangs descending from her gums were eager to chomp into Vivian's jugular as a reminder of who was actually in charge.

Bianca's devilish smile curled at the thought of consuming the life of the person who hurt her the most. Bit by bit, she opened her mouth, excited to put an end to the torment her mother subjected her to. People called Bianca evil— the Killer of Men. But if it hadn't been for her mother treating her like a throwaway, Bianca would not have all the rage that fueled her destruction.

Looking at her mother, now helpless under her mighty hand, felt like redemption. *YES, SHE HAS TO DIE,* Bianca thought to herself. "This about to be more satisfying than killing that nasty wench, Lucy."

She opened her wanting mouth wider, leaning in slowly, preparing to savor the moment when revenge would be sweetest, when she saw the spark of excitement and the curl of a slight grin come across her mother's face. Bianca paused her attack to grasp the joy her mother showed in the midst of her demise. Bianca loosened the grip on her mother's neck, allowing the grin to transform into a smile of elevation.

"Yes, B. Take my life. Make me like you, though. Let me rule beside you as your second in command." Vivian said between gasping breaths. "Don't stop, Baby. Make me like you because you don't have it in you to kill me. Your only mother. The only resemblance of real life you have left."

Bianca looked hard into her mother's eyes and could see the desire for the power being a vampire can wield. Bianca removed her claws from her mother's neck and allowed her teeth to retract calming the desire within her to kill Vivian.

Vivian then fell to the floor, holding her neck and rapidly convulsing as her body felt the relief of freedom from Bianca's hold. She looked up at her daughter from the floor as she began to gain her composure. She wiped her tears of stressed pain away before she spoke again. "Why Bianca? Why can't you see we can run The Block and rule the world together?" She said in a hoarse and raspy voice now that her throat was bruised from the crippling grip. "My plan for us is bigger than this 'lil shit you got going on. Let me be the mother that can guide you into the future we both want."

Bianca stared with anger and frustration at her mother before she spoke. "You want to be a mother to me finally?! What the hell do I need a mother for?! Look at me! At 16, that dumb drunk nigga tried to rape me because your raggedy ran-through pussy won't good enough no more!!! Where were you then??" Bianca's bottom lip began to tremble, so she pulled it tighter to her mouth to keep it still as the memory of her tortured past began to bubble up within her.

"But he didn't, B… I was—"

"You were gonna what?! Tell me it was my fault he wanted me and not you??" A small tear began to swell in her eyes as the image of that night began to make her skin chill and develop goosebumps. "But you could have left me with my Nana Gene while you hoed around that funky ass town. You could have just left me with someone who really loved me, but you took her away from me because she cared too much! I HATE YOU FOR THAT!"

"B…." Vivian said softly. She could see the deep sadness Bianca was actively reliving. She had to be cautious with her words, not knowing how she would respond with the monster of the vampire running through her veins. "Nana didn't love you like you think she did. I was paying her money to keep you, and when the money ran out, she sent you back and blamed me. And before I could clear things up with her, she died."

"You a liar and always will be a LIAR! My Nana was the only person who loved me, and you HATED it!" Bianca's tear fell fast from her eye as she wiped the rest of her pain away. "We can't have nothing together… especially ruling this fucked up ass world." Bianca turned again to walk away but looked over her shoulder to see Vivian's head hopelessly bowed into her hand. She said to her, "Me and you together? Yeah, right. All you'd do is take this away from me just like you took everything else. Ain't no way I'm going to give you anything of mine. This is my power. MINE!!" Bianca turned and stormed out of the penthouse, slamming the door behind her.

"Yo, Boss! Why you slamming doors like that?!" Phaizo spilled a little of his drink, startled by the bangs the door made. "Fuck you, Phai! Stay out of my damn business!"

Bianca pushed through her group of flunkies and through the exit doors to take the steps down to the streets. "What's wrong with her crazy ass now?" Phaizo asked Lance. "I don't know, man... She may be a vampire but she still acts like a regular moody-ass female." He looked at his watch and noted the time. "She probably hungrier than a muh-fukka 'cause she late for her regular feeding time."

"I hate to be the joe who gets to be her dinner tonight. She probably gonna mangle the fuck out they neck." Rell lamented.

"Probably?? Man, it's guaranteed to be messy." Polo responded.

Marco put his hands up in surrender as he shook his head. "Well, I'm not cleaning up behind her tonight. She fitna fuck The Block up for sure with that nasty attitude. Lance, put me on hoe patrol or collections tonight. I can't stomach the blood tonight."

"Y'all a bunch of punks! Fuck your weak ass stomach!"

"I'm for real, Lance! She messy as fuck as is! Tonight, gonna be brutal!"

Lance thought for a minute before responding. "Man, just get a crew of junkies then and have it clear by dawn."

The crowd of girls scattered once they saw Bianca emerge from the front doors of the Hoe-tel full of rage. "Minah!" Bianca screeched, "Minah! Let's go!" Bianca folded her arms across her body with anger filling her eyes.
"Min—"

"She not out here." Roxanne rushed up to Bianca, hoping the update would calm her enough for her to move on.

Bianca turned to Roxanne quickly with irritation all over her. "Well, where the hell she at?"

"She umm... She's probably out hunting for you. We haven't seen her all day."

Bianca angrily stared through Roxanne as she thought about where Minah could be.

"Do you want me to send one of the girls out looking for her?"

Bianca blinked to clear her thoughts before she spoke. "Nah. I'm going to look for myself." Crossing over some streets and checking their regular places to feed, Bianca didn't find her. As her hunger pains grew, Bianca began to see men as they walked down the streets as meals instead of customers. She licked her lips at the dark, tall stranger by the alley watching her as she watched him. *PREY*...

She walked over to the stranger, reached out, and assertively grabbed his crotch, tickling and fondling his meat as she seduced him with her eyes. He grabbed her by the head as if palming a basketball and began pushing her to her knees, but Bianca resisted by removing his hand and placing it on her breast.

"Let's go fuck." She said as she felt his cock become engorged with desire. She grabbed his big, strong, muscular hand and led him to the dark alley behind him.

"So, you don't talk much?"

"Not much to say."

"Good. I like the strong silent type."

As they walked further into the alley, it became darker. Bianca felt her desire to kill grow under the guise of the shadows. She stopped walking and turned to her victim. Her eyesight, keener than the average human's, saw what the darkness would usually cloak. The man was almost half a foot taller than her and didn't look like the usual type. His grimaced face showed a lack of desire her victims usually displayed once being unsuspectingly chosen to be her feast under the guise of sexual fantasy with an unnaturally breathtaking woman. She approached him and pressed her hand on his solid chest. Bianca hadn't seduced a man in a long time and was out of touch with how to be personal. *This would have been an easy kill if Minah was here. She could have distracted him so I could have caught him off guard.* Quickly reverting to her days on The Block, Bianca decided it was time to have some fun.

"So how much you willing to pay for some pussy?"

"Who said I was buying?"

"Oh, so you think I am going to give you ass, or are you finna just take it?" There was a long pause between them. The man dug into his pocket, pulled out a fifty, and tossed it on the ground in front of her. Bianca took steps toward the tossed money at the tip of her shoes. She looked down at it and then stepped on the crumpled bill as she approached him. Standing as close as she could, she opened her mouth slightly, allowing her fangs to slowly descend and rest atop the plump of her bottom lip.

"Enough of this fake shit..." She spoke with malice intent while her hand darted to his neck, her fingernails forcefully digging in as if trying to pierce his skin. Her fangs bared, she hissed menacingly at him.

"You obviously ain't trying to fuck, and I'm hungrier than a muh…" She leaned into him and spoke her next words. "And you my type of bite." She opened her mouth wide as the man raised his hand from behind, holding a shiny object that caught Bianca's eye. Just as she halted her bite to grab the man's object from his hand, she heard the fearful yell of her concubine.

"Bianca, stop!" and then rapid click of her heels on the cobblestone alley coming her way.

"Stop, B! He not ready! I'll get— I mean, I got someone else for you to try tonight." Minah said through gasps of breaths.

Bianca turned around to see Minah stumbling and rushing her way. She rolled her eyes, irritated by the interruption. "Bitch, what you talking about! I'm fucking busy!"

"Sawyer, No!" Minah ran past Bianca, reached up quickly, and grabbed his raised hand, pulling the razor-sharp dagger from his grasp and tossing it further into the dark alley.

Bianca caught a glimpse of Minah's swift action. She looked at her victim and then at Minah suspiciously. Her skin flushed with rage, causing intense heat to course through her veins and making her feel like she might spontaneously combust. Seeing the panic in Minah's eyes made her realize what was plainly obvious. She rushed at Minah, pushing her against the wall and holding her under her superhuman strength.

"Who is he to you?" Bianca said in a low growl, reverberating through her body and causing her skin to pimple and blister. Bianca got closer, inhaling Minah's tell-tell smell of a new owner.

"Bianca… your skin…" Minah watched in awe and fear as the blistering pimples gathered, swelled, and popped on Bianca's arms.

"Answer me!" Bianca ignored the question. She was more focused on regaining control of her Minah. With her teeth bared, she snapped them together forcefully as a threat to Minah, bringing her attention back to her for an answer. "Now, where the fuck you been? You been with this nigga?" She flicked her head in her victim's direction while keeping her eyes on her possession. "You trying to leave me for that bitch made nigga over there? That's who you love now?"

Sawyer made a move to confront Bianca, but Minah's eyes widened, and she put her hand up to stop him. "Stay right there, Sawyer! This is between me and her… Please don't come any closer."

Bianca flashed him an angered glance before she turned her glare back at Minah. "You better answer me before I kill you both."

"B…" Minah said nervously, knowing a wrong response could get her and Sawyer ripped to shreds. She tried to give a reassuring smile before explaining. "You know I'm loyal to you and only you." She reached her hand up and grazed Bianca's cheek softly with her index finger. The gesture slightly softened Bianca's jawline, which had hardened at the thought of abandonment. Minah noticed Bianca's tenderness peak through her tough exterior, and she seized the opportunity and lovingly grabbed her hand. "Why would I ever leave you? Our bond is so strong, and the sex is so good..." Minah leaned in to kiss her, seductively suckling Bianca's bottom lip before slipping her tongue into her partially opened mouth. She looked over at Sawyer, who surrendered his will to attack and lowered his eyes as it was too painful to watch her grovel for their lives. He couldn't watch the sad display, but he knew why she felt she had to do it.

Bianca returned the kiss and embraced Minah allowing the affection given by her whore to be a reminder of how much she had missed her touch. Bianca gripped and then tightly squeezed Minah's backside as a sign of ownership, aware that the tall stranger watched their interaction. Bianca wasn't sure who the man was to Minah, but she knew he could be a wedge between them. She pulled Minah from their kiss and quickly turned her around to face the man who tried to attack her previously and who Minah tried to save. Bianca inhaled Minah's air, convinced that the stranger caused the shift in her familiar scent.

"You've been with him, haven't you."

Minah's body slightly stiffened at the revelation, but she knew she had to answer honestly for any hope of salvation. "Yes... but only for your enjoyment."

"Mine? You think I want you with someone who hasn't paid for the pussy and you acting like I can't bite?!" Bianca's mood began to shift towards rage once more. The blistering pimples on her arm now started to cover her chest. "You been happily giving my pussy away to this nigga when you supposed to be in these streets hunting?" Bianca gripped Minah by the forearm, twisting it back and holding it between the shoulder blades. Sawyer flinched to rescue her from the pain-inducing hold, then hesitated, knowing what was between him and Minah was stronger than any choke-hold she tried to squirm from. He knew she could handle herself. His butting in at this phase could ruin everything.

Bianca cut her eyes Sawyer's way when he tested the urge to save her. Without hesitation, she swiftly sank her teeth into Minah's neck, suckling the blood that spilled out of the wound.

He tightened his mouth, clenching his teeth together, trying to remain composed. Attempting to kill her now could put Minah in harm's way. No longer able to watch the maddening display, Sawyer turned to leave. As his heels clicked the pavement, he could hear Bianca continuing to slurp as Minah moaned in sultry agony. "Yeah, you think you can take her from me, but she ain't going nowhere! She's mine!" Bianca yelled the taunting words as he continued to walk out of the dark alley.

Sawyer balled his hands in anger and restraint as he thought, *you think she is yours, but she will be mine, and you will be dead.*

Once Bianca saw the stranger was no longer in hearing distance, she turned her attention to Minah, who was now slumped over and half coherent from being drained of her blood. "So, this is what you been up to?" Bianca grabbed Minah's face by her cheeks, turning her to look Bianca in the eyes. Dizzy, Minah could hardly keep her flopping head still while trying to regain her strength. "You supposed to be working The Block, but you out here fucking for free. I see why you not pulling money." Bianca flashed back to the torture she endured with Daddy and how she spent her time with him before Kilion scooped her up. She was naive then, and Minah was falling into the same trap she'd fallen into.

"What you fail to realize is I'm the only one that got your best interest at heart, and I got everything you need and want." Bianca used her fingernail and sliced open her wrist. The thick crimson-red serum flowed steadily from her open cut. She then laid her wrist on Minah's lips and allowed her potent mixture to nurse Minah enough to bring her back from the brink of her demise. Bianca yanked her wrist away before Minah could benefit from the elixir's power. She noticed the blisters that had formed on her arms had begun to heal and settle. She then licked the self-inflicted wound on her wrist to seal the power of the blood back into her body.

She watched as Minah regained consciousness and control of herself. Still too weak to escape but strong enough to walk home to the prison that awaited her, Bianca continued her taunt. "Like I thought. This shit I got in me is too good for you to leave. Yeah, hoe. Yo' skinny ass not going nowhere, and can't no one save you from me or these fucking streets. Don't ever think you leaving because if you do, you gotta take the dirt road out." No longer hungry, Bianca grabbed Minah by the top of her thin arm and partially pulled her to the River Towers.

The hustle of the night's energy slowly fizzled when everyone saw Bianca and Minah headed their way towards the front steps.

"Dang Boss. You full already? You back early, and the sun ain't even all the way gone yet." Phaizo said with a half laugh in his voice while playfully pointing to his watch.

Bianca snapped a glance his way as she made it up the concrete entry stairs. Phaizo immediately saw Bianca's eyes flash fire red. He took that as his signal to lose the silly grin and playful tone he tried to use to ease the awkwardness of her being there. Bianca walked past him while staring him down with her scary scowl. She moved swiftly through the lobby and kept hold of Minah, who stumbled while keeping pace. They exited the elevator at the penthouse, where Bianca shoved her toward the door. "Get your ass in there and get undressed."

Chapter 15

Whimpering in silence and limping on her broken high heels, Minah slowly made her way down the hall to Bianca's bedroom, knowing her fate, worse than death, would be sealed behind the heavy, dark wooden double doors of the master bedroom. Still too weak to manage the weight of the ornate doors, Minah's attempt to open them on her own was futile. Bianca walked up behind her and, with the least effort, pushed the doors open, flooding the room with the lights from the hall.

Being drained of her blood made her weak but also intensified her other senses. It was a phenomenon she'd experienced previously with Bianca but never experienced with Kilion. Kilion never drained her as far as Bianca would. The draining was always the beginning of the torture she'd have to endure for hours or days on end as her re-entry into the submissive position she was lowered to. During the times her blood was low and she teetered on the line between life and death, Minah's eyesight was sharp. Her thinking was clear, and the combination of the two allowed her to see things that the normal eye could not. There were times in her weakened state, locked in Bianca's closet, when "The People" would come to her and whisper about things in her past she regretted or about her future that she knew would make her happy and cheer her up. They would keep her company in the darkness Bianca would subject her to and speak of random things that didn't connect to the past, present, or future. "The People" would come and go as if the closet door was open, and Bianca never questioned them when they were around.

Whenever she heard the closet door open while trapped there, she would never look up for fear of seeing something scary with her keen eyesight. She'd keep her head between her knees and just listen for Bianca's familiar voice or "The People" to see what message they would deliver. When "The People" were talking to her, she understood those were the times she was nearest to the other side of life, like no one could ever come back and report on. Minah was sure "The People" kept her on this side of life instead of slipping away. She appreciated them for that and was more assured that she wasn't going to die from Bianca's torture no matter how bad it felt… at least for now.

When Bianca opened the door to her bedroom and breezed by, Minah heard her say, "We got company." Minah raised her bowed head and looked around the room. She couldn't tell if Bianca was talking to "The People" who would visit her in the closet or was telling her someone else was in the room with them.

"We do, Love? Who did you bring me tonight?"

Minah looked over at the bed and saw a shirtless Mahlon lying across it. He smiled devilishly at Minah before throwing his head back with a giant laugh.

"That?! You bought me her?!" He laughed again, rolled off the bed, and made his way over to Minah. He smiled as he stroked her mangled hair. He then grabbed her hand gently as he looked her over. After his inspection, he cupped his hands under her chin and kissed her forehead softly. "Darling, where in the hell have you been? You've gotten this household all shaken up since you disappeared."

He looked at her with concern before he couldn't hold his laughter in any longer.

"She smells like shit, B! Where did you find her? Under a pile of fat greasy fuckers?"

Bianca walked back from her closet dressed in her favorite strappy leather crotchless, assless, exposed breast ensemble. Her leather headpiece masked the upper half of her face, and her sharp fangs were ready to dig into Minah's supple flesh. "What you smell is the funk of a mortal she has been sneaking around with. Seems like he's marked his territory all over her, but I'll take care of it."

Mahlon's eyes opened wide with delight and surprise seeing Bianca in her bondage outfit. "Oh, Darling, where did you get that ensemble from?" Mahlon turned his attention to Bianca as she stood close to the bed. He grabbed his erect penis and massaged it as it tried to force its way out of his silk pants.

Bianca smiled when she saw the desire in his eyes. He walked over to her, drawn in by the seductive attire. Once he got to her, he reached out and let his fingers slide down the side of her arm, across her flat stomach, and down the outer side of her thigh.

"I have to have you right now…" He said as his fangs slowly exposed themselves from his mouth. Without another word, Bianca and Mahlon grasped each other in a passionate kiss. Their teeth sank into the flesh of the other. Their blood dripping on and from one another. Finally, Bianca pushed him away and wiped the mixture of their blood from her mouth and wiped it on her exposed derriere. She looked over at Minah and signaled with a nod of her head for her to come over. Minah slowly obliged. Excited and curious, Mahlon laid back on the bed to see what Bianca had planned.

"Get on your knees."

Without a word, Minah slowly went down, knowing the routine.

Bianca stuck out her thick, blood-stained hip towards Minah and said, "Lick me clean." Minah looked at the blood, desperately trying to restrain herself. Her vision was clear even though her perception was off. She quickly looked around the room to see not just Mahlon and Bianca but others whose bodies were blurred behind theirs. Echoes of their anxious mutters filled the room. *The People. I don't want them to see me like this. I'm about to do things I don't want them to talk to me about.* Conflicted in her desire for the blood and to resist its call, the thick crimson color ooze no longer looked like blood to her but a serum with healing powers. The smell of it floated to her nostrils, and she inhaled its delicious aroma. She licked her lips with desire, excited to taste the addicting concoction but sad she was succumbing to the feen mentality she wanted so desperately to kick.

"Lick it, you little bitch. You know you want it." Bianca commanded Minah once more.

Minah clamped her hands to Bianca's hips and began licking the blood off her mistress' hot brown skin.

"You two have a little role-play thing going on, don't you." Mahlon said with delight.

"Yeah… and you're going to join us."

"But Darling, the smell… Her smell is gagging me. It's like an ancient old man smell. Nothing about it is appealing."

"Don't worry. I'm about to bathe my little bitch right on up." Bianca looked down at Minah, whose head was bowed as she sat on her knees, waiting for her next command.

"Crawl that little ass into that tub over there. Mahlon's gonna watch me treat you to a nice bath, and then we gonna fuck the shit out of you.

Chapter 16

Rested, Mahlon stretched with a deep yawn and gradually opened his eyes, allowing them to adapt to the dimness, faintly illuminated by the red glow from the lightbulb in the corner. He untwisted himself from Bianca and Minah, who were both sleeping soundly together after several rounds of make-up sex. He shook his head at the thought of how, in one moment, Bianca would be ready to rip Minah's throat out for any misstep but would then forgive her once she'd had her way with her weakling of a minion. Mahlon couldn't fully understand Bianca's draw to Minah but did understand the appeal. For just one pull of the strongest blood on the planet, Minah would do any and everything. She was utterly hooked on sucking that blood from Bianca; she would slut herself out just to get some on her lips.

Mahlon chuckled to himself as he thought about how he had Minah's legs folded above her head while he leaned over her enough that he could dip his dick in and out of her mouth. *The ultimate deep throat, I'd say.* Mahlon rolled onto his side and checked the time. It was still too early in the night for them to retire. He looked over at Minah cuddled into Bianca as if she'd fallen asleep suckling her bare breast, and it instantly reminded him of the night he had with Kingston at the sex club. A devilish grin formed as he got excited about his next adventure.

"B… wake up." He whispered in her ear. She stirred slightly but didn't wake. "B… wake up. Let's get out of here. I want to show you the town."

"What…" Bianca said slowly as she woke from her slumber. "I already know this stupid city." She pushed Minah off her so she could turn over and go back to sleep.

"Get up."

Annoyed with his prodding, Bianca whipped her head around and glared at him with fury in her eyes. Mahlon held his hands up in surrender and then flashed Bianca a wide, harmless smile before he spoke.

"But you don't know it through my eyes, and boy, do I have an eye." He winked like a used car salesman trying to convince a customer to buy a questionable vehicle, which they were uncertain would be valuable.

Bianca gave an exasperated sigh while looking away and slowly got out of bed. "This better be worth it."

"Oh, what I have planned for us tonight will please you so much." Mahlon quickly got dressed and watched and waited as she primped herself in front of the tall mirror. She put on her dark plum purple satin see-through lace slip dress that barely covered her larger-than-average nipples. Never wanting to show a panty line, Bianca skipped putting on even a barely noticeable thong but grabbed her crystal-studded six-inch stilettos with silver satin ankle ties and undid her smoothed-out coils to let her thick black hair cascade down her back. To finish the look, she pierced her wrists with the tips of her nails, allowing her blood to pool within the open wound. She then smashed her writs together, smeared the blood into her skin, and dabbed the scented excrement onto her neck and between her full bubbling cleavage. She then grabbed her Black Opium perfume by YSL and sprayed herself from head to toe.

"Oh… so that's how you get your prey." Mahlon said with a sly smile.

"It's one of the ways I can make myself irresistible. The pheromones and just a hint of the blood drives them wild." She walked past Mahlon, and he couldn't help but catch a whiff of the alluring scent trailing her.

"Oh my God, you smell amazing!"

Bianca smiled as she watched him follow behind her in a trance. "Yeah, it only works on anyone who consumed the blood. Sometimes, I don't kill all my dinner. Sometimes, I like to have seconds; if they are out, they'll come to me if they can smell me." She laughed at her previous encounters with victims and their second time around. "A feen finding me out leads to some very interesting and fun times."

"You mean to tell me you aren't always mad and killing recklessly?" They came to the front door of the penthouse, and Mahlon opened it so she could walk into the hallway.

Bianca shrugged her shoulders, unbothered by the question. "I mean, sometimes I like to play. It can get a little boring just ripping people apart." They headed for the elevator but eyed the open window. They looked at each other, smiling knowingly as they headed for it.

"After you…" Mahlon said, bowing and using his hand to gesture at the window.

Bianca perched on its sill. She took in the cool night breeze before she pounced to the rooftop of the building in front of her. Bianca landed gracefully on the tips of her toes. Her crystal studded stilettos catching the light and making it appear she coasted to the rooftop on a bunch of tiny stars clustered together. She looked back just in time to see Mahlon landing a few feet from where she stood. He looked strapping in his fitted black suit. The jacket opened, exposing his dark, shirtless skin. His grayish-green eyes filled with delight at his eye-catching date.

"You really are a stunning piece of work."

"The baddest bitch around." Bianca walked to him, leaned in, and gave his cheek a tiny, playful lick.

Mahlon grabbed her close by the waist and stared deeply into her eyes. It was hard for him to contain his desire to explore her beauty once more in the cool air and on the roof. He swallowed his yearning with a gulp and let her go slowly, as she never disconnected her gaze from his. Their attraction to each other was undeniable, and she could tell exactly where his naughty thoughts would take them.

"Enough." Mahlon broke their intense pull by looking away towards the city across the James River. "We are headed that way." He pointed towards the west end of the city. "Have you ever been to The Fan? It's this weird little eclectic neighborhood."

Bianca quickly thought about her days on the college campus near that area where she recruited several young ladies for Daddy. The faces of the many young girls she coerced into "The Life" came to mind. A slight smirk of pride appeared on her face when she recalled the first three girls she charmed into an epic foursome she'd almost forgotten about.

Angela and Renee were two of the three girls from that first day out scouting. They wanted to have it all, so they continued to go to school part-time while working for Daddy. Renee finished her undergrad and went to law school in California. Angela got her business degree and opened a high-end nail shop in Belgrade on the far south side of Richmond, which Bianca sometimes frequented when she chose to venture off The Block and live like the living. Renee and Angela stayed loyal to Bianca even when she became a vampire. They contributed their mind-blowing encounter that first time in their dorm room as the moment that changed their lives forever. In return, they helped Bianca whenever she called.

She chuckled slightly at how inexperienced they were when she turned them out, but then her fond memory faded when she remembered the one girl of the three, Jade, who took her place as Daddy's favorite. Jade, the third girl, and Angela and Renee's best friend were introduced to "The Life" that night. Jade was a different story. Her betrayal of Bianca was too deep to forgive. Death was too good for her. When Bianca took over The Block, Jade stupidly tried to have her killed, but Bianca turned Jade into a zombie vamp and left her to be killed by the paranormal hunters Minah told her to be aware of when she first was turned by Kilion. She shook the memory from her head, rolled her eyes, and then sucked her teeth at the tainted recollection. That girl's betrayal was the last time she was ever going to let someone take her place as Head Bitch In Charge.

"So, what do you say? Can I show you your city?" Mahlon bowed slightly and extended his hand for Bianca to take in agreement.

She smiled sweetly at the offer and placed her hand in his before saying, "How can you show me my city? I know way more about it than you do."

"That may be true, but you don't know it like I know it. The most you know is what The Block brings you, and look around you, it's changing every day. The city is pushing all of you out with the building of all these new apartments and shopping centers."

Bianca looked down at The Block beneath her. He was right. Her neighborhood was changing more and more. The chief of police swore she could still run it like she wanted as long as she kept her end of the bargain and stayed within The Block when she first took over, and he saw the power she wielded. The deal was he would let her pick off the degenerates, making his job of keeping the city crime-free, but when the city started tearing down buildings and making a way to revitalize her territory, she had no choice but to expand her killing field. The chief sent a warning through Bianca's crew that she'd crossed a line. She sent a message back, releasing half dead men and women all over the town, making it look like a drug epidemic, but the chief understood loud and clear. After that, construction stopped for a while, which somewhat restored the balance that had teetered. However, construction had picked up lately, and Bianca knew she had to think of a new way to kick them back out.

"I'm going to take you to the excitement." Mahlon said, pulling Bianca back into their moment. "You're going to be a guest of the city's tonight and not the feared devil whore you like everyone to see you as."

Bianca turned defensively away from Mahlon's playful stare as his words felt like an attack. "You don't know me well enough to judge."

"But I do know you." He said as he walked towards her. He placed his arms around her waist and held her tight. Her rigid stance began to relax in his embrace. "You've been hurt. You're angry because no one cared. You're bitter because you didn't stand a chance at being loved because everyone around you selfishly wanted you to love them." Mahlon turned Bianca around and stared into her dark brown eyes that shimmered in the night's light. "Even my brother couldn't love you without you loving him first. It wasn't fair how he took everything from you… your life, your opportunity to make changes to your world on your own terms. He gave you this curse of a power without your consent and then left you alone to find your own way, not knowing how this curse running through your veins would torment you."

Bianca's head bowed in sorrowful solidarity. A small tear fell from her eye and landed on the top of Mahlon's hand as he held hers. He looked down at the tear, seeing it as a lost and forgotten symbol of the humanity she'd hidden inside her since she turned. Mahlon gently tilted her head up so their eyes could meet.

Bianca stared into his, surrendering her will, allowing him to be the one person who loved her without expectation… if only for one night. Her delicate smile assured him it was okay to lead her without pause. To allow her to be free from the rage and anger she keeps in the forefront of her persona. Tonight, she would be the young woman before the change Kilion tricked her into. Before the sway of the glamorous life Daddy promised her. And before she realized how much her mother despised her.

Ready for their night in "his city," Bianca wiped her eyes and levitated slightly above his head. He looked up at her, the starry night sky as her background enhancing her beauty. He began to levitate to meet her in the air. Mahlon smiled playfully and tilted his head in the direction he wanted them to go.

"That way."

Chapter 17

"There." Mahlon pointed downward to a small, barely lit diner on the corner of a quiet street with an uneven brick sidewalk in The Fan. From her perched position on top of the roof of a Victorian-styled house lining the shadowy street across from the diner, Bianca leaped from the roof to the pointed destination with Mahlon behind her. As they landed, they grabbed hands, and Mahlon led her towards the diner. Bianca hesitated and pulled him back towards her, unsure of why he wanted to be there.

"What are we doing? Are we actually going in? I thought you were going to take me to see 'your Richmond'. This diner is far from enticing."

Mahlon smiled as he pulled her by the hand towards the diner. "Consider this me easing you into society. Let's sit down in here and enjoy a slice of real life. That twisted sense of reality you live in has warped your connection with humanity."

They walked into the old, cozy diner and sat in a booth with cracked red plastic leather seats. Bianca looked around the place to explore the faces of the eclectic mix of customers. A single man eating at the bar. Two young girls sharing a basket of fries laughing while carrying on an easy conversation. A middle-aged man scrolling his phone at a table for four while two kids sit at the same table eating their meal. Bianca's eyes landed back on Mahlon, who was smiling and staring her way.

"Well... what do you think?"

"About what?"

"The people, this place, the mood... Real life."

"I think nothing about it except I'm hungry." Bianca licked her lips as her sharp teeth slithered from the top of her closed mouth, exposing their intention.

"Put those back. We aren't eating here." Mahlon playfully reprimanded Bianca by tapping the back of her hand, which sat on the table between them.

She smiled, licked her lips, and her sharp canine teeth retreated as he requested. "So, what are we doing here if we aren't killing these people? Those girls look like a real good suck and fuck." She stared at her potential victims, who continued to laugh and eat their fries ignorant of how close they were to being her meal. Their outfits for the night made visible their young, buoyant, and supple skin. Bianca hadn't had the flesh and blood of a young, eager woman in a long time. She could feel the yearning for their innocence rise in her. The instinct to kill without fear or trepidation was becoming overwhelming.

Mahlon could see her reaction to them. He, too, fought the lull of the blood desire, but he was determined to show Bianca another way to kill without it being a massacre. "Hey..." Mahlon snapped his fingers loudly, very close to her eyes, to divert her attention before she exploded into a veracious killing machine. Her eyes darted to his. Her intense glare, along with the heaving of her chest, felt like he was now the prey. Unafraid, he grabbed her hands, which were still folded peacefully on the table like there wasn't a monster lurking in the depths of her soul. "Calm down. We're in public. Not in the shadows. Look around. No one knows you. They aren't scared of you… right now. Let them all enjoy their peace. Let them live tonight…and you live with them in this moment. Be human right now. Calm yourself." He kept her gaze as he watched the intensity melt from her face and her breathing slow down to a relaxing state.

She began to blink herself out of the spell the alluring blood pumping under the young girl's skin had put her in. The trance the metallically thick red life water had her under made her want to pounce on them without regard. Bianca had power and influence. She didn't care what anyone saw when she was ready to feed. But this night, as she took another look around the diner, she caught her breath, which made her realize she was not under the cloak of The Block.

"I know you are triggered sitting here. I mean, you could take all these people away from their loved ones just as quickly as they could comprehend what's happening to them, but do you really want to do that all the time? Do you really want to kill everyone once you bite?"

"Yes." Bianca said with a deadpan expression.

"No, Bianca. You don't. You really just want to eat and be on your way. Or maybe you want to have a light snack and then have a girl's night with the ones you've pricked. Sometimes, Bianca, it's good just to let them live. Look at them. They are just trying to live."

Bianca took another look around the diner with a more humanistic perspective. The man and his two kids were headed out the door. The two girls were now huddled together to take a picture with their phones, and the man at the bar was drinking a coffee. The call of the blood still beckoned her, but its pull was no longer as strong. She could now focus on Mahlon as her craving subsided. "None of that makes any sense. Who cares about human life? One less person on this earth will not change anything. It is my right to kill. I can kill, I can destroy, and I can do what I want. If I weren't supposed to, I wouldn't have these powers."

"Just because you can doesn't mean you always should. Of course, we can. Of course, these people should bow to us, and fear us, and beg for their lives. That's the fun part of our existence. But blending in, taking what's ours without detection, being the monster in disguise is an art and there is joy in art."

"An art in what Mahlon? Stop talking in circles."

"The art in the vampire seduction. The art of the tease, the back and forth between human and beast. The playful game the predator plays with the prey. You still have the power with all the control. We are very powerful, Bianca. Not just powerful over humans but we are powerful over other vampires. There isn't any other vampire stronger than us… except…" Mahlon paused and drifted back to a time long forgotten. He thought on the night he and Kilion were mauled, chewed, and left for dead by the beast that changed them forever. "Except for the one that made me." Mahlon looked at Bianca with stuttered tears holding in the bow of his eyes.

The vulnerability Mahlon expressed in that moment relaxed Bianca; no longer focused on her own desires, but the truth of what flowed inside of him was also flowing inside of her. "The beast… he's in you too? Its blood is our blood?"

Mahlon nodded his head in agreement. "I never saw it. Kilion never saw it. Before we could understand what happened, we were already dead."

"Are there any more like it?"

"I've never cared to find out. I've just lived past my death. And I've enjoyed every minute of it." His smile returned. His playful mannerisms lightened the mood. He slightly brushed Bianca's cheek, admiring her glowing beauty. "I can see why Kilion chose you. I just wish he would have done it differently, but to spend an eternity gazing in your eyes would make any man do the craziest shit." Mahlon laughed but meant every word.

Bianca blushed. Her dark brown complexion hiding the redness of her cheeks that embarrassment brings. "Well, you're right.

He went about it wrong. He could have just told me what he wanted. I may have agreed. It wasn't like being alive was working out for me."

"Yeah… your mother is a piece of work."

"The worst piece. But never mind her. Get back to telling me about the art of the vampire seduction."

"So yeah. The vampire seduction." Mahlon clapped his hands and rubbed them together vigorously as he readied himself to explain the ins and outs to her. "When a vampire bites, it is an act of desire and temptation. We seduce our victims, drawing them into a web of forbidden pleasure." He licked his lips temptingly before he continued. "Because biting, for us, is an assertion of power and control, we can dominate our victim, both physically and psychologically. The art in biting is when we only mix the psychological aspect with a sweet and tender, undetectable touch." Mahlon looked around the diner and spotted the waitress leaning on the bar, talking and flirting with the cook. Mahlon snapped his fingers and waved his hand to get her attention. As she began to walk over, Mahlon turned to Bianca in hushed tones and said, "Watch how it's done."

"Y'all ready to order?" the waitress asked.

Mahlon grabbed the menu and looked it over quickly. "Yes, I'll have… wait..." he said as he pretended to sniff the air. "Is that you? Is that your perfume I smell?"

The waitress lifted her wrist to her nose and smelled the White Diamonds knock-off she dabbed her wrists with before her shift.

"I guess so. It's nothing special. Just something I splash on from time to time."

"If I may…" Mahlon brought her small, delicate wrists to his nose and sniffed the bland aroma. "This smells delightful." He put the writs again to his nose but lowered them slowly to his mouth as he looked her in her eyes and asked… "May I…"

Their eyes locked, and Bianca saw the waitress instantly lost in his. "Uh-huh…" was all she could say in response.

Mahlon smiled and gave her a quick wink while he kissed the wrist of the waitress once more. He then placed his lips on her wrist and rested them there. However, what looked like an innocent kiss had the waitress's eyes rolling and her slightly moaning. Bianca looked at her face. Seeing her aroused by Mahlon turned her on. She discreetly slipped her hand under the waitress's short skirt and began to fondle in between her shaved mound until her secretions saturated her fingers. Mahlon let her wrist go at the moment Bianca retrieved her hand and wiped the woman's juice across her lips. The lady stumbled back into the moment, clearly unaware of the minutes before but entirely aware her body had been aroused.

"Excuse me, you two. I'm feeling a little woozy. I'm going to catch my breath, and I'll be right back."

"By all means, go take care of yourself."

The waitress walked away in a rush and ducked into the bathroom.

"You see… just a quick demonstration of the art of the seduction. No harm, no foul. Everyone happy."

"Yeah. She looked very satisfied." Bianca said with a chuckle.

Mahlon chuckled, too. "Let's get out of here. I have somewhere I actually want to take you, and I guarantee you'll feel like you're at a buffet. You can practice the art there."

Chapter 18

"I can't believe you made me walk." Bianca complained as she tiptoed on the unevenly bricked sidewalk, hoping not to get her heel stuck between the cracks.

"Don't act like you forgot how to walk… or is pouncing the only way you travel these days."

Bianca tilted her head back and groaned at Mahlon's response. "We could have just traveled like we usually travel. Walking is slow and bothersome… especially in these fucking heels and this stupid sidewalk."

"Walking is human. You need to reconnect with your human self. You're so bitchy all the time. It's got to be because you don't appreciate the little things in the before-life anymore. You've gotten uppity, Bianca." Mahlon shook his finger to shame her playfully.

Bianca shot him a look of frustration as her eyes flashed red. Mahlon understood the glare was a warning that his time was almost up trying to show Bianca his version of Richmond. He cleared his throat with an uncomfortable cough. "We're almost there. I promise it will be worth it."

"We better be because I'm real tired of your 'human experience' at this point. I mean, who cares about walking long distances? This is so—"

Mahlon pointed to an all-black square building. "There. Right there." He said as he looked at Bianca with a sneaky smile. "Tryst. This is where our night takes a turn for the better."

"What's so good about this place? It looks like nothing."

"It's not supposed to look like anything. That's the allure. Aren't you curious about what goes on in there?"

"Knowing you, it's probably something nasty." Bianca giggled with all the mystery about the night's events and finally got to the place Mahlon wanted to enjoy. She realized then that she and Mahlon were on an actual date— something she hadn't had in a long time. *Look at me. I'm someone's date. He really is taking me out on the town.* Bianca looked at him up and down with delight as he rummaged through his pockets.

"What are you looking for?"

"The access code to the door so we can get in. I wrote it down so we could breeze right through like we own the place, but now I'll have to go through the dreadful process of getting let in." Mahlon huffed a breath of annoyance at the thought. He grabbed Bianca's hand to walk across the street to the entrance. He knocked on the door and patiently waited for the rectangle peephole to open.

"What." The flat-toned voice behind the pair of eyes said as they stared down at Mahlon and Bianca.

Mahlon sucked his teeth before he spoke. "I'm on the list. Could you let me in?"

"If you're on the list, you wouldn't need me to let you in; you'd use the keypad and let yourself in." The flat-toned voice and dead stare eyes disappeared once the peephole closed.

He folded his arms in frustration. "I swear I hate this part." Mahlon knocked on the door again, and the eyes reappeared at the peephole.

"What."

"Look, I lost my code. Just check the list and let me in."

"No. It's not my job."

"What do you mean it's not your job? Why did you answer the door if you aren't the doorman?"

"Who said I was the doorman?"

No longer wanting to play the game, Mahlon flashed his deadly teeth in irritation. The eyes behind the peephole widened in shock and then dimmed with realization.

"Oh, you are one of those guests." The eyes shut the peephole again, and Mahlon and Bianca could hear the door being unlocked and opened. "Welcome." The eyes, which now had a feminine pale face with stringy red hair on top and a small framed tattooed body, stepped aside so Mahlon and Bianca could enter.

Bianca looked around, seeing nothing so special about the room where they stood. "Welcome to Tryst. I trust you know your way around?"

Mahlon smiled and nodded in agreement. "Yes, I can manage."

"And your friend…. Does she know the rules?"

"She will be briefed." Mahlon nodded once more.

"Well, we love when our special members show up to surprise our regulars. I'm sure you will be discreet about how you interact with them. Obviously, we would like it if you didn't drain them dry."

"Yes, of course, we will be discreet." Mahlon began to head down the hall into the main lounge. "Oh," Mahlon turned around and looked back at the lady at the door. "Is Tantra and her harem here tonight?"

"Actually, no. She and her baby mothers left Tryst. She said they are preparing for the next coming."

Mahlon laughed, thinking *I should have cleared their thoughts when I had the chance. They are going to be waiting forever for those babies.* He then went to where he and Bianca could be free to roam. "Are you ready, my love? Tonight, we can explore your wildest sexual desires and drink without rage. Tonight, your thirst will be quenched, and the ravenous pit within you that keeps you hungry for death will finally be filled with something rage cannot do. Tonight, your human soul will remember and be satisfied because it craves more than what you have fed it. It craves comfort and love. Here, you will get fulfilled."

Bianca nodded, understanding how Mahlon, describing her unfulfilled desires, called on her to feed that "Bianca" who had walked amongst the living long ago. She thought that person didn't exist anymore, but now, standing at the door of pleasure and not carnage made her think that what she destroys is what she's trying to bury within herself.

"So, are you ready now?" Mahlon pushed the heavy black door to the den open, exposing the dimly lit bodies enthralled in their own pleasure. Bianca quickly took in the scene of the natural and unnatural contortions of the moaning men and women. Their bodies pressed together, writhing with each other. Sweat could be seen glistening from their bodies as they humped rhythmically to a beat they could only hear.

Mahlon grabbed Bianca's hand as they slowly entered the sex den. The door closed behind them, and the light in the room dimmed more so that it could have been hard to see. But Bianca was used to the light of the night, and her already keen eye adjusted quickly.

As they walked through the crowded space of half-naked bodies, a sexual appetite she never knew had begun to arise in her. Sex for Bianca was never a problem. With Derick, her mother's pedophile of a boyfriend, she was prey. For Daddy, sex for him was work. With Kilion, it was manipulation, and with Minah, it was control. The sex in this space was for pleasure. Seeing sex in this lens stimulated her in a way she had never had. Walking through the room, watching the people kiss on the flesh of another, lick in places rather than each other's groin, made her nipples hard and her clit sweat. She could feel how moist her thighs were becoming underneath her delicately flimsy dark purple plum slip dress.

"Them." Bianca's eyes fixated on a couple in the corner, away from the crowd enjoying each other. "I want to be a part of them."

Mahlon's eyes followed Bianca's gaze. He smiled at the thought of sharing a moment with the couple while tasting their delicious, sweaty nectar. "They look very tempting indeed. I'm sure the sexually charged blood running through their veins probably will taste as delectable as they look." Mahlon kissed Bianca on the cheek for choosing the perfect couple. "Good choice." He lightly grabbed her hand to lead her to them.

Mahlon quietly sat beside the beautiful woman. Her slinky top rested around her waist. Her plump melon-sized breasts relaxed and free atop her chest. With her white lace panties circling her ankles and her dark metallic green patent leather pumps covering her toes, she was very occupied with the gentleman massaging her thighs and kissing her glossy red lips. Mahlon began by massaging the woman's head. He ran his fingers through her tousled hair, using his finger and the tips of his sharp nails to send a tingle up and down her spine. He could see her body respond to his touch. The small chill bumps sprinkled her bare arms. Her body began to wind slowly from the intense pleasure of his contact. He turned his attention to Bianca and signaled her to join them by sitting next to the young woman's handsome partner. In a deep, seductive tone, Mahlon said to her, "Take your time, Darling. Indulge in the pleasure now, and we'll delight in the feast of the flesh soon."

Bianca licked her lips with want. With the eyesight of a nocturnal creature, she could see the thin sheen of sweat glistening from the beautiful woman's meaty thigh. It took everything in Bianca not to sink her teeth into the woman and eat her pulsating pussy. Still, she remembered how Mahlon wanted her to experience the difference between devouring a meal and enjoying the prey. *Remember, my dear, it doesn't always have to be a slaughter. Be discrete, and you'll always be welcomed back for more*. He'd said that to her while they snuck a taste of the waitress earlier in the evening. She swallowed hard and turned to the man sitting on her other side. Their eyes met, and his smile invited her to sit down.

"Are you finally finished watching your man taste my woman?" He said as Bianca slid into the booth beside him. "They do look kind of sexy together."

Bianca eyed his thick neck, imagining how tough it might be to rip his skin open with her teeth. As much as Mahlon enjoyed the art of seduction, she took great pleasure in the bloodshed she created. She loved seeing red splattered on walls and staining floors. The fear of the horror forever fixated in the eyes of a dead human pleased her beyond expectation. Bianca rapidly blinked her eyes to wipe the thought of opening his jugular with her clawed nails and baring her teeth to expose the monster within her. *Stay in control, B; now is not the time.* Mahlon's voice rang in her head as if he were sitting beside her and coaching her in her ear. She looked over at him, astonished she could hear him so clearly. He just nodded slightly in her direction and continued to kiss the beautiful woman on her chest and massage her supple breasts. *Yes, I could always communicate with you in this way. I just choose to hear myself speak. It's the narcissist in me.* He chuckled out loud while he continued to seduce his dinner.

The man put his finger on the corner of Bianca's chin to guide her gaze back to him. "You have some very pretty eyes. Your stare arouses me." He then grabbed her hand, kissed the top of it, and guided it to his crotch, where Bianca could feel the solid rock hiding in his trousers. She glided her fingertips along his shaft. He rolled his eyes with ecstasy as her fingernails continued to glide slightly from his tip to his groin. He laid back in the booth, more relaxed that he finally had her attention. Bianca leaned in and let her glossy lips kiss the thickest vein in his neck. As her hand still played in his crotch, her tongue began to slowly roll and lick and flick as she deliberately kissed his exposed skin until her mouth made it to his sexual region.

"Damn…" The man whispered and then gulped in hopes of subduing the excitement building from Bianca's touch.

She unbuckled and unzipped the man's loose trousers and stuck her hand into his pants as if she'd put her hand in a jar to grab a treat. She pulled out the thick bulge from his pants. A dense, clear stream spilled from the opening. Bianca wrapped her serpent tongue around his warm, fleshy member and licked his sweet serum as it slowly made its way to the lap of his trousers. She then let her tongue glide up his pole, and when she reached the tip, her lips planted on top of its head. Her neck held steady as she twisted and turned her tongue, her teeth retracted, and her slippery saliva polished his extension. He moaned loudly and tried his best to grip the back of the seat to stop from exploding from Bianca's skill.

"Oh my GOD…" the man said breathlessly. Bianca looked up to peek his way. His eyes spun with amazement. His mouth gaped open in awe.

Flashbacks of how she enjoyed making men fall to their knees in praise because her head game was nothing they'd ever experienced came to mind. Lucy had trained her well, and she was able to put her own spin on her mastery of the craft. Bianca stopped swirling on the tip and tightened the suction. She sucked him like a lollipop and then freed him from her mouth's grip. He gasped from the sensation of the release, but before he could gather his composure and decipher what kind of magic her mouth possessed, she wrapped her lips around him once more. Her mouth discharged a batch of thick saliva that drooled and dripped from her fat bottom lip, which sent a shiver up his legs, making him get even stiffer in her mouth.

Once Bianca decided he was ready to begin again, she loosened her mouth's grip on his shaft so that the rim of her lips only grazed his solid pole, allowing the slippery spit to assist her lips with the slow glide down his phallus. Her mouth's journey to his groin was slow; he could barely tell she was moving until he felt her tonsils touch the tip of his dick. His body stiffened with delight when he realized what was to come. She tightened her mouth and opened her throat, and her head began to fiercely bob up and down while gagging on his hard dick. The move sent shivers through his body, and he began to tremble uncontrollably.

The beautiful woman, captivated by Mahlon's tongue exploring her hidden crevices, glanced at her man curiously. "What's… What's she doing to him?" She said in between moans.

"No worries, Love. She's got him under her control now. Be under mine if you will allow."

"Yessss…." She said, sinking back into her own ecstasy. "Take me…" Mahlon welcomed the invite by allowing his sharp fangs to slide into bite position. He opened his mouth ever so slightly. His tongue licked his teeth for a bit of lubrication, and he pricked her inner thigh enough to bring her blood to the forefront. He took his teeth out of her sweet, tender meat to see the two drops of blood begin to grow in circumference. His victim under his trance, not knowing he had pierced her skin. His eyes widened, watching his beautiful prey ready for him to attack.

Bianca smelled the aroma of the blood from Mahlon's victim, which then turned on her desire to bite. *Be discreet, my dear. The time has come for you to dine.* Without stopping the repetitive flow of the insatiable deep throat. Bianca slowed the motion of her head and focused her mouth work where the shaft and the groin met. She wrapped her tongue around his piece, and her lips bumped up to his groin. In a startling move, she twisted her body and her mouth never left his member. Her silky slip dress shifted upwards, exposing her bare round ass, which was now his focal point as her feet were placed over each of his shoulders and the back of the booth used to stable her footing.

"God help me…" The man whispered as he watched her round bottom rotate slowly in a hypnotic way as she continued to give fellatio. He rolled his eyes into the back of his head once more, knowing precisely what heaven felt like, as he sensed his eruption building in his member. Then, he felt the graze of her teeth disrupt his vision of bliss. He winced from her teeth scrape. His eyes clenched from the nip, and he said, "Ease up, Baby…"

"Mmmhm…" Bianca said as the trickle of blood began to make its way onto her tongue and sliver down her throat. Once the warm metallic flavor awoke her taste buds, she tightened her mouth's grip on his dick and began to pull the blood with her suck. She slurped and drooled. The sound effects stirred him more, and the blood flowed harder. She then arched her back to plant her butt on his face. Smothering him, which elated him further. He grabbed her thighs and squeezed them in delight.

"Yes, Baby… YES!" He said in muffled tones. His voice reverberating in her butt crack.

He began thrusting his pelvis into her mouth as he was unable to control his ejaculation. Bianca took her hand and held his sack at the base to prevent him from cumming before she was ready for his release. She took her mouth off his dick and pressed her ass into his face more. "Control yourself. Don't cum until I say."

He nodded his head and relaxed. Bianca eased her ass from his face enough for him to breathe, and he took in a deep breath. "You ready?" she said to him as she loosened the grip on his sack.

"Yes. I'm ready." He said eagerly.

"Good. Bite my ass. I want to feel how you hurt me."

With a big smile, he opened his mouth wide and then clamped down on the roundest part of her rump.

Bianca shuddered at the pain the bite sent through her body. She giggled at the thrill of the control she had over the man and began swallowing his dick once more. As her deep throat was bringing him back to arousal, she stuck her tongue out and began to lick his balls and fondle them simultaneously.

"Ooooh my GOD!" The man's moans were no longer low and seductive but filled with thrill and surprise. His phallic was now at full attention, and he was no longer in control of himself. And as much as she wanted to take his explosion on her terms, she knew he'd refrained as long as he could. *He's not trained to take orders just yet, my dear. Let him go and have your meal.*

Bianca released her mouth's hold on him and planted her tongue on his tip as she began to vigorously jerk him with her hand to his climax.

"Ooooh my GOD!" His shaft filled with a rush of seaman. Bianca felt the buildup expand his dick to a massive size. Her eyes widened with delight. She quickly put her mouth on it and slurped and sucked until he screamed out louder than a victim crying for their life. While he was distracted by his orgasm, Bianca quickly went back to the open wound and began sucking his blood from it. The delicious nectar exploded in her mouth. The sweet and salty blend fulfilled every sensory moment a meal could do.

She pulled his blood in long draws and did not dribble one drop from her mouth. His body was no longer ridged and stiff but relaxed and almost limp. His dick began to droop between her jaws and began to retract from its erect position. Bianca felt a tap on her bottom, which she ignored until she felt the tap again.

"Darling… it's over. You've had enough."

"Bianca ignored his words. Her instinct to kill had overtaken her. She was now ready to devour her victim."

"Darling let go. He's almost dead. His death is not part of tonight's date."

Bianca flashed her angry red eyes at Mahlon, but he didn't flinch. Instead, he grabbed her waist and hoisted her over his shoulder. The grip of her mouth was not firm enough for his muscles. "Put me down! I wasn't finished!"

"Oh yeah… you're done. This isn't the buffet. This was a test. I can see you are not ready yet." Mahlon began to walk towards the exit of the den. "Look how you left him. He's half dead." Bianca looked at her victim, breathing hard from exhaustion. His orgasm had filled her up but drained him.

"He'll survive, but it will take him a while to recover. Luckily, he'll just think he had the best head he's ever had in his life. Kudos to you for that." Mahlon said with a laugh as he stepped over a couple who was fucking doggy style in the middle of the walkway.

"But I need more!" Bianca growled.

"Another day. You've had enough for now." Mahlon opened the door to Tryst and planted Bianca on her feet. She folded her arms and tapped her right foot in frustration. Mahlon walked over to her, stroked the side of her face, and smiled affectionately.

"You have a lot to learn, but you did good tonight. Next time, I'll take you someplace that's not so stimulating." He kissed her on her lips, and she reciprocated.

"But I'm still hungry. And I need to kill. You've aroused me, and I need to finish."

Mahlon rolled his eyes at the thought that Bianca learned nothing from tonight. "Fine. Let's go back to The Block so you can have your fill of degenerates."

"Thank you." Bianca said as she pounced to the top of the building in front of her and headed back to The Block. Mahlon followed.

Chapter 19

As Vivian woke from her night's sleep, she heard the stumbling and clumsy thumps followed by giggles and laughter of Bianca and Mahlon while they attempted to crawl back through Bianca's bedroom window. Irritated by their noise, she threw the covers off her and swung her feet off the bed. When she heard another huge thump and a burst of laughter, she hastily put on her slippers and robe, fiercely snatched her bedroom door open, and headed down the hallway to Bianca's room.

"Uh-uh. You can't go in there." Minah stopped Vivian in her tracks before she could pass her in the hallway.

"I sure the hell can." She pushed Minah aside and continued on her way.

Minah quickly got back in her path and blocked her with her arms and feet spread wide. "You can't go in there. She's probably a bloody mess and still hungry. You can't go in there because she'll devour you before she thinks about you. I've seen her do it. Don't go in there. You have to wait until she is rested before you can see her. She's like a raging Pitbull after she feeds."

"You think I care about her scary ass?! I could give two fucks what she feening for. That's my child, and she knows better than to harm a hair on my head whether she's some trifling lil' girl, a fucking vampire, or a damn Pitbull. I'm in charge, and I can say and do what I damn well please! Besides, listen to that noise in there. That girl ain't a bit more a monster than any other drunk hoe trying to sober up."

Minah tilted her glance to the sky and intently listened to the noise coming from Bianca's room. As the muffled giggles, laughter, and sexual moans continued from behind closed doors, Minah's rigid stance became more relaxed. Her look almost confused. "Yeah. Ain't no monster behind that door." Vivian said with her hands folded across her chest. "That's a drunk bitch, and her fucked up man."

Minah put her hands down and closed her legs, allowing Vivian to push past her once more. "That's what I thought, little bitch. Stand the fuck down." Vivian said, looking back at Minah and opening the door to Bianca's bedroom.

She flicked on the light, filling the room with brightness. Mahlon and Bianca instantly stopped their carefree banter, bared their fangs, and hissed in anger at Vivian for disrupting them. "Turn that light off, Ma! You see, we just got in!"

"Nah, I HEAR you just got in! It's too fucking early for you two to be thumping and bumping in here like you are teenagers! People in here sleep, and y'all in her wildin'!"

Bianca couldn't hold her mean glare any longer and burst into laughter, falling over Mahlon, who was also rolling on the floor laughing. "Y'all two look a mess! Where y'all been anyway?"

"Fucking!" Mahlon belted out between laughs. "We've been out fucking, and sucking, and bucking!"

"Boy! Don't be telling our business! Tell her we been out killing. That's what she wants to hear. She likes when I kill." Bianca said with laughter.

"I don't give two wags of a dog's tail about you killing or fucking. What I care about is you acting like you give a fuck about what's going on in this organization you supposed to be running! It's like all you care about is that lame-ass nigga over there and dead bodies. How about rule over these people like you claim to be doing because Bae-Bae... this shit in shambles!"

"What?" Bianca said as she turned away from the passionate kiss she and Mahlon were entwined with.

"You heard me. You so busy listening to that nigga you forgot you have a corporation to run, and these niggas definitely need a leader. They out here doing shit ass-backward, and you ain't even notice. Do you even care them girls ain't brought no real money in here? And the clean-up crew leaving limbs in the trash, and the cops been coming around because of it? The ship ain't tight, B. The ship sinking."

Bianca rolled her eyes in irritation. "Well, tell them I said, tighten up and correct all that shit before I wake up because if not, I'mma rip them across the chest and eat they booty holes for lunch."

"What? Eat booty holes? One night in the den, and now you think you're a stone-cold freak." Mahlon fell out laughing, and Bianca followed.

"I said I'm eating booty holes?! I said that?!" Bianca questioned her outlandish response in between laughs.

"Yeah! You said booty holes for lunch!" Mahlon repeated. They both began to struggle to get up off the floor and proceeded to clumsily strip out of their clothes and head to the bathroom.

"Listen, Ma!" Bianca shouted from her master bathroom. "Tell 'em tighten up 'fore I fuck 'em up! I'mma take this nap and handle business when I get up!"

Vivian unfolded her arms and relaxed her stance while thinking about how now she was finally in charge. "Good!" She shouted back. "I'll get them fools under control. You just rest up while I handle this." She smiled devilishly and walked out of the room, passing Minah on her way back to hers. "Tell the crew we got a meeting in an hour. Some things fitna change while I got my hand on the wheel."

Minah shook her head in defeat of her orders. *Why in the entire hell would Bianca let this grinch run her territory?* Minah walked back to her small quarters near Bianca's, where she could hear her and Mahlon in the bathroom making out as the running shower muffled their noise. *It's like the Bianca I met is no longer here since that man came around. I mean… She is a bit nicer, but on the other hand, she's not handling business.* Minah's arm began to itch, the uncontrollable itch of her body's system still detoxing her from the powerful drug that is Bianca's blood. She hated when she had to go through withdrawals. Bianca never kept her supplied well enough with her fluids. She liked to keep her on the edge of addiction so that she could assure Minah would never have the power to leave her but still function in the capacity she needed.

Minah looked at her dry and torn skin. She'd scratched raw scars into her arms, and when she looked down at her thin legs, she still saw the scratch marks from Bianca's wounds trying to heal. Bianca always left marks on her. Kilion never handled her so roughly. He never took advantage of their relationship. Yes, he supplied his blood. Him offering his blood to her was only part of what kept her craving his attention. His tender touch. His delicate care of her while he drank from her and the nurturing way he allowed her to do the same. He was a comfort, and even though he kept her at a distance, what was between them was unbreakable.

She would have given herself to him forever, never minding if he had others he pined for. She knew about all of the others. It wasn't a factor in their relationship. She would have allowed them to drink from her if that was his wish because he cared for her, but Bianca was nothing like him. She had a coldness, and a bitter taste mixed in with the powerful fluid she inherited. The mixture of Bianca's chemical makeup and the most purest unfiltered blood tasted so different than Kilion's. When the blood ran through him and flowed into her, she felt calm and safe. He gave her just enough to live for as long as she wanted and pass away whenever she grew tired of the years leaving her.

All vampire blood is addictive, and Kilion was careful enough only to allow her to feed from him when she was clear in mind, body, and soul. Minah's detox from Kilion was more in tune with her body's natural detoxification process of her monthly cycles. She could go for long periods of time without the desire for him. In fact, he would sniff her out when she menstruated for an elixing encounter.

Bianca was nothing like her maker. She purposefully forced herself on Minah. She took most of her pain and anger out on Minah when she was ready to feed. Bianca enjoyed the fact that she had so much control over her as if she hated that Kilion could care for Minah the same as he cared for Bianca. Bianca also hated that Kilion was obligated to take care of Minah. However, Bianca could not destroy her in good conscience, and Minah believed it was because she was the last connection to him, and she took out all of her anger on Minah about what Kilion did to her.

Shaking her head to release the thoughts about her relationship with Bianca, Minah grabbed a coat because she stayed cold all the time and went to the lobby, where Bianca's crew stood around, barely managing their obligations. "Y'all…" Minah said with low interest. She noticed no one responded or acknowledged she was there. She straightened her back, held her head up, and spoke again. "Y'ALL!"

Startled, Phaizo turned to see Minah standing behind him with her hand on one hip and an irritated expression. "Damn! I didn't see you there. Wassup, Baby Girl."

Minah used her thumb and pointed back to the elevator, gesturing they were needed upstairs. "Ya'll need to go check in with Vivian. Bianca left her in charge."

"I know you fucking lying!" Kingston belted from the middle of the crowd. His voice was heard, but his face was unseen in the sea of women he was crowded by.

"Bianca nose that wide open, she letting her damn mama fuck up what we got going on?"

"Stop Kingston. If B said her mama is management, then her mama is management. Would you like to go tell Bianca you ain't feeling this?" Roxanne said in support of Minah, who was definitely having a hard time getting the crew to the penthouse. "Y'all, come on and head on up there so we can hear what Viv got to say." Roxanne shrugged her shoulders before she continued. "Maybe we'll like what we hear. Besides, it's probably temporary. Bianca ain't crazy enough to let that woman have all this."

"Maybe we won't like what we hear, and Bianca don't want to do this anymore." Rell wondered.

"That may be a good thing. I'm tired of the shit she doing. Got us all on pins and needles because we never know what mood she's in." A random woman under Roxanne's control said.

"Well, y'all all need to shut up. Whether we like it or not, Vivian is in charge until Bianca say… which still means Bianca is in charge. So just go on up there and see what she want so we can move on." Minah said as she turned back to the elevators.

All of the heads of the crews slowly emerged from the group of people standing around and made their way upstairs. Once at the penthouse, they begrudgingly packed themselves into Bianca's open living room, which shared space with the kitchen area. Most of the heads of the smaller crews had never been inside the penthouse. Their eyes wandered the room slowly, taking in some of the elaborate décor and modern contemporary furniture. For them, it was a surprise to see their hellish boss have taste in home decorating as calm and welcoming as it was, considering she was such a dark and monstrous entity that plagued their streets and owned their lives. To expect a space full of carnage and animalistic appeal but instead see a comfortable and cozy space did not make sense to them, and their expressions of confusion showed without having to say a word.

Vivian closed the door behind the last to enter and leaned on the back of it with her arms folded in satisfaction. *My army now.* She smiled easily at them while they eyed her with indifference. "So, you've probably heard I'm the head bitch in charge right now." She began. "So that means what I say goes. Nothing more, nothing less." She pulled herself from the door and casually walked around the room, inspecting the men and women under her command. "Yeah… I've seen you all in action." She nodded to affirm her statement. "I've been watching this whole operation since I got here. Minding my business… just watching and not saying nothing… to y'all." She said as she suddenly stopped walking. Her index finger pointed and coasted around the room to single out every individual for emphasis. "And what I've seen…" She began her slow walk around the room once more. "Is a bunch of ig'nant ass niggas fumbling the bag." She began laughing at her statement. "Y'all are all pathetic when it comes to running this block like you supposed to. Y'all so scared of my daughter that you do the bare minimum to keep her at a distance when instead you should have immersed yourself in her orders and took control of not just here but this whole city." Vivian put her hands in front of her and slowly gripped the air as she closed her eyes while thinking of how triumphant her reign could be.

She opened her eyes again to look at the crowd. "Yup. I've got big plans for this rag-tail crew my daughter has put together. And while I'm in charge, I'm going to take this organization to the next level." Some of the people in the crowd nodded their heads in agreement with Vivian's statement. "We need to make this city our own. Nothing should stand between us and having everything we want because next stop is total dominance." Filled with excitement and authority, Vivian walked over to the first man in her sight and kissed him hard on the lips. He looked surprised once their lips separated but smiled proudly anyway. "Now, get back out there and muscle up. Go across the line drawn between the The Block and the rest of the city. Do your worst and let them know we are ready to finally take what's ours!" Most of the crowd clapped in agreement and headed out the door, but Roxanne flashed Minah a look of annoyance, and Kingston saw them both. He grabbed their arms and led them out into the hall to talk in private.

"What the hell is going on here?" Kingston harshly whispered.

Minah folded her arms across her chest and rolled her eyes. "Chile, Bianca, and Mahlon came home wasted. She ain't no more thinking about us than she is his dick all up in her ass."

Roxanne covered her mouth to stifle the loud laugh she was about to belt out. She playfully hit Minah repeatedly in excitement about the naughty tea Minah spilled. "Girl, is you mad your girl got a man, or is you big mad her mama think she running thangs!"

"Girl, no." Minah said and giggled. "She can have him for all I care." A tingle of an itch under the skin on her arm made her begin to want to scratch as she rethought her statement. Of course, if Bianca were gone out of her life, so would the blood, and she was not ready for that, so she fought to resist the urge to scratch as a symbol of resistance to the desire of the addicting nectar. "I have a man now."

Kingston and Roxanne gasped with their eyes wide open. "Girl, stop playing! Who you fucking!" Roxanne said as she giggled with excitement again. "I'm so happy for your little skinny ass!"

Minah blushed and cupped her mouth to subdue her joy before she began again. "Well, he ain't my man… yet, but I think we gonna be together." Her eyes glazed over, thinking about her statement. Her smile dissipated when she considered Bianca's warning for her to stay away from him. "I just gotta find a way around the beast. I gotta get away from her."

Chapter 20

"Boy, stop grabbing my butt!" Bianca swatted Mahlon's hand away from her bottom as he playfully pinched and squeezed her jiggling cheeks.

"You don't have on panties under that little dress you got on, and you expect me not to fondle and caress your blessing? Darling, you must have gone mad." Mahlon wisped her up and hoisted her over his shoulder. Her bare bottom perched by his face. With an open hand, he slapped it.

"Ow! Why you got to hit it so hard?" She laughed. When they made it to the living room, he tossed her on the couch and then dived on her, showering her with kisses all over her neck, making her giggle and laugh.

"Ummm... is there a meeting today or what?" Marco said, startling both Mahlon and Bianca.

They gathered themselves from their playful positions on the couch and saw several members of Bianca's crew hanging in the kitchen. "Oh. I forgot I told y'all to come up here." Bianca laughed at her forgetfulness and then kissed Mahlon on the cheek. "Babe. We got to be serious for a minute. I got to handle these fools first." She waved her hand at the crew, motioning them to come into the living room.

After they gathered, Bianca stood up. Staring them down and examining who showed up. She cleared her throat and ran her hand down her hair to straighten it out, knowing it was disheveled from her and Mahlon's brief week's long sabbatical. "So, it's been a while since I've been around. Been sort of busy." Bianca turned her head slightly, winked, and smiled at Mahlon, who returned the gesture. "So, we got a lot to catch up on."

"Sorry, I'm late. Don't start the meeting without me." Vivian opened the front door and made her way to stand by Bianca. "Hey, Baby." She planted a big kiss on Bianca's cheek, which Bianca quickly wiped away. "Glad I made it in time. Didn't want you to start without me being here. I can give you the rundown on what we've been doing since you've been…" Vivian turned her body in Mahlon's direction and ushered her hand to him. "busy." She stated with a sly smile.

"Well, all you've had to do was maintain order while I took a few days off. It's not like you had to build this thing from the ground up."

"Well, Dear, you've been preoccupied for more than just a few days, and since you left me in charge, I saw a need to tighten up a few areas and lean heavy on a few other places as well."

Bianca looked at Vivian with confusion. "What do you mean tighten up and lean heavy? I run my shit just fine."

Vivian patted Bianca on her shoulder reassuringly. "I'm sure you think you do, but honey, your shit is ghetto, trust me."

Bianca pulled her shoulder away from her grip. "My shit straight. These people in this room work for me with no problems and with no worries."

"Yeah, but you have limited them to this measly part of this little city, and y'all ain't in charge of nothing but what's around you."

Bianca's body tensed, and her hands began to ball up to a clenched position. Her dark brown eyes began to lighten to a warm amber as her brow slowly furrowed. Her anger with her mother's criticism fueled the fury that began to brew within her. The playful demeanor she'd worn earlier was slowly disappearing. She was no longer a young woman in love but becoming the beast they all bowed to, and her mother never met.

Vivian could sense the change in her daughter but continued speaking out of defiance. "Now, don't get so uptight about what I'm saying to you. The little changes I've made will only enhance what you have going on and take you to the next level."

"Oh yeah? What level is that?" Bianca said as she cocked her head in a condescending way.

"I mean, do you really want to stay stuck in this shit hole?" Vivian said with a laugh. "Yeah, this little apartment you're in is... cute. But you could have so much more. Like... there is an adorable neighborhood in the Northside that has huge homes. Let's expand this little operation a bit, and you can have your pick of homes that are way better than this dumpy neighborhood because, face it, you're going to lose it to the mayor anyway. He's already started his little revitalization campaign in your territory to win election votes."

Not able to contain it any longer, Bianca quickly grabbed her mother's throat and forced her to a wall. Her teeth bared, and she let out a low, thick growl that resounded through her fingertips and was only fueled by rage and a desire to destroy.

Everyone looked on in shock and fear, not able to stop Bianca from ripping into her mother's flesh to get to her blood. The image of Bianca mindlessly killing her mother in front of everyone showed how merciless she could be. "You always think you know better than me! You come in here thinking you are going to control what I have done because you have fucked up your whole life, but you can't! This is mine! These people are mine! Fuck what you think the dumb mayor got going on! You can't take care of them! You couldn't even take care of me!" Bianca squeezed Vivian's neck a little more. Vivian began to choke, and her brown skin was slowly becoming ashen. Her lips turning purple.

Seeing the strain Bianca was putting on Vivian, Mahlon eased his way over to her side. He stroked her hair and moved it away from her ear. He kissed her neck before whispering. "Don't do it. She's not your victim. She, in fact, wants to be you. Look at all the power you have over them. She wants that. I know you. You're not going to kill her because your natural instincts won't let you do that… and that's okay. But you will, in fact, make her your minion… someone who will be around for longer than we all want. Biting her will not help. It'll only make it worse. Let her go. She hasn't done enough damage to your empire than she lets on." He felt the tenseness in her shoulders melt and her body relax. She let her grip on Vivian's neck loose, and she fell helplessly to the floor.

"Take your raggedy ass back to where you came from. You can't stay here no more."

"But Baby…" Vivian struggled to regain composure. "I was just trying to help. You need me." She said through several coughs.

"I don't need you. I have never needed you."

Vivian finally stood up. Her chest heaved as her breath slowed to a normal pace. "But you do. All little girls need their mother. I can admit I wasn't there like I should have been, but I can see you need me now more than ever. Look around you. All these people depend on you to keep them safe and to help them make money, but you have abandoned them for that… that man over there." Vivian wagged her finger at Mahlon. "He has taken you away from your responsibilities, but I can handle the operation until you are ready to come back and be in charge." Cautiously, Vivian stepped closer to her, not wanting to be slammed against the wall again. "Just give me a chance, Bianca. Ask around. While you were busy, I handled things, and I handled them well. I moved us into new territory. I made us more money in these past few weeks than you average in a few months. The police? I let them know we're here and not to fuck with us. I—"

"You what??" Bianca quickly looked Vivian's way.

"I— I let the police and the mayor know to just stay out our way while we are expanding." Vivian shrugged her shoulders while smiling meekly.

"Why would you do that? I have an understanding with them! They don't bother me, and I don't bother them!"

"But unlike them, Baby, they scared of you. You put that fear in their hearts. They will lie down and do whatever you say. You would have known that if you weren't so scared, you could just take what's yours, and I'm here to help you do that." Vivian quickly embraced Bianca, thoughts of opportunity swirling in her mind. "Oh, Baby… just think about it. Me and you. Us. Living like we are supposed to. We can take them all on and have a future together. We can forget the past."

Bianca shoved her aside, the force of her emotions evident in the sharp, sudden movement; her hands trembled slightly after the response, her eyes simmering with fury at just the thought. "Just because I spared your life doesn't mean I got love for you. I hate you from the depths of my soul. You are nothing but a thorn in my side. I'd kill you now. You just lucky I'm not ready to see you squirm until I can squish you under my foot."

Vivian's head dropped in defeat. "I just want the best for you. Ruling this city is what's best for you. What's best for us. I came here to mend our relationship, but you won't let me in. You won't let me love you. Is there anything left inside of you that resembles the Bianca I knew? The little girl I raised?"

"You? You 'raised' me? The LIES! You are a deadbeat parent in the worst kind of way! I'm probably this way because of you!" A small tear formed in Bianca's eyes and spilled onto her cheek. She used her fingertips to wipe it away quickly. "No, I AM this way because of you. I hate because of you. I'm angry because of you.

Look at Mahlon. He's more powerful than me. The blood that runs through him is more pure than mine. He was loved. He is at peace. He has joy. The blood that runs through him fuels that part of him. Even Kilion… The one that turned me; he was loved and wanted to love. That's why he chose me. He thought I needed love, and he was right, but what he didn't know killed him. The hate buried inside of me and my anger that fought to keep in KILLED HIM! You created that part of me!

Before the blood, I was sad and unloved and ran through. Daddy may have exploited that part of me, but you CREATED that part of me! WHO I AM— WHAT I AM IS ALL BECAUSE OF YOU! And now you want to use the worst part of me to get what you want… and that's more control of me. You don't care about this city. You care about you and what I owe you. What life owes you. LIFE don't owe you nothing! I don't owe you nothing!" Bianca didn't realize that she was no longer holding back her sobs. A tear-stained face startled her, and she quickly gathered herself together and headed towards the door. "FUCK YOU MOMMY!" She opened it and stormed out.

The room was now empty. Vivian hadn't realized the crew had left long before Bianca did, and it felt too quiet for her to process the words Bianca spat at her. Each word, sentence, and all of the emotions behind what Bianca felt all of those years rang in her ears. She slowly walked to the couch and sat bewildered at all she'd heard. *Was I that bad of a parent? Did I really hurt her so badly?*

When Bianca left, Mahlon escaped the penthouse through the open window to the streets below in search of her. As he landed in the alley in between buildings, he saw Bianca turn a corner headed away from him. He knew what she wanted, and he also knew the way she was going to get it was not going to be pretty. He picked up his step and followed her down the street. Unfortunately, he saw she'd already chosen her prey and had already forced him onto the backstreet close to her. "Bianca!" he said, but she ignored his voice.

He picked up his pace and got to her in just enough time to stop her from sinking her teeth into her victim. Approaching cautiously, Mahlon could see the fear in her victim's eyes since his screams were muffled by her strong hand across his mouth.

"Bianca! Let him go!"

She turned to Mahlon quickly in anger. "Why!" She said loudly.

"Because. This isn't what you really want. Killing this innocent man is not what you want to do. I saw you up there. You were all undone. Don't take it out on him. He won't taste as good if you do."

"Your charm isn't going to fix this."

Mahlon eased up to her with his hands held high, baring his palms to indicate he wasn't up to any tricks. "My charm fixes everything." His lure showed through his slow, casual smile. "Let him go, and let's talk."

"I can't let him go. He's seen me. My prey never see me and live. That's how this works."

"It doesn't have to be this way." He walked to her, placing his hand over hers to help loosen her grip on the man. "I can charm him into thinking none of this is real. He can walk away from here and just think he got lost, and he can go home and never think of this place again. I can make him do that." Mahlon took Bianca's hand off the man's mouth. Her victim's eyes were still filled with fear. His body shook uncontrollably.

"You don't understand…" Bianca said as her bottom lip quivered."

"I do understand. Your mom's a bitch. That's understandable."

Bianca dropped her head at the realization. With her guard down, Mahlon took control of her victim. He snapped his fingers, bringing the man's glance to his attention. "Hey, guy. Look at me." He waved his hand to make the man focus. "What's your name, guy."

"It's— It's Ed. My— My— My name is Ed. Ed from Fulton." Ed whimpered with fear, not understanding what was exactly happening but knowing he should have never come to The Block to meet friends for drinks.

"Okay, Ed from Fulton. Watch this hand." Mahlon waved his right hand vigorously. Ed's head turned to watch as ordered, exposing the thick vein under his sweaty flesh that spanned the length of his neck. Mahlon quickly dug his fangs into the vein. Sucking hard on the blood that redirected from Ed's arteries to Mahlon's mouth. As Mahlon did, he sliced his wrist and placed the open wound on Ed's lips. Ed sealed his lips around the wound and began to suck instinctively. Mahlon cleared his mind and only thought of the blood connection he and Ed created. He envisioned Ed leaving The Block and finding his way home safely and starting tomorrow as if it were the best start of the rest of his life and never wanting to come to The Block again. Forgetting he ever met a woman who pushed him into a dark space on a dingy, grimy street. Mahlon exchanged the image with Ed through their transference of serum. The grip Ed's lips had on Mahlon's wrist loosened, and Mahlon stopped himself from sucking Ed dry. Mahlon licked the wound to heal it, and it began to close.

"Wait right here." He said to Bianca as he hoisted Ed over his shoulder and walked him to the street they turned from previously. Mahlon stopped a car and put Ed in it, handing the driver a stack of bills he had in his pocket and instructions to drop Ed off at the medical college on Broad Street. The driver took the fair and pulled off with Ed in the back seat. Mahlon quickly headed back to Bianca.

"Now. Let's go somewhere and talk. We have a lot to process." Mahlon grabbed her hand and interlocked her fingers with his as they walked out of the darkness together.

***

Vivian sat at the dining room table in the dark. The smoldering red light of her cigarette could be seen rising to her lips as she smoked and then brought down to her waiting ashtray while she thought about everything Bianca said. *It's not true. I wasn't that bad. I couldn't have been. I was gone most of the time working at the restaurant. She lying to me and herself about how it really was.* She puffed on her cigarette before dimming its light in her ashtray. *She act like she didn't survive. Like I didn't teach her how to survive and depend on no one but herself.* She opened up her pack of cigarettes and pulled out a new stick. *So what. So what I stopped her from seeing her grandma. That was a good thing. That woman wanted to baby her and tell me what to do all the time. My mama was too damn nosey for Bianca to be over there telling all my business. I did right to keep her little butt at home.*

She lit her new cigarette and took a pull of it. Exhaling the first hit of the menthol-laced tobacco out of her nostrils in a slow, easy breath. The smoke flowed out of her like steam from a train's blastpipe. She sucked her teeth in irritation as her next thought formed. *We ain't have no problems until she pushed up on my man. Acting like she was hot in the ass. Her fast tail stayed in his face, and then she tried to blame him for wanting to fuck. I was always enough for him, but nah... she was jealous and wanted him. Stupid motherfucker fell for her childish games and lies, and it got him stabbed. Can't blame him for leaving after that though. Couldn't even get his ass to look at me after what she did to him. Then act like he don't want me and up there living with that hoe, Torie. Seem like everybody had my man but me. But he got what he got in the end, though. Had he stayed with me like I said, he wouldn't be dead now.*

She put down her cigarette, picked up the shot glass full of Brandy, and swallowed the rest in one gulp. She then got up from her chair and walked back to Bianca's room. She took in the scene, screwing her face up at all the lavish things she saw sitting around. She looked down at her shoes and well-worn, outdated jeans, more aware of their vast differences in life. *Designer this… Designer that… she act like she can't share the wealth like I shared with her. I had to share my money with her black ass, and apparently, I had to share my man with her too. But that's okay. I'm going to find a way to get what she owe me, and we going to be sharing everything like old times.*

***

Chapter 21

"So, talk to me, B. Tell me what you're feeling. That rage in there was crazy."

Bianca looked down at the sidewalk as they strolled hand in hand on a path to nowhere. "I don't even know. She just gets on my nerves. I don't even know why she is here all up in my business like we are best friends or something."

"Bianca, don't be foolish. You know why she's here. She knows what you are capable of, and you are showing her how much power you really have. I'm pretty sure she wants to be you at this point. She would welcome a bite from you." He said with a laugh.

"Yeah. She been gunning for me to bite her so we can run The Block together."

"And that's where we should have a long talk."

Bianca looked up from the sidewalk and at Mahlon with curiosity. "A talk about what?"

"About The Block... about this life you lead."

"Oh, so now you want to help me run The Block?" Bianca stopped mid-step, let go of his hand, and folded her arms disapprovingly.

Mahlon stopped walking as well and turned to look at her so he could explain further. "No. Not at all. I don't want to run The Block at all. It's so much work and so little reward." He said with a half-laugh.

Shocked at his words, Bianca dropped her arms to her side. "What do you mean 'little reward'? I work my ass off keeping these people in line and money in their pockets… and, of course, me fed."

"B… this is all so… low rent. Look around you. The Block ain't nothing but a big ole' trap house. It's the bottom of the barrel for any respectable vampire. It's like you are ashamed of who you are and are now wallowing around with people and vermin who could never be as powerful as you, even if they had the blood you have running through them." He went up to her and grabbed her shoulders to emphasize his point. "You are more than this. And the money and the control over the people you govern isn't keeping you satisfied. And what happened to all the money Kilion left you? He had so much money that took him several hundred years to amass. You couldn't have possibly blown it living here."

"No… I haven't touched it. I don't even want it. He only gave it to me because he wanted me to be his mate. It's like that's the money he owns me with, and no one owns me anymore."

"Geesh… That money is your way out of here. Take it and go."

"Well, what do you want me to do? Where else do I go? What… you want me to be like you? Just roaming free and fucking on anyone that will let you?"

"Yes! Yes! I want you to roam free. Live your life without restrictions… without a hold. You let this blood run you. It controls you more than you control this block. You haven't left here because the blood wants you close to a never-ending supply of that crimson crack. But with me by your side. You can control you. You don't need any of this to survive and feel powerful. You are the power. You are the control, and with that, everything you desire will come to you. The wealth, the source, the love, and the peace you want. Come with me. Leave here, and we can roam the world together."

Bianca saw the hope in his eyes. It almost sounded appealing. She shook the dream from her head, knowing the reality of her being amongst the living, with all the anger and destruction she held within herself, would only result in total chaos. "You know I'm not going to leave here." She spread her arms wide and looked up to the sky with exhilaration. A slight breeze wisped through her loose locs. "This is my block." Her eyes sparkled with the satisfaction of her boundless freedom. "This is my city. This is where I belong. I roam free… here. I get money… here. I have no fear…" She put her arms down, and her head followed with sorrow, realizing what really kept her from embracing Mahlon's proposal. "… here."

They walked silently a moment longer, thinking of what would happen next. "I have no fear here," she said after a deep exhale. "I don't know what else is out there. I know what is here. I control everything with no inhibitions. I can be everything I want to be right here on this block. No one questions me, and no one tells me what to do. No one can beat me into submission. No one can manipulate me to do what they want me to do. No one can trick me out of what's mine. I'm the boss. I do all those things to everyone else, and if I don't need them for any of that, then they die by my hands. And that's the end of that."

"Bianca, I understand how powerful all of this may seem to you, but staying here only drains you of everything you can be. You should know that all of this anger and resentment you stew in every day in this dreadful place is just going to deteriorate you. You have got to get out of this sunken place. Beyond this depressing wasteland where misery is your comfort is a world with its arms wide open. I know you think Kilion cursed you with this beastly thing, but in reality, he freed you. You can walk away from all of this right now… in this moment, and be greater than anything you ever imagined.

Bianca stopped walking to think about what Mahlon said. His words were almost cutting.

"Bianca, you aren't the boss here. You think you are, but you aren't. You're still a hoe turning tricks for the real boss… that beast inside of you that's keeping you under mind control. And I'm not talking about the blood." Mahlon leaned in, gave Bianca a soft kiss on the cheek, and then started walking in the other direction. Bianca watched him walk away while his words stayed present in her thoughts.

Chapter 22

Mahlon took the long way back to River Towers as his conversation with Bianca replayed in his mind. To see her being held back by her own self-worth was something he remembered all too well before he was changed. Back then, Kilion wanted him to be more. To work hard and become more. But Mahlon never wanted the life Kilion and his family had. He wanted to roam. His desire to be free was more potent than his desire to work the land and make a family. Kilion judged him for not being committed to their way of life. Mahlon resented him for being so dedicated to something he knew deep down he didn't want.

That terrifying night when they both were mangled and left for dead by a monster neither could describe, Mahlon thought his life was over. But when he woke from what seemed like the deepest and longest slumber and felt rejuvenated and stronger, he took that as his way out. He left and never looked back. Freedom was his. No longer bound by obligation. He was his own man. It took a long time for Kilion to understand that their destinies were no longer the same. For years after their rebirth, Kilion wanted them to stay together, build a coven of mighty vampires, and become a family. Mahlon disapproved and finally made Kilion see that freedom was Mahlon's way.

Once he got to the Hoe-tel's entrance, he took the elevator. He would usually pounce and scale the building to Bianca's penthouse, but he was in no rush to get back. As he walked into the building, he could almost see why this place had a hold on her. He thought about all of the many people he'd met since he started hanging around. Some of the people he was fond of like Kingston with his charismatic and feisty ways, but others were definitely not his type, like Bianca's five-guy crew that handled all of the rough and tough business around the area. Mahlon didn't trust them, just like they didn't trust him.

Getting off the elevator, he headed for Bianca's door. He could see Roxanne hanging in the hall across from it. She stood gazing out the hallway window, watching the dusk of the day turn into the night. Mahlon caught her attention as he got closer and greeted her by nodding slightly. She smiled pleasantly and watched him as he approached. Mahlon jiggled the door's knob and realized he was locked out. He patted himself down as if he had a key, knowing he didn't.

"Looks like you are having problems with getting in." Roxanne smiled once more.

"Yeah… it looks like I'm actually locked out. I should have taken the window like I always do but I wanted to try something different."

"Sometimes sticking to what you know can be better than trying something new… like leaving a place for a new place." Roxanne said knowingly.

Mahlon paused his movement and looked at Roxanne now that she had his attention. "Pardon?"

"Yeah, it's like, you already know what works. You know what's comfortable, why would you put yourself up to searching for something else that may or may not work? Why would you want to grab birds in the bush if you have a bird in your hand?"

"Because there are so many more birds in the bush than there are in the hand. If you could have more, why not go and get it? Especially if you know you can catch the birds in the bush." Mahlon said with a wink and a sly smile.

Roxanne smiled, too, as she thought on his words. "Well said." She dug into her pocket and pulled out a key. She leaned in close and opened the door for him. "It would be something different for all of us if she went out there to catch those birds in a bush with you. Might do us all a world of good."

"But mostly her. It's time she sees what's out there." Roxanne nodded in agreement and shut the door behind him as he entered.

"Oh, you came back, huh." Vivian said as she strolled from the kitchen with a drink in her hand. The glass was half full of her usual. "She ain't with you?" She said as she looked around him, expecting Bianca to pop up from behind.

"No. She's out on the streets prowling… she needs to get some things off her mind."

"I guess. Tonight was really intense. I didn't mean for it to get out of hand." Vivian sat her drink on the living room coffee table and settled on the couch. She patted the space beside her as a gesture for Mahlon to have a seat and talk. He obliged so their conversation could continue. "I don't mean to get her so riled up every time I want to talk to her."

"Well, you two do have a very contentious relationship that isn't going to mend in just a few months. It's going to take time."

Vivian nodded in agreement and then took a sip of her drink. "It's contentious, alright." She said as she rubbed her bruised neck. "If it gets any more contentious, I'm going to end up dead."

"But maybe that's what you want… to end up dead… or undead." Mahlon looked at her with a curious stare.

Vivian almost choked on her drink after hearing his accusations. "Me? Are you saying I want her to bite me? What good would that do?"

"Vivian, don't play dumb. We all know what you want. I've heard you say it; she knows your goal. Just admit it."

Vivian chuckled. "Yes… I guess the gig is up and the cat's out of the bag." She shrugged her shoulders to gesture it wasn't a big deal to want that for herself. "I do want to rule with her. I feel it will mend our relationship."

"I don't believe you want to mend anything. I think you want control of your relationship with her, and the only way you see you can do that is if you are as powerful as her. And you want to rule over everything."

"Ummm… almost right. I do want to be bitten, but only to help Bianca gain what's rightfully hers… this city. I can do that if I'm on the other side of life. Not stuck in this vulnerable body with no powers. She needs me beside her to help take this to the next level.

"Well, I don't think she needs any of this."

"Good, then take her with you, and I'll run things here."

"Easier said than done. She won't budge."

Vivian huffed at the thought of how hard her plan turned out to be. But then she had an idea that she felt would work. She put her hand on Mahlon's thigh and began to rub.

"Listen… I know you don't like me. You aren't the first and won't be the last. I know you think I'm out to get all that Bianca has, but I assure you I only want the best for my baby. I want to bury the hatchet with you. I want to start over. I think if we all get along, Bianca will like me more, and then the three of us can come up with a plan for her to live her best life. What do you think about that?"

Mahlon uncomfortably watched Vivian massage his inner thigh meat as he listened to her proposition. Once she was done speaking, he removed her hand and placed it back on her lap. "I mean, getting reacquainted couldn't hurt, but I'm not into you like that. We should just keep this friendly."

Vivian put her hand to her mouth, and her eyes widened in disbelief at his insinuation. "Oh no! I didn't mean to get to know each other like that." She laughed before she continued. "You're almost like a son to me at this point. I'm talking about lets you and me go out and have a conversation over some drinks at the bar around the corner. You up for that?"

"Well, drinking does give me a slight buzz. I guess I can enjoy a glass or two with you."

"Great. Let me get my purse, and we can head on over there." Vivian got up from the couch and grabbed her things. Mahlon headed for the window.

"Um, sir." Vivian said, headed for the front door. "I will not be hopping off the sides of buildings and coasting fifty feet in the air... finna kill me before I'm ready. We gonna use our feet like normal folks."

Mahlon put both hands up in the air, surrendering to her will. "However you want to get there is fine with me. We shall walk... or maybe we'll drive."

"Who got a car?"

"Not me, but I'm sure with the power of my persuasion, somebody will let me borrow theirs."

Stepping off the elevator with Vivian following not too far behind, Mahlon spotted Marco in the lobby with his phone nestled to his ear.

"Say there, Marco. Do you mind if I take a spin in your car?"

Marco looked over his shoulder as Mahlon headed his way. He touched his neck, where the bruise from being strangled was still noticeable. "Man... I'm going to call you back." He said to the person on the other end of his call. He then turned back to Mahlon to respond. "Nigga, you know we not cool. Why the fuck you think I'm going to let you use my car?"

"You're still mad over that little tiff?" Mahlon chuckled at the thought. "Don't be a bitch about it. What's happened, happened. I'm over it; you should be, too. Now, about that fancy automobile you have parked outside… may I get the keys? Old Viv and I want to take it for a spin."

Marco sucked his teeth and pushed past them both. "Ain't no way I'm finna give up my keys."

Before he could get any further, Mahlon stepped in his path. "Okay. This is the last time I'm going to ask."

"You ain't got to ask me no more! I said no!"

Mahlon flashed his teeth. His menacing snarl a mere hint of the possible damage his bite could inflict if his answer didn't change. Mahlon saw Marco's thuggish demeanor melt away, exposing the fear he harbored. "So, you're going to let me use your car, right?"

With a trembling hand, Marco placed his keys in Mahlon's palm. "Yeah… man… whatever." He cautiously backed away from Mahlon and ran out of the back exit.

Mahlon retracted his teeth and smiled pleasantly at Vivian. "See, no problem." He raised the keys and jiggled them excitedly.

Ten minutes later, Mahlon put the chromed-out all-white Supra they borrowed from Marco in park when they pulled up to the bar. Mahlon opened the door of the car to get out, but Vivian grabbed his arm and gently pulled him back in.

"Don't get out yet. We gotta prep before we drink."

Mahlon closed the car door and looked at Vivian curiously as she rummaged through her purse.

"Prep? We're only here to drink. Why do we need to prep, and what are you looking for?"

With a big smile, Vivian pulled out a pre-rolled blunt, placed it under her nose, and took a long whiff of the tightly rolled tobacco leaf. She then pulled out a lighter and lit it. Watching the blunt begin to smolder, she said in a low tone, "This is the prep. I like to smoke before I taste." Once the blunt was ready, Vivian put it to her lips and took a long pull, held the smoke in her mouth, and then exhaled, filling the car with the smell of tree bark and an undertone of warm chocolate. She took another quick pull, exhaled, and handed it to Mahlon for him to try. Looking a bit confused, Vivian gestured for him to take the blunt and have a few hits as well. "Go on, get you some of this. It's only going to enhance the taste of whatever you going to drink and gonna really get you relaxed."

Mahlon hesitantly took the blunt from her fingers and shrugged his shoulders with doubt. "I already told you, it's hard for me to get high or drunk the way you can. None of this does anything for me." He took a pull from the blunt and mimicked how Vivian had taken her first pull, but he wasn't able to hold the smoke in his mouth as long as she did and coughed his exhale out in a frantic fury instead.

Vivian laughed at his response to the potency. "Yeah, you think you can't get down like we get down because you so strong with that vampire blood, but I got something for your ass!" She pointed and laughed at the blunt he took another pull from. "That right there is the devil's garden mix. I put some shit in there that will have you laid out on the floor talking to them floaty things you see in your eyes sometimes. That shit right there ain't for the weak, so I know you can handle it. Go on and get another pull, and then we gonna go in and drink."

Mahlon's pupils began to enlarge as he felt his body become warm and then relaxed as he took one last pull. "Oh yeah... I see what you mean. I've never tasted anything like this."

"Yeah, it's not a creeper. It'll hit you if you not prepared. Me, however, I'm used to it, so I know how to pace myself." She smudged out the blunt, laying it to rest in the empty space of the car's console, and then got out of their ride. Mahlon slowly followed and made their way to the bar's entrance. It was a dark and drab place with dirty windows, and the old, thick air when breathed in when the heavy, beaten-down metal door swung open, gave the essence of how aged the building was. Vivian first walked into the nearly empty bar and hollered at the barman who was wiping down the counter to send over two Brandy's. "And make 'em neat. No ice or I'mma smack the shit out of you." Never stopping her stride, she went to the small table for two and sat down. Mahlon sat across from her. The bartender was not too far behind them with their drinks. Mahlon handed the bartender a twenty-dollar bill, and the bartender walked away.

"Cheers to my fucked-up ass relationship with my fucked-up ass child." Vivian held her drink up as she spoke, then put it to her lips and downed it in one gulp.

"I'm not drinking to that." Mahlon said with a chuckle.

"Well, drink to whatever the hell you want then."

He thought about it momentarily and then held his drink high in the air. "Cheers to new beginnings." He put the drink to his lips and downed the Brandy in one gulp as well. Mahlon was surprised at how much Brandy burned his chest as it flowed through his system. "Geesh! That's strong! I mean, I've had Brandy plenty of times before, and it has never been that strong. Wha— what… is it a concentrated blend or something?"

Vivian laughed and raised her hand to the bartender. She caught his eye and said to him, "Keep them drinks coming!" He nodded and prepared their second round. "Ain't nothing to that drink. That's the effect of that blunt. See, I told you it'll make you feel something."

"Yeah. I haven't had alcohol hit me like that in a long time."

"The weed powerful, man. My batch got a little kick to it. Gotta get the edge off. Life's a bitch."

"What's in it?"

"Just a few mushrooms. I grind them bad boys up and lace my blunts with it. 'Shrooms already get you seeing crazy shit, but when you put it with some weed… you gonna feel a lot more than what you see. And alcohol only makes the trip even better. Trust me.

By the third drink, you gonna be calling me mommy." Vivian doubled over in laughter, and Mahlon followed in amusement. When the bartender put the drinks on the table, this time they both put their glasses in the air.

"What are we cheering to now?" Mahlon asked.

"We gonna cheer to a good ending to a crazy night."

"The night's over?"

"Oh no. It's just getting started."

Chapter 23

"Call the fellas and tell them to come clean up." Bianca wiped the bloodied saliva away from where it dripped from her lips. The splash from one of the bloody droplets landed beside her, drawing her gaze to examine the tiny pool forming amidst the grime blanketing the decrepit warehouse floor. In that brief moment of thought, she felt the pressure of leaving her life behind and going with Mahlon to explore the world as he described it. She shook the thought out of her head as she turned her eye away from the puddle and back to the massacred remains before her. Barefoot, her heels tossed in the corner of the dilapidated building where the homeless would come when they were turned away from shelters, Bianca took her time to return to the building's entrance. The double metal doors of the warehouse clung precariously to their hinges, swaying as if they were on the brink of collapse, mirroring the inner chaos she wrestled with regarding her very existence. By the light of the moon, she looked down at her arms and legs. Both were splattered in sticky blood from her victim, whom she allowed to scream as loud as they could when she tore into their midsection in the deserted building.

Their insides flowed out of them, and the blood that spewed from their gashes drenched them both. She delighted in the bath of blood her victim's wounds submerged her in. Just like a pig waddling in a mud pile, she enjoyed the fluids his body offered. The acidic taste from the bile his organs produced, mixed with the heavy metal taste the blood gave, enhanced her craving and fueled her intention to destroy anything or anyone that intended to stop her. She felt powerful ending another worthless life.

She raised her hands and arms to the moon to watch the remnants of the blood shimmer and dance on her skin. She sighed deeply as her gaze wandered, staring at the stars. Her thoughts taking her to a place where she doubted she was right to settle with the life she currently lived. She looked back at her dead victim. Minah sat beside the carcass as she gave orders and their location to the guys.

It hit her just like that. The emotion she'd tried to stifle for so long finally filled her like water poured into a bowl and welled up behind her eyes, trying to push through in the form of tears. Seeing Minah half alive, Her emaciated body struggling to stay upright, and the cadaver of an unknown dead man proved this was all she really had, and it all pointed to death. She truly was dead. Surrounded by destruction was her coffin. She began to hyperventilate. The image of her reality was too much for her to handle.

Minah saw the panic in Bianca's eyes and how uncontrolled her breathing had become, so she rushed over. "B… you good? You okay?" The look in Minah's eyes darted down Bianca's body, checking for wounds, but she saw none. Still breathing hard and now shaking, tears flowed heavily down her face; Minah was astonished to see Bianca in this manic state. She wrapped Bianca as tightly as she could in her meatless arms and began to whisper softly. "It's okay, B. Whatever is going on, it's going to be okay." She slowly rocked Bianca, which somewhat calmed her down. "Don't worry, B. I got you. I'm here forever. Calm down. It's okay." Feeling that seeing the dead body may have caused the reaction, Minah began to walk Bianca out of eyeshot of the macabre scene. With the phone still in her hand, Minah called Rell.

"Yo…"

"How close are you to getting here?"

"Man, we just hung up a minute ago. I just left the house." He snapped, his voice tinged with frustration.

"Look, just get here quick. I'm going to need you to take Boss Lady back to the crib."

"What happened?" Rell replied. The irritation in his tone now turned to concern.

"I don't know, but she won't stop shaking… like something made her panic, and now she won't stop shaking and crying."

"Yo… that's not like her…"

"I know. May have been a mix of all that happened these last couple of days. Or this blood she drank from this man is really nasty stuff."

"Alright, well, I'll be there in five."

Minah ended the conversation and strode Bianca out of the warehouse, hoping the cool air would calm her more. "Bianca, keep it together. Rell is on his way, and he's going to take you home and get you comfortable. No more hunting for you tonight."

Bianca nodded her head yes vigorously because she couldn't control her breath long enough to respond with her words. Minah walked her around the parking lot, which was overrun with tall weeds and dirt from years of neglect. Bianca's breath was now slowed, but she still hadn't uttered a word, which quietly relieved them both. Minah took the opportunity to distract her from her thoughts by talking.

"B… remember when we first met? I didn't know how to feel about you. I never fell for a girl before… but I guess that was the blood talking more than my heart. But now… I think we got a good thing going. I mean… we could be better… we have our days… but for real… I think it's good."

Bianca's breathing finally steadied as she listened to Minah. Her words made her body tense, and the anger again began to simmer. She felt the blistering abscesses percolating under her skin, ready to expose themselves at the moment Bianca would lose control. Her eyes dimmed to a slit as she continued to remember the encounter unlike the fond memory Minah recalled.

"Yeah... In the beginning, we were two peas in a pod." Minah stated with loving remembrance. "It wasn't a place you went that I didn't go. And the sex... oooh, the sex was top-notch." Minah giggled, but Bianca fumed at the recollection.

"All in all, I'm grateful because, without you, I don't know where I would be."

"Probably still strung out like you are now because all you are is a junky bitch clinging to my pussy lips for your next fix!" Bianca halted their pace and pushed Minah off of her. Minah fell to the ground from her force. Just then, Rell pulled up. His headlights brightened the scene of their conversation.

"Y'all good?" Rell yelled his question as he rolled down the window.

Bianca put a hand over the one boil that pierced through her skin in an attempt to shield it from speculation. She stared at Minah coldly while she stayed where she fell. "We ain't nothing. We ain't never going to be nothing. I own you, and that's it." Her temper began to resign as she looked at her helpless underling. "Get all that fairy-tale shit out your mind. You are in a fucked-up situation that you put yourself in, and now you trying to make it feel right." Bianca spit at the ground in front of Minah with disdain. "Get your junky ass up and get your shit together. You been avoiding me lately because you been out hanging with that nigga I seen you with. Yeah... you say it's been me and you, but now it's you and him. Run these streets without me again and watch what happens. I better be able to find you when I call your name." Minah put her head down in shame. Her one hand gripping her other arm for comfort.

"Fucking junky… like I would want you for real. I can have any nigga I want! I can have any bitch I want! Why would I choose you?" Bianca turned, got in the car with Rell, and then rolled down the window. "And you better be back at the spot in an hour, or I'm gonna fuck you up."

Chapter 24

Bianca tossed the key to her place on the counter when she entered. Rell continued his update on everything he'd seen on The Block the last couple of days.

"... But what's so crazy is, three cops came up to me and was like, they were finding dead bodies again like a few years ago, and news is spreading through the city that a monster was prowling Richmond. They basically talking about you, B. The cops was saying that you broke the treaty, and now the regular folks scared. It's not good for business, and this they last warning."

"I broke the treaty?! Are they serious?! Clearly, they forgot they started building in my territory! They crossed the line first! I ain't have no choice but to expand out!" Bianca pinched the pressure point between her eyes, and she processed Rell's update. "Ain't y'all supposed to be getting these bodies off the streets, though? Where y'all been? Where is the cleanup crew?"

"That's the thing..." Rell said while scratching his head. "Yo' mom's pulled them off the streets. Said she was letting the city know you not hiding on The Block no more. I guess nobody put the cleaning crew back on duty."

Irritated by the news, Bianca sucked her teeth and sat on the couch, exhausted. "Well tell Lance to set up a meeting with the chief. Let him know the treaty been broken because of them, but I'm willing to close the gap when they stop coming over here and tearing up my place."

"A'ite, but when mom's was in charge, she really changed a lot of things you don't know about."

"I won't gone that long Rell." Bianca said exasperated.

"Yeah, but no offense, you ain't been paying attention to business since that man got here. Not to say you ain't been on game, but you have basically been… well… in love and shit."

Bianca rolled her eyes at the thought because much of what he said was true. "Well, I'll deal with it tomorrow or something. Tell Lance we'll meet to come up with a plan to shut this shit down." Bianca stood up from her couch and began to head down the hall.

"Yo, boss," Rell said loudly. "Yo, you just left the nastiest stain on your good furniture. It's all bloody and shit."

"Well, have Roxanne and King—" Bianca opened her bedroom door shocked at what she saw.

"What you say Boss?" Rell said as he walked down the hall. "Something wrong?" He said, hurrying his steps to see what halted Bianca in her tracks.

"Oh shit!" Rell said with awe as he put his hand to his mouth. "You a fowl ass nigga for this one!"

"Baby! It's okay, right? I didn't think you would mind… seeing y'all share everything anyway." Vivian said with a sneaky grin.

Mahlon opened his eyes in a groggy way upon hearing Bianca's voice. "Hey, Baby. You just getting back?" He rubbed his eyes to focus and stretched his arms wide. "Why are you standing in the doorway looking? Come on in and hop in the bed." He said through his yawn. As his eyes began to focus he felt a kiss on his cheek. Surprised by the lips, he quickly focused on what was happening and was shocked to see Vivian lying beside him.

"Vivian! What are you doing? Why are you in the bed with me?!" He then looked under the covers with surprise. "Naked?!"

Vivian giggled coyly. "Don't act like we just didn't fuck. We had a great time, Baby."

Mahlon jumped out of the bed, his body fully exposed. Rell, put his hands over his eyes. "Man! Cover your shit up! I ain't trying to see that!"

"B! It's not what you think! I don't know how this happened!"

"You don't know?! I can clearly see how the fuck this happened!" Bianca said. The rage in her began to boil over. Her razor-sharp teeth were now exposed as her mouth opened wide, and her voice pierced the air with a raw, primal scream that echoed through the room, filled with a mix of unfiltered anger and distressed emotions was the only way she could express her frustrations. As her body tensed with fury, she raised her hand and swiftly sliced Rell across his chest with her protracted claws. Blood oozed from the four slashes in his shirt.

"Oh shit! Why you slice me?! I ain't do nothing!" Rell screeched through the agonizing pain as he stumbled backward from the bedroom door. He ran down the hall and out of the penthouse, screaming for help.

Still in a rage, Bianca pounced on the bed and yanked Mahlon from it, throwing him against the wall.

"GET THE FUCK OUT OF MY HOUSE! GET THE FUCK AWAY FROM ME!"

"Bianca, you have to believe me! I don't know what happened! I would never do anything to hurt you! I love you!" Mahlon said cowering in the corner where he landed.

"But you said you loved me when you was pumping my ass with that dick, so who you really love?" Vivian chimed in.

"Shut up, Ma!" Bianca yelled over her shoulder.

"Get your shit and get out." Bianca said in a low grumble. Her stare pierced through Mahlon's pleading eyes.

"But Baby, it's not what you think…" Mahlon said in a helpless whisper.

"I SAID GET YOUR SHIT AND GET! THE! FUCK! OUT! AND DON'T COME BACK! WE ARE DONE!" She yelled and then ran out of the room and out of her home. The door slamming shut behind her.

Vivian began to giggle once more and then escalated to a loud laugh. Mahlon looked over at her bewildered. "What the heck happened? Why is this funny to you?"

Vivian pulled her blunt out of her purse lying beside the bed and lit it. As the blunt began to simmer she took a pull from it and blew the smoke at Mahlon. "I've been waiting for my time to get your ass back for fucking up my chance with my daughter, and all it took was a few pulls from this right here." Vivian said as she tapped the blunt with the index finger helping to hold it. "Yeah, nigga. You think you invincible. Like you ain't vulnerable to what we got going on, but you ain't shit. You just like all of us and this proved it. Yeah… you caught up but now you ass out. Get yo' shit like she said and get the fuck out. Me and my daughter got some making up to do."

Vivian wrapped herself in the sheet she was under, slid out of the bed, and walked out the room. She turned her head slightly to address Mahlon. She pointed to the window and said, "The exit is that way." And then shut the door behind her.

Chapter 25

Sawyer stood on the rooftop five blocks away from River Towers. He could see the random lights on in the other towering buildings while thinking about the text he received from Mahlon requesting they meet at the designated location. Suspicious by what Mahlon wanted, Sawyer stood in the shadows, guarded, waiting for the meetup to begin. Not having to wait too long, Mahlon landed on the rooftop. His shirt open revealing his tatted chest. His pants were half buckled, and his shoes were missing. His expression was dire. Mahlon raised his hands in surrender. "I've come alone, and I mean you no harm. I know you're here Sawyer."

A silent pause between them, Sawyer stepped out of the shadows and put his silver sword back in its sheath. "So, I'm here. What's up."

Mahlon ran his fingers through the curly locs his outgrown caesar haircut produced. Stressed about all that had taken place. "It's over, my guy."

"What's over."

"Me and Bianca. It's over. Me and her mom… We uh… we… I guess we slept together, and Bianca caught us, but I swear I don't know how."

Sawyer scoffed at the revelation and shook his head at how pathetic the situation was. "I've never known you to turn down pussy. Not even old, raggedy, sour pussy. But you crossed a line with this one. Why would you sleep with her? She's the worst type of woman. I've been watching her since she got here. She's a problem. She wants this life more than Bianca does and if she gets it, all hell is going to bust loose."

"I know. She's been trying and failing, but I think she found her way in by sleeping with me. I don't know how this happened. All I know is she wanted to go for drinks to clear the air between us, and the next thing I know, I wake up with her lying beside me and Bianca yelling."

Sawyer looked confused at the retelling of Mahlon's story. "You had a drink, and then you woke up next to her mom? Unbelievable. That excuse can work on regular humans, but you are a vampire. Alcohol doesn't affect you."

"It doesn't unless I've had way too many and I've fed off drunken people, but a glass or two never leaves me inebriated. And she knows that. So, she gave me a blunt, and I smoked it before the drinks. She said it would enhance the alcohol and get me tipsy. So, I tried it. She said it was laced with mushrooms so I could really trip." Mahlon ran his fingers through his hair again in disbelief recalling the details of the night's events.

"Mushrooms? Psychedelic mushrooms?" Sawyer asked.

"I guess." Mahlon shrugged.

Sawyer threw his head back in disbelief. "Man…that's a bad combination for you. Don't you know that?"

"What? Mushrooms aren't good for me?"

"They are not good for anyone or anything. They have you seeing things and hearing things, and then she had you smoking weed and drinking. That combination will definitely enhance any moment."

"But I don't understand. Nothing affects me. I'm not even alive."

"But mushrooms can re-animate anything. Mushrooms are a fungus that grows on dead things better than anything living. You are undead.... Half dead... basically not really alive. That mushroom took ahold of you really well. Your kind can handle anything but mushrooms... they are a whole new level. People think it's garlic that will take you out, but mushrooms are really your weakness. And don't forget silver. Silver is definitely a kryptonite."

Mahlon absorbed what Sawyer said, thinking about how the night played out. "But I never knew that. Why have I never known this and how did she know this?"

"I don't know how she knew this. Probably a lucky guess. There isn't anyone out here feeding her information about how to take you down. She just took a guess about how to get you wasted." Sawyer shook his head awe struck at the coincidence of Vivian's unfortunate win. He then thought of Mahlon's other question and began to respond. "There's no handbook to this undead, vampire life. And besides, you've never even probably come in contact with a mushroom to even know. Your lifestyle has you all over the place, but I'm sure you haven't even thought about mushrooms. No one ever does. Not even the living. The ones they eat are harmless, but the ones they smoke and consume for recreation purposes have them astral projecting... out of body experiences. They talk to spirits and all of that messing with mushrooms."

"Amazing... I never even thought of it."

"I can see you didn't." Sawyer said with a chuckle and a pat on his shoulder. "The mushroom may not kill you, but it definitely will have you fucked up for a few days."

Mahlon paced the top of the building deep in thought and then finally paused his stride to look at Sawyer "I'm not staying. This is too much for me. Her lifestyle, her mom… her rage. She's all messed up, and I can't handle this. My lifestyle is too free. I live my life on my terms. I come and go as I please. She wants to be stuck in this rotting hell, so be it. I can't go down with her."

"I hate to tell you this as well, but since you say it's over might as well let you in on another little known vampire fact."

"Geesh… Again… Why isn't there a vampire course about these things? I don't think I can take another fact."

Sawyer chuckled, knowing what he was going to say would make Mahlon question everything he felt about his beloved. "Well, that love feeling you think you have with Bianca? That instant passion since the day you laid eyes on her? Well, those feelings aren't real. It's just your blood connection. If she had some other vampire's blood running through her veins, you would have definitely killed her without hesitation. The blood connection strengthens that familiarity and is perceived as love. Nothing more."

Mahlon shook his head no, not wanting to accept Sawyer's fact. "Not true. I loved her."

"In a sense, yeah, but not the romantic love you think it is."

Mahlon stood with his hand on his hip, baffled by what Sawyer said. "But I loved her, Sawyer. Don't you believe it?"

Sawyer walked up to him and extended his hand for Mahlon to shake. Hesitantly, Mahlon accepted the gesture and placed his hand in his to shake in agreement. "If you want to believe you loved her, I'll believe you loved her too."

Mahlon scoffed but accepted Sawyer knew more about being a vampire than he did. "I give." Mahlon said as he raised his hand in surrender. "Whether I loved her or not is of no consequence now. Whatever you do from here on out, I will not refute it. It's probably best if you do her a favor and free her from this life." Mahlon pulled Sawyer in for a soldier's hug and then released him. He breathed in deeply before voicing the rest of his retrospection. "… and when you do, take out her mom, too. If she gets ahold of any type of vampire power, she will definitely be a problem for all of us… the lifestyle, the treaties we've created with the living and the unliving, The Council… oh, The Council will surely have your head if you don't kill her too." They both laughed, thinking about how The Council feels about vampires not being under watch and control.

"I guess what has to be done, has to be done." Mahlon stepped closer to the ledge, preparing to take his leave. "When you do finally free her. Just let her know I tried to love her. I really did care."

"I could tell you did, Mahlon… Even though what you felt may have been strong nepotism, you cared for her like she was the one. She changed you, and I thought you had changed her enough so that you'd make my job easier. But she's different. She's holding on to her past. She should have let that go when she died."

"Probably." Mahlon shrugged. Sawyer turned to walk away. "Hey!" Mahlon said. Sawyer stopped walking and turned. "You going to free Minah too? She's in pretty bad shape."

"I'm going to free her, but not like I will with Bianca. I feel I can help her."

"So, you're in love too." Mahlon said with a grin.

Sawyer chuckled at the thought. "Maybe. But what Bianca has done to her doesn't mean she's lost. She's made it this far… Two vampire masters in her lifetime? Not all Assists make it to two masters. She's seen a lot. Suffered a lot. It's time for her to live her long days in peace. I'm going to get her some help, and once she's clean… who knows. She may want to come with me and hunt vampires, too."

"Maybe." Mahlon laughed. "I swear, I've been all over the world, and it's got to be something in Richmond's water to make me fall as hard as I did for Bianca."

"Same." Sawyer said. "It's got to be something in the water." They both laughed at their bewildered hearts.

Mahlon raised his hand goodbye, and Sawyer did the same. "See you around, my guy."

"Yeah. I'll be seeing you before you see me. Don't get into any trouble."

Mahlon raised his hand and pinched his fingers together. "Maybe just a tiny bit... to keep you on your toes." They both smiled at each other, and Mahlon turned and jumped rooftops until Sawyer could no longer see his friendly foe's silhouette.

Chapter 26

"Yeah…"

"We have a new assignment for you."

"Where?"

"It's still Richmond. It's more of a side job. We still need you on Bianca."

"So far, she's been laying low. There's been a few reanimates popping up here and there, but I've been able to neutralize the situation."

"Yes, we've been watching. Your new assignment is on the line of that."

"Okay, what's going on."

"A few level three vamps are trying to occupy the city. We can't allow them to meet up with Bianca. We need them burned."

"I'll handle them."

"Our scout has located their den and will send you their coordinates. We expect them to be in the sun within the next days."

"Acknowledged."

"And the status on Bianca... Where are we on her. Was Mahlon successful with getting her to relocate?"

"Negative. Mahlon has left Richmond. Him and Bianca are no longer an item. He has given me the go-ahead to neutralize. He has included her mother as a target. He believes she will try to find a way to turn."

"We don't neutralize humans. Leave that to the streets to do."

"We don't, but this time, I'm making an exception. I've seen this woman, and her kind can't be left to her own devices. She will be a problem if she finds a way to turn."

"Fine. Handle it discreetly. There should be no record of her death."

"Acknowledged."

"Check-in is in four suns. We expect artifacts of their neutralization and hopefully of Bianca's as well."

"For those level three's, I can guarantee. Bianca is going to take a bit longer. I have to overhaul my plan of attack since I have already made contact with her. She will know I'm up to something if I attack now. I'll let you know when my new plan is in motion."

"Fine, three suns for the first assignment. Two suns to begin Bianca's annihilation."

"Acknowledged."

Sawyer ended the call with The Council. He pulled out his small pin and pad and jotted down a few notes. A text came in, as The Council said, and he read the instructions and the location of his next targets. He then put his phone back in the inside pocket of his long leather jacket for safekeeping as he prepared for his mission.

It had been a few weeks since he'd last seen or spoken to Mahlon, and the city felt a bit quiet now that he was gone. Since her breakup with him, Bianca could no longer be seen smiling as she walked the streets to engage in illicit activities. It was like when he left, she vanished into a hidden void, emerging only to satiate her morbid hunger. Unfortunately, her disappearances perfectly aligned with the spike in gruesome murders that had caught the police's attention, with viciously bitten corpses appearing throughout the city.

The police knew there would be significant challenges in handling the surge in brutal killings since the uncertain treaty between the city and The Block was considered a quiet matter. However, with the turmoil boiling in the streets, the surrounding communities that slept without fear of the unknown were becoming deeply shaken by the wave of mysterious killings. Fear and anxiety began to spread through Churchill, The Bottom, Scott's Addition, and Manchester, with many residents feeling unsafe in their neighborhoods.

Sawyer got another notification on his phone. He looked at the message, which showed The Council sent a profile of the level three vampires he had to kill. None of the faces looked familiar. *Freshmen.* He deduced. The location of their den wasn't too far of a car ride from where he considered his headquarters. While he mapped out his plan, he leaned on the corner of a building where he could keep an eye on River Towers, hoping to catch a glimpse of Minah. He hadn't seen her in weeks hunting with Bianca and could only assume she was being held at her captor's place until she could be freed.

Not ready to give up hope on his fleeting look of Minah, he lingered at his post for a few more minutes. In his eye's peripheral, he caught a glimpse of a familiar person, someone he'd seen around but never engaged. He looked in their direction as they walked towards him, not knowing who he was. However, he knew them very well from his talks with Minah. Just when they were right at a speaking distance, Sawyer spoke.

"You headed to see Minah?"

Kingston paused in step at the deep voice coming from the man with his head down. He looked at him curiously before he responded. "What you know about Minah?" Intrigued, Kingston walked closer to the man for more information.

"Not much. She's someone I know. Just haven't seen her around lately."

Kingston put his hand to his chin as he considered giving him more information about his friend.

"Well… I see her all the time. She's here and there lately. Can't really say where she's going to be next. You know how Minah is."

"Yeah, I do. Especially when I know she's tied up with Bianca and strung out on that blood."

Kingston gasped at what he'd heard. No one ever talked about Minah's blood addiction. "She told you about that?"

"Ummm-hm. I know a lot about her. She's someone I care about. When you get a chance, tell her— and only her, her friend is looking for her."

Kingston nodded in agreement and smiled slyly. "Oh, you, that friend-friend I heard something about." Kingston did a hop-skip and giggled with enjoyment at the thought of Minah having someone who truly liked her. "Yeah, my girl mentioned you, but what she didn't say was you was this type of fine. She ain't say she bagged her some man candy!" Kingston said loudly in between laughs. "She ain't say you couldn't dress, though." Kingston said with disdain after he took a good look at him once he'd stopped laughing. "Yeah… friend. You need some help with that. Minah may not be a good dresser either, but y'all ain't got to look like two goofs together! Get you some better clothes and step your game up if you want to get with my friend!" Kingston rolled his eyes and folded his arms in a pout.

Sawyer took a deep breath to restrain himself from grabbing Kingston by the collar and shaking him straight. "Look. Just tell her I'm looking for her and don't worry about finding me; I'll find her. When the time is right."

Kingston took one last look at him, letting his eyes swiftly glance over him several times before he finally agreed. "Yeah… I'll tell her you looking, but just make sure you clean yourself up…

looking like a dirty Jolly Green Giant. Yeah, you cute in the face and thick in the chest, and them legs could probably snap a bitch in two, but your style got me questioning your ability to make good decisions, and my good-good sis need a man who can guide her to the light." Kingston rolled his eyes one more time before walking away. Sawyer shook his head, his frustration evident in the tightness of his jaw and the furrow of his brow, and headed in the other direction. He hit the button on the key fob of his car, and the car's headlights flashed to let him know the door was open. Hopping in, he input the destination of the vampire den into his car's navigation system and headed to the outer county of Richmond to reach their layer.

Twenty minutes southwest of Richmond, Chester was a county far enough away from the city for a clan of vampires to lay low and close enough to get to the urban jungle when they were ready to feed. Level three vampires are still weak and lack cohesiveness; they only think about hunting and eating. They move as a pack, appearing like a gang when seen from afar. However, once they strike, their true nature is revealed as they turn on each other in a deadly frenzy, each vying to be the one to claim the victim's life. Killing level three vampires is always messy and chaotic. It usually takes several vampire hunters to kill a den of level three's, but Sawyer was up for the challenge and liked to take the mission on himself.

The Council didn't mention who was responsible for creating them, but his instincts told him it was the work of the messy cleanup Bianca's crew did. If, while attacking and her saliva or any of her blood splattered, her excrement could contaminate anything picked up by vagrants. Discarded needles were a common way Bianca's fluids could be transferred. If her splatter were on used needles that were picked up by junkies and shared in that area, there was a higher chance of infection. Since Bianca had been the only vampire in the area, he's sure it's her victims he's up against. Preparing to dismantle the vampire den and dismember its occupants, Sawyer's thoughts turned to Minah and how she hadn't turned into a vampire like the ones he was assigned to assassinate.

He could only imagine that Bianca kept her on the edge of turning or dying because she's probably the only person in a worse position than her. Any vampire, whether they are half-breed or full blood had a sense of power and freedom. Minah was neither. She lived for the blood, and Bianca was her only supply... or at least she thought. It was almost like Minah was a trained elephant bound by the twig stuck in the ground they held onto, which kept them in captivity. For him to be with Minah, he knew he'd have to free her from not just Bianca but also the blood. He had to be the one to do it.

Sawyer pulled up to the vampire den and turned his car's headlights off. It was still daytime but closer to the evening, and the sun hadn't set. He checked his watch and found that there were fifteen minutes left until dusk. He could easily burn the den where they were sleeping, but that would take all of the fun out of the kill, and he definitely needed the practice. Fifteen minutes allowed him to explore the den and set up for the slaughter. Entering the den, there were several carcasses rotting in the hall. From the amount of dead bodies, he assumed there were at least seven vamps he'd have to kill. The smell of decaying dead flesh was pungent, but he was used to the stench of death as part of his line of work.

The den, which was just a shell of an old and dilapidated 1920s duplex on the edges of the county and close to the James River, had a second level. He took the stairs to the top and searched the rooms for any indication that they had organized. More dead bodies and a half-eaten dog were found on his trail of discovery. It wasn't unusual for level three vampires to experiment with other species, wondering if they could get a fix from something other than humans, but animal flesh was tough to rip through, and the blood was too thin to satisfy their desires. The flavor wasn't as appealing, either. He could only determine the taste was different because of the human diet, which consisted of butters, sugars, and carbs. Seeing half-eaten animals was par for the course.

He continued to search upstairs. In some cases, there was a leader of the den, a vampire with whom the others naturally flocked to. Sawyer found that the leader would look the most decomposed and usually nested alone in the den. Killing the leader first usually dismantled any organization the vampires had started to create. Sawyer likened the killing of the designated lead to when an ant's trail is disturbed; all the other ants behind the lead ant lose their way when the trail the lead ant made is severed. If the lead vampire were found before they began their killing spree, it would make his night easier.

He checked his watch, *two minutes...* He crept down the long hall, pushing open each door, and as he made his way to the last door, the smell of death was more potent than it was on the first level. *The leader...* He put his hand around the handle of his sword that remained in its sheath, prepared to pull it out before the vampire arose. He slowly pushed the door open to the last room at the end of the hall. He could tell the room's windows had been darkened, making it difficult to see by the unnatural night. Sawyer quieted his steps as he made his way through the room. He listened to the quick and heavy breath of the vampire sleeping restlessly. He knew it was almost time to kill. Once he got close to the vampire, it would pick up his scent and instantly attack.

Sawyer slowly pulled out his sword and aligned himself with the sleeping vamp. He raised his hands, clasping the sword high in the air. The sharp end pointed directly at the vamp's chest, where his heartbeat at a slower pace. As he began to bring the sword down, the vampire's eyes shot open abruptly, and his mouth instantly opened, showing its sharp and rotten fangs. Thick, cobwebbed saliva dripped from its lips. The vampire unleashed a blood-curdling screech that echoed through the den to alert the other vamp's danger was upon them.

Sawyer did not hesitate to plunge the sword deep into the vamp's heart. His body began to sizzle and smoke and shake as the silver blade reacted to its dead internal organs like heat to plastic. He then took out his short knife and slit the vampire's head off its neck. The vampire died with its eyes open, and the head rolled off its neck and next to Sawyer's foot. He kicked it to the opposite corner in enough time to see the other vampires from the first level of the den rushing through the door, ready to feast on him.

He pulled out several silver daggers and began throwing them in the direction of the attackers. The daggers hit the targets but were only meant to put them off course. The vampires that were struck by the daggers fell to the ground, writhing in pain as the other vampires rushed past them to continue the attack. Sawyer swung the sword in a circle above his head and let his body follow the flow of his weapon as if he and the sword were in a dance. Sawyer spun around enough time to slice through one vampire's torso. The severed pieces dropped in two different directions. Another vampire attempted to attack from his side. He lifted his hand with the sword in it, and the other hand went underneath the sword. His dagger in that hand stabbed the vampire in the heart. He twisted the dagger halfway to the right and swiftly sliced upward, cutting right through the vampire. His arm slid off its torso. Sawyer then guided the dagger to rip into its neck. His head fell to the floor.

He kicked the other coming his way in the chest, knocking him back to the wall. The vampire stumbled, charging toward Sawyer, and it gave him enough time to pull out the gun he had in his holster and fire two rounds into the middle of the vampire's head. The vampire fell backward to the ground, dead. Sawyer wiped his brow and turned his attention to the two vampires with whom he had initially begun his fight. They were still writhing in pain on the floor. He took his gun and shot them both at close range, finalizing their initial death by the bullet's impact. Sawyer walked out of the den and checked his watch. It was ten minutes after sundown. The sky was now turning to night, and there was an orange glow in the sky, remnants of the sun's aura. He pulled out his phone and sent his text to The Council with the one word, "clear." In about an hour, The Council would have scrubbed the den of any indication that he or the vampires were there concealing their tracks from human suspicion and curiosity. He got back in his car and turned it on. The engine rumbled like thunder and then revved high and loud. Finishing it's starting ritual, the engine's sound lowered to a comforting grumble, letting him know he could pull off when ready.

He turned on his music and backed out of the driveway of the vampire's den. His thoughts began to make their way back to Minah. His plan to get her from Bianca was now his mission. Sawyer was a loner. He'd lived on this earth longer than anyone had known and learned never to get attached to anything living or dead, but Minah was different. She was tender and innocent and caught in a way of life she never expected. Kilion was her master. Sawyer had seen him go to her over the years. He'd never seen her up close out of respect for Kilion because he was of no consequence to the balance of the living and the undead, so Sawyer and The Council allowed Kilion to go unhunted, just monitored. Kilion didn't parade Minah around or glorify his lifestyle with her. He also didn't abuse it. Bianca ruined Minah, but Sawyer was ready to build her back up. He didn't know what love was, but he knew he had never felt anything for anyone until he met her. He put the car in drive and headed back to The Block ready to free his woman.

Chapter 27

"So, what are you going to do?" Roxanne asked Minah as they sat in her small room in Bianca's penthouse while combing out the mats in Minah's hair. Since Bianca confined her to her room for her antics while supposedly working, Minah hadn't bathed or groomed herself, too depressed to do anything else. Over the last few weeks, Minah felt she had officially crossed a line with Bianca she thought she could never come back from. Not answering when she was called and playing on Bianca's vulnerable moments was one thing, but Bianca had had enough when she showed interest in Sawyer.

Being ordered to her room had taken its toll, and Minah's look and self-care had taken a downturn. Her skin was ashen, her hair brittle and knotty, and her nails yellow and broken. Her eyes were bulging from dehydration, and her already slender frame was now skinny and gaunt.

"I'm strung out. I can't do nothing but wait for her to come fill me and feed me." Minah said as she picked the dry skin from her toenails.

"But you can try to get away and go get you some help."

"How? She doesn't let me out anymore. She knows Sawyer likes me, and she's paranoid that if I leave to help her go hunt, I'm going to escape. But look at me? I ain't getting far. How? How can I go anywhere? I'm too weak to go anywhere."

Roxanne thought over Minah's circumstances. "But Kingston told you, right, that he's looking for you? I'm sure if you could just get to him, he could get you out of here."

"Probably. But how am I supposed to get out of here good enough so he can get me? This place is guarded and when Bianca finds out I'm gone, she is going to go on a rampage. You could even get hurt messing around helping me."

"One thing is for sure; Bianca don't scare me like she scare y'all. She is pretty dangerous, and she would probably take my life if she gets that angry, but I don't live in fear of no one or nothing. I live this life in this neighborhood because that's what I want to do. I'm on these streets because it's where I want to be, but she don't keep me here, and she don't keep me from what I want to do." Minah chuckled at Roxanne's boldness because what she said, she believed, and so did everyone else.

When Bianca began formulating her crews, Roxanne assigned herself to be in charge of the women since she was good at arranging hook-ups for the men who came around for a thrill. Roxanne began on The Block hustling right around the time Daddy was murdered, and she was already running with the boss Bianca took The Block from. Not waiting for anyone to assign her fate, she let it be known her role in the organization, and no one objected. Roxanne was the type to go with the flow until the flow dried up and because of that, she could live the life without a care.

"Yeah... I wish I had your strength. It's like you're here living this life, but you don't see it like we see it. It's like nothing gets you down." Minah began to remember times when Roxanne could have been cowardly and run away from challenging situations with Bianca or the crew, but Roxanne would stand her ground and always came out on top.

"I make my world how I want it, Minah. I understand where I am in life. I know I'm a hoe, and I run with gangsters. Living was and always is hard for me. Don't get me wrong, though. I'm running from some things, too. I got some monsters in my closet I don't want to let out. And truth be told, I could leave The Block and try to exist somewhere else and do something different with myself. I could probably find a man to take care of me, and have a few babies, and get a regular job, but that would mean I'd have to deal with those monsters in my closet, and I'm not ready for that. There's some work here that I must do first. There are people here that I have to take care of before I can begin my journey to my next level."

Roxanne turned Minah's head towards her and looked her in her eyes, hoping what she said next would get through to her. It was obvious to anyone who cared that Minah wouldn't last if she stayed. "I was given a chance to save myself a long time ago by someone who loved me deeply, but I didn't take the opportunity." Roxanne's lip quivered as she held in her tears, thinking about her past. "You're one of the people I want to save before I leave this place. I can't go until you get up out of here. I'm not saying you are holding me back, but what I'm saying is I owe it to myself and my past to help you be better. Once I know you're free, I'll take my chances with my own monsters. We got a deal?"

Minah saw the tear slide down Roxanne's eye and wiped it from her cheek with the tips of her fingertips. She nodded her head in agreement. "We got a deal." Minah wrapped her hands around Roxanne's neck to embrace her for her grace. They both let go of each other and giggled before Roxanne returned to combing out Minah's tangled and matted hair.

"So, what's the next move, Minah. Are we going to plan your escape?"

Minah sighed heavily at the thought of trying to get away. "But how will I survive? I'm not in the best shape." She began to scratch her arm. Her dry skin began to flake under her brittle fingernails. "This addiction is rough. How am I going to get away when I need that blood?"

"Haven't you gone long times without it before? I mean, you and Kilion had a thing, and you told me before you would go months without seeing him. You'd get your fix, and he'd be out. Why can't you do the same with B?"

Minah shrugged her shoulders in bewilderment. "I honestly don't know how to explain it, but maybe because she takes so much blood from me when she feeds and then has to refill me with hers, it's just more of her blood fueling me than anything else.

Roxanne shook her head in disgust. "No offense, but it just sounds so nasty to me. Like, who wants to suck on blood? Like, I'm so scared of seeing a little prick of blood on my finger, let alone seeing you drooling over an open vampire wound. Bleh!"

"It does sound pretty gross when you say it like that, but it's my way of life for over a couple of hundred years."

"Dang… You been chasing after a man for that long… girl, I would have been dropped his ass after the first fifty." Roxanne said jokingly.

"Girl quit. You know you would have chased dick longer than that if you could." Minah responded in jest.

"Wait…" Roxanne said as she stopped combing Minah's hair. "I got an idea. What if we just get you out of town, and I can get you to that rehab Kingston told you about. I don't think they rehab blood feens, but they rehab everything else, so I'm sure they can rehab you."

"I could try…" she shook her head no before she spoke again. "But again, I wouldn't get too far. Look at me."

"But me and Kingston can help you get away from here. Kingston can be a distraction, and I can sneak you out. Then, when we get to the streets, we can get someone with a car to take you out of the city, and then your man can scoop you up and take you away."

Minah's eyes lit up at the plan Roxanne had figured out, but slowly, her eyes dimmed, and her defeating thoughts crept in. She shook her head slowly again. "No." She said with a heavy sigh. "It's not going to work because as soon as he sees the mess I'm in, he's going to leave me where I stand. Nobody wants to take me on as a project. And plus, I don't have nothing to offer this man. He has his own shit going on. He don't even look like he like people that much, and then to have me dragging behind him… Nah… that's not going to work."

"Girl, don't think like that!" Roxanne shoved Minah playfully on the back of her shoulder. "You got to think positive. You got to believe the plan will work, so it will work."

"But you already know—"

"No, I don't know! I don't know what's going to happen next. I don't know what's going to happen tomorrow, but I do know what the past looks like. I know you been in this same cycle with Bianca for too long, and if you don't change at least one thing about your situation, you gonna end up repeating the same situation every day and for the rest of your life." Roxanne sucked her teeth with slight frustration at Minah's resistance. "Girl, just imagine yourself on the other side of your addiction. Living your life with your man and being far away from here. Think of yourself a year from now, praising yourself for having the courage to make that change. To get up from this space on the floor and just walk out the door and never come back… ever. Because I know Sawyer going to fuck that crazy bitch up over your ass if she ever THINK she can have you back!" Both Minah and Roxanne laughed at the thought of it.

"She does need her ass kicked." Minah said before she covered her mouth quickly to stifle her giggles.

Roxanne laughed loudly before saying, "Yeah, she does! Somebody gotta beat that ass! Can't be me, though. I know she can toss me across a room." They both laughed again.

"And my skinny tail, all she would have to do is blow her breath strong enough, and I'm through a wall." They both laughed again.

"But seriously. You think you ready, you think we got a plan?" Roxanne said as their laughter died down.

"Yeah… I think we can try it. It's not like I got a whole lot to lose. I'm already half of nothing." Minah said as she looked down at her bony legs and pronounced knees.

Roxanne patted Minah on the back of her shoulder. "Don't worry about that part. If we got to carry you out of here or fold you up and stuff you in a duffle bag, we gonna get you out of here and healed. God got a plan for you."

Chapter 28

"Hey, boy." Kingston said loudly but not in a yelling way. He was sure he said it loud enough to catch Sawyer's attention while he walked in front of Kingston on the crowded downtown sidewalk. Sawyer didn't turn when Kingston shouted out. He kept moving with the crowd. His height and black leather jacket were among the factors that made him stand out. Kingston had been looking for him since early that morning. He'd gotten word from Roxanne that Minah was ready and wanted to see Sawyer as well. As a favor and for a small finder's fee, he set out to look for him but found him hard to locate even though he was not someone who was as forgettable as any other person. Sawyer had a look about him that would make anyone feel uncomfortable to be around because of his towering presence and the cold way he stared at anyone. But that same presence also had a way of making anyone feel secure. His strapping physique and the darkness behind his eyes felt like he was a vigilante on a mission.

"Sawyer, I know you can hear me back here yelling for your ass. Stop walking so I can catch up... damn."

Sawyer stopped moving, and the people behind him rerouted their paths to proceed around him and dared not complain about his abrupt halt. Kingston caught up with Sawyer just as he turned around to see him walking up.

"What." Sawyer mumbled, his voice devoid of energy.

"Your girl looking for you. She want you to come get her."

Sawyer's unbothered stare turned into a look of interest as soon as he heard Minah was waiting for him. "Come get her? You mean she wants me to come see her."

"No, nigga. She ready to bounce. Go. Leave. Get the fuck out of Dodge."

"Where is she."

"She at Bianca's."

"Where is Bianca?"

"Out fucking... killing... we don't know. She been funny acting since her and Ol' Boy broke up."

"Yeah. I heard they were no longer together. Mahlon told me on his way out of town."

"Wha— you mean to tell me he gone?! That nigga was supposed to help me on the come up!" Kingston stomped his foot, folded his arms, and pouted once more.

"Yeah. He left a few weeks ago. Bianca's turmoil was too much. The trick Vivian pulled really put a wedge between them."

"That old bitch been fucking shit up since she got here."

"Seems like she's been like this way before she got here."

"Yeah, I guess you right about that."

"So, Minah's ready to go."

"Yes, she's ready. She just needs a little bit more convincing, and I think if she sees you, we think she'll be ready to leave just like that."

Sawyer smiled slightly, thinking of Minah jumping into his arms and them leaving together. He could teach her his way of life and allow her to grow strong. Then, they can hunt together. "Well, I definitely want to see her, and I definitely want to take her away, but I have to complete what I came here to do. I'm here for a purpose."

"I mean… what do you do exactly? What's so important you got to put your job before your boo? What, you guarding a celebrity or something? I see you walking around in all black and I know you packing some heat. That can't be all you in those tight-ass ashy black jeans you got on." Sawyer let his black trench close in front of him to cover the resting bulge in the crotch of his pants. "Oh…" Kingston covered his mouth and laughed. "I guess that is all you." He said as he belted out a rhythmic laugh. "So, what is it, you protecting a celebrity or something?"

"Something like that."

"Ohmygawd…" Kingston said with excitement while waving his hands wildly on either side of him. "You got to let me meet them. I swear I'll be good. You can tell them I'm your assistant. I just want to meet them. Once they see me, they'll want me to be in their inner circle. Like… Me being with them is just going to level them up." Kingston said proudly. "Just look at me. I'm so stylish, and you already know I know all the hot spots in town, and everyone knows me. Just let me come with you, and I'll handle the rest."

"Not that kind of celebrity."

"Ain't no other kind!" Kingston huffed. "You just don't want me to come up and be the megastar I know I am. But it's cool though. I'm going to be back on top for sure. Just wait."

"Enough of this." Sawyer said with a straight face. "Take me to her."

Kingston sucked his teeth in annoyance and folded his arms. "Y'all don't treat me right. I swear I be doing too much for all y'all weird ass muthafucka's."

"Take me to her!" Sawyer said. He wasn't the type to use force to get what he wanted, but Kingston delaying his meeting with Minah took him to the edge of his emotions.

Startled by his sternness, Kingston changed his attitude and calmed down. "Ok. Listen. I'll take you to her, but it's going to take some time. Bianca's place… that whole building is on lock. She got all her goons watching and patrolling. See, the cops been heavy in the neighborhood lately because of all the killings Bianca been doing. She been keeping a low profile around there, and she hasn't really been at her place either. She still mad at her mama, so she avoiding coming home, and ain't no Mahlon, so we don't really know where she be. All we know is them bodies adding up, and the police are on her trail."

Sawyer listened but knew where Bianca was since he'd been tracking her. He only had a few more days before The Council demanded her head. He'd been given several extensions on expiring her, but his grace period had run out. What he knew that they all didn't know was most of the killings the cops were running into weren't all her doing. The level three vampires had made a mess of the city and interrupted Bianca's truce. Between the cops and The Council, Bianca was on the brink of a war. He had to strategize to get Minah out and neutralize Bianca before the battle came to Richmond.

"Let her know to meet me at her window in the morning. Just as the sun hits the sky, I'll be there. When the living are outside, we can talk."

"Yeah…" Kingston nodded, confirming the plan to meet in the day was perfect. "I see what you doing. Bianca crazy ass can't stop y'all from seeing each other during the day. I don't know why someone won't just kill her during the day anyway. That mean bitch needs to go."

"You don't mean that."

"I do… a little bit anyway. I mean… she once was nice. I know she got some good in her somewhere, but foreal… I think that's gone. She just pure evil and hate at this point."

"Well, killing her in the sun is harder than you think. Vampires have automatic protection in them during the sun hours.

They are sleeping mentally, but their bodies are still functioning. Vampire blood is conscious and aware. The actual vampire... not in control. Their bodies only play host to the blood. And also, vampires as powerful as Bianca can walk the day for a little while and being a melenated vampire gives another layer of protection from the sun's rays. Mostly before the sun is at its brightest, but they aren't that strong during the day. Basically, they are still vulnerable. Their best bet is just to rest while the sun is up."

"Sounds crazy." Kingston said as he thought on Sawyer's explanation. "But how you know about them so much? You one of them?"

"No, and I'm not a fan. I just like to be aware."

"Oh... a smart type... but I guess you have to know a lot about stuff if you're protecting celebrities. Never know who or what wants to harm them and take all their money. Well, I'll let Minah know to be at her window in the morning."

Sawyer nodded goodbye and turned and walked away. Kingston turned the other way and headed to the penthouse while Sawyer's words swirled in his head. *Vampires aren't alive or dead. Vampires can still fight your ass in their sleep. This shit too much. But I do feel bad for Bianca. I mean, she cool and everything if she wasn't such a bitch. But Minah does need to get from her. That girl look a mess.*

As Kingston walked back to River Towers, he spotted a storefront filled with women's clothes. *Umph... if she gonna meet that man tomorrow morning, she got to look halfway decent. Because Lord, have mercy on the way she look now. She done fell all the way off. I mean... it's not her fault but damn. She looking too much like a Skeletor.* Kingston entered the store and browsed through the garments hanging on the racks. Several dresses caught his eye, but the one that stood out was a creamy cotton slip dress that hit right below the knee. *I mean... nothing really is going to make her look appealing, but white always adds a few pounds to any frame, and she gonna need something to help her look less bony.* He grabbed a long, wide, woven scarf that Minah could drape around her lean shoulders to complete the look. He also grabbed a few things for himself. After paying the attendant, he headed out of the store and continued on his way to Bianca's.

When he got there, he saw the two guards at the door. "Excuse me, fellas. I'm going in to see Minah. Y'all good with that?"

"Bianca said no guest."

"You's a lie. Rox was in there the other day doing her hair. Plus, I ain't no guest. I'm the help."

The guards looked at each other, both assuming he was right. Kingston always came and went as he pleased. The one guard opened the door and stepped aside. "Alright, you can go, but don't do nothing crazy. Boss Lady probably show up tonight. We ain't trying to get fucked up because she see you in there with that girl."

Kingston patted the guard on his chest reassuringly. "Don't worry about that part. Me and the boss have an understanding. It'll be fine." Kingston walked through the door and shut it behind him. "Minah, you here, girl!" Kingston yelled.

Minah popped her head out of her room. Her hair was no longer a matted mess but smoothed out and curled under just below her ear. She smiled when she saw Kingston, knowing he would probably have an update for her. "Yeah. I'm here. Come on back."

Kingston smiled, too. He was happy that Minah looked much better, though her frail frame was still very jarring. "I got something for you, girl," he said, holding the bag of garments up for her to see. Once he got in the room, he put the bag down and sat on the bed beside her.

"So... what's in the bag?" Minah said and pointed to it as it sat in the chair by her vanity.

"Never mind that right now. I got some real news to tell you." Minah's expression perked up at the thought of an update. "It's about Sawyer. I found him today, and we talked." Minah's eyes widened with delight. "He said he ready girl. He coming to see you tomorrow morning. He want to talk to you. He said he coming to get you."

Minah clasped her hands over her mouth in shock. "What you mean he coming to get me? I said I would talk to him and see what he wants. I'm not ready to go yet. Look at me," she said while referencing her physical condition. "I can't get out of here safely."

Kingston shook his head, not wanting to listen to her excuses. "Ah-ah, girl. Roxanne said you said you was ready and that we was going to get you out of here by hook or by crook. I know she telling the truth because she wouldn't lie about a thing like that. Now, that man said he coming for you tomorrow, and you just need to accept the fact that he coming for you tomorrow."

Minah folded her arms in a huff and then began to cry.

"Aww, Baby, what's wrong?" Kingston put his arms around her shoulders and held her.

"I can't go... like I'm scared. I'm scared I'm not going to make it without Bianca or the blood. We do all this to get me out of here, and then because of what I am, It'll fuck everything up, and someone is going to end up dead. Bianca already said she would kill Sawyer if he came back around. He promised me he would stay away, but now he wants to meet me tomorrow and take me away just like that! This is too much, too fast. I'm just not ready."

"And you'll never be ready thinking like that. That's why we here, girl. We gonna be brave for you. You just do as that man asks, and I promise, you going to make it out here and off these streets and Bianca will never find you. You'll be safe."

"You think so?"

"I know so." Kingston planted a kiss on Minah's cheek, got up, and grabbed the bag. "Now, this is for you."

Minah opened it and pulled out the cream-colored dress. "Kingston, oh my god! This is too pretty!" She stood up and held the dress to her. "What you buy me this for?"

"For tomorrow. Sawyer needs to see you in something nice."

"But I have plenty of dresses in my closet. We could have pulled one from there."

"No, Honey. Those are your freakum dresses. Not respectable lady-like dresses at all. Not a one." Kingston screwed up his face at the thought of all the spandex and latex attire hanging in her closet. "And they probably got cum stains all over them too. Your man don't want nobody else cum on you but his."

"Oh, Kingston, you always saying too much!"

"But it's all truths! You know you ain't washed not a damn garment hanging in that closet of yours. But that dress right there... that's what you meet your man in. I picked white because you skinny as hell but also, white is pure. White is sacred. White is matrimonial. Y'all may not get married. He don't look like the type to want marriage, but he'll see 'commitment' when he sees you in that white."

Minah continued to hold the dress up as she looked at herself in the mirror. She was disappointed at how she appeared physically, but the dress made her look soft and wispy. She smiled at the thought of Sawyer seeing her as a delicate lady and not a hard street girl. "You're right. I got to take a chance. I'll do it. I'll see him tomorrow."

"Perfect! Make sure you get up early enough to look your best. When the sun is high in the morning, he said he'll meet you at your window... this window. You don't even have to leave your room." Kingston went over to it and looked down at the ground below. "I don't know how he's going to meet you here, but he said this is where he'll be."

"I'm sure he'll find a way."

Chapter 29

"Alright girl… stop wiggling. I got to finish putting these eyelashes on you." Kingston called Roxanne to come help get Minah ready for Sawyer. The night before the meetup, Minah couldn't sleep. She could hear the whispers of "The People" in her ear. Trying to decipher what they said would make her wake several times during the night to decrypt their jumbled and scrambled words. Her dreams about the days to come seemed to be nightmares, giving her feelings of panic and dismay. When she finally woke for the day, she was exhausted and fearful but also determined to meet with Sawyer as he requested.

"I'm trying, Roxanne, but I'm so nervous. My anxiety is so up right now."

"Well, let me get you a lil' sum-sum." Kingston said while sauntering out of Minah's quarters to grab an alcoholic beverage from the bar near the dining room.

"Try to relax, Minah. You wiggled so much while I put on your makeup that I barely got it on well. If you don't hold still for these lashes, you gonna look like caterpillars are sleeping on your face."

"Between my anxiety about meeting him and me not getting my fix, I really can't control all these movements, but I'm going to try. You almost done, right?"

"Yeah. Give me a few more minutes. These individual lashes take a bit more hand control than a lash strip, but they look more real, too. He ain't gonna know you only got one or two real ones left." Roxanne and Minah laughed.

"But for real, where is Bianca anyway? I'm used to being locked in here for a little while, but this has gone on for a long time. She really not fucking with me, huh?"

Roxanne shrugged her shoulders. "I don't know Minah. She really has been out here hanging at these underground clubs and hunting by herself. The crew been checking for her and telling her she need to come back on The Block, and they'll bring her what she needs, but she just been ignoring them. It's like that breakup really did something to her. She still mean as a bitch, but she just seem a little more vulnerable lately."

"But she know I'm here struggling, and she ain't even checked on me. Like I'm really going through it."

"Minah, that's a good thing! Why you want her here? We just said you was ready to get yourself together. Besides, you just going through a little withdrawal pain. You'll feel much better when you are off that blood."

"Here go your drink, girl." Kingston walked back into the room and handed Minah a shot glass half full of dark liquor. Minah took a tiny sip and handed it back to Kingston.

"Girl! I know you gonna have more than that!" Kingston said, shocked.

"I thought I could, but it taste gross. My appetite ain't what it usually is. Really want that blood."

Kingston sucked his teeth, rolled his eyes, and folded his arms. "Girl… I'mma be glad when your ass over that shit because I can't with you." He sniffed the drink he bought her and then drank it himself.

"Alright, look in the mirror." Roxanne turned Minah around to see her reflection. Minah looked shocked at how beautiful she turned out.

"Girl… you can work some magic! I ain't never looked this pretty." Minah's bottom lip began to tremble as tears formed in the wells of her eyes.

"Nope. Don't you start crying like a little bitch. Not after I put all that work into that face." Roxanne began using her hands to fan Minah's eyes to stop the tears from forming. She then smiled and said, "You are already beautiful. It wasn't hard to enhance what God already gave you." She said with a wink and a quick peck on the cheek.

"Now come on here so I can help you put on this dress. Oh, I got you some flats because you barely can walk now. Didn't want you to look like a baby giraffe as that man confessing his love to you."

"Y'all two got all the jokes." She said with a laugh. "But that's okay. My man coming." Minah spoke with a bit of sass in her tone. They all laughed as they assisted her in stepping into her dress. Roxanne checked her watch as the sun was now higher in the sky.

"Minah, I think it's about that time. He said he gonna meet you at the window. I don't know how since we all the way up here. You sure he not one of those vampires? You know that's how Bianca got caught up with Kilion."

"I don't think he's a vampire, but I think he be finding ways to get around." Minah's long conversation with Sawyer before she was confined to her room filled her in on what he did. He wasn't a vampire but had agility and strength just as strong as them. And because he had the ability to live longer than most humans, he was able to track and kill vampires. *I should have let him kill Bianca when he had the chance, but I was confused back then. I'm not anymore. I know what I want.* She thought to herself, and as much as she wanted to fill Roxanne and Kingston in on his extraordinary life, she didn't want to expose who he was to even her closest friends because there were eyes and ears everywhere, and she didn't know exactly what that would mean for him.

She walked over to the now-open window, and a cool morning breeze flowed through the tiny room. Kingston bought her a small stool to sit and wait for Sawyer. As the birds flew by and the sound of traffic and the bustle of the day drifted up from the streets below, excitement began to build in her at the thought of finally getting to lay eyes on the man she loved once again. It had been such a long time since Bianca had locked her away in the penthouse for her own needs; she hoped he didn't hold the memory of how she used to look but remembered how she felt in his arms, lying in the hotel bed.

She wasn't the person he met walking home from turning tricks. Back then, she looked healthy and confident, and the fear of changing so drastically simmered underneath her growing excitement. Just as the panic began to overcome her joy, she saw the silhouette of a tall man walking on the rooftop of the building right in front of her. She straightened up her back to get a better look at him, sure that it was Sawyer, but she wanted to be positive so as not to have gotten her hopes up. She waved her fingers cautiously at the man standing on the rooftop across from her window.

He stuck one hand above his head as if in a wave. Minah smiled brightly and waved back with delight this time. Before she knew it, Sawyer had leaped from the building and landed on the terrace at her window. She stepped back to make way for him to come in. Minah looked at him in amazement as his tall and wide physique filled the window frame as he entered her room. He stood in front of her straight-faced. His square, solid jawline clenched tight. However, his eyes held the excitement he tried so hard to contain.

His breath was drawn in as if waiting to see Minah's reaction to him being there in her space before he could exhale. It didn't take long for him to breathe out. Minah rushed into his torso to be smothered by it and wrapped her arms around him as far as they could go.

"You really did come for me." She said in muffled tones, her face buried in his fitted black top.

"Okay, Mr. G-Q! I see you made an effort!" Kingston said loudly and with a bright smile on his face. "You came dressed to impress with them black motorcycle boots and in all black like an omen! You giving mystique! You giving… Edgy! You giving… I got a motorcycle out back, and I'll fuck all these motherfuckers up!"

"Boy, will you shut up! You know people right outside the penthouse! What if they hear you!" Roxanne hissed at Kingston.

Kingston cupped his hands over his mouth for his blunder. "My bad, y'all." He said in hushed tones.

"Come on, Kingston, let's get out of here so they can talk." Roxanne walked out of the bedroom, and Kingston followed behind.

"Don't worry, girl; we'll keep them guards busy so you and him have y'all some alone time." Kingston tiptoed out of the room and closed the door behind him.

Minah pulled herself slowly away from Sawyer and looked him in the eyes. His gaze now seemed more relaxed, and a slight smile warmed his face. Minah smiled back and hugged him once more. This time, Sawyer wrapped his arms around her tightly at first but then eased his grasp, remembering how delicate Minah had become.

When she let go of him, he let go of her, and Minah led him to the bed to sit and talk, but all she could do was look, smile, blush, and then look away. Sawyer awkwardly rubbed the nervous sweat off his hands on his pants legs, realizing this was his first time ever feeling excited about anyone. He barely remembered his parents and their love for him, who were the only people he ever felt close to. Connections with people outside of vampire hunting were never a thing he did. But Minah was not just anyone. He knew she understood this other life and was fearless, straddling the world of the undead and the land of the living by any means necessary. She wasn't like anyone he'd ever met, and he knew he would never find anyone like her ever again. Taking a chance to save her was something he felt drawn to do.

"I missed you." Minah said bashfully.

"I— I've thought of you often since we saw each other last." Sawyer stammered as he tried to think of the right things to say. He quickly grabbed her hand and held it carefully in his.

"This isn't something I usually do. I mean… I usually don't do relationships of any kind… I mean… my line of work… it just… it just keeps me from making connections." His head hung low as he thought about his words.

"I know what you mean. I don't make connections, either. I'm here for her needs. I only have one purpose."

Sawyer looked up quickly and into her eyes, wanting to say something comforting. He opened his mouth to speak and looked up at the sky, hoping something eloquent and meaningful would find its way into his thoughts, but he couldn't think of anything supportive or understanding to say. He lowered his head in embarrassment. "I'm not good at this."

Minah put the tip of her finger underneath his chin and lifted his eyes to hers. "It's okay. You don't have to say a thing." She put her other hand on his chest, feeling the fast and steady beat only feelings and emotions can create. "I know your heart."

He rushed his next words because he couldn't hold it in any longer: "I want to take you away from here."

Minah let his declaration hit her. She sat quietly for a moment, weighing the impact of what he wanted, and answered truthfully: "I'm scared."

"I know. I can tell. But I can take care of you. I can get you better. I can make you strong, and you don't have to be scared anymore."

Minah scratched her arm. The itch was back. Sawyer watched her scrape her skin. He noticed how dry and flakey it was. He then actually noticed how weak she had become. Makeup couldn't hide the sunken cheekbones, bulging eyes, and mediocre wig that probably covered damaged hair. She didn't look like the woman he'd met not too long ago. But it all didn't matter to him. All of that could be fixed with healing, support, and protection.

"I'm not well, Sawyer. I don't think I can even make it from here without falling apart. I'm really too weak to walk too far."

"I can carry you."

"I have a blood addiction problem."

"I can get you to a place that will give you a transfusion. Whatever is left of Bianca's blood that is in your body will be gone, and I'll burn that blood. We can get fresh, clean human blood in you, and then you won't be addicted to her anymore."

Minah's eyes perked up. "A transfusion? I could have a transfusion and be free of her? Free of the blood?"

"Yes. I have someone who can get it all out. You'll be healed."

"But she'll come for you. She'll kill you. She'll kill me."

"Her days are numbered. She can't defeat me. I've fought better."

Minah grew silent. She continued to think. "But I have to pack."

"You don't need to take anything with you. I'll take care of you."

"How will you get me out of here? There are guards everywhere."

"The same way I came in here is the same way we are leaving."

Minah grew quiet once more. He had an answer for everything. There wasn't any response he gave that she could say no to, and that he would accept.

"When can we go?"

"Right now." Sawyer walked over to her closet, grabbed a coat for her, and stood by the open window. He reached out his hand for her to grab.

Minah stood up, walked over to him, put her hand in his, and kissed his lips. "I have to tell Kingston and Roxanne goodbye," she said.

"They'll understand if you don't."

Minah hugged Sawyer tightly and whispered fearfully, "I'm ready."

Chapter 30

Bianca walked up to Tryst's door and banged hard. She'd become a regular at the club, having fun and dining with the other patrons. Tryst was a member-only place. She didn't want the hassle of her identity being known, so she used the power of persuasion Mahlon taught her to find her way inside their walls. On most nights, she could be spotted in the den of Tryst exploring the ins and outs of an unknown body having fun sex and then the ability to nibble on their necks, or inner thighs, or any other soft spot she could bite on.

The nights at Tryst easily end in the mornings at Tryst. After spending all her time in the throes of experimental kink for the past few weeks, she was sure she'd bitten everyone there at least twice, and the best part of her evenings there was the time right before dawn when she would enchant everyone who crossed her path to forget they ever had the pleasure of her company.

Being at Tryst had comforted her, soothing her angry soul about her fight with Mahlon, whom she hadn't seen since their blowup. He stopped staying at the penthouse since she put him out, and even though her time at Tryst was for her enjoyment, she secretly hoped one of the nights she was there, they'd bump into each other and make up. That hadn't happened. Until it did, she chose to carry on with her private feasts.

Tonight was no different. Tryst allowed her to be seen and unseen. None of the patrons wanted to be named. None of the patrons wanted to be remembered. It was all about the hook-up. Bianca walked through the doors of Tryst as usual and headed to the den. She was one of the first to arrive. She paused and watched the featured entertainer swing angelically down the shiny chrome dancer's pole, landing in a handstand. Her legs separated like scissors, revealing the soft tuft of curly hair between the dancer's legs. Bianca wrapped her arm around the dancer's waist while she was still upside down and leaned in, French kissing the woman's pussy covered in sparkling dust. The dancer's clit twitched with every flick of her tongue. The soft pubic hairs tickled Bianca's upper and bottom lip, which turned out to be one of the endearing elements of cunnilingus.

Before she released the woman, she took a sniff of the performer's natural musk, making Bianca's nipples hard with arousal. She lifted her head from in between the woman's legs and stuck a few of her fingers in the wet pussy hole and then brought the fingers to her upper lip, taking a long whiff and allowing the aroma to linger in her memory for the rest of the night. Bianca then pulled a few hundred-dollar bills from between her cleavage and tossed it in the air over the dancer, who had finally flipped and landed in a split. The dancer blew Bianca a kiss and mouthed, "Thank you," while Bianca continued to make her way through the den.

She found a place in a cozy corner where a plush, dark blue smoker's chair awaited her. On her way to her seat, she stopped by the bar for a shot of their best liquor. The bartender poured her an elixir in a short glass and passed it to her. The smell of the alcohol was strong, awakening the prowess inside of her. She gave the drink a sip, letting it burn as it went down her throat, warming her slowly. The experience was comforting.

In her chair, watching the door and listening to the low music playing in the background, Bianca observed strangers slowly become lovers. The interaction between two people rushing the process to get to know each other well enough to engage in sexual activity played out almost the same for everyone every time she was in Tryst. The sexcapade between two potential lusters unknowingly began with the initial offer of a drink by either person. Then, there was the chat at the bar to cover the surface-level pleasantries. After a few tastes of their drink, they would make their way to the dance floor, where maybe one or both would pop a pill or smoke something potent to relax their moods even further. One or two songs later, they officially paired up, arms draped around each other, laughing and flirting and not beating around the bush about what they both came to Tryst for.

Bianca enjoyed the interaction. She loved watching a couple play the game so they could get to business. She also liked to masturbate as she watched the couple lay each other down on the couches or anywhere comfortable and explore each other.

The couple, currently in her view, had gone through all the motions, found a spot on a small pallet, and began to discover each other's sacred spots… the places that would make the other secrete the sweet nectar they both craved to slip their fingers in to taste. The sweeter the juice, the better the experience.

"Excuse me, is this seat taken?"

Bianca looked at the young woman who appeared at her side. Her thigh-high white mini-tube dress highlighted her slender but curvy frame. Bianca smiled slyly at the young woman and gestured with her hand to the empty seat beside her. "By all means, be my guest. Have a seat."

"Thank you." The woman said. The young lady had a cropped wavy haircut. Her skin was luminescent in the dimmed room. Bianca slowly looked the woman up and down as she took the seat beside her and crossed her legs, one on top of the other. Approving the lady's appearance, Bianca nodded yes instinctively before turning her attention back to the couple on the pallet. The man in the coupling had his hand in the woman's open shirt as he kissed her neck. Her head resting backward. Her eyes closed while enjoying the moment.

"I haven't seen you here before," the woman said as she watched the couple play.

Bianca turned her attention to the woman sitting beside her, assured she wouldn't miss too much of the couple's performance since they'd only just started. She looked at her company once again. Her pointed, manicured, glossy gold-painted nails rested on her crossed legs. Her glossy gold pedicured toenails looked like perfect little squares on her dewy skin. The work of the ten-toe perfection awoke her foot fetish. Bianca slightly shifted in her chair to subdue the excitement from the woman's cute feet brewing between her thighs. Bianca continued to admire the woman's style. Her gold anklet matched her gold bangles and bracelets, that matched her thin gold chain, that matched her thin gold glistening hoops. Bianca took another sip from her shot and then put the glass back on the side table between their chairs.

"I don't come here often." She lied.

"Is it your first time?"

"Not really my first time, but I'm not a regular."

"I'm not either. A friend of mine who actually became my husband turned me on to this place a few years back. Since my friend and I are divorced now, I thought I'd give it a go again."

Bianca lifted her glass. "Cheers."

The woman lifted her glass, too. "Cheers to old flames." The lady said as she clinked her glass against Bianca's.

Bianca smiled, and they looked into each other's eyes as they drank to the toast. They set their glasses back on the table, and Bianca turned her attention back to the couple. The man had the woman's legs spread open as his face was buried in her lap.

"Looks like fun." The woman beside Bianca said.

"It does."

"My husband loved going down on me and massaging my pussy with his tongue."

"You mean your ex-husband."

The lady giggled over her blunder. "Yeah. My ex-husband." She said and giggled again. "Forgive me, the divorce is still fresh."

"Totally understandable. My ex and I broke up recently as well."

"Oh my. I'm so sorry for you," the woman said, softening her expression to show her sympathy.

"Thank you. But it was a whirlwind of a relationship. We started hot and heavy and ended cold and dead. But just like your ex-husband, my ex gave good head as well."

The lady raised her glass once more, and Bianca joined before saying, "Cheers to the men with the good head!" They clinked glasses while looking at each other and sipped from them. Bianca watched as the woman drank the rest of her drink and noticed how pure her eyes appeared to be. *The eyes of innocence. I remember when Minah's eyes looked at me with such virtue….* Bianca shook the image of Minah from her thoughts. Minah was a betrayer and a user, and she was of no use to her anymore. Their relationship had run its course, but she hadn't decided whether it was the end for Minah or not. Keeping her locked in the penthouse was not enough, and not wanting to be tempted by the scent of her captive's blood kept her away from her prison. She wasn't in love with her at all, but she wasn't ready to destroy her yet. Her indecision about Minah had to have been Mahlon's influence. Before him, she wouldn't have thought twice about her choice.

"You got kids?" The woman asked, which broke Bianca's thoughts.

"Kids? No. I can't have kids."

"How does that make you feel?" The woman asked as she put her hand on Bianca's knee in compassion.

Bianca shrugged. "I don't think about it. I don't think I ever really wanted any."

"I don't have kids either." The woman said as she lowered her head in regret. "I wanted one, but he cheated, and I didn't want him to touch me after that."

"Men suck. Mine cheated, too."

The woman looked up, surprised. "Yours too?!"

"Yup. But with my mom."

The woman's eyes widened, and her bottom lip dropped open with shock. "What in the world?!"

"Yeah. Family is always your first and truest enemy."

"But what about your ex? Did he apologize?"

"Don't know. I cursed them and left. Haven't been home since."

"Oh wow. That's pretty bad." She signaled for the bartender to bring her another drink. "But where are you staying if not with them?"

Bianca shrugged her shoulders. "Here and there. Get a hotel for a few days and then get another one somewhere else. I'll go back home when the time is right." Bianca switched her view back to the couple having sex. A few more people had arrived, and the dance floor was not as full as before. Other couples had finished their rhythmic ritual and had retreated to other dark, intimate spaces in the den.

"It just seems like you lost it all because of that unfaithful man."

"Oh no…" Bianca slowly placed the young woman's hands in hers and brought them to her lips, and she kissed the top of her hands softly. Her tongue licked the young woman's skin ever so discreetly. *I can tell she is going to taste so sweet, probably like Minah used to.* "I haven't lost a thing. They can have each other for all I care."

The woman felt the kiss Bianca had placed on her hand. Her cheeks blushed pink, and she felt her temperature had risen. The heat from her arousal made her glisten with a sheen of sweat all over her skin. "If I had a family I had to walk away from, I'd be so torn. I don't have any family here. My husband was all I knew."

"No family?" Bianca said as she leaned in to kiss the woman's nape. Her lips aimed for the thick vein that ran down her neck. *Keep it slow and steady. The bite will be more delectable the longer you let heat from their arousal simmer inside their veins...* Bianca could hear Mahlon's words in her ear as if he were right beside her. She quickly turned her head to the left to know for certain he was not there, but a lingering memory ringing in her ears. Her eyes darted around the club, looking for a trace of him. She sniffed the air to pick up on his familiar scent, but neither was there to confirm his presence. She put her attention back on the young woman. She leaned in again to kiss the main vein but hesitated. She didn't want to hear Mahlon's voice again. She took her hand, reached down, lifted the woman's foot, and slipped off her gold strappy sandals.

"For tonight," Bianca licked and began to suckle the woman's big toe. The woman's body relaxed and tensed from the sensation the foreplay gave. "I'll be everything you need. I promise my tongue will make you forget about your ex, and I'm sure that pussy between your succulent thighs will make me wish I were a lesbian." She kissed her ankle and lifted the woman's leg just enough to kiss the soft space on the back of her knee.

The woman pulled away, confused by what Bianca professed. "You're not a lesbian? I came here tonight to swear off men." The lady got up to walk away and grabbed her shoe from Bianca's hand in a huff. Bianca grabbed her elbow just in time before she mixed in with the crowd in the den and gently pulled her back. The woman was now sitting on her lap. Bianca looked deeply into her eyes. Minah's face replaced the woman's. Bianca shook the image from her head. Minah was not what she wanted. She pulled the woman's other shoe off and began kissing her feet while lustfully eyeing the thick life vein in her foot that mimicked the one in her neck.

"Hey, let's not label. Let's just be two souls together, not worried about being a wife, a girlfriend, or an ex. Let's start over in companionship. Let's just be us… together. The mix of Bianca's words and the enchanting charm she used to relax the woman worked. Bianca led her back to her chair beside her. She placed small kisses on top of the woman's feet. Her fangs slightly pricking the lady's main foot artery.

"I've never had anyone kiss my feet before." Her eyes fluttered in enjoyment.

Bianca pulled her teeth from the puncture she created in the foot. The blood drooled from the wound, and Bianca licked it with delight. "Your feet turn me on in so many ways." She placed her tongue on the bite, and she could feel the pool of blood smear onto her lips. She licked it away from her mouth and began to kiss the woman passionately on her lips, puncturing it discreetly and sucking on it to draw more fluid. An appetizer for what was to come.

The lady moaned in ecstasy as she felt Bianca's tongue dart and flicker in her mouth. She gently pushed Bianca away, impressed by her skills. "My husband never kissed me like that. Do all girls kiss like that?"

"I don't know. I've never kissed a girl before tonight." Another lie. Bianca stood in front of the woman and unbuttoned her fitted collar shirt, exposing her braless and plump breasts. Her dark nipples became stiff from excitement. The woman reached and fondled one of them before grasping Bianca's hips and guiding her to her knees. They were now face to face. Bianca took one of her hands and opened the woman's thighs. Her fingernails grazed the inside of them. The sensation of Bianca's touch made her open her legs more. Her head slowly fell back to continue enjoying what she knew was next.

Bianca massaged the woman's privates. She felt the subtle hint of a fine layer of soft hair. *Oooh… another pussy patch to play in. I ain't know full muffs were back in style…* Bianca grabbed at the hair, gently pulling just enough for the woman to feel the hint of pain. The lady slightly winced at the pulling but oddly felt good. She opened the woman's private lips with two of her fingers and used her fingertip to play around her clitoris, arousing it to make it respond to another's touch. The woman began to discharge her clear, thick, sticky fluid at Bianca's mastery of the finger fuck. She pulled her moistened appendages out of the woman's pussy and put them up to her nose. "My gawd woman…" The scent of her juice reminded her of ripe mangos. "I love how you smell." She stuck the two moist fingers in her mouth to taste. "Ummmm…. You taste sweet, too."

Turned on, Bianca put her hands down her pants and felt how wet she was. She pulled her hands out of her pants, placed them in the woman's open mouth, and then kissed her after. "You like how that taste?"

"I do."

With a smile, Bianca placed her face in the woman's lap and allowed her tongue to find its way around the woman's puss. The woman moaned while Bianca dined on her soft, delicate, sexual fruit. From her place between the woman's legs, Bianca peeked to see the pleasure in her playmate's face, only to find a man massaging her breast and fondling her nipples while the woman's hand stroked his erect and bare penis as his welcoming. The newcomer to their sexual encounter looked down at Bianca, winked, smiled a cocky grin, and nodded his head in solidarity. Not mixing words, Bianca gave him a wink back.

"I'm about to climax…" The woman whispered as she could feel the moment of her release build inside of her.

"Would you like to cum with her?" Bianca turned her glance slightly to the left to see the "eye" of a stranger's dick. The stranger, placed his hand in between the woman's vagina and began to rub her clitoris rapidly. The woman's moans grew deeper and huskier in tone as her orgasm began to make her legs tremble with expectation. Bianca took her pants down, sat back in her chair, and spread her legs. He then licked his lips hungrily as he placed his face between Bianca's legs, writhing his head back and forth until her silky-to-the-touch secretions were smeared all over his face, the rest of her juices; he slurped them into his mouth, making the *whoosh* of his inhale vibrate her privates. The sensation of his tongue flicking the tip of her clit, and his lips puckered just enough to suck it made Bianca feel her orgasm wanting to explode. The two women locked eyes as they both came at the same time by the stranger's advanced manipulating skills. Bianca's orgasm spilled on his face. The woman's poured out into his hand. Once he got what he wanted from them, he licked their cum into his mouth and smiled brightly.

Hours later, it was close to sunrise when Bianca finished her evening at Tryst. The people in the orgy she created were still all nestled together. She had suckled from each of her partners, and now she was satisfied with her feeding. However, she was disappointed that this, too, was a night she could not meet up with Mahlon.

"B, is that you?"

Bianca heard Kingston's whispered tone at the entrance of Tryst while walking out. She turned to see him standing next to a guy he was in conversation with before she walked up.

"Yeah, it's me." She said with a flat tone.

"Girl, everyone looking for you. You ain't been home in a minute."

"So, it's my home. I can come and go as I please."

"But you left Minah to fend for herself."

"She a big girl. She can figure it out."

Kingston rolled his eyes knowing Bianca knew she left Minah there to rot. "You so messy. Like… you just sooooo messy."

"Whatever." Bianca turned to continue walking towards the exit.

"You need to go home and check on that girl." Kingston hollered at Bianca.

"When I'm ready to deal with those traitors, I'll go home. Right now, they are lucky I'm staying far away."

"Oh, you still mad about your mama and Mahlon too. I get why you staying away."

Bianca turned back around and swiftly walked back to Kingston. "Yeah, my mama and that fuck-boy, Mahlon. I should kill both they asses!"

"Well, don't be mad at me about them. They the ones who did you dirty, not me, and besides, Mahlon gone. All you have to deal with is your mama and take Minah off punishment. The girl is practically skin and bones."

Bianca's interest peaked when Kingston mentioned Mahlon hadn't been staying there. "What you mean Mahlon's gone? You mean he hasn't stayed there because I'm not there?"

"No, he gone-gone. I got it on good authority that he left the day you put him out."

Shocked, Bianca grew silent. "But that was weeks ago."

"Yeah, it was. You ain't been paying attention and couldn't nobody find you to let you know. Where were you staying at anyway? Like you've been ghost."

"Mahlon is gone…" Bianca ran her fingers through her hair in a state of stressed bewilderment. "He left me. He said he wouldn't leave. He left me, but he said he wouldn't leave. He left me and didn't keep his promise." The thought of Mahlon breaking his vow grew the rage inside of her.

Kingston felt anxious over Bianca's rising anger. He turned to his friend with fear in his eyes. "Listen… get out of here. Go tell everyone inside the den they need to go out the back door quick. Tell them you smell smoke or something, but everyone got to go. I got to calm this girl down before she go off."

Kingston's friend heard the urgency and panic in his words. Without hesitation, he swiftly returned to the den to relay the message. Kingston turned his attention back to Bianca, whose body was now heaving in anger, and the skin on her arms formed the small blister-like boils that were making more frequent appearances when her fury became uncontrollable. "Now, B… y'all fight was huge. I can understand why he went— but maybe he only left for a little while." Kingston said with hope in his voice. "Yeah, maybe he left to let you cool off… you know, give you some space. Like, give you enough time for you and your mama to work things out." Kingston said nervously. Scared, he patted Bianca on the back fearfully in a feeble attempt to comfort her. She quickly turned her attention to his hand, patting her. Her eyes glowed red from irritation, and she let out a low growl.

"Get your fucking hand off me."

Kingston put his hands up and backed away. "Just trying to help a friend in need, that's all. I understand, though. I'll give you your space." Kingston opened the door from the hallway they stood in that led into the den to head out the back. As he did, the woman in white that Bianca was with all night walked through and into the hallway with a smile on her face. Still in sexual bliss from Bianca's experience, she didn't notice the scowl on Bianca's face.

"Ma'am… don't go that way… we all leaving out the back— Ma'am!" Kingston put his hands out to grab the lady and pull her back in the den but she was out of reach.

She put her arms around Bianca to embrace her. "Hey, Babe. Thanks for last night. I hope I can—" The woman began to choke and gag from Bianca's sharp fingernails that had dug into the middle of her torso and were now grabbing and squeezing her internal organs.

"B! Stop! You killing that girl!" Kingston screeched with awe.

Bianca let out a loud shrieking noise which startled Kingston. He bolted into the den and out of the back door with the others. Running as fast as he could, he reached into his pocket, pulled out his phone, and hit the dial button. Roxanne was the last person he called, and on the second ring, she picked up.

"Whaaaat…" She said, still groggy from her deep sleep.

"GIRL THE BITCH IS OUT! BIANCA IS MAD AS HELL!"

Chapter 31

The reflection of several red and blue lights shined off the slick black marble tile of the cube-like building of Tryst. Cops, detectives, and forensics teams moved in and out and around the building, gathering evidence, taping off the area, and making it an official crime scene. The chief of Richmond's police would never come out for a standard homicide victim, but this one was different but very in line with several of the victims being found all around town. They all had the makings of being killed by a vampire.

Standing across the street from Tryst, watching his subordinates manage the area while simultaneously being briefed by his second in command, the thought of Richmond's gory past began to mimic itself with the killing of the young lady in the building. Anger glazed his perception of how things were unfolding while listening to his second-in-command and observing the organized chaos before him. Memories of that treacherous day with Detective David Foster and the infamous hooker Lucy began to replay in his mind.

Several years ago, Lucy's serrated body parts were stacked a pile high at the intersection of Ruffin Road and Harwood Street, and

Detective Foster blew his brains out at the horrific sight. Apparently, she was his lover, and now, dead and dismembered. That was the night the police realized they had something on their hands bigger than their regular reality.

"…and from what's being reported by a few bystanders and club patrons, she was engaged heavily with a woman all night. Some people believe they saw that woman leave out the front after the young lady was killed and walked away like nothing happened. We believe if we can find the woman, we can find the killer— if she isn't the killer herself."

The chief slowly turned his attention to his second in command, more tuned in when he heard the description of the accused. "You say a woman might be a suspect?"

"Yes, I know it sounds crazy because the wounds of the victim do not correlate with the force or scarring a woman assailant can make— it doesn't even match any normal weapons anyone would use to slaughter a victim. The lacerations and the way her insides are spilled on the floor beside her— not to mention the blood splatter at least ten feet high towards the ceiling match that of a wild animal. Chief, I got to tell you, this is Richmond city, not the county. Where would a beast that wild come from? The closest zoo is in Amelia, and that's at least a good forty-five-minute drive from here on the highway. I doubt an animal of that size is roaming in Richmond unnoticed."

"What about the other victims who were killed in almost the same fashion?"

The second in command pulled up a briefing he'd prepared about those killings to bring to the crime site to match up similarities. He skimmed through his several pages before responding. "The wounds from the other victims compared to the wounds of our current victims seem to match up in some aspects. Previous victims have bite marks like our victim inside the building. There are rips and tears in the previous victim's skin as if scratched and mauled while dying. However, our previous did have ripped limbs tossed aside and found other places. This victim is whole with the exception of the gaping wound where her internal organs fell out."

The second in command had a revelation in his train of thought and wrote it down in his notes. The chief turned his attention back to the scene and then shook his head with shame. He knew he had to make the call he was dreading to make, but the time had come. The treaty between Bianca and the Richmond City Police Department was now permanently severed. Not only did Bianca cross the line by leaving The Block to do her killings, but she had become too reckless with her actions. With the young lady dead and found at the dawn of a new day, it only proved it was time to go to war. The chief pulled out his phone and dialed the contact labeled "Phew". The phone rang twice before his call connected.

"Yeah." Marco sighed heavily, knowing what the call was all about. "I already know it's bad. We got word about that girl about an hour ago."

"You do? And you left this dead body for me and my guys to clean up? Let alone, she's out of her territory... AGAIN."

"What can I say?!" Marco exclaimed, his voice tinged with frustration. "You think that treaty really was going to keep her under control?! She's a fucking POWERFUL VAMPIRE! She's not just some lady boss from the streets! She's a VAMPIRE!"

Marco's escalated tone made the chief's anger boil. "Don't talk to me about what she is! I know what the fuck we have on our hands, but I told you! I told you all when this thing started years ago! When I saw my best detective dead on the streets! I told you then I was going to level that putrid place you call The Block! I should have burned it down with you all there! Especially that vampire BITCH! You and your fucking goons and your lowlife whorish women and all the drugs that come out of that place?! I should have shut you down! But YOU SAID! YOU! I TRUSTED YOU because my sister... God rest her soul... my SISTER said, 'Watch over my boy.'

And that's what I've been doing since she's gone! Watching over her fuck-up of a son! You only got away with all of this because we're blood, BUT NO MORE! We're coming after you guys, and we're coming HARD! You fucked with the wrong police department! Count your days, nephew, because your years of destroying this city are OVER!"

The line went dead.

In a panic, Marco dialed his uncle once the call ended, but the call was sent straight to voicemail. He began to pace the floor, hoping a plan would come to his mind. *Shit! How did I get myself into this?!* He continued to pace the floor while he processed the imminent demise of all that he and his crew had built up.

For five years, he and his friends ruled The Block alongside Bianca. Five years ago, he met Lance, but the encounter wasn't friendly. He was by himself that day, and Lance approached him with a gun pointed at his chest under the guise he was getting robbed. Lance forced him into an alley so Bianca could officially introduce herself with her teeth bared. He was shocked to see how much she'd changed when he recognized her through her relationship with Daddy. When she was with her pimp, Bianca was his beauty, and Lucy was his partner in crime. He also remembered how Daddy shitted on Bianca by kicking her off the pedestal he created for her, and when Daddy was found murdered, the slot had opened for someone else to be on top. A light bulb must have gone off in Lance's head by then, and he convinced her she could be the new boss. Marco agreed and gathered his crew to work for Bianca.

He'd tried to take the crown for himself when The Block found out Daddy was dead. He and his crew tried to muscle their way to the throne, but it proved hard. But when Bianca cornered him, and Lance came up with the idea of leveraging her power to finally get what they all wanted, he knew he could eventually take what was his under her lead.

Bianca agreed with teaming up, but with that came the fear that they had no real loyalty. He knew she could turn on him anytime, but he and the crew decided to take that chance. With his uncle being the Chief of Richmond Police, he was certain he could make life a little easier for them all. And he did. He got his uncle to look the other way when they found that detective dead. He even convinced his uncle that he had to agree to walk away and never think of The Block anymore unless he wanted to explain more dead cops. And he agreed as long as "The Trash" didn't come off the four-mile radius he and his crew claimed as theirs.

For five years, there wasn't a problem. They did what they wanted, and Bianca was able to satisfy her desires as long as she stayed within the invisible walls. Now it was all over. Their empire was crumbling, and there was no stopping his uncle from sweeping in with their ammo and killing everything in sight. But Marco couldn't let them take what he'd worked so hard for. He had to get his uncle to back off. Not just because he didn't want to see The Block in ruins but because Bianca would kill them all... He and the crew included. Marco understood Bianca cared for no one or nothing. Everything was expendable.

He had to come up with a plan. In a moment of clarity, he remembered that his uncle wasn't his only connection to the force. He pulled his phone out of his pocket and dialed his friend Cherry.

"Hello." She said in a flat tone. He could hear the other office phones ringing and her nails clicking on the keyboard in her background.

"Hey Boo." He tried to sound upbeat as his voice shook.

"Don't 'hey Boo' me. I ain't talk to you in months, and now you calling me all early in the morning. You know my shift done started and I'm mad busy. Shit popping off too early in the city this morning."

"Yeah... I heard."

"What you hear?" Cherry said inquisitively.

"About it." Marco said without saying too much.

"How you hear about what's going on? The news crews ain't even picked it up yet. We using a whole different communication system to keep up and track what's going on. We ain't trying to get this out to the city yet. If we even do. They say the shit bad this time." She started chewing her gum loudly as her brain started to connect the dots. Marco could hear her nails abruptly stop clicking her keyboard, knowing she had figured it out. "Hol-up!" She said in elevated but hushed tones. "I know this ain't y'all out her wilding!"

"Sort-of kind-of… but it ain't our fault. You already know what's up. Don't act like you don't. You used to work for her until you got that certificate to be a cop dispatcher."

Cherry sucked her teeth, not wanting him to bring up her days on the streets. "And so! That ain't me no more, and I'm glad too! Y'all in hot shit!"

"And that's why I'm calling. I need your help."

"Nah! I can't get caught up in y'all shit! I like my job, and I want to keep it! I shouldn't even be talking to you!"

"But you owe me! Who helped you get that good job?"

"I don't owe you shit! You owe me! My pussy kept y'all laced! You still got a tab to pay, bitch!"

"Fuck you hoe!"

"Retired hoe!" Cherry disconnected their phone call.

Marco redialed Cherry's number.

"Hello!" Cherry said in an angry tone.

"Man… look. I'm sorry. I'm just stressed. I shouldn't have called you a hoe, and, yes, your pussy made me and the crew. We owe you for all your hard work."

"Thank you." She said with an attitude.

"Now, will you help me?"

There was a moment of pause before she answered. "I guess I can help you." She said reluctantly. Marco could hear her nails clicking on the keyboard again as she continued to type. "What you need me to do?"

Marco clapped his hands and rubbed them together optimistically as he ran the strategy down to her. "All you have to do is keep me posted on when they plan their attack on The Block."

"They finna go to war with y'all?!" Cherry said with shock in her tone.

"Yeah… Unc said they coming in hard and heavy, and they gonna air this bitch out. I can't let them do that. These my streets."

"Listen… I ain't for no one getting hurt. Not even these cops. Some of them are my friends."

"But we family, Cherry. Your loyalty with me."

She sucked her teeth once again and grew silent as she pondered if she was doing the right thing. All Marco could hear was her clicking her nails on the keyboard as she typed.

"Come on, Cher… We not trying to kill them, we just trying to stop them, but you know people going to get hurt— or even killed… on both teams. That's the price we all play on the good and the bad side. Some are just going to have to die."

"You going to die?" Cherry asked in a soft, childlike voice laced with fear.

Marco put his hand to his heart and felt it beat as reassurance before he responded. "I ain't dying, girl. And when we done— with your help— I'm coming to see you."

"We going out?" Cherry asked happily.

"Yup. You and your kids. I'm going to take y'all out."

"Oooo!" she squealed. He could hear her hands clapping with delight instead of her nails clicking on the keyboard.

"Now, are you going to help me over these pigs or what?"

"Yeah, you got me. I'll keep you updated. I'm going to have my cousin text you on her phone what's going on over here."

"Your girl gonna snitch later?"

"Nah she not like that. Just let her get at Polo funky ass. She like your brother real bad."

Marco laughed at the small request. "Yeah. I'll hook them up after this all done."

"A'ite, Boo. Call me when you finish playing stupid games with these fools here so we can go out."

"A'ite, then. I'll holla." More relaxed, Marco disconnected the call and sat back on his couch to plan his next moves. He picked up his phone once more and dialed Lance.

"Bro, where you been? I thought you would be here by now. Shit bad at the penthouse. Me and the boys were ending the night up when Bianca came home looking like HELL!"

"Oh yeah? Where is she now?"

"She went to her room. It's been quiet. I guess she's sleep."

"Where she been all this time?"

"I don't know, but she been fucking shit up outside The Block."

"Oh shit! She get caught?"

"Yeah. My uncle called and told me we started a war."

"Oh fuck! A war?!"

"Yeah. I got Cherry who work police dispatch keeping me up to date on when they are going to attack, so you and the fellas get over here so we can come up with a strategy."

"A'ite, bet. I'll get the rest of the crew, and we coming through."

Marco disconnected the call. He then turned over crates and placed flattened boxes over top of them to use as a table where he could roll his blunt and lit it. *This shit about to be a blood bath.*

Chapter 32

It only took a matter of minutes before the crew of men were huddled in his apartment. He looked at all their concerned faces. None of them knew the extent of the damage Bianca had caused. He let out a deep sigh and proceeded to summarize the destruction. "It's bad..." were the only words he could use to describe how deep they were in.

"How bad?" Polo asked.

"There's a dead woman in a nightclub. Bianca bit a hole into her stomach."

They all groaned in misery at the update.

"Man! She been out here making it worse for us! It's bad enough there are extra dead bodies out there that we know nothing about, and they trying to pin it on us!"

"They not trying to pin it on us. They already have. I got a text from Cherry letting me know the report is Bianca got bodies on her." They all hung their heads in defeat. "Unc said he getting his boys ready to come take us all down."

"Basically…" Lance stood beside Marco to speak to the crew. "We got to prepare for war."

"Yeah," Marco said in agreement. "We can't stop what's coming. We can only prepare. We can either give up quietly or go down in a fight. Either way, we're done."

"Us, one, two, three, four, five guys against all of them? Man, this is not a war; this an annihilation of a dying breed!" Phaizo complained.

Lance perked up and said, "But we have B on our side! We can use her to take them all out."

"But if they come in the day, we don't have her as an advantage. Shit, all they got to do is arrest us and burn her in her bed." Rell said.

"True, but they not. They trying to do this on the low. Everything that's wrong about The Block that we like… that we make money with, they trying to take from us. But I got Cherry watching their every move."

As Marco continued to explain the police's intentions to the group, Lance slowly paced back and forth in thought.

"Yeah… they could have taken us today, but they didn't. I think they want to take Bianca alive. I bet they think they can round her up if they attack at night."

"They can't possibly think that." Marco said.

"Well, why would they come at night unless they want a showdown. They up to something. They want her alive and not dead."

"You got a point." Rell said.

"Well, we can't let them have her, and we can't let them take what's ours. We gonna fight."

"Yeah!" they all said in unison.

"Y'all go back and prepare for war. Tell everyone that you can to stay inside until we say it's okay to come back out," Lance commanded.

"If they want what's ours, they gonna have to take it out of our cold dead hands." Marco said as the men left his apartment on a mission.

Chapter 33

Summertime in Richmond was always humid, and as the day grew into night, more people would come out on the streets to enjoy the last moments of the day without the humidity. However, due to the crew's directives, the residents of The Block were instructed to remain inside until the streets were calm. The war with the RPD was coming to them, and the crew vowed there would be no casualties.

Marco may have had the connection of his uncle that allowed them the power they wielded on the streets and Cherry as his friend on the inside to keep them aware of what the police's next moves would be, but Lance was the one with brains in the crew. He was quick to get plan "A" jumping and plan "B" to the ready. He took his title as the lead of the crew seriously. Bianca trusted him to call the shots when she was busy, so he knew he'd have to prepare her for what was about to happen in the next couple of hours.

From Marco's intel, the cops were going to strike at midnight. The police knew they would have a better chance at the height of the nightlight. He headed up to River Towers to ready his soldiers.

It was 11:50 pm. When he pulled up, there was no one hanging outside like they usually did before the night's activities started. When he told the crew to get everyone inside, he meant it, and they did. The streets were quiet. He could hear nothing move but the soles of his shoes hitting the pavement. For him, it was eerily reminiscent of that night he got caught in the alley for the first time he met Bianca, except his meeting didn't go like the myth of her seduction. She was dangerous that night. He remembered how her intriguing beauty took him off guard. He thought she was just another beautiful woman walking alone that he could holla at and hook up with later. But when she spotted him, she forced him into a small walking space between two buildings. She ripped his shirt off, and she forced him to submit so she could tear him to shreds.

The fear of a woman killing him was no match to the fear of the monster she transformed into. Her snarling and grotesque scowl, her sharp fangs so pronounced and protruding, were ready to rip his muscular flesh to get to his internal meat. The hungry glare in her blank stare made his veins grow ice cold, and he was ready to submit to his untimely and tortured death. But something in him clicked. His survival mode kicked in, and he had to use the only thing stronger than her monstrous strength, and that was his words. He was a natural hustler. Someone who could get anything and anyone he wanted.

When he looked into Bianca's eyes right before she was about to rip him apart, it was like time slowed down, and he was allowed to see the vulnerability that haunted her. He could see her uncertainty of the newness her powers gave. He glimpsed her insecurities staring back at him, begging him to free her from this form. It was all in a flash, but it was all he needed to see so as not to be her victim.

When he felt her nails dig into his skin, it brought him back to the moment right before what could have been his last. "Baby, Baby, Baby, Baby, please don't hurt me." Stammering over his plea for mercy. His fear-filled sweat dripped from his head and into his eyes, mixing with his tears. It then all rolled down his face, blending with the heavy mucus oozing from his nose and seeping into the corners of his mouth. "You— you— you— you don't want to do this to me." He said in between sniffling. His body shaking while she had him backed into a wall.

"I do what I want." Her heavy, growl-like voice said in a slow, menacing way.

"But you can use me for other stuff. I can get the people to come to you; you don't have to go nowhere. You can just be here, and I'll take care of the rest."

Bianca licked his neck before wrapping her fingers around the back of it and squeezing. "I don't need your help." She put the tips of her fangs on his neckline and began to apply pressure.

"But if I get them to come to you, you can stay in the shadows, and no one will know about you. It'll keep the heat down about what you are. You can become a myth and live peacefully. Nobody will know anything about you. And— and— you can rule here, and no one can tell you nothing. You'll be in control."

Suddenly, Bianca forced her teeth into his flesh and forcibly sucked on his neck. His blood oozed from the crevices of her mouth, staining his shirt. He screamed in horror and tried to push her off him, knowing these were his last moments. But she loosened up her grip, retracted her teeth from his jugular, and licked his wound to help it close and heal. She pushed him into the wall just behind him, and he fell to the ground while gripping his repaired wounds. He breathed in frantic huffs, not believing he was still alive.

"Bring them to me then."

"Yeah. I can do that." Lance said as he stood up, patting his body down to make sure he was, in fact, intact.

He shook the chilling memory from his head. Now, it was time to focus on what they had to safeguard. The police were coming, and he and the crew were ready. Hours ago, he sent Phaizo to let Bianca know that the police were on their way and that he was just waiting for them to show up. He checked his watch as he heard a set of heels approaching. He looked up to see Vivian walking side by side with Phaizo. His jaw almost dropped when he saw them together.

"Don't act shocked, bitch. I'm still her mama, and I am going to do everything I can to help my baby."

"But where is Bianca? We need her if we gonna win."

"I don't know where she is. Phaizo told her what we were up against, and she took off. I thought she would meet us here."

Lance looked up at the sky, hoping to catch a glimpse of her, but it felt futile. Bianca couldn't be spotted anywhere. Worried, Lance wiped the sweat from his brow before turning his attention back to Phaizo.

"Is the crew ready?"

"I guess. I mean, we got everyone we could get together. It's like forty of us hustlers and street niggas with they straps." He shrugged helplessly. "That's all we got."

"I know the police about one hundred strong if they only just the one precinct. If they bought others into this, we definitely outnumbered."

Before they could speak another word, Lance heard the faint sound of several big trucks coming up The Block's main road. Lance pulled out his phone and called Rell. "Y'all in position? We got the vantage. This our turf."

"We got you, Boss. We see them coming."

"Alright, well, spread the word. But don't fire until I shoot up."

"A'ight." The phone call disconnected, and Lance put the phone in his back pocket and readied his weapon.

"Phaizo? You good?"

"Yeah. I'm ready."

"Viv, you sitting this one out, or are you strapped?"

"Don't worry about me, muthafucka. I can handle my own." She said as she put bullets in the chamber of her Black Pearl Sig Sauer P238.

Five big trucks stopped at the crossroads of L Street and 25th Avenue, one of the main roads of The Block. The chief got out of one of the trucks, and when he did, several other cops dressed in all black got out of their trucks as well. None of the officer's uniforms were labeled as regular police gear. Lance could tell this was a very undercover mission, and once they settled the score tonight, there wouldn't be another word from either side. There was only one war to control this area, and tonight would be the answer.

The chief walked over to Lance. Lance met him at the center. "You giving up, or we gonna have to level this waste y'all call home? It's only a matter of time before the mayor puts you all out anyway. Give up now and make this easy."

"Ain't nobody coming here to take what we made. You nor the mayor can take what's ours."

The chief looked up at the buildings and saw people in the windows looking down at them in the street, waiting for the action before he spoke again to Lance. "Where's that killing whore you're protecting?"

"We still protecting her."

"You give her up, and you can have this rotten space. I can convince the mayor to finish up the buildings he started renovations on and then just leave. Just pack up the construction workers, call off the revitalization campaign, and just leave. We can find another way to get his votes. It'll be like we were never here."

"No deal. She is a part of this area whether you like it or not. You gotta kill us because even if you take her, we coming for her, and it ain't going to be pretty."

The chief laughed at Lance's stance, knowing he and his crew were no match for Richmond's Boys in Blue. "So be it." The chief tipped his hat at Lance and then turned around to walk away. As he returned to his all-black Suburban, he heard a faint curdling scream from one of his men. Then he heard another one of his men shriek in pain, and then his cry for help was cut short like his air supply was abruptly severed. Before he could say anything, one of his dead officer's head landed on the windshield of his SUV and slowly slid towards the window wipers while the mixture of blood and other organ secretions smeared the windshield. The chief gasped to see the blood running from the dead man's opened eyes.

"Men! Attack!" The chief yelled.

With a smile of relief, knowing Bianca had shown up, Lance shot a bullet in the sky, and his men ran out to join him. Their guns drawn and ready for action.

Rell took the first shot, skimming a police officer's arm. The cop screamed in agony and went down from his injury.

Phaizo began shooting at anything moving his way, hoping his aim would be better than Rell's. His fury to protect The Block fueled his purpose.

Marco loved the feeling of killing with his hands. He put his gun in his back pocket and tackled the first distracted officer he saw, who landed flat on his back. Marco pinned him with his legs and proceeded to punch the man in the face. The feeling of his pommeling fist connecting with his victim's jaw with all his power was a thrill for him. He yelled in triumph once he saw the police officer was unconscious by his stoned knuckling.

"Come on, bruh! There's some police over there!" Polo yelled as he pulled Marco off the unconscious cop. "I think they got Lance!" Marco and Polo took off running towards the gang of police, who were taking turns beating Lance with their fists and clubs. Polo stretched his arm out with a gun in hand and shot three policemen in the back. Marco grabbed another and hoisted him in the air and then slammed him to the ground and began stomping him in the stomach.

Bianca emerged from the shadows and rushed to their side and swiftly dismembered the two remaining cops. A shot rang out from behind Bianca. She turned around, stunned, to see an officer falling to his knees, dead before his face hit the ground.

"I got you, Baby! Mama's here!" Bianca looked up to see her mother's gun pointing at the now-dead officer. Bianca gave her a half smile and a nod of approval before she made her way to the black Suburban, where the chief sat fearfully on the passenger side. Before she could make it to the truck's door, a bullet hit her in her chest, and she fell to the ground. Dark, thick blood began to ooze from the wound quickly. She wailed in pain before her body went limp.

"Bianca!" Vivian yelled in horror. She pulled out her gun and shot, but her chamber was empty. She and the crew began to run to Bianca's side, but out of nowhere, several cops with their guns cocked ran in front of them, holding them back.

Quickly, the chief got out of his SUV and ran to Bianca in triumph. "Come on, boys! Whose left to help me get this dead bitch off the street!" His tone filled with excitement over her death. Two cops followed him to her body. When they got to her, the chief kicked her in the side to see if she would move. Her body remained lifeless. "See, boys! This is how it's done! Can't nobody fuck with Richmond City!" The chief raised his gun high in the air and shot a bullet into the sky. The cops cheered at their victory, and a few of them fired a bullet in the air in solidarity.

"You two, grab her and throw her in the back of the truck. We'll take her to the incinerator and watch her burn." The two cops reached down and they both grabbed an arm to raise her from the street. When they had her upright, the chief looked her up and down, admiring his kill. "She sure is a pretty thang… even for a dead bitch." He laughed at his statement, and the two cops laughed as well. He lifted her head to get a better look at his trophy. When he did, he was met by the anger in her red eyes. The chief's mouth dropped in surprise and horror at the realization that the bullet didn't kill her as he thought.

"And don't forget I'm dangerous too." Bianca's lips curled into a sinister smile, her eyes gleaming with a malevolent glint. She opened her mouth wide, and her fangs sank into the face of the cop holding her up on her left. His screams muffled as Bianca gnarled on the middle of his face. The cop on the right began to scream hysterically because of the horrific visual and took off running.

"Yeah, B! I knew your ass won't dead!" Lance yelled and cheered from behind the police line.

"Get 'em, B! Fuck his ass up!" Another yelled.

The chief took off, running back to his SUV, knowing he was on her list. Before he could open the door, Bianca stood in front of him. Her face was smeared with his subordinate's blood, and her eyes were glowing red with anger and power. "Your city belongs to me now."

The chief shook his head nervously before he spoke. "Yes— yes— anything you say."

She grabbed him by the middle of his shirt, clenching it tightly to bring him closer to her. Her breath was warm on his cheek as they were now just nose to nose. He began to whimper in fear, knowing he was next in line to die. She stuck her tongue out and took a long, slow lick of his face from his jawline to his hairline. She then pushed him away from her, and he fell backward to the ground. She glared at him hard as he curled up into a ball on the ground and cried, waiting for his demise by her hands. Instead, he felt something hit him on the head. He looked at it and saw that it was the bullet that went into her chest. He peeked up at Bianca in bewilderment when she said, "And don't come back here."

"Yes. Never." The chief said as he scrambled to his feet.

Bianca scanned the area to see the bloodshed the war's end had brought. Her crew remained standing and ready to do what was needed to keep them on top. She cocked a half-smile of accomplishment and began to make her way home.

"Pack it up!" The chief said to the remaining cops. "Y'all, let's get out of here!" The remainder of his team lowered their guns and piled into the cars and trucks they came in. The crew cheered their victory and fell in line behind Bianca on their way to River Towers.

Chapter 34

In her home, the crew could be heard cheering and laughing as they recalled their win. Bianca came out of her bedroom, showered, and redressed in fitted jeans and an oversized halter top. Her hair was oiled and wet, and her feet were bare. Her look was feminine compared to her furious, beastlike manner with the police.

"Baby, you were so good out there! I never seen you in action, and I must say, Mama is impressed!" Vivian proudly stated as she rushed to her daughter and hugged and kissed her on the cheek. Lance put his hand up in a high five, and Bianca smacked her hand to his, blushing over her accolades.

"Yeah, Boss Lady. It's been a minute since I seen you go crazy on a fool, but you still got it." Polo said as he rushed in and hugged her, sweeping her off her feet and twirling her around.

"Yeah, them pigs know now to leave us the fuck alone. We ain't gonna have no problems from now on. We back on top!" Rell exclaimed with joy.

"But what we not gonna do is call attention to what we got going on. It's business as usual. So y'all get some of these people around here together and get them bodies off the ground out there and dispose of them like we used to. Ain't nothing changed." Lance commanded. They all agreed and left to dispose of the evidence like nothing unusual had ever happened.

Bianca surveyed the room. She, Lance, and Vivian were left. There was an awkward silence between the three. Bianca sat on the couch and put on her Louboutin spiked-heel boots. Vivian and Lance also took that as a directive for them to have a seat.

"So, here we are." Vivian said as she looked at Lance and Bianca. "What's next for us?"

Lance looked at her, about to respond, but Bianca put her hand up to stop him. He closed his mouth and allowed Bianca to speak for both of them.

"What do you mean 'us'? You not a part of this."

"But Baby, I was out there fighting with you… for you. Can't you see I just want to be part of what you got going on? That I just want to help? I thought tonight would let you know that I'm ready to be the mom you need."

"I don't need a mama. I'm grown."

"But Baby, you do need me. I can help you make decisions. I can lead the crew while you out there doing what you want to do. Didn't I prove to you I can handle myself?"

"Lance can handle anything I need. He's been my second since we started this. I don't need you."

Lance could see Vivian's desperation, and Bianca was conflicted about letting her mom in, so he spoke from his heart. "B, listen. She did step up when you were out with Mahlon, and tonight she showed she not scared of nothing. She was really out there handling hers. Let her come on with us. I can teach her the ropes and give her an assignment, and when you feel she is ready, maybe she can be third in command. You know… now that the police not going to fuck with us no more, we can add more business, and she can help me manage it all. And, like she said, you can be out there doing what you love. We can handle the rest." Bianca stared at her mom while thinking of the potential of bringing her into the business.

When Vivian first showed up on The Block, Bianca was set on not letting her into her life. Bianca owed her mother nothing for all the pain Vivian had put her through growing up. If anything, Bianca could have done her the favor of ending her life because it was worth nothing to everyone. But she stayed and endured the insults and the shutting out Bianca put her through. She persevered, never wavering on just wanting to be by her side. In some respects, she knew her mom's ultimate goal was to be a vampire, but she wouldn't take it that far. She knew if Vivian got that type of power, she would try to destroy Bianca and take over The Block and more. Vivian wasn't to be trusted. It wasn't lost on Bianca that her mom slept with her man, but she could be a decent ally on the streets because they both wanted the same thing, which was the power The Block offered.

Bianca looked over at her mom; her anger towards her betrayal with Mahlon was at the point of forgiveness, and she finally saw her differently. Her face not as hard and her glare not as resentful. Instead of supple skin, there were subtle wrinkles. Her soft, salt and pepper, coily locks framed her face in a haloing afro. She looked like a mother she would have loved to have had when she was younger and needed one. Vivian resembled a wholesome woman with a daughter she loved and was proud of. The Vivian that stood before her was nurturing and supportive. She was not the person she ran away from in fear all those years ago. *Maybe her time here has made her see me as her child and not her enemy.*

Vivian witnessed Bianca's heart melting for her as they sat silent in thought. She walked over to Bianca and wrapped her arms around her in a warm embrace. "Baby, it's me. I'm your mama. I'm here for you. I'm ready to start over if you are ready for us to begin, and I'm so sorry for what I did with Mahlon. His love wasn't my goal. You are my goal."

She pulled away from Bianca to search her eyes for redemption. Bianca nodded her head and said, "Yeah, Ma. I guess it's time to work on us side by side." She grabbed her mom's hand and turned towards Lance. "Lance, meet your second in command."

Lance clapped his hands joyously. "Alright now! Looks like a family affair!" He said with a smile.

"Finally, me and my baby are going to run things like they should be— after I go through you of course, Lance." Vivian said humbly.

"I get it, Ma-Dukes. You just excited. I can dig it. I'll probably hook you up with Roxanne and the girls. You can oversee what they got going on. Roxanne be too nice to them sometimes, and the money be short fucking around with her."

"Well, that's nice and all... you know, girl power. But I'm not with hanging with a bunch of females all day. Can't I run with the guys? Go hustling with you all, or go kick someone in the nuts because they short on our cash?"

"Nah," Lance said with a chuckle. "We ain't got to do all that all the time. Just stick with the girls until you learn the ropes."

"Or how about I handle the money? I was a waitress all my life, so I know my way around the books and shit. I probably can tell you where you need to beef up and stuff like that."

Lance thought about it for a moment and agreed. "Yeah, I guess you're right. We probably need a fresh pair of eyes on the books. You get with Minah, and she'll tell you where they are. She don't usually do the books, but she keeps the info in a particular place. She can tell you where the money is coming and going."

Bianca looked up from doing her fingernails when Lance mentioned Minah. "Where is she anyway? She still in her room?"

Lance shrugged. "You put her there a week or so ago, and no one has seen her since."

Bianca looked up at the ceiling as she thought about Minah's whereabouts. "Yeah, I guess I did put her ass on punishment a few weeks ago. Dang. It's been a while, to be honest. I don't think she's fed in a minute." Bianca chuckled at her revelation.

"I mean… I guess. You ain't really been here. You been out in those streets. We had to clean up a lot of damage you did on those bodies in the city."

"That wasn't me. The cop said the same thing, but I ain't out here killing folks like that."

"You think it was Mahlon?"

Bianca's thoughts wandered to Mahlon. His leaving was a sore wound she didn't want to nurse. "Maybe. I don't know. It's not the way he moves, though."

"Yeah, well, there was something else out there beyond The Block killing like you kill."

"You out here turning people, Baby?"

"Nah, Ma. I'm not like that. I'm never going to make a vampire. I will never put this curse on anyone. It's bad enough I got to deal with it. To make a vampire, and they have as much power as me and as much anger as I do? The world doesn't need two of me. Besides, I like it being just one of me."

"I get it, Baby. No need to make another one of you." Vivian said as she began to formulate her next statement. "But if there were another vampire out there like you… as angry as you… with your strength, wouldn't you want some help in getting them in line or, better yet, having them killed?"

Bianca stared at her mother inquisitively. "No, Ma. I don't think I need help killing another vampire. I can handle my own."

But I'm saying. It could be deadly for your crew if another vampire is out there trying to edge in on your territory. Maybe you should consider… you know… rethink turning one of us. You know me or Lance."

Lance backed away from the conversation with his hands up in surrender. "No, Ma'am. I don't want that life. I'm good dealing with the living. I don't want to deal with this afterworld shit. Keep me out of your decision."

"My decision is final. I'm not turning anyone." Bianca said with annoyance.

"Okay, okay." Vivian said. "I get it. No one turns. You don't need the help being a vampire, and you can handle any other vampire that comes your way. But if you do feel like you need some help. I don't mind offering myself as the person you turn. Trust me. I have been living long enough to know sometimes you're better off dead. And if you can be dead with perks, then I'd rather be dead with perks."

Bianca rolled her eyes with annoyance. "You always gunning for my spot. I can't trust you to just be my mom. You want to be my mom and extra. Just learn how to be a good mom. You ain't mastered that yet. Be my mom and help me manage the money, and that's all you need to do."

Vivian rolled her eyes again. "Fine. If you don't want me dead, then I'll be alive. Either way, I got your back."

"Good. Then go check on Minah." Bianca looked at her pointy nails. As strong as they were, some of the paint had gotten chipped, and at least two were broken during the fight. "Lance, remind me I need to hit up Angela's to get my nails fixed tomorrow." She picked up the glass on the new coffee table that replaced the one broken in the fight she and Mahlon had the first day they met. She smiled, thinking about the combat and how she'd never been so turned on by any man or woman, living or dead. She pierced the inside of her wrist with the sharp, pointed index fingernail. Her thick red blood began to ooze out. She hovered the wound over the glass and squeezed her wrist tight enough to allow her blood to pour faster and evenly. Once she had the glass half full she handed it to her mother.

"Here, take this to Minah and tell her to drink all of it. I'll be in later."

Vivian looked at the glass full of vampire blood. She jiggled it, making the blood swirl. The color was hypnotizing to her. *All that I could do with this one little shot of her vicious blood…*

"And no. Don't even think about drinking it, thinking it's going to turn you into a vampire like me or give you any type of power. All it's going to do is give you a taste for it, and then you gonna be a feen like Minah, and then I really can only get rid of you by killing you. I can't have two needy bitches all up in my face wanting my blood every time I enter a room. Just take her that glass and let her drink it. She probably need some to take the edge off."

Vivian looked up from the glass and at Bianca with irritation. "Why would you think I would even think about tasting your blood? I know what it does to people."

"Yeah. You just looking a little desperate right now. Just take her that glass."

Chapter 35

When Vivian got to Minah's closed door, she gently knocked. "Minah. Bianca's back. She got something for you to take the edge off." Vivian waited for Minah to respond but didn't get an answer. She knocked harder the second time before raising her voice a bit to say, "Yo, Minah. It's me, Vivian. I said Bianca here. She got something for you to drink to get your strength up. Do you want me to come in and give it to you because you are too weak to come get it, or are you going to open your door?"

Vivian waited for a response, but there wasn't one from the other side. She rolled her eyes in irritation. "Girl, I'm just going to come in and give it to you." She closed her eyes, and as she swung the door open, she said, "I hope you're dressed, but if you aren't, I got my eyes closed because I don't want to see your skinny, lil', raggly goodies." There was more silence as she stood in the middle of the room. She opened her eyes to look around. "Minah, you in here, girl?" She waited to hear a faded muffle of a voice from anywhere in the room, but there wasn't. "Minah? Where you at, girl. I know you ain't dead." She put the drink down on the dresser and began to walk around the small room, looking for Minah in the corners and closet. "Minah? Is you in here? You under the bed? Say something if you not dead." But Minah was not in the room.

Vivian walked out of it and into the hallway and hollered, "Bianca, that girl ain't in her room."

"Well, check mine. She might be in there even though I told her to stay in hers."

"Alright, I'll check." Vivian walked down the hall to Bianca's before checking the hallway bathroom for any sign of Minah. She wasn't in the bathroom. Vivian walked across the hall, opened Bianca's bedroom door, and flicked the light on. Bianca's room was massive. It had one wall of just windows curved outwardly, giving her a panoramic view of the Richmond Skyline. The heavy drapes were open on either side of the windows, softening the window's frame. Vivian walked through Bianca's closet, gaping the rack of clothes open to see if Minah was passed out or hiding behind clothes, but she was not there. She then went to Bianca's bathroom. She checked in the double-sized whirlpool jetted tub and in the four-person shower closet, but there were no signs of her. Vivian walked out of the bedroom and hollered down the hall once more. "Bianca, she not in your room or the bathroom across the hall."

Bianca thought for a moment about Minah's whereabouts. She knew she hadn't allowed her to leave. She got up from her place on the couch and met Vivian at her bedroom door. She walked in and looked in all the places Vivian had previously looked, confirming Minah had seemingly disappeared. She then went to Minah's room, looking for any signs of escape. "Who the fuck gave her permission to leave the crib? Didn't I say for her to stay here?" She thought about it some more, knowing that Minah should be in the apartment. "Lance, call down there to them boys and send for the two guards I told to watch the door."

Lance pulled out his phone and called Marco, telling him to send the two guards up. Within five minutes, the guards on watch were inside the penthouse, slightly nervous to be called in by her.

Bianca walked over to them. The beads of sweat began to show on both of their brows. "Which one of you two fools let Minah out of the house?"

Both men looked at each other, confused, hoping the other would confess. Once they realized neither had let Minah out, the bigger guy of the two reported, "It wasn't us. We were on post the whole time. She didn't leave, not one bit, or we would have seen it."

"You two are some lying muthafuckas. The bitch ain't here, so where is she?"

"We don't know, Boss. She was here when we left, right before Rell said we could go. We ain't see her leave or nothing."

"So, the whole time y'all been here, she ain't leave?"

"No Ma'am. She ain't even peek her head out the door, and we ain't even hear nothing from her the whole time we were on post."

"Did y'all even check on her? Did you ever even see her while I was gone?"

"No," the men shook their heads nervously. We were told to stand guard outside the door and not let her out, so we just stood outside the door."

Bianca rolled her eyes with irritation. It didn't make sense to her that Minah would be gone if she didn't leave the house. They were too high off the ground for her to have gone out of the window. "But did she have guests?" She asked with irritation.

"Yeah, Boss. Just her regular two… Roxanne and Kingston. They came over a couple of times. They haven't been to see her in a few days, though."

Bianca's ears perked up, hearing Kingston and Roxanne had come over. *Them two got something to do with this. I'm sure of it.* "Lance, call down to Roxanne and tell her and Kingston to get up here."

Lance nodded and made the call. A few minutes later, Roxanne and Kingston came through the door.

"Hey B. What's up. I got the girls on the block now that the police are gone, and I got a few other things I need to get back to, so what's up." Roxanne said.

Bianca walked over to Roxanne authoritatively with her arms crossed over her chest. The distance between them was too close to comfort. "I'm looking for Minah. She supposed to be here, but she isn't. You two were the last to see her. Where is she."

Roxanne crossed her arms as well and swiveled her neck to make her head roll. "I don't know where she is. She not with me."

"How you not know? Out of all the people in the world, you two know everybody business. I know you know where she is." Bianca's eyes began to glow red with anger, but it did not scare Roxanne. She continued to stand in defiance with her arms folded.

"Put it like this. If I knew where she was, I still wouldn't tell you."

"Yeah." Kingston chimed in. "That's our girl, and we love her. You've had her trapped in her damn room for I don't know for how long. You don't care nothing about her. It's good she gone."

Bianca roared a low growl and snapped her head to Kingston and quickly back to Roxanne. "You two. Y'all think y'all better than me, and I don't run y'all. But I do. I've told you before to stay out my damn business. Minah is my business. If I wanted her here, that's where she should stay until I put her out. Now, where is she!"

"Ain't nobody scared of you, B—" Kingston could not get all his words out before Bianca wrapped her hands around his mouth and covered his nose. She began squeezing his lips until they mushed together and pressed her hand against his nostrils to cut off his air supply.

Surprised, Roxanne ran to Bianca's side. "B! Don't do it! Don't hurt Kingston! He didn't mean nothing by it!"

"Where is she!" Bianca said as her glare turned to Roxanne. Saliva drooled from her mouth like a rabid dog. Her body trembled, fueled by the rage she could no longer contain due to their insubordination. Kingston could be heard struggling to breathe under the clasp of her firm grip.

"Bianca, we… we don't actually know. She left here with that guy, Sawyer." Roxanne said in a meeker tone than her previous stance.

"Who the fuck is Sawyer!" Bianca yelled as she tightened her grip around his mouth.

Roxanne could see the color changing in Kingston's face as he was starting to lose oxygen, and his skin was becoming pale. His struggle to stay alive was also waning. Roxanne was becoming frightened that she could lose both Kingston and Minah if she didn't say something to make Bianca release him from her grip. "Listen… I— I can get her on the phone. She left a note for me to text Sawyer if I need her. I— can get her here. Just give me a few minutes… but you have to let Kingston go. Look at him, he's dying."

Bianca briefly glanced his way. His deathly state did not move her to release him. However, she wanted Minah back, so she freed Kingston, and he dropped to the floor like a worthless rag doll. Roxanne rushed to his side, fanning him and pumping his chest in an attempt to get him to breathe.

"Get Sawyer on the phone." Bianca said in a low, growling voice. "Get him on the phone now."

"Let me make sure Kingston is okay." Roxanne said as she continued to try to help Kingston regain consciousness. Bianca walked over to him and swiftly kicked him in the ribs. Kingston flinched, and with a gasp of air from the pain, he was conscious and holding the place where Bianca jolted him back to their reality.

"You didn't have to do that!" Roxanne pleaded.

"Get that fuck boy on the phone NOW!" Bianca yelled.

With tears in her eyes, Roxanne pulled out her phone and texted Sawyer to return to the penthouse and bring Minah. She put her phone back in her pocket and looked at Bianca with a huff. "It's done. You happy?"

Bianca did not respond. Instead, she walked back to her balcony and looked at the skyline. *Who the fuck is Sawyer?* Bianca thought to herself. She then remembered the tall, strange man that Minah tried to protect from her claws. *Oh, that's Sawyer. She actually did choose him over me.* She balled her fists and clinched them so tight that streams of blood flowed in between the fingers of her constricted grasp. *She thinks this man gonna take her out of here like she don't belong to me? I own her. She doesn't go anywhere until I say so.*

Bianca walked back inside. Kingston was now sitting up and breathing normally. Roxanne had gotten him a drink of water from the kitchen. Her mom was leaning against the wall, watching her every move. Lance stood by the door with his phone hugged tightly to his ear. Roxanne reached into her bag when she heard the notification for a new text on her phone. She read it and then put the phone back in her bag. She looked at Bianca with a sullen expression and said, "They are on the way in about fifteen minutes. But I can text them back and tell them not to come. You don't need to do this. You have had your fun with Minah. Just let her live. Let her be with that man. You don't even like her. Let your mama be your little feedbag. She want to be a part of this life so bad anyway. Just let her do it and let Minah go."

"It's not for you to tell me what I can and cannot do with that girl. You don't know the things I've endured. Y'all think she is so innocent, like she didn't have a part in what's happened to her. Y'all pitying the wrong one. She begs for this every night. I didn't turn her into a feen. I met her this way, and if she didn't want it, then she knows what she could have done."

"What, kill herself?"

Bianca shrugged her shoulders without a care in the world. "If that's what it takes, then so be it."

"You know, you just cold-blooded." Kingston said in a weak voice.

"Cold-blooded ain't me. I'm real. I'm the realest bitch you are ever going to meet because can't nobody hustle me no more. All Minah want is for someone to take care of her, and what she fails to realize is that ain't nobody going to do that. She got to learn like I had to learn… don't nobody care. And If I have to suffer for what Kilion did to me, then she gonna suffer for what Kilion did to us."

"God, I wish someone would just kill your bitter and hateful ass."

Bianca laughed maniacally at Kingston's spoken desire. "I'm too powerful, Baby. Too bad for all y'all. Kilion chose me to carry his legacy. He picked the right one because he damn sure ain't have more fun than I have." Bianca began to laugh again when she heard a knock on the door. Lance opened it up, and Minah walked in with Sawyer by her side.

"Hello, Bianca. I hear you're looking for me.

Chapter 36

Bianca watched Minah walk in with Sawyer. Minah looked stronger. Her frame still small but no longer frail. Her hair was cut into a pixie and shaped nicely. Her clothes fit all of her soft and petite curves. Her confidence was also restored. She looked powerful and assured as if Bianca were seeing Minah for the first time so long ago. Bianca looked Sawyer up and down. His broad and solid frame appeared to protect Minah from anyone or anything. Bianca quickly made her way to Minah, where they stood nose to nose. Bianca grabbed her wrist, but Minah quickly snatched it from her.

"Where have you been?" Bianca demanded.

"Free." Minah smiled slyly at her response and walked past Bianca, standing on the opposite side of the room to get distance between them.

"I never said you could leave. You were supposed to stay here until I returned." Bianca said. Her anger slowly grew. She looked over at Sawyer with a snarl on her face. He opened his jacket slightly, exposing a hint of his weapon.

"I'm glad I didn't. I'm glad I got the courage to leave you. I feel so much better." She said with a laugh.

"Oh, you think you're free? You aren't free. I can still smell my pussy all over you. Yeah… you my bitch, who came home for me to lick her wounds." Bianca nodded slowly as she turned her head towards Sawyer, letting him know Minah was returning to her. "Now go on and tell your little friend bye." She quickly turned her head back to Minah in anger. "And let him know don't come back here looking for your tired ass!" She rushed over to Minah with her fist balled by her side and her eyes glaring red. "I should kill you right now for prancing around with him on your arm!" She said through clenched teeth. "You tried my hand for the last time, you little whore!" Bianca raised her hand to slap Minah across her face, but Sawyer rushed over and pulled Bianca back, and she flew across the room.

Everyone in the room gasped, having never seen a human overpower Bianca before. Shocked, Bianca stood up and rushed over to Sawyer. Her fangs ready to rip through any part of his exposed body.

"Stop Bianca! Your beef is with me, not him!"

Bianca was not listening to Minah. She tried to rake her claws against his face, but he arched back, barely missing her attack. Bianca screamed with rage and frustration. She never missed her target.

"BIANCA!" Minah rushed to her and held her former mistress' arms, pleading with her eyes for Bianca to look at her and see she was not the same person. "Look at me, Bianca! Look! I'm no longer under your spell! I'm clean!"

Bianca's eyes softened as she finally started to see Minah as she was. Her body began to relax, and the color of her eyes began to slowly turn back to her dark chestnut brown color. "B, look at me." Minah pleaded. She let go of Bianca's arm and stepped back closer to Sawyer. "I've changed since you left. Sawyer loves me. He saw me through all that you've done— we've done to me. Yes, I played a part in what I've become. I should have got out when I had a chance—when Kilion tried to free me a long time ago. He tried to tell me that he no longer needed me. That he had you." She said as she thought about one of her last moments with her former master. "I refused. I did everything I could to keep him coming back because I was jealous he chose you instead of me." Minah grabbed Sawyer's hand for comfort. "I should have never done that. I got myself in the mess of your world, but Sawyer and with the help of Roxanne and Kingston, I found the strength to get away from you."

Bianca's face softened. She could see Minah was different. She stepped closer to her and could no longer smell her blood seeping from Minah's pores. "How did you get clean? How are you free of me and not dead?"

Minah looked lovingly at Sawyer and then back at Bianca. "Blood transfusion. Sawyer and The Council—"

"The Council? What's that?" Bianca asked with shock.

"Sawyer and The Council were able to get me clean, and I no longer need you the way I used to. I can go live my life now." Minah walked over to Bianca and grabbed her hand. "And maybe we can have a different type of relationship where you don't rule over me, and I don't leech off of you." Minah smiled softly and graciously as she gazed into Bianca's eyes. "I would love a life where you are still in it. Where we can all be free of all of our demons. Even you, Bianca. You can be free too. There are other vampires out here that live a happy and fulfilling life. Kilion and Mahlon did." Bianca grew tense at hearing Mahlon's name. "The Council and Sawyer allowed—"

"Allowed?!" Bianca said in anger and shock.

"Yes, allow. The Council monitors the undead and regulates when needed to and they have allowed Mahlon to live an afterlife without interference as long as he minds vampiric law. Like I said, you can live free under their law if you are ready to change." She held a golden necklace up with a pendant on it that had a raised symbol in its center. "I've taken an oath with The Council because I have changed. I'm going to help track vampires with Sawyer and be in service to blood junkies like me. I'm going to assist them get off the blood and back into a normal life."

Bianca listened to all of this in silence as a tear fell from her eye. She held her head low and walked away. Minah looked at Sawyer, and he nodded his head in the direction of the door. "Well, I guess I'll go. I just wanted to tell you in person that I'm okay and that I've found my calling."

Bianca walked to the balcony, leaped off of it, and disappeared into the night. Minah rushed to the balcony and yelled out in desperation, "Bianca! Bianca, come back!" Her voice echoed as it bounced off the sides of buildings until it dissipated.

Sawyer walked over to where Minah was still leaning over it in hopelessness, looking for Bianca. He put his hand on her shoulder and gently moved her away from the ledge. "It's okay, Minah. You knew there was a chance that she wouldn't take it well." She buried her head into his chest and began to sob. "It's over Minah. You know this was her last shot at redemption. I have to do what I have to do now."

Minah nodded her head vigorously as she continued to sob into his shirt. "I know you do. I just didn't think it really was going to happen. I thought I could get through to her. To stop with this and live at peace."

"Mahlon already tried that, and he failed. I knew there wasn't any hope. Say your goodbyes, and let's head out."

Minah nodded in agreement and turned to face everyone else in the room. "Well, guys…" Minah said as she sniffled and wiped her tears and nose with the back of her hand. "This is it. I'm free." Minah stretched out her arms and flapped them slowly as if they were wings. "I'm going to start a new life with Sawyer. We're going to be a team."

Roxanne was the first to walk up to Minah and give her a hug. "Girl, I'm so proud of you! You made it out of here just like I said you would! And look at you! You turned it around quick! My girl is back to that skinny little cute thang I saw walking up and down The Block years ago!" Minah giggled, thinking about how Roxanne used to tell her she had a lightbulb for a head. "You and that big sexy man go and save some vampire souls."

"I will. I got a lot of practice being a blood junkie. I'm going to put that to good use and help who I can. I know there are others out there."

Kingston slowly made his way over to her with a humble smile. His mouth still sore from earlier. He wrapped his arms around her and squeezed her tightly. "I'm so proud of you." He whispered in her ear. "Take care of yourself and never bring yourself back here. You are loved. There is no reason for you to return just to remind yourself of that." He gave her a kiss on her cheek before pulling himself away from her. "I love you." He mouthed as he walked backward to stand beside Roxanne.

"Well, don't look my way for some kind of goodbye. I hate yo' ass and been hating yo' ass since I met you. You don't deserve my daughter's grace. You a traitor in my eyes." Vivian said as she poured a glass of wine and headed back towards Bianca's room. "Someone let me know when my daughter gets back. Until then, I'll be cleaning out the trash this girl left in the room and making it mine.

Minah rolled her eyes and said, "That's one trifling bitch. I won't be missing her."

"Don't worry. I have something planned for her, too." Minah looked up at Sawyer, who had mumbled his statement so that only she could hear.

Minah turned to Lance, who was standing by the door. Making their way towards it, she stood before him for the last time. Lance was straight-faced. She couldn't tell how he felt about her departure, but she smiled, and he slowly smiled as well. She wrapped her arms around him, and he did the same. "A'ight now, Shorty. I don't know how you pulled this off, but you got out of the game with not one hair harmed. I'm proud of you, girl."

"Thanks, Lance. We didn't spend too much time together, but I know you didn't mean me any harm."

"Yeah. You was cool. But don't let me see your ass around here no more. Ain't no telling what B gonna do if you come back. Consider yourself lucky."

Minah pulled herself out of their embrace and opened the door. "Yeah. I do." She looked up at Sawyer and smiled. "I'm very lucky." Minah put her hand up and waved at everyone to say goodbye. "Okay, guys. Wish me luck!" Minah said with a big grin. Sawyer walked past her and out into the hall, and Minah followed as the door closed behind her.

Chapter 37

Walking The Block felt different with Sawyer on her arm. Sawyer had gotten her clean. He'd freed her from Bianca and was ready to take her on to work beside him under the direction of The Council. Almost like Sawyer could read her thoughts, he put his arm around her shoulders and squeezed her close to him. She looked up at him and smiled as he looked down at her and smiled.

"I can't wait to get in your car and just drive off like I never lived this life."

Sawyer smiled humbly. "I can't wait until we are out of here, but you know what I have to do."

Minah nodded in agreement and then began to frown, thinking about Bianca's demise. "You know, I feel like a part of me is going to die with her." Minah said solemnly.

"I understand there was a connection between you two, but that was the blood. You have to remember she does not care for you. She doesn't have the capacity to feel anything for you. You are just a tool for her that she possesses. Now, mind you, vampires can develop binding connections that equate to a feeling of love. They can almost mate for life, but she didn't choose you."

"It hurts to hear, but you are right. For all that I've gone through with her and for as much as I was there for her, she didn't choose me. Just like Kilion didn't choose me."

"I chose you. And I'll choose you over and over." Sawyer placed a soft kiss on her forehead as they continued to walk.

"You know I have been watching her for a while. I was sent on a task to annihilate her way before Mahlon met her. For a while, she has slowly become a problem for The Council. You were part of that plan for elimination, but I chose for you to live. I believed you had the ability to break free, and you did. Her mother? No. She must go, but Bianca is the first priority. Mahlon was her redemption. The Council approved her stay of execution if Mahlon could have gotten her to leave here. The Council and I both felt she had bonded with Mahlon enough that she would have left quietly and could have been rehabilitated, but with her mother as a force in her life, the plan failed. We all tried to save her, but she doesn't want to be saved. She has to go."

Minah thought on his words for a moment before she responded. "I agree. You are right. It is time for her to die. Her hate is too strong, and with her mother now in the picture, there's no telling what those two can do. They do have to be stopped."

"Exactly. So, when it's done, allow your pain from all of this burn in the fire I plan to put her undead corpse in."

"Whose undead corpse you throwing away?"

Sawyer and Minah turned around to see Bianca standing in the middle of the street to exit The Block. With her arms folded in vexation, her eyes blazed with intensity, and her lips pressed into a thin, hard line. Her nostrils flared slightly as she took a sharp breath, and a faint flush of anger colored her cheeks. Her entire demeanor radiated fierce, unyielding irateness that seemed to crackle in the air around her. Sawyer saw the dangerous wrath mounting in Bianca.

For the sake of caution, he gently guided Minah to stand behind him as he addressed his nemesis.

"Yours. Your lifeless corpse will be in the fire by morning. It's time for you to leave this earth, and I'm here to do it."

Bianca looked him up and down. She casually walked over to him. The sharp click of her Louboutin's echoed along the asphalt. "You think you gonna kill me? You think just because you pushed me into a wall, you are strong enough to kill me?"

"Not only am I strong enough, I got enough balls to do it. I've killed better vampires than you."

"You think you've killed better vampires than me." Bianca confidently retorted. "Can't nobody hurt me. I've been through all types of pain, and I've probably died a couple of times when I was alive by the hands of some of the most notorious street niggas out here. You ain't nothing to me. I'll beat the hell out of you."

Sawyer opened his coat. His long sword aligned with the length of his leg. Bianca looked at it and stepped back with taunting caution. "What you think that's going to do? Make me scared and beg for my life? Nigga, please. I don't need nothing but these muthafukin' hands to fuck your shit all the way up." Bianca gestured for Sawyer to do his worst. "Come on nigga. Let's end this."

Sawyer pulled off his coat and dropped it to the ground. "I'mma make it fair. I'm not even going to use my sword." He took his weapon off and let it drop to the ground. "And I definitely don't need these knives." He pulled the daggers from his waist and let them drop to the ground as well. "And this gun?" He pulled a gun from the back of his waist. "And this gun?" He pulled another gun from the front of his waist. "And this gun?" He pulled it from underneath his pants leg and held all three up for her to see. "I don't need these either." He dropped them to the floor. Sawyer rolled up his sleeves in preparation. "So yeah, let's end this." He took off running towards Bianca and tackled her at the waist, forcing them both to the ground.

Minah let out a frightful scream as she saw them beating on each other like wild animals battling for territory. Bianca hoisted Sawyer off of her and lunged him into the car on the other side of the street. He fell off the car and left a crunched indention on its side. Sawyer gathered himself from the ground, and before he could attack, Bianca was on top of him, repeatedly scratching at his chest. His skin ripped open, and his spilled blood was flung from her nails.

Sawyer screamed in agony from the pain of the gashes. He grasped her tightly around her tiny waist and squeezed with all of his strength. The crushing effect made Bianca wince in pain, slowing her from continuing to tear into him. With the rest of his strength, he stood up while still holding Bianca by the waist and began to twist his hands as if he were wringing her out to dry, and she writhed at the effect of the pain he inflicted on her.

She began to draw her legs up, and she used them to dig her stiletto heels into his abdomen. Sawyer buckled over from her attack, letting her go. She dropped to the ground and began breathing hard and deep as if grasping for air. She looked up from the ground to see Sawyer's fist come crashing into her jaw. Her face violently twisted in the opposite direction. He grabbed her by her loose tendrils and laid her out in the street. He stood over her and raised his foot, and with all his strength, he forced his foot with its steel-toed leather boot to come crashing into the middle of her face, but Bianca was quick enough to move out of the way while simultaneously kicking her foot into his groin.

Sawyer fell backward onto the ground. The pain was excruciating. Bianca hurriedly went over to his stack of weapons and grabbed the long sword.

"Bianca! Don't!" Minah yelled.

Bianca looked at her in disgust. "I told your dumb ass to leave him alone! Now he gonna die because of you!" Bianca spit the blood from her bruised jaw out of her mouth towards Minah. "Go on and lick that up. It'll give you a start to being back as my worthless whore once I finish beating his ass."

She turned back to Sawyer, who was now charging her way. She raised his sword at him and swung it, aiming to slice him through his abdomen, but she missed. Sawyer had quickly jumped far enough back to barely skirt the sharp edge of his own sword. He charged at Bianca again. She held the sword with both hands above her head and swung it down and at an angle, aiming to slice through his neck, envisioning his head rolling and stopping at her feet.

"Bianca I said STOP!" Minah shouted as she quickly moved in between the sword and Sawyer.

"MINAH, NO!!!" Sawyer yelled as Bianca wielded his sword right through Minah's neck. Her head fell off and rolled and stopped right at Bianca's foot. Bianca's mouth dropped in awe and shock, seeing Minah's lifeless eyes looking up from the pavement in fear.

"NO!!!" Sawyer screamed out.

Bianca dropped the sword, surprised at what she'd done.

"LOOK WHAT YOU DID, YOU STUPID CUNT!" Sawyer yelled. Minah's body dropped to the ground like a crumpling piece of fabric.

"MINAH!" Sawyer yelled through tears full of panic.

"I— I— didn't mean it…" Bianca said meekly. "I wanted to kill you…"

Sawyer grabbed Minah's headless body and cradled it in his arms. "I'm so sorry Minah… My sweet, beautiful, caged bird. I'm so sorry."

"I was aiming for you…" Bianca whispered, half dazed as she came to the realization that Minah had died by her hands. "I WAS AIMING FOR YOU!!" She screamed at him, but Sawyer never looked up or acknowledged her. She looked into Minah's eyes once again. Tears instantly sprung from her own as all of her regrets about their life together overwhelmed her. She frantically wiped her tears and took off in a blur.

Chapter 38

Sawyer scooped Minah's body up from the ground and cradled her in his arms. Blood continued to drip from her open wound and down the back of his arms, but he didn't care. He then picked up her head, placed it on top of her body, and closed her eyes. Her final look of fear had already begun haunting him. He took her to his car, opened the back seat door, and placed her inside. Once the door was closed, he leaned on the car, and his knees buckled from the agony he felt, and he slid down to the ground. He was defeated in battle and love. Before her, he'd never decided to help anyone. He was a loner and lived like he didn't exist to anyone. He felt a kinship with Minah; she saw him like no one ever had. She was the first person to actually see through him, and he let her down. Hyperfocused on killing Bianca, he didn't see that he needed to take care of her problem before he could take care of her. Before he could free her.

He knew Bianca was a loose cannon. He should have obeyed The Council's orders and killed her when he first got to Richmond, but he played by a different set of rules, and Minah lost. That wasn't the plan. Minah was never part of any of his plans. Not the plan to fall in love or the plan to save her. The plan was to kill Bianca and move on. Now, Minah was gone. Bianca was still free, and he was in shambles.

His infuriation because of his pain could no longer stay contained. He went back to the spot where Minah died and gathered his weapons. He stoically placed every knife and every gun back where it was previously placed on his body. He returned to his car and looked inside the backseat. His sadness hit him again, and he began to weep. "I tried Minah. This was not supposed to happen to you." He said between sniffles. His chest began to heave, and his breath flowed in and out of his nostrils quickly. As he grappled with his emotions, he balled up his fist and tensed his body, the strain visible on his face. His gaze turned skyward as he released a howl of anguish, rippling through the night's stillness. The sudden outburst startled the birds nestled amongst the branches, rousing them from their slumber and prompting a flurry of activity as they took flight, their chorus of chirps and flapping wings adding to the chaos of emotions echoing through the air. He grabbed his gun from his side and fired several rounds toward the sky as he continued to yell, "WHY!!!"

He got in his car and turned the motor on. The car roared and grumbled when he started the engine. He looked in the backseat at Minah once again. Her body was there, but he knew her soul was gone. He felt like all the good in his world left with her. The small ounce of humanity he'd carried within his heart to remind him that being part of the living was important no longer chained him to this world. He knew at that moment he was fully committed to being part of the underworld. The world that never associated with alive beings. The world that only kept the balance between the undead and the living. Being a person alive and enjoying life was no longer a thought. He was now only a vessel to destroy monsters like Bianca. He took the car out of park and put it into drive, and when he stepped on the gas as hard as his foot could slam to the floor underneath the pedal, his tires squealed, and smoke rose from the whirling they did. He sped off, headed out of the city.

"This was our plan, Minah. We were going to leave tonight. We were going to head on to the next mission together." From Broad Street, Sawyer got on the highway going 95 South, using all three lanes to dip and dodge traffic until he made it to Bells Road and took the exit to the heart of southside Richmond. From there, he drove as fast as he could through the industrial park, where no one could slow him down in the early dark of morning. With his foot pressing steadily on the accelerator pedal, he did not see the bump in the pavement that was supposed to slow a driver's speed before crossing the uneven railway tracks, and his car almost flew across them. When his car hit the ground on the other side of the railings, he continued to race through, making his right turn onto Jefferson Davis Highway and then a quick left onto Maury Street.

Trees lined both sides of Maury in a dense collection of various kinds of foliage native to Richmond. There wasn't enough lighting to brighten the two-way street, but he knew where he was just by the way the area held a reverence for its resting occupants. He'd been put on missions in this zone by The Council to make sure the newly dead did not come back, so he recalled the best obscure place to not be noticed. He parked his car near the "Maury & Mt. Olivet Cemetery" sign and got out. He opened the back door of it, extracted Minah's body, and then secured her separated head in the front passenger seat. He shut the door behind him and trekked through the cemetery grounds, the sound of crickets and croaking frogs his only company.

He searched around the grounds, looking at headstones, and noticed the shovel leaning by a tree. The light from the nearest streetlamp made a glowing halo over and through the spaces between trees, branches, and leaves. He made his way over to it and looked around. He then realized this was the best spot to put her to rest. He placed her body down next to the tree and began to shovel. With his first strike at the ground with the shovel's edge, he was able to lift a considerable hunk of soft grass. He hoisted the shovel over his shoulder, and the grass and dirt fell behind him. He dug again and again until the hole was deep enough, and the dawn of the day began to show through.

He finally looked up from his place in the grave once he felt he had done enough, assuring he was as tall as the grave was as deep. He tossed the shovel out before he pulled himself from the hole. His clothes, now dusty and grimy, didn't stop him from his obligation. Loose and compacted dirt was all over his face and hands, and he shook and patted it off before he took off his jacket and laid it on the ground. He then placed a headless Minah in the middle of it and enclosed her delicately in it, wrapping the sleeves of the coat around her body as if he were still embracing her. With her in his arms, he jumped back into the grave and placed her body in the space he prepared for her. He bowed his head and began to pray aloud.

"Dear God. I tried to protect one of your souls. I tried to protect her life from the hell that got her here. I did your work and found love with this woman, but evil won this round, though the battle is not over. I will prevail for her and for you. Bianca is an abomination… one of the worst of their kind. She has lost her way and has chosen a path of darkness. And because of that choice, she will never prosper; as long as I am alive, I will kill her. In my darkest hour, I vow that this beast will never see the light of day once I get my hands on her. I will bring her to justice, and thy will, will be done. Please forgive me, Father, for not following your guide. I know now Minah was my sacrifice for not adhering to your word. No longer will I be swayed away from my mission to keep balance between these two worlds. Bianca will die on the cross she created. In all that I do, I say, amen."

Sawyer pulled himself out of the hole again and began using the shovel to cover Minah with dirt. Once done, he placed the shovel against the tree and walked away, knowing he would never return. Minah was now free, and so was he. He walked swiftly back to his car, and once he got in, he looked over at the passenger side and saw Minah's head sitting in the seat.

"We got one more mission together, and then I'm done."

He turned his car on and sped away, headed back to Bianca's layer.

"She dies by the light of the sun as I said she would. She dies today."

Chapter 39

The door of the penthouse flew open, and Bianca rushed in. "Who out there?" Vivian yelled from Minah's room, which she had started redecorating as her own.

"Who else would it be?!" Bianca yelled back.

Vivian peered from the room to see Bianca huffing and puffing angrily, pacing the floor, and mumbling to herself.

"Baby, you alright? Where have you been? When you left without killing him, and that mangy girl, we got a bit concerned." Vivian said as she carefully approached Bianca and placed a hand on her shoulder as an empathetic gesture. Bianca yanked her shoulder from her mother as she continued to pace and process what she had done. "Don't touch me. I'm not in the mood for your fake ass caring."

"Here we go with this shit again." Vivian threw her hands up in defeat. "You never give me the opportunity to help you. Why don't you trust me already?"

"Because you fake! You can't ever be trusted!" Bianca yelled as she continued to move back and forth. "Besides! This ain't about you right now! I got bigger shit on my mind than you!"

"Well, let me help you! You want me to call the guys?"

"Nah. They outside watching for Sawyer."

"Sawyer? I thought him and Minah left?"

"They did. And I caught up with them, and we got into it in the streets."

"So, you beat that ass, huh, and now he mad." Vivian said with a laugh. "I knew my baby ain't nothing to play with! I just—"

"Would you shut the fuck up?! I didn't kill him! Why would I be worried about him if he were dead or some shit like that!"

"You got one more time to tell me to shut up! I am still your mother, got-dammit!" Vivian retorted irritably. She folded her arms in a huff, watching Bianca continue to pace. "Why the hell you just ain't kill him when you had the fucking chance? You've had several times to do it, I'm sure, and now he's still walking around ALIVE with your bitch." Vivian shook her head and chuckled. "All this talk about you being so big and bad, and you got your ass kicked and your bitch stole by a mortal."

Bianca's face contorted in fury, and with a bellowed growl, she unleashed her anger onto her mother. She grabbed Vivian and slammed her into the coffee table, which then collapsed from the impact. "You just don't know when to shut your fucking mouth!"

Vivian winced on the floor in pain and then slowly got up. "He after me because I killed Minah! Me and him were fighting, and Minah jumped in trying to save him, and I killed her with his sword!" The words finally made the moment real. She actually had killed Minah. Minah was no longer with her.

Vivian rubbed her back, which was tender under her touch. "Good. That skinny hoe needed to go anyway. She was holding you back. Now you can find someone else that's not so clingy."

"Who?? Like you?!"

"Why not me?! I've been here dedicated to helping you and expanding your business, and all you want to do is destroy everything you built!"

"Who said all of this was important to me?! You think because I have money and bitches and niggas to fuck, I want this?! I don't fucking care about any of this shit! It can all burn to the ground as far as I fucking care! Yeah, it's mine, and I don't give a shit about it!"

"Then let me have it! Let me run it, and you leave! I want it more than you!"

"And that's why you CAN'T HAVE IT! Why would I let you live like a queen on the shit that I built?! Your ass don't deserve nothing! You treated me like shit, you've always treated me like shit, and you only here because you want my shit! You can't have any of it! My life was fine before you got here, and now everything is falling apart, and it's because I let my guard down when you walked into my life with your hand out! I HATE YOU!"

"Well, then, just kill me! I'm tired of this back-and-forth! Just kill me and get it over with!"

Bianca rushed over to her mother, invading her personal space. Her thoughts raced with ways to kill the bane of her existence. "I would love to kill you! I would love to take your life and live without you in mine! But what I would love more is to see you suffer without me! Without my money and without my power! You can never be me! You could never have all of this, and you never will!" She paused and looked Vivian over slowly. The tense and quiet moment between them cleared any doubt about her feelings for Vivian. In that moment, it was obvious their relationship would never work. "Get the fuck out of here, and don't come back."

"You don't mean that!" Vivian said as she pushed Bianca away. "You don't hate me! I'm your mother! I raised you! For good and for bad, I raised you, and no matter what, you and I are the same! You can never get rid of me! I will be here! I'm staying here! I'm never going anywhere! If you don't give me what's mine! What's owed to me! I'll just take it! Just like you took the love of my mother from me! You think because you were a child, you were so special to her! That was my mother! You took my man! You tried to act like Derrick wanted you! You tried to take him too because you didn't want me to have nothing! You just wanted me to slave day in and day out to make you comfortable!"

"I was a CHILD!"

"You knew what you were doing! You think I'm stupid to believe you weren't trying to take him from me?! And now you living good! You invincible! You powerful! And you don't owe me?! YOU OWE ME BITCH! You owe me everything!"

There was a loud crash at the door, and both Vivian and Bianca looked over to see it hanging off the hinges and Sawyer coming through it. His face full of vengeance and rage. With his sword in his hand, Bianca looked at it and saw the blood from Minah still on it. He reached behind him, pulled Minah's head from the bag on his back, and tossed it over to her.

"This should have been you!" With a yell, he entered the penthouse and began to wield his sword in an attack on Bianca. Vivian quickly headed for the door as they readied themselves in combat. "I'm going to get the fellas!" Vivian yelled as she left.

Across the room, Bianca braced herself for the attack. Her razor-sharp teeth glinted by the chandelier hanging above her, and her claws flexed in anticipation. With a swiftness, Sawyer drew a dagger from his waist and forcefully threw it, aiming to hit between her eyes. Bianca twisted in mid-air, spinning away from its ragged edge, but the blade grazed her arm. Blood from the cut sprayed Sawyer's face, temporarily blinding him and giving her time to retaliate with a thunderous kick. Her heel aimed directly at the center of his chest. He tried to block the blow with his forearm; his voice rang out with ferocity as the impact from her strike pushed him back into the kitchen area. She rushed him, her claws aimed for his throat, but he countered her advance by dropping to the floor and rolling to the side. He stuck his leg out, clipping Bianca at the ankle and making her tumble to the ground.

Quickly, he pulled out another one of his daggers, rolled over onto Bianca, and straddled her, ready to plunge it into her heart, but she twisted the lower half of her body, and her leg barred him in the chest, making him fall backward off her.

On her hands and knees, she swiftly crawled to where he was and pounced on him. Her nails slashed him across the cheek. He yelled out in pain, grabbed his gun, and slammed it into the side of her jaw. Bianca fell off him, but the force of the steel didn't stop her. She picked herself up as quickly as she could. He fired several rounds her way, but she moved in a blur, missing his target by inches. He spotted her and grabbed the sword that he had left by Minah's severed head and lifted it high. She charged him with all her might as he ran towards her with all of his force. The sword came down as he got close, but he moved out of the way just in time and ended up behind her. He kicked her in the back, causing her to fall over and lose her grip on the sword.

Neither with a weapon; the two now clashed like titans. Sawyer's movements were precise and controlled, and his training was evident in every step. Unlike him, Bianca fought wild and feral. Her attacks were unpredictable and savage. Finally, Sawyer saw an opportunity. He dropped to one knee, pulled his last dagger from his back holster, and stabbed Bianca in her side, forcing the silver blade deep into the wound. Bianca's screech of pain was high-pitched and piercing, like that of a wounded animal. She fell backward in agonizing distress. Her body flailed, and her insides seemed to sear as she frantically tried to dig the dagger out of her side.

Sawyer picked up his gun and limped over to her while she tried backing herself into a corner. "No need to say a last prayer because you're going to hell." Sawyer aimed the gun at the middle of her forehead and pulled the trigger, but the gun jammed. He pulled the trigger again, but nothing came out. "What the…"

As he dropped his gun and pulled out another, the crew came in with their firearms cocked and ready, and they began shooting. Sawyer ducked and then dived from their spray of bullets. Lance followed him to the balcony, and they struggled to overpower the other. Sawyer pushed him away and jumped off the balcony as the only way to live and fight another day. The crew rushed to the balcony and began shooting in the direction they believed Sawyer fell.

Lance pushed through the guys and headed over to Bianca, who was wounded in the corner and pulled the silver dagger from her side. Her blood poured out of the wound and was smeared all around her. She coughed up a dark, thick, gelatin-like substance that put fear in his heart; thinking they were too late to save her as she also appeared to be very weak. "B, you ok? What do we need to do."

"Get me to my room." Bianca said through her coughs. I'll be okay. Just get me to my room." Before Lance could scoop her up, Vivian pulled him aside.

"You don't have to do this." She whispered to him.

"She's dying. We can save her."

"Why do we want to, though?"

"Get me to my room!" Bianca said as she used the wall behind her to pull herself from her place on the floor.

They both looked back at her to see her very badly bruised and almost helpless. Her eyes were swollen shut from the punches inflicted by Sawyer. There were cuts and lacerations all over her, which were also dripping and oozing dark-colored blood and green puss.

"Look at her. There is no way rest is going to fix her. Let's just get her to her room and then kill her with one of those weapons Sawyer left. Once she's gone, we can rule The Block the way we want to."

Lance snatched his arm away from Vivian. "You talking crazy. I don't care how bad of a condition she is in. I would never betray her."

"I would." Rell said. Vivian and Lance look over to see the rest of the crew standing together.

"I would, too." Said Phaizo.

"I'm down if y'all down." Said Marco.

"And whatever my brother do, I'm going to do too." Said Polo.

Lance looked at them in shock. "I can't believe y'all niggas would turn on her! Look at our girl! She's halfway dead and would still beat y'all asses! Don't listen to her greedy ass mama! Let's get her back to her room!"

"For what?! For her to just wake up and be mad as fuck and probably kill us anyway? She don't need us! We kill her, we can run this shit on our own!"

"Fuck y'all niggas man! I ain't selling out!" Lance began to walk over to Bianca, but there was a gunshot, and a bullet went through his back. The smoke from the bullet wound could be seen floating up to the sky as if his soul was leaving his body. Lance choked as he stumbled to the floor and fell flat.

"Y'all killed him!" Vivian said, shocked but pleased they acted on her command.

"Lance!" Bianca said as she whimpered in the corner.

"He wasn't down. We don't need him." Said Rell. "I can run this." He put the gun back into his waist belt.

Angered that Rell assumed he was next in line to be the boss after all Marco did to get the crew to the top, he began to raise his gun to kill him, but Polo quickly grabbed his brother's hand, making him lower it. Polo gave Marco a quick look to let him know they'd take care of Rell later. Marco slightly nodded his head in agreement and stood down.

"Yeah, with my help. Don't forget that." Vivian responded as she made her way over to stand beside him."

The other guys nodded in agreement. Vivian walked over to one of the daggers on the floor left by Sawyer and then crossed the room to Bianca. She pulled Bianca's loose and tangled hair, and she yelled in pain as Vivian tossed her to the floor.

"Yeah. See. I told you I wasn't going anywhere." Vivian then kicked Bianca in her wound, and Bianca screamed out in pain once more. "And I told you, you owed me. I told you we could run this together, but your greedy ass wanted to keep it all to yourself like everything else you took from me." Vivian kicked her again and again, harder each time. "You feel that?! That's what you did to me!" Vivian stood over Bianca and pulled her up to where her neck was fully exposed. "You getting back everything you took from everybody… especially me."

As she stuck the dagger into her neck to slice it to the other side, she felt a bite on her own, which made her drop the knife. Blood began to trickle and then pour steadily from her neck while she continued to be fed upon.

"Y'all let's get out of here!" Rell yelled at the guys, and they rushed out of the front door.

Forcefully, Vivian was thrust away from Bianca, her feet losing their grip as she crashed onto the wooden, unforgiving floor. She frantically grasped her wound, hoping to salvage any more blood loss, but found her neck too mangled to save it as she felt her life draining from the life-ending gash.

Choking on the blood pooling in her opened neck, she looked up to see Mahlon towering over her. The glare in his pale green eyes was wild, and her blood was painted all over his face and down the front of his white V-neck t-shirt. He wiped himself as clean as he could and picked up the gun that jammed before Sawyer could kill Bianca. He checked the chamber and saw one bullet ready for the next round. He closed the chamber and pointed the gun at Vivian.

Her eyes widened in fear. Her plea to be spared gurgled in her throat so it couldn't be heard. She put her hands up as a sign, begging him not to kill her, but he pulled the trigger without hesitation. With one shot, Vivian's body fell flat. Mahlon immediately turned to Bianca, who was half-conscious in the corner and rushed over to her.

"You came back." She said weakly.

"I couldn't stay away." Mahlon said with a soft smile as he began to weep.

"I didn't want you to." She smiled faintly before she passed out.

Quickly, Mahlon used his fingernail to open his wrist and cut his vein. The blood from it slowly pooled and then began to spill. He hovered the open wound over Bianca's slightly open mouth and dripped the blood into her gaping lips. The nourishing fluid slowly began to restore Bianca's strength, and she started her healing process; as she grew stronger, she was able to pull herself up to Mahlon's offering and nurse from it. Each pull from his wrist began to heal her faster. The swelling in her eyes went down, and the cuts healed, and her brown skin began to glow again. Once restored, Bianca stood as beautiful as ever. She kissed Mahlon passionately as his reward.

Satisfied with the payment for his chivalry, they pulled away from their embrace to gaze lovingly into each other's eyes. "I missed you so much." Mahlon said as he fondled her tousled hair.

"I missed you, too" Bianca said. She looked over his shoulder to see her dead mother. She instantly felt her hate for Vivian dissipate and a feeling of relief took its place. She then saw Lance, her faithful servant, slumped over and lifeless. She closed her eyes in remembrance of his loyalty and sent a quiet 'thank you' to his soul wherever it rested.

Mahlon looked around the smashed room and the dead bodies. "It's over. Your world has crumbled."

"It has." Bianca said as she looked around the room as well.

"You ready to go now?"

"I have nothing left here. I think it's time."

They grabbed each other's hand and walked out of the penthouse.

Prelude

The plane landed in Cairo, and all the passengers departed. The air outside once he got off the plane was dry but tolerable. Sawyer left the airport in a small taxi and headed to the quiet town where he was scheduled to meet his connect. Two hours later, the cab stopped at his destination. A tall, slender man in a worn baseball cap, a casual navy blue linen blazer, a crisp white-collar button-up shirt, khaki pants, and brown hiking sandals stood by the door of the hotel he'd booked for his stay.

Sawyer got out of the yellow vintage-style cab with his two bags, and the man anxiously waiting for him walked over to assist. When he tried to grab Sawyer's bags, Sawyer gave him a quick look and moved them from his range. "No worries. I can handle my own."

The man smiled generously. "Allow me to assist. You are, in fact, my guest."

"I'm not your guest." Sawyer said as he grabbed the handle of each bag. "I'm here to do a job." He strode past the man without another word. The man looked at the cab driver and then at Sawyer, who was steadily walking towards the hotel. The man looked back at the driver and pulled out his wallet. "My apologies. Here is your pay and a tip."

The taxi driver nodded in appreciation and drove off. The man quickened his step to catch up with Sawyer, who was already in the lobby checking in. Slightly out of breath, the man patiently waited behind Sawyer to finish his business at the check-in desk. Sawyer turned around and looked the man up and down. However, his gaze hidden behind his dark glasses. He then tipped his head toward the direction of the elevators. "Let's go," he said as he headed that way, and the man followed quietly. When they reached the elevators, Sawyer hit the up button on the wall between two elevators. The doors of the first opened, and they got in. Sawyer hit the button for the sixth floor, and the elevator began to hum with upward movement.

"Thank you for coming. We really need your help."

"Wait until we get to the room."

The man nodded vigorously. "Of course. Of course."

The elevator stopped at their destination. Sawyer walked to his room, got to the door, and opened it with his key. The room was big enough for a living space and a private bedroom. Sawyer put his bags in the bedroom and returned to the living area. The man was standing in the entryway awkwardly. Sawyer waved his hand to gesture for him to sit down. He smiled happily at the invite and crossed the room to the couch. Sawyer went to the bar area and made two drinks of scotch and ice. He sat opposite the man and handed him one of the glasses.

"Oh no, I don't drink." With his hand up to motion, he declined the drink but still smiled graciously at Sawyer's offer.

Sawyer shrugged his shoulders and put the drink down. He gulped the scotch he had made for himself, then picked up the other and drank that one as well. He set the empty shot glass aside and opened his pack of cigarettes, pulling one out and lighting it. He grabbed the ashtray on the coffee table and tapped his cigarette so the ashes could fall into the tray. The man continued to sit with quiet patience while waiting for Sawyer to get comfortable.

Taking another pull from his cigarette, he relaxed backward into his chair and blew the smoke out. "Now, explain to me again why I have been called here."

"Yes sir. Gladly." The man rubbed his hands on his pants legs nervously before he began. "Yes, my name is Ish. I was put in contact with The Council a few months back after searching for some help with a problem my town and I have."

"I don't work for The Council anymore." Sawyer said as he continued to smoke.

"Yes, they said you didn't, but they believed you would want the assignment since you hunted these two before."

Sawyer nodded. He got back up and grabbed the bottle of scotch he left at the bar. He returned to his seat, poured another drink, and sat back down. "Go on." he said as he sipped his scotch.

"Right. So, years ago, a couple came to our town on a visit. They enjoyed our way of life, and our people welcomed them. They decided to stay, and for years, they have integrated into our community without problems." The man's smile of remembrance began to fade as he continued. "But recently, there have been murders— rare but not unusual in our town, but these murders have been different. It is like the victim has been eaten... gnarled on... their bodies almost unrecognizable." His head bowed in sadness. "My wife..." he said with tears beginning to form. "My son..." He put a hand over his eyes and began to weep. "They were both killed this way." He said as he sobbed. Sawyer poured a drink and handed him the glass. This time, Ish took the cocktail and swallowed it all in one gulp.

"Continue." Sawyer requested.

"Yes..." He said as he straightened back up; composing himself to finish his story. "Our town— Our town didn't know what to do. We began hunting the beast. It took days to pick up a trail, and we traced it back to the couple. With great surprise, the beast entered their home! We were scared that the nice couple would be their next victim but soon realized the beast was theirs!" The man said with shock. "How could such a lovely couple harbor such a brutal beast that is killing our people?! So, we gathered some men and marched to their doors. The man came to greet us, and he looked exhausted. He looked sick. We could tell there was darkness within him, but we demanded he bring us the beast. Instead, he begged us to leave. Told us to stay away and never to come back, but we would not stand for it! We demanded that we came to kill the beast! But Sawyer, what we saw next… we knew we could not fight alone. He himself transformed not into a beast but his face! His face morphed! His teeth grew, his skin tone changed to the color of the dead! He was a vampire! We had never seen one before but we knew it was one! He yelled for us to leave, and in fear, we did!" Sawyer poured Ish more liquor into his glass, and he took another sip of his drink. His hand shaking as he put it down on the table.

"Once we saw we were no match, we went home. The next day a note was on my door saying to get in contact with The Council and to find you."

"Enough." Sawyer said. He patted the man's shoulder in sympathy. "Go rest. Tomorrow night take me to the home. Is it safe for you to be out at night?"

"We don't go out at night since the murders. We don't go out at night knowing he is a vampire."

"Fine. I will go to them. Send me their address." Sawyer got up from his chair, went to his bedroom, and pulled out one of the bags and unzipped it. His artillery showed he was prepared for any possibility. "You stay here tonight. I will be back in the morning with a report."

"You will go tonight?"

"Yes. I'm going to check it out."

Sawyer arrived at the address Ish gave him. He crept up to the window where a light was on. He could hear murmurs of people talking. Their voices rose and fell as if in a heated discussion. Outside of the house, Sawyer crept around the home until he could find where the voices were coming from. Then he heard, "No! I'm going to lock you up! You can't do this anymore! You aren't even the same!" Sawyer looked into the window and saw the back of a man's head. There was a shadow of someone else there, but he needed a better look. He peered around the closest corner of the house and saw a window open and crawled through. He heard the shatter of a glass breaking and then the thump of two people tussling around. "Don't do this! We must get you some help!"

"Get off me! There is no help! This is what I am now!" Sawyer crept through the room. There was more thrashing, and he saw the man fly across the room. Sawyer peeked in and saw Mahlon lying on the floor. He was the man who'd been thrown. He looked across the room and saw a horrendous beast of a monster almost double his size. Mahlon saw Sawyer standing there, looking at the beast in awe.

"Sawyer! You came!" Sawyer looked at Mahlon. The beast looked at Sawyer and, with rage, charged his way. Sawyer pulled out his blade to prepare for the attack.

"No Sawyer! Don't attack!" Mahlon yelled and got up from the floor, reaching the beast in enough time to halt it from charging.

Sawyer jumped in and began helping Mahlon wrestle the beast into submission. "Hold her down!" Mahlon yelled as he opened his wrist and poured the blood into its mouth. Almost within moments, the monster transformed into a female. Sawyer jumped off her in surprise as his rival, Bianca, lay before him and passed out. He looked at Mahlon in shock.

"Sawyer, we need your help. It's gotten pretty bad."

END

Acknowledgments

Whew, CHILE! What a RIDE! Did you enjoy it as much as I loved writing it? I had a whole blast composing part two of our girl, Bianca. She is such a character! First, I want to say, "THANK YOU!" to all of the fans of Vampire Whore. You waited patiently while I did life. I appreciate that. I wanted to make sure Vampire Whore II: Blood & Lust was on point just for you, and I hope it didn't disappoint.

To my Belle, Arielle… we did it again! We are such talented writers and a great team. I can't wait for us to be the next big thing because we definitely have some more stories to tell.

To the hubs, my "Stacks". I love you! Thanks for letting me bounce all these ideas off you and for holding down the fort while I created. You believe in me so hard. I feel I can do anything.

FYI… Roxanne, Keith Walker, and Danette are real people. Shouts out to you guys for allowing me to commandeer your essence for this project. Especially you, Roxanne! You have been a character in at least three of my books because you my Bookie-Boo! I'mma let you rest now!

Family, friends, and RVA… Y'all know what it is! I love y'all real bad!

Until next time,

Adenike.

ade_b_lu@outlook.com

    ade_the_writer

www.ingramcontent.com/pod-product-compliance
Lightning Source LLC
Chambersburg PA
CBHW060947030726
47503CB00003B/763